THE GOOD PEOPLE OF NEW YORK

THE
GOOD PEOPLE
OF
NEW YORK

THISBE NISSEN

ALFRED A. KNOPF   NEW YORK   2001

THIS IS A BORZOI BOOK
PUBLISHED BY ALFRED A. KNOPF

Nissen

For my parents

I have done nothing but in care of thee,
Of thee my dear one, thee my daughter

—William Shakespeare, *The Tempest*

It's a rough road to travel
Mama, let go now
It's always called for me

—Joni Mitchell, "Let the Wind Carry Me"

Contents

1 The Rather Unlikely Courtship of Edwin
  Anderson and Roz Rosenzweig   3

2 Honeymoon in Omaha   16

3 Joshua Ezra Rosenzweig's Illegitimate
  Bar Mitzvah   31

4 Thou Wast That Did Preserve Me   41

5 The Incipience of Their Discontent   52

6 A Proper Farewell   64

7 The Mess Under the Bed   75

8 Where Your Parents Are   91

9 Wrestling Jailbait   101

10 Spitfire   123

11 The Perils of Orthodontia   130

12 The SS Steven Stone   137

13 Any Strange Beast There Makes a Man   149

14 Horror   161

15 The Night After the Night After the Night
  After That   170

16 Lov   183

17 Christmas in Lincoln   190

18 Youth Dew   201

19 New Wives and Old Husbands   207

20 Think About If You Want   211
21 Enter Certain Nymphs   221
22 Just Like a Pretty-Boy   235
23 Inclement Weather for Travel   246
24 The Ardor of the Liver   255
25 The Good People of New York   276

THE
GOOD PEOPLE
OF
NEW YORK

1

THE RATHER UNLIKELY COURTSHIP
OF EDWIN ANDERSON AND
ROZ ROSENZWEIG

DURING THE SUMMER OF 1970 FRAN KORNBLAUSER
was renting a fifth-floor walk-up in a building whose buzzer system was partially and perennially incapacitated. When she threw a dinner party—which she did with characteristic frequency—her guests were able to buzz up to Fran's to announce their arrival, but Fran could not, as the system only worked in one direction, buzz back down to open the door. Thus, when the bell rang, Fran would hoist open one of the large front windows that overlooked East Eleventh Street, her jangling necklaces and voluminous breasts dangling over the window box and crushing the petunias planted there by the former tenant, wave hello to her prospective company stranded on the sidewalk, their necks craned upward like gawkers at a rooftop suicide, and toss a spare key out the window to the cement five flights below. "Turn it left and push hard," she'd holler. "It sticks like a motherfucker."

Roz Rosenzweig, who with her crazy ostrich legs and excruciatingly bright and irrevocably short Marimekko minidress looked remarkably like a strawberry lollypop, and Edwin Anderson, seersucker suit rumpled to Kennebunk perfection though he was himself not a Mainer but a Nebraskan, arrived on the stoop outside Fran Kornblauser's simultaneously and became acquainted on their knees as they scrounged in a bed of impatiens for the elusive key which had ricocheted off a third-floor balcony and landed in the little cordoned-off flower patch. A sign hanging from the chain requested that dogs kindly be curbed elsewhere; still, Roz was unsurprised when, instead of the key, her hand brushed what one hasty sniff proved to be a mostly but not completely hardened pile of dog shit.

"Dammit," she said.

"I've got it!" he exclaimed, procuring the key and holding it up so that it glinted in the light. He raised himself to standing and offered her a hand, but she declined and pushed herself to her own feet. His arm was still outstretched. "Edwin," he said, "Edwin Anderson," and he extended his hand further toward her.

"Roz Rosenzweig," she said, "but I think we should wait and shake on that later."

"Oh," he said. "OK."

She shrugged. "Whelp . . . up to Fran's?" she suggested, and when he gestured for her to go ahead she said, "No no, after you," knowing full well all he wanted was a good view from behind for five flights. So then it was he who shrugged, and pushed open the door.

As it turned out, it was neither her ass nor his gallantry that had prompted Edwin's offer to allow Roz ahead of him, but the simple fact that he was a man who walked with a dreadful limp and knew that taking the steps behind him was bound to make for an unbearably slow and frustrating climb.

From the fourth-floor landing, they could see Fran hanging out the open door, a plastic tumbler of drink in hand. "Come on, Gimpy," Fran called, not yet drunk, just naturally crass. She turned and yelled into the apartment: "One more flight and the Gimp'll have made it."

Now doubly horrified—by her tainted hand and by Fran's unconscionable ridicule of this poor limping guy—Roz watched as Fran herded Edwin through the apartment door, and then she flicked a wrist and whacked Fran on the rather substantial flank of her upper arm. Ice cubes clunked in the jostled tumbler.

"You rat," Roz scolded, her face contorting into an overly dramatized approximation of appalled.

Fran gave Roz a reciprocal whack that nearly sent her sprawling down the stairs she'd just so arduously climbed.

"What's next?" Roz hissed. "You going to start hanging around St. Vincent's poking fun at the bedridden?"

Fran guffawed, flapped her arm toward the apartment door through which Edwin had disappeared, then gave another amused snort. "You mean the Gimp?"

"Fran!"

"Roz-Roz," Fran said, wrapping her arm around Roz and guiding her, too, into the apartment, "things are hardly as they appear, my darling."

EDWIN "THE GIMP" ANDERSON, IT SOON BECAME clear, was not a cripple but a casualty of the Mad River Glen Ski Area. Fran's party guests were all skiers, except Roz, who had lived her twenty-nine years on the island of Manhattan and could imagine nothing so unpleasant as a vacation in the middle of God-Knows-Where, Vermont, frostbitten on the side of a mountain with six feet of deadly fiberglass strapped to the bottom of each of the only two feet she had. There was much debate throughout the course of the evening as to what his accident said about Edwin's downhill prowess. Roz, having washed her hands thoroughly, sat on the floor of Fran's sparsely furnished bachelorette pad trying not to flash her underwear to absolutely everyone in the room, sipping her Vodka Collins, and pondering how she might offer herself up as an object of ridicule just to save poor Edwin from the barrage of attention which she was sure he had never before attracted in his short little library-squirreled life. Though he was taking it remarkably well (some, including Barb Carpenter, who always found it within her to come to the defense of any marginally attractive male in distress, did, after all, believe that Edwin's fall on a particularly icy stretch of "the Goat," a double black diamond slope, in no way indicated that the mountain had gotten the better of him), Edwin was taking it mostly in the face, his blush a shade of magenta not dissimilar to Roz's minidress, the purchase of which she was growing to regret more with every passing moment, vowing that, if she managed to escape Fran's without spilling anything particularly disastrous on herself, she would return to Marimekko the next day on her lunch hour and exchange it for the turquoise she knew she should have gone with in the first place. Her down-the-hall neighbor, Loralee, whom Roz had consulted for final fashion inspection that evening before she'd headed over to Fran's, had assured Roz that only she could pull off a dress like that so fabulously. Roz wasn't convinced. She had always wanted to be a devil-may-care girl, proud and irrepressibly fuchsia. The fact was, she felt a lot more comfortable in blue. With maybe a few more inches of material to cover up her rather nice but very white thighs.

Edwin Anderson, a newly anointed lawyer fresh from the heartland—who wanted, he avowed earnestly, to do work in civil rights—cornered Roz in Fran's kitchen, where she'd retreated for a few moments of reprieve under the pretense of replenishing the bean dip. She was in the process of adding another jigger of vodka to her Collins when the door swung open to yield Edwin, carrying the near-empty potato chip bowl like a monk begging for alms.

"Fran sent me for chips," he announced.

"What are you, the lackey?" Roz tossed another jigger into her drink for good measure and pawed around the countertop for the screw cap she'd set down somewhere. "Fran sent you to shame me out of raiding her liquor cabinet, is what you've actually been dispatched to do." Roz waggled the bottle toward him.

"In that case," said Edwin, "she picked the wrong spy." He set his chip bowl on top of the fridge where he'd be sure to forget about it completely, and started opening Fran's cabinets one after another in search of a clean glass. "What're you mixing?" he asked.

"Over the sink, on the left," Roz said. "Collins." She paused. "Collinses? Collinsi?"

"It could be like lice?" Edwin suggested.

"Ice? In the freezer," Roz said. "Do I look like a bartender? You've got arms."

"No, I, no, I mean, I meant the plural. Louse, lice. Mouse, mice. It could be like that. Or even like children. You know: child, children."

"Edwin," Roz said, facing him dead on, "tonight we're making yours a triple."

EDWIN ANDERSON HAD NOT ONE IOTA OF NEW YORK savvy, yet he managed to surreptitiously extract Roz's phone number from Fran's kitchen address book, and telephoned Roz the very next evening not two minutes after she'd walked in the door from work, the new Marimekko bag in hand, to ask her out on a date.

"To see the symphony," he said.

Roz was trying to wriggle out of her panty hose, the phone clamped precariously between her shoulder and her jaw. "Is that the bargain deal for people who can't afford to go and *hear* the symphony?" she asked him.

Edwin didn't laugh. "Actually," he said, "I've only got one ticket. I thought you'd watch while I listen. We could switch at intermission if you'd like."

Roz was utterly unprepared for sarcasm from the mouth of a Nebraska farm boy. And a lawyer too, no less. A legal secretary, Roz spent her days surrounded by lawyers and found them, on the whole, to be a humorless lot.

"What'd you do?" Edwin asked. "Drop the phone?"

"No," she said, grabbing hold of the receiver. She lifted her feet from the floor in front of the couch, panty hose still bunched around her ankles, and scissored her legs apart and together thinking such an exercise might have surprising effects on her butt, which she was sure would be the first thing to go as she sagged her way into middle age.

"I could pick you up," he suggested. "Tomorrow evening, say around seven . . ."

Suddenly it felt like a challenge. "OK, sure," Roz said. He seemed harmless enough. And, honestly, when she thought about it, she could not remember once, ever, having had a man ask her to something so elegant as the symphony.

"IT WAS PERFECTLY ADEQUATE," ROZ TOLD LORALEE, who came knocking voraciously on Roz's door for details when she returned from her date with Edwin Anderson. Loralee was a bombshell, about as savvy as a tulip, and monogamously devoted to her incurably philandering boss, which, Roz told her regularly, quite obviously stemmed from Loralee's deep-seated fears of dating in New York City.

"So, any mushy stuff?" Loralee sat on the carpet, her back up against Roz's front door as if to block all means of escape.

"Actually, yes," Roz said. She was flopped out on the couch, conducting Brahms in the air with her left foot. "We went for an ice cream."

"Mmmmm. What flavor?" Loralee demanded.

"I had Butter Pecan."

"No, the gentleman," Loralee prodded.

"Vanilla."

"Sugar cone?"

Roz nodded.

"Uh-oh."

"You said it," Roz concurred.

WHEN EDWIN CALLED A WEEK LATER TO INVITE ROZ on an architectural walking tour of Harlem, she lied, right through those mildly crooked but admirably white teeth she took such pains to brush and floss. "I'm sorry. That sounds lovely, but I'm spending the weekend up in Westchester. My aunt and uncle's place, you know?"

"Sure," Edwin said, about as suspicious as a ballpoint pen. "Some other time."

"OK, well, actually, I've actually got to get off the phone, Edwin. Thanks for the thought."

"Sure," he said. "No problem."

"Well, bye," she said, taking the receiver from her ear before he had a chance to sign off, though there was no doubt that he would anyway.

EIGHT MILLION PEOPLE IN THE CITY OF NEW YORK, what could the numerical odds possibly be of running into the one person you've told you'll be out of town? But it was Sunday afternoon, on the Fifth Avenue bus, right by the Metropolitan, when someone brushed Roz on his way toward the back door and paused there, his breath just behind her ear.

"Westchester, huh?" he said, his voice cold as chrome, and she didn't even have a chance to turn around before she spotted that telltale seersucker jacket mounting the steps of the Museum of Art.

Without thinking, Roz yanked on the signal cord, hollered "Getting off!" and plowed her way to the back door. She dashed up the museum steps and grabbed at the sleeve of Edwin's jacket. He turned, calm as only a nonnative New Yorker could be, and faced Roz on a landing halfway up the imposing bank of steps that served to weed out the faint of heart and bar the cardiovascularly unfit from access to the world's great art. Now that Roz was there, panting from her sprint and still clinging to the material at Edwin's elbow, she was at a loss for words. Any excuse would be paltry and disingenuous. And Roz, who took silence to be a sign of nothing less than death, couldn't bear it. "I just . . . I mean . . . I'm—," she stuttered.

Edwin interrupted. "That was rude of me," he said. "Not to mention juvenile. I apologize."

"What?"

"I said I was sorry for—"

She cut him off this time. "You're apologizing to me? You can't apologize to me. You've been nothing but perfectly nice and I lie, and then I get caught like a kid in the cookie jar and now you think you should be—"

"—Apologizing for baking the cookies in the first place?" He chuckled.

"Exactly." Roz couldn't identify her own emotions, but was afraid she sounded annoyed, or self-righteous, as if she'd just said *I told you so* and was waiting for Edwin to concede his own mistake.

Instead, he said, "Have you seen the Goya exhibit yet?"

"What?" Roz was disarmed.

"Goya," Edwin said. "That's what I came to see."

"Well, I, but . . . You want me to come with you?"

"Sure," he said, and there was nothing left to do but accept. If it was a game, she didn't know the rules. If it wasn't, if he was actually this trusting and forgiving a human being, the man was going to last about another week in New York before he fled on a train back to Nebraska, where the waves of grain were amber, the plains fruited, and the girls as simple and blond as sunflowers.

THAT EVENING THEY ATE INDIAN FOOD BENEATH billowing purple tapestries at a little place on Sixth Street where the curry was so hot Roz had gulped her own glass of water in one breath and then moved on to Edwin's, which he had pushed insistently toward her without a word. They went to Little Italy the next weekend, and for drinks one evening after work in a tiny brownstone yard turned garden bistro. They strolled the Bronx Botanical Garden, and prowled Greenwich Village, Edwin's architectural guide in hand, and when they stopped for hot dogs on a bench beside a playground, he read to her descriptions of Gothic facades and flying buttresses that sounded, through his Midwestern appreciation and awe, as much like poetry as any verse she'd ever heard.

It was her apartment they'd retire to at the end of an evening since his roommate, a law student at NYU, seemed never to venture out of doors, and though Edwin almost never stayed the night at Roz's (he worked early in the morning, and as the firm's underling lawyer, he liked to be fresh when he arrived at the office), he almost always stayed until Roz was just on the edge of sleep, when he would kiss her softly, gather his clothes, and dress in the dark before he let himself out, pulling the door silently shut behind him.

He was not, in any way, a man Roz would have imagined for herself. He was four years her junior, for god's sake, and he'd never really even *known* a Jew before Roz, let alone kissed one. He still limped a bit from his injury, and though he wasn't short—five eight, the same as Roz—he certainly wasn't tall. He had fair and honest good looks but lacked even an ounce of the dark mystery, furtive heart, or swarthy sophistication that Roz had clambered after for most of her adult life. But there was a point at which one tired of clambering, and Roz wondered if maybe she was reaching hers. A point when you stopped looking for Eden and set down your bags right where you were just to have the weight off your back. And maybe you stopped and built yourself a little house then, not because you'd found paradise but because the land was fertile, the view pleasant, the water clear and cold. When Loralee pried Roz for details about the clean-cut and exceedingly polite young man she often encountered late at night in the lobby of their apartment building, he on his way out, she on her way in, panty hose tucked into her purse, all Roz could manage to say on Edwin's behalf was, "I don't know, Loralee. He's not a shit," disbelieving her own words as she spoke them, as though she'd always understood shittiness to be an intrinsic male characteristic, as essential to attraction as musk.

ONE NIGHT IN LATE OCTOBER, WHEN THE DIE-HARD were still trying to milk a few final outdoor café evenings before they succumbed to the winds of fall, Roz was wide awake at eleven-thirty, having had far too much black tea at dinner due to an unexpected chili pepper in the Duck Wok's cashew chicken, and as she watched Edwin gather his clothes from the floor at the foot of her bed, she had the sudden but certain sense that Edwin actually had someplace to be.

"Hot date?" Roz asked, a brash attempt to quell her own unease.

Edwin froze, his khaki trousers clutched at his crotch like an adulterer caught in the act. "Oh," he said. "No." He tried to recover his composure, but, naked, there wasn't much to work with. "Just meeting a few folks for drinks, over by Fran's."

Roz was a bit startled. They'd been dating nearly four months. She knew Edwin socialized without her on occasion—of course he did—but somehow, late-night drinks with Fran's crowd—a big-drinking, smart-talking, easy-fucking crew of peripheral socialites and overgrown trust-fund babies—didn't strike Roz as a perfectly innocent evening's activity.

"Which folks?" Roz asked. She knew what she sounded like: a mother reprimanding her reticent teenager, out too late with the wrong crowd.

"Oh, you know . . . Fran, Steve, Barb Carpenter . . ." He trailed off, having spotted his boxer shorts among the bedsheets. He snapped them up and on in about the time it took for Roz to realize and identify her present emotion: she was jealous.

"Hmmph," she snorted. Barb Carpenter was a vampire vixen. Gorgeous (if one happened to find that sort appealing), and as smart and sexually conniving as she appeared vapid.

Edwin seemed to be regaining a bit more personal wherewithal with every garment he succeeded in finding and getting onto his body. "We haven't made this an exclusive relationship," he pointed out.

Roz was well aware of that fact, as it was she, not Edwin, who'd insisted upon noncommitment. It seemed like decades, though, since she'd dated anyone else. Since she'd had the desire to. But Roz was the first woman Edwin had dated in New York; surely it would be wiser to let him play the field a little . . . But how? They were together practically every night. Whether it was a good idea or not, they were clearly a couple. Suddenly, Roz was defiant. "Well, maybe we should!" she declared, as surprised as Edwin at the suggestion issuing from her kiss-chapped lips.

"Excuse me," said Edwin, glancing around him as if to register familiar sights, "I was looking for Roz? Roz Rosenzweig's apartment?"

"Cranky sort?" Roz asked. "Rather easy? Lousy taste in clothes?"

"That's my girl!" Edwin cried.

"Yeah? Well, I can't find her either. What'd you do with her?" Roz demanded. "What'd you do to the real Roz Rosenzweig?"

Edwin smiled, but he didn't speak. Then finally he said, "Are you serious about all that, Roz?"

"Yes," she snapped, utterly baffled by the source of her conviction. "I think you should move in here with me." It was almost a question the way it came out, like she was asking herself if that could actually be what she was suggesting.

Edwin looked mildly troubled. "Maybe we could talk about this at some other time?"

"Fine," Roz snapped. "What? I'll pencil you in a week from next Thursday? Don't give me that crap."

"Maybe just when we're feeling a little less emotional . . ."

"Stop speaking to me like Queen Victoria. *We* are perfectly calm and prepared to discuss this right now. But perhaps *we* would rather go toss back a few with Barb Carpenter . . . ?"

"Is that what this is about?" he asked.

"This!" Roz yelled, then caught herself. She began again. "This is about me inviting you to move in with me and you hedging the question completely and acting like some prepubescent dimwit at a Sadie Hawkins dance. For Christ's sake, Edwin."

Roz was going to have the conversation right then, whether Edwin wanted to or not. He looked resigned. "I don't know about the whole idea of living together," he said.

"Oh fine," Roz shot back.

"No, no," he said, "I've got a problem with the whole living-together paradigm. Living with someone is hard, but there's no commitment. It's too easy to leave if—and they're bound to—so, *when* things get rough. What's to keep us from jumping ship if the ride gets a little rocky?"

He had to be the only man she'd ever known who could get away with a metaphor like that, and she knew then that she loved him, rotten metaphors, unflappable composure, good manners, and all. "Well," she said, "well, so maybe we should do something trite and banal like get married."

Edwin looked like he might burst out laughing. "Is that a proposal?"

"Why not?" she said. She was warming to the idea. One could do worse than trite and banal. She wasn't getting any younger.

"What's the most awful thing that could happen? We get divorced?"

Edwin was thoughtful. "You're certainly not the kind of girl I expected to bring home to Mom . . ."

It was not a compliment, but it explained something: it told her something of who she was to him. Not the sunshiny corn queen that Edwin had been meant for, Roz cast shadows into Edwin's full-lit life. She lent depth, added dimension; she made everything more interesting. Roz was not the person Edwin was supposed to love, but she could not manage to register that as insulting. Rather, it was a choice, and Roz chose to be complimented by it. She chose to be extraordinarily pleased with the classification. "Well, you're not exactly the rabbi's son yourself!" she said. *Jesus,* how on earth was she going to broach the issue of his goyness with her mother? She couldn't tell her mother she was *dating* a non-Jew, not to mention *marrying* one! Perhaps they could avoid the topic entirely? Perhaps no one had to know they were marrying at all? *Oh, this is ridiculous,* she thought. Then she smiled, mischievous, the whole world a dare: "Come on, Gimps, whaddaya say? You game?"

But Edwin was already slipping his trousers down over his feet and clambering back into the bed beside her.

2

HONEYMOON IN OMAHA

THE WEDDING WAS A VERY LOW-KEY AFFAIR: ROZ IN A pale blue knit dress cut well above the knee; Edwin in khakis and a blazer, less formal even than the fledgling lawyer costume he wore on weekdays. They held the ceremony on a cold day near the end of 1970 at Fran Kornblauser's apartment: no family, a few close friends, justice of the peace, a couple of quiches, Fran's pineapple upside-down cake topped with a bride and groom she'd snatched from a bakery display at Gristedes, and enough champagne to keep them all drunk for a week. Their hangovers had been their honeymoon, since Roz and Edwin both worked and decided they'd simply have to take a real one when they could (a) afford it, (b) agree on someplace to go, and (c) concede that they were ready to venture further out of New York City than Jones Beach. Roz, one hundred percent urbanite, had no yearnings for tranquil countrysides or tropics of paradise, and saw no reason to go to any other city when they lived in the best one there was. And Edwin couldn't yet fathom having the desire to get away from "it all" since "it all" was all he'd been trying to get *to* his entire life. Thus, the first time they ventured together outside the state was to visit Edwin's folks. In Nebraska.

SOME MONTHS AFTER THEY WERE OFFICIALLY MAR-
ried, the mail brought a mimeographed invitation in Edwin's Aunt
Annibelle's hand inviting them to attend the upcoming family
reunion, Elks Club Lodge, Papillion, Nebraska, R.S.V.P.

"Let's go," Roz said. She was seated at the breakfast bar that
separated the kitchen area from the living-room area of her
apartment. It was a studio, but a sizable one, and when Edwin
had moved in with her just after the wedding they had built a
divider to create the sense of a separate bedroom. Roz sat on a
stool, her legs straight out in front of her, a plastic grocery bag
hung on each ankle. The sacks were full of the ingredients for a
spaghetti dinner and a gallon of vanilla ice cream that Edwin
would have liked to see her put in the freezer already, but Roz was
using these makeshift ankle weights in an improvisational muscle-
isolation exercise. Roz, at thirty, had become quite concerned
about sagging.

"My mother has nine sisters," Edwin said, as though that were
reason enough to skip the family reunion.

"But I've never been to Pa-pi-yon, Nebraska," Roz told him, as
if that weren't just the sort of place she'd spent her entire life
relentlessly mocking.

"Pa*pill*ion," Edwin corrected her. "It's not a Parisian butterfly.
Pa*pill*ion. It rhymes with gazillion."

"Of course it does," Roz said. "Hand me that pen." She flicked
her hand at the coffee table. Edwin tossed the ballpoint across the
room. Roz caught it gracelessly. "We'll drive," she declared. "We'll
make a honeymoon out of it."

Edwin groaned dramatically. He slumped into the couch, an
extravagant display of misery.

"Come on, you old goat," Roz chided him. "They're going to
have to meet me someday."

Edwin made his voice a plaintive whine. "I don't see why that's necessary at all . . ." He drifted off as if to demonstrate how very close to certain death she was drawing him.

"*Dear Aunt Annie,*" Roz began, orating the letter as she penned it. "Edwin and I will—"

He interrupted her: "Aunt Anni*belle,*" he corrected.

"Aunt Anni*belle,*" Roz repeated. She turned to her husband. "You'll have to write it all out for me beforehand. The whole family tree. Marriages, children, divorces, nicknames, affairs, everything."

Edwin was disappearing into the couch cushions. "You realize," he called out in his best imitation of Roz's mother's guilt-inducing tone, "you realize this is my worst nightmare."

"Be strong," Roz said, hoisting the shopping bags from her ankles and joggling the ice cream into the freezer. "Buck up, young friend. We've a long and dusty road ahead of us."

ROZ WAS EAGER TO MAKE A GOOD IMPRESSION AND show Edwin's family that she wasn't just the loud, crass New York Jew she was sure they imagined. "Do they *have* Jews in Nebraska?" she asked Edwin as they sped along the interstate through Pennsylvania, past farms and pastures still brown with winter.

"Nope," he said, his voice taking on a hillbilly drawl, "but we seen 'em on the television."

Edwin had family with a capital F. Roz's father had died when she was thirteen. Went in for a routine appendectomy, died on the table. Her mother, Adele, lived in Yonkers, went to shul every day, sent money to the Israeli children and the Sons of Jerusalem and the United Jewish Appeal, played mah-jongg on Tuesday and Scrabble on Thursday, and made the chopped liver for the weekly bingo game at the senior center on Monday night. Roz and her mother were close, in a proximal sort of way, but tolerated one another's actual presence infrequently. They picked on each other once a week by telephone. That was what Roz knew of family. The brood from which Edwin was descended seemed to Roz a staggering mystery, a miracle of copulation, from the beginning of the line to the present day. There was something oddly appealing about it too. She thought perhaps having a big family turned you into a competitive breeder, a collector greedy with acquisitions. If Cousin Bob had a daughter, you wanted a daughter too. You wanted to see his little girl and raise him a younger brother. And then he'd need to see your son and raise you twins, triplets, a gaggle of generations. The spirit of the game would overtake you, the thrill of the ever-upping ante irresistible.

A perfectionist, Roz was determined to know the entire family story cold before they arrived in Papillion, Nebraska. She planned to march up to Edwin's relatives and be able to say: "You're Cousin Rusty. You're a manager in the Sears automotive department and you punched Edwin in the stomach at Thanksgiving dinner when you were seven and made him vomit mashed potatoes into Aunt Laverne's potted ficus plant." Roz was intent on impressing the crap out of everyone.

"God bless the foresight of Sairy and Frederick Friske," Roz declared. Edwin was driving; Roz sat in the passenger seat of their rented Plymouth, a box of animal crackers clamped between her knees, an open notebook spread across her lap. She had a pen in one hand and a beheaded lion in the other. Perhaps, she thought, children were like cookies: once you'd had one you just couldn't help wanting another, and another, and another.

"In the beginning," she intoned, "were Sairy and Frederick, who dwelt in the land of Omaha. Now Fred knew his wife, Sairy, and ten times she conceived and bore him ten girls: Annibelle, Bonnie, Constance, Dorothy, Esther, Freida, Gertrude, Hazel, Imogene, and Joy, not to mention Freida's stillborn twin sister, Franny."

Edwin was looking over at her with amusement from the driver's seat.

"Watch the road, Gimps," said Roz. "Now," she resumed her recitation, "now Annibelle knew her husband, Mack, and in the interest of genealogical organization bore Arthur, Anne, and Arnie.

So too did Bonnie know her husband, Judge, and she bore Buster and Barney. Constance married Carl and bore him Cordelia, Corinthia, Cassandra, Connie, and Carl Jr. before God struck her dead as a post."

"A little respect for the deceased, please," Edwin requested.

"Sorry, Connie," Roz said to the roof of the car. "No offense intended."

"Thank you," said Edwin.

Roz read on. "Oh! This is sad," she said. "Dorothy, known as Dot, and her husband, Harlan, had only one child, a little girl called Daisy, who was hit by a car and killed at the age of ten." She paused, then continued. "And Esther and Bob Anderson begat our own young Edwin.

"Freida found she could bear no offspring by her husband, Maurice, and they enjoyed a long and happy life together. It was Gert, the seventh daughter of Sairy and Fred and something of a rebel herself, who married a first-rate gent named Mort Seahorse, and they begat three sons, who, in a willfully shocking breach of a family tradition which Gert thought to be utter horseshit, they named Paul, Samuel, and Gerald." Roz turned to Edwin and chomped the rest of her lion cracker. "So did they turn out any more interesting than the rest?"

Edwin shook his head sadly. "Mort tried, but Gert died young. He remarried a hard-ass. The boys are bland as custard."

"Sad." Roz consulted her notebook. "Now Hazel, the eighth Friske daughter, and rather a wet blanket, say reliable sources, was a superstitious little bug who believed that her sister Gert, with her randomly named sons and her wacky old husband, was somehow to blame for sister Dot's daughter's death—whew! Say *that* ten times fast—*and* sister Freida's inability to conceive, and Hazel was going to be the one to get the family back on track. So she and her husband, Nestor, brought unto the clan Harry, Henry, Hannah, Hope, Hettie, and Howard. Poor Nestor then dropped dead of exhaustion, and Hazel sank every penny they'd saved into the

Evangelical Church before she died an early death for which no laying on of hands could do a damn thing."

"Amen," said Edwin.

"Now now," Roz chided. She went on: "Sister Ida joined the convent and no one's heard from her since 1947. Easy. Thoughtful of her. Anyhow, and last but not least, dear sister Joy, the youngest of the Friske girls, knew her husband, Clyde, but like her older sister Freida was unable to conceive and instead adopted a Chinese baby named Hwa Ling, which so scandalized stubborn sister Hazel that until her death Hazel referred to Joy's daughter only as Ling, lest the little slant-eyed creature be mistaken for one of her own 'H' brood." Roz paused and flipped back a few pages in the notebook. She studied the lists. "I can do this," she said. "Three days. No sweat."

"That's the easy part," Edwin told her. "You've got another generation, two in some cases, and they're all unalphabetized."

"You underestimate my genius." She paused. "Maybe I'll only speak to people over thirty."

"That'd be friendly of you," Edwin observed.

"Won't there be name tags?" Roz asked.

Edwin looked thoughtful. "Let's pray," he said. And they drove on.

THEY ARRIVED IN NEBRASKA AT AN UNGODLY HOUR of morning, a good twelve hours later than they'd planned due to a bout of unforeseeable car trouble in Iowa involving a flat tire and a faulty jack. Their eyeballs were prickly with sleeplessness as they pulled into the driveway of Bob and Esther's home, yet Roz could detect an expectancy in her husband: prodigal son returning home. It wasn't excitement in Edwin's eyes so much as a kind of relief she hadn't anticipated. The first rays of light were beginning to creep into day and the clock on the dashboard said five-fifteen.

"Maybe we should sleep in the car awhile," Roz suggested. Her heart was beating at an alarming rate and she couldn't tell if it was the roadside coffee or the fear of impending doom.

"Oh no," Edwin said, unbuckling his seat belt. "Esther's up and at 'em by five. She'll probably have breakfast made already." And though he moved wearily, it also seemed that he might be truly anticipating that meal, his taste buds perking up at the thought of those sweet familiar comforts: Sara Lee pecan rolls and crisp-edged fried eggs and fat-dripping bacon that no one would ever dream of blotting down with a paper towel.

"Oh good lord," Roz moaned.

"Probably best not to take the Lord's name in vain around her either, especially at this hour of the day."

"Jesus, I forgot."

"Jesus, we're in trouble," Edwin said to the sky. They climbed out of the car.

ESTHER ANDERSON WAS INDEED AWAKE. SHE WAS puttering about in the kitchen in a long quilted housecoat in a shiny fabric of pastel flowers. Esther's hair was the white of ice so cold it was blue, matted awkwardly against one side of her head. "The woman went completely white at forty," Edwin had warned Roz. "She's been waiting for her chance to be an old lady since my father slid the ring onto her finger. She covets arthritic joints." Esther's face was disconcertingly free of wrinkles, and Roz wondered if this was a source of lament and frustration in her life.

"So this is Roz," Esther said, sizing her up from a few feet's distance.

Roz, in the throes of near delirium, extended a hand for shaking. "It's good to meet you, Esther. I've heard a lot of stories."

"Mom, please. Please, Roz, call me Mom," and Esther spread her wings and enveloped Roz in a hug that was a cross between Mother Hubbard and Joan Crawford.

"Mom," Roz repeated. She didn't even call her own mother "Mom" anymore. Her eyelids were being drawn shut by a seemingly magnetic force. She wondered if she appeared drunk. Edwin, beside her, looked composed as ever. Roz wondered, as she did occasionally, if her husband was perhaps not human after all. *Her husband!* The whole thing was bizarre.

"Let's get you kids to bed." Esther was proving to be impossibly good-natured. Roz was never going to be able to keep up. Esther would find out sooner, not later, that her dear son was married to an ill-tempered, foul-mouthed, and thoroughly unsuitable woman.

"Yes," Edwin said, palpably relieved. He turned to Roz. "Let's get the things from the car."

Roz's face displayed clear and utter dismay. All she wanted was to fall onto a bed and lose consciousness.

It was Esther who came to the rescue. "Eddie," she said, "leave it for later. Come. Poor Roz is exhausted." She put an arm around Roz's shoulders and the other around her son and pulled them in to her as she led the way toward the spare bedroom. "I've got extra toothbrushes," she was saying. "Some night crème, if you need it, dear?" She looked to Roz, who could only shake her head that, no, night crème wouldn't be necessary. "Oh fine, fine," Esther said. She seemed to be talking to keep up her own spirits mostly, as if she knew the kids needed sleep but she couldn't help but be disappointed that they weren't ready to sit down with her at the kitchen table and chat away the morning. "Your room's all ready for you, and there's towels in the powder room. And, Roz, I've got an extra nightgown you'll borrow."

"That's OK," Roz said through the fog of sleep in which she was walking, "I don't wear one."

They were approaching the guest room door. Esther stopped, removed her arms from their shoulders, and turned to Roz. Her nod was businesslike, but her intake of air was audibly shaky. She spoke slowly, and with an edge of something that even through her exhaustion Roz could readily identify as marked disapproval. Esther said: "I'll lend you one anyway."

They collapsed onto the twin beds Esther had prepared in the guest room. The floor was carpeted in a green shag, with matching hand-crocheted coverlets over the beds, and as Roz looked over at her new husband slumped atop his thin mattress she saw for the first time that morning the exhaustion in his face as well, his color so drained he appeared to be melting, and she wondered if perhaps she continued to underestimate him. If perhaps he deserved a few more grains of credit for his rebellion, for all the things he would have to give up, for the transgression perpetrated by this sweet Nebraska boy to marry the crabby New York Jew he loved.

THE ELKS CLUB LODGE IN PAPILLION WAS A CONverted bowling alley. The bar was set up at what had once been a front desk, liquor bottles stored horizontally in cubbies that used to hold pairs of bowling shoes. The slots were marked with the name and type of alcohol to be shelved therein, but some of the tags had fallen or been ripped off, which left some bottles to be housed under the dubious headings 8W, 11M, or 3½ KIDS.

"A drink?" Edwin suggested. Esther had woken them that afternoon in time to shower, dress, and drive to Papillion for the "opening ceremonies." Roz felt as if she were seeing the world through an enormous cotton ball. Edwin's eyes were puffy, but his cheeks had regained a rosy splash. He looked even more youthful than his twenty-five years. Home did that to a person, Roz thought. A day in Mom's house and you were always fifteen again, for better and for worse.

"Yeah," Roz said, peering at the selection, "yeah, I'll take a 6½ W. On the rocks. No twist."

"How 'bout we make that a triple?" Edwin smirked at her conspiratorially.

"How many children did Hazel have again?" Roz asked. She had dreamed all day in her fitful guest-room twin-bed sleep of children and alphabets and God's deathly finger pointing down from the clouds to smite someone dead in the flick of an instant, vanishing from the earth in the insignificant smoke-fizzle of a burned-out matchstick.

"I haven't the foggiest idea," Edwin said, "and I'm sure no one else here does either. Two bourbons, please," he said to the bartender.

Roz turned and leaned her back against the edge of the bar, gazing out onto the sea of relatives. A band was set up on the far side of the vast windowless room, and a few couples were swaying awkwardly out on the makeshift dance floor, which still sloped down, though the lane dividers and ball-return tracks had been removed, at an angle that turned a simple two-step into a calf-straining, hamstring-wrenching ordeal.

Someone sidled up to the bar beside Roz. He wore cowboy boots and needed a haircut. He smelled of Brut. "Buy you a drink, pretty thing?" he asked, looking unabashedly down the length of Roz's body and finding with great satisfaction, it seemed, that the minidress was still in vogue.

"Thanks," she said, "but my husband's already ordered me one." She turned before he had a chance to react and grabbed for Edwin. "Honey-nuts"—she pulled him to her—"Edwin, are those drinks ready yet?"

He stuck a tall bar glass in her outstretched hand.

"Edwin!" said the cowboy. "Little Eddie Anderson?"

Edwin's face washed in bland recognition. "Hello to you!" he cried, though it was unclear whether it was a cry of joy or agony.

The cowboy clapped him on the back and pumped his hand. "Eddie!" he cried again. "Eddie Anderson!" Then he appeared to spot someone over Edwin's shoulder and he stopped the hand-shake, grasping Edwin's hand between both his own. "Wait," he said. "You-all, you wait right here. There's the wife, she'll be pleased as anything to see you." And with that he took off shouting some woman's name into the scotch-and-Aqua-Net air.

"Who's that?" Roz whispered.

"I have no idea," Edwin whispered back.

"Oh Jesus, it's going to be a long night."

"Watch it with the Lord's name," he cautioned. "I wonder if this would be an appropriate time to say *I told you so*."

"Yes," Roz said, "perfectly appropriate. Is it an open bar, or do I have to pay for another one of these?" She jiggled her ice cubes at him.

"It's a family reunion," he said, "you think they want anyone here sober?"

"If it's free," Roz said, "maybe they could just hand us over a bottle."

"I see a darkened corner over there we could hide in."

Roz said: "You're my hero."

THEY FOUND A SPOT IN A POORLY LIT CORNER AND SAT on the floor, their backs propped against the side of a boxy tweed couch, the bottle of Evan Williams stuck between them on the floor. Roz rested her head on Edwin's shoulder. They sat with their legs stretched out before them, and her feet extended a good three inches farther than his. The couch reeked of cigars, but Edwin was the pure clean of Ivory Snow and shaving cream. She let her eyes fall closed.

WHEN SHE AWOKE THE EVAN WILLIAMS AND EDWIN were both gone and Roz's cheek rested painfully against the bowling alley's stucco wall. Her stockinged toes stuck out in front of her, but her shoes seemed to have disappeared. She sat for a moment, disoriented, trying to understand where she was, and perhaps why, when there was a shuffling sound nearby, followed by a yelp, clatter, and thud, as a small child in a red jumper tumbled into Roz's lap.

"Oops," said the child. Roz stuck her hands beneath the girl's arms and hoisted her to her feet. She too was only stocking-footed, but Roz could see a few paces behind her a pair of awfully familiar-looking Pappagallo heels sprawled guiltily where they'd fallen.

"Hi," Roz said. The girl looked at her curiously. It made Roz feel nervous. "Hello," she said again.

The girl craned her head around and peered at Roz's shoes behind her. Then she turned back to Roz. "How come you wear those if it's so hard to walk?" she asked.

"Well," Roz said, "that's actually a very good question." She paused. "And if I could answer it satisfactorily I'd probably be heralded as a great feminist thinker of our time." The girl, five or six years old, Roz guessed, appeared quite interested and Roz went on. "As it is, I'm afraid I can be somewhat of a sellout to the very culture I criticize."

The girl looked at Roz thoughtfully. She had light brown hair and dark, narrow Asian eyes. She was, on reflection, quite an exquisite child.

"What's your name?" Roz asked.

"What's yours?" the girl countered.

Roz stuck out a hand. "Roz Anderson."

The girl shook it daintily. "My name is Gertrude."

Roz had to fake a cough to keep from bursting into laughter. She swallowed hard. "Pleased to meet you, Gertrude." There were an awkward few moments of silence during which Roz tried to think of what it was you were supposed to talk about with a child. She had never been a kid person, not intrinsically. She liked children the way she liked people: discriminatingly. You didn't get any points with Roz just for being a kid; you had to be an interesting person too if you wanted to turn her head.

"How old are you, Gertrude?" Roz asked finally.

"Six," said Gertrude.

"Ah-ha," Roz said softly, and they were silent again. Roz glanced around the room. "And who do you belong to?" at last she thought to say.

Gertrude fixed Roz with a puzzled stare, crinkling her nose distrustfully. When she'd pondered the question thoroughly enough to speak, she did so with one hand on her hip, the other pulling at the tights that were twisting annoyingly around her leg. She said, "Me."

Roz smiled. "*That*, Gertrude, is a very smart answer. You're going to go places in this world."

"I want to go to Mars," said Gertrude.

Roz laughed. "You know," she said, "I think I'd actually like to go to Mars too."

"We could go together," Gertrude offered politely.

"It's a date," Roz agreed, and she realized in that instant that she wanted it to be true. She wanted to make plans with this child, a future of interactions with a little person who would grow and change in all the fascinating, enthralling ways that grown-ups, or most grown-ups at least, didn't do, or had given up doing. Mostly they had given in to their selves as immutable facts in a way that Roz prayed and swore she would never do.

Suddenly, in a whoosh Edwin swooped in from behind and scooped Gertrude up into the air by the armpits. "A date! Are you trying to steal my wife away from me, Gert? Is that what's going on here?"

"Uncle Edwin!" Gertrude cried.

He set her back on her feet. "I see you've met my wife, Gert. Gert, Roz. Roz, Gert."

Roz nodded vigorously. "We've just been discussing some of the finer points of feminist theory."

Edwin ruffled Gert's hair. "Gert's mom is Hwa Ling," he explained.

Roz gasped. "Adopted daughter of Joy and Clive!"

"Clyde," Gert and Edwin corrected her simultaneously.

"Clyde," Roz repeated giddily. "Clyde." And all three stood nodding for a moment until Roz exploded with another revelation. "You're named for Great-aunt Gert!" she cried. "Wife of Mort Seahorse! Mother of Paul, Samuel, and Gerald!"

Gert stood with her hands on her hips looking at Roz like she was a crazy-woman. "Yeah," she said, her voice leading, prompting Roz toward some explanation of the point of all this enthusiasm.

Roz sat on the floor by the smelly tweed couch watching her husband smile down at this outspoken little spunk of a girl, and she felt something start to break and spill inside of her. It was something that, once opened, would flood through her body more swiftly than bourbon—more powerful than cyanide, faster than a speeding bullet—and stay in her system as long—longer!—than a shot of plutonium. It surged up in her throat like tears and came out in words: "Edwin," she said, "let's have a baby!"

"On Mars!" Gert cried. She didn't miss a beat.

"I think that clashes with some law of the Talmud," Edwin said.

Roz sank into her corner, the coziest corner in all the world, she thought. "Talmud, Schmalmud."

"Did my mother offer you money?" Edwin queried. "Is this a setup?" But he was grinning wildly, shining with an elation Roz had not yet seen in the young man she'd married less than four months before.

Roz glowed. "Yes, Eddie darling," she said. "A setup. That's absolutely exactly what all this is. The great setup of fatherhood."

Gert tugged on her tights. "Are you going to get lovey now?" she said, crinkling her nose with displeasure.

"Yes, Gert, we are," Edwin said, settling himself down on the floor beside Roz.

"That's how babies are made, Gert," Roz said. "By being lovey."

"You guys are weird," Gert said, and, still shoeless, she sashayed off, zigzagging her course into the crowd. The room was huge and humming, all the grown-ups sucking at their fizzy, sparkling drinks like desert flowers. In her stockings Gert could spin and slide as if on ice, or air, and she flitted around the spacious room from adult to adult, from mother to cousin to great-great uncle once removed, all their dresses and pocketbooks and pressed suit-pants swinging in the breeze of her wake, their slip ruffles and paunched bellies and saggy-hose legs and coattail wings all swirling 'round her as she buzzed and zipped and darted among them.

3

JOSHUA EZRA ROSENZWEIG'S ILLEGITIMATE BAR MITZVAH

ROZ'S OLDER SISTER MONA WAS A GIRL BLESSED WITH the cheekbones of a Vermeer and the guile of a tax attorney. In 1959, when she was all of twenty-three years old, she had given birth to a son, Joshua Ezra, born, as they say, out of wedlock. Roz was eighteen at the time and a freshman at Barnard, and although such things had long ago been perfectly well explained to her, she still could not help but find the phrase "out of wedlock" misleading. It made it sound like the child had been born of parents who were locked together in wed. Roz's sister Mona was quite certainly not wed.

As far as anyone could discern, little Joshua's father was either the cellist in Mona's quartet, one of the workmen from Queens who'd painted her apartment during the summer of '58, or Mona's boss at the consulting firm where she earned her living as a secretary/dry cleaning retriever. Roz suspected the last of the three; she could see in young Joshua the darting eyes and smirking grin of Mona's intractable employer. Mona did seem to live extraordinarily well on a secretary's salary, and hardly appeared to toil commensurately at the job. A job from which Mona had been given a generous maternity leave at a time when most women would have been fired simply for carrying the illegitimate child in the first place. A more than suspicious coincidence, Roz thought.

Joshua was eight years old when Mona, for reasons far too complex and illogical to reconstruct, reclaimed her latent and largely ignored Judaism. Compliant a child as he was, Joshua soon thereafter conveniently claimed his own. On the strikingly beautiful Mona, Judaism was as fashionable as Rive Gauche; she wore her freshly excavated piety like a new blouse from Bendel's. Joshua Ezra, on the other hand, began to resemble a geriatric rabbinical student. He insisted on sporting a yarmulke to school and went to his Hebrew classes as eagerly as if they handed out banana splits along with the Torahs. He was a diligent, if unremarkable, pupil, and by the age of thirteen was well prepared for his bar mitzvah. It was, after all—and this Joshua Ezra appeared to believe quite sincerely—his initiation into manhood.

THE SPRING BEFORE THE BAR MITZVAH, MONA CAME pleading. Roz was already pregnant, ready to heave at the mere thought of ingesting anything more exotic than a saltine. Mona let herself into Roz and Edwin's apartment and strode across the living room as if it were the Givenchy runway. Mona never failed to make an entrance.

"I need Edwin," she announced, flopping down onto the sofa. "January sixth. Ten a.m." She scrounged in the depths of her handbag, finally emerging with a somewhat squashed Whitman's Sampler box. She tossed it onto the coffee table. "I brought you chocolate."

"Whoa whoa whoa!" Roz waved her hands as if to hail Mona like a taxi. "Back up," she said.

"The ceremony," Mona said, as though that should have explained all.

Roz raised her eyebrows expectantly, and with sisterly annoyance.

Mona took a deep breath. Her voice was the grudging monotone of a forced confession. "We need a man," she said. "A relation. Daddy's gone. Joshy's father—." She let the sentence go midstream, as if the man had been killed in the war, the memory too painful to speak of.

"Yeah," Roz said, "what with the immaculate conception and all."

"Right," said Mona. "Exactly. Which means that Edwin is Joshy's closest living male relative." Roz could sense Mona closing her case. *Matter of Fact,* by Mona Rosenzweig.

"Might I remind you, my pet," Roz chirped, "that my dear husband is about as goy as a goy can be."

"Which is all well and good," Mona said, as though she had fully expected to encounter this argument, "because *I* know that, and *you* know that, and *Edwin* certainly knows that . . ."

Roz was nodding. "I get it, I get it," she groaned, "but our sweet lovely mother does *not*."

"And," Mona pointed out, "unless you'd like to send dear Adele Rosenzweig to a premature grave, I think it would behoove you, baby sister, to keep it that way."

"Is this extortion?" Roz demanded.

Mona gathered her things. She bent over and bestowed a kiss on Roz's nose. "No, love," she said, "this is what is known in these parts as family."

And so over the next six months it seemed that everyone was in training: Roz for childbirth, Mona to host the bar mitzvah party of the century, Adele for grandmotherhood, and Joshua and Edwin for the recitation of their Torah portions and their entrances into the covenant of Jewish manhood. Mona transcribed the text of Edwin's speeches completely into phonetics, and the memorization was, Edwin told Roz, much like learning the Latin hymns and chorales he'd sung in the church choir as a boy in Nebraska. He was a remarkably good sport about the whole thing, considered it a learning experience, and allowed himself to be dragged by Mona on a number of occasions to the bar mitzvah services of various boys whom Mona didn't even know. She wanted Edwin to get a sense of the whole shebang, a feel for what he was about to encounter.

IN MID-DECEMBER, NEARLY NINE MONTHS' PREGNANT and about ready to yank the goddamn baby out herself, Roz stopped on her way home from her last official day of work to buy a spur-of-the-moment present for her husband, just for being such a trooper through it all—Lamaze, Hebrew phonetics, Roz's nightly *need* for a small chocolate Carvel cone with rainbow sprinkles. She was so laden with packages by the time she got home that she had to ring the doorbell with her elbow and wait for Edwin to let her in.

"Ho ho ho!" Roz cried as the door swung open.

Edwin's face was a jumble of amusement and confusion.

"I figured," Roz explained, forging her way into the apartment as Edwin tried to divest her of some of her burdens, "I figured if one is going to be as fat as goddamn Santa Claus"—she looked down at the shelf of her belly—"then one might as well have the lousy trimmings to go with it."

They set up the tree in a corner of the living room, and Edwin puttered around it, happy as an elf, hanging lights and tinsel and a set of tiny, tiny green glass balls Roz had purchased at Woolworth's. Edwin popped some popcorn and ran down to the corner market for cranberries, which they strung into chains and draped around their tree, which was so small they wound up eating most of the popcorn and calling Edwin's mother in Nebraska for her cranberry relish recipe so the bag would not go to waste. Then Edwin made two mugs of cocoa and sat on the couch with his hugely pregnant wife and they watched their little glowing, sparkling tree as if it somehow proved that the two of them, together, were actually capable of creating something quite truly lovely.

Roz was on the Ninety-sixth Street crosstown bus headed east when her water broke. The temperature outside was such that she had on a number of layers, including thermal underwear and a fur-lined raincoat she'd inherited from her mother during Adele's last fashion overhaul, and though the mink never really looked the same again—but the damage was all on the inside, so who ever saw?—its insulation saved Roz any leaky embarrassment on the bus, which she disembarked calmly and in turn. She walked the three blocks uptown to Mount Sinai Hospital, approached an admissions desk, and told the attendant seated behind it—an expressionless woman whose name tag, as if in an attempt at irony, read "Trixie"—that she was having a baby.

Someone called Edwin, who left work, took a cab uptown, grabbed Roz's prepacked overnight bag, called Adele to let her know what was happening, and—as an afterthought which dawned on him halfway out the door and made him drop everything and dash back into the living room, his arm through only one sleeve of his forlornly dangling coat—scooped the little Christmas tree up from the corner and stashed the entire thing—balls, lights, baubles and all—into the first hiding place he encountered: the coat closet.

Which, he congratulated himself, turned out to have been a very fortunate move, as Roz's mother took it upon herself to stop by while Edwin and Roz were still at the hospital. Adele thought she'd just drop off some bagels, put a kugel in the freezer, make sure they had milk and juice, butter, eggs. Tidy up for them a bit, she figured—they'd have their hands full and more when they returned with the little kindela. What a nice thing if the dishes were done and the carpet vacuumed, the trash set out for the garbage men.

THREE DAYS AFTER THE BIRTH OF MIRANDA GERT Anderson, Adele summoned Edwin to dinner, alone. "Give the mother and child some time together to bond," she said, and Edwin did not stop to remind her that he worked all day while Roz and Miranda were at home together so alone-time was not something in which they were lacking. However, one did not say no to Adele Rosenzweig, ever. Edwin hadn't before been faced with his mother-in-law alone, without buffers or diversions, with no one else around to take up the slack. He confessed to Roz: he was a little bit afraid of her mother.

They met downtown, near Edwin's office, not in order to be convenient to Edwin, but because his office was close to a kosher delicatessen, which was the only kind of restaurant in the city of New York where Adele would deign to eat. She was waiting for him, Edwin later told Roz, already seated at a table when he arrived. "Hello, Adele." He bent down to kiss her cheek. She seemed pleased by that. Edwin pulled out his own chair and lifted his trousers slightly so as not to bulge the knees and ruin their pleats. A waiter appeared.

"I ordered for myself," Adele said, "you don't mind. The pastrami's good—a little fatty but tasty. Don't get the matzoh ball—I make it better at home. Oh, you're a grown man. Eat what you like." She turned Edwin over to the waiter.

Edwin perused the menu. "Blintzes, please, to start. And a corned beef, on whole wheat. With mayo," he added.

The waiter looked down at Edwin with a stare that could curdle coleslaw, then turned to Adele as if she might be able to provide some explanation for her table companion. She sighed audibly and waved the man away.

"You're looking well," Edwin told his mother-in-law.

"Thank you," she said, and Edwin had the feeling he'd just made it possible for her to check off another item on a mental list.

"How are Roz and the baby?" Adele inquired politely. She seemed disinclined toward the baby's name and had not yet, to Edwin's knowledge, ever used it. Miranda was the Baby. He wondered how long that might last.

"Fine. Good," he said. "Fine, fine."

"Oh good."

"Yes," he agreed, "all good. Quite good."

"Good," Adele said.

"Yes," said Edwin. He straightened his silverware, then looked around the room as if trying to commit the decor to memory. When the waiter appeared with his blintzes, he felt a wave of relief.

"They're hot enough?" Adele asked the waiter. "That didn't take so long. They cooked them through back there in the kitchen?" She was pointing accusingly at the little doughy rolls.

"Yes ma'am," the waiter promised, "of course." He paused to see if there might be anything else they needed. But before he could inquire—and before Edwin could pull his blintzes to him and begin to eat—Adele, whose hand was poised threateningly over the plate, suddenly plunged her index finger deep into one of the blintzes and, with it stuck there up to the first joint, said loudly, in proclamation: "It's cold like ice." At which point she removed her finger, held it in the air at some distance from her person as if it were now contaminated, and handed the blintz plate back to the waiter, who scuttled off toward the kitchen, whether perturbed or embarrassed it was impossible to say.

Edwin stared at Adele, too taken aback to speak. She didn't appear to notice. She took a deep breath, as if preparing for a long speech.

"Edwin," she said.

"Yes?"

"Edwin," she looked off to the proverbial horizon. "Edwin, I've come, in short, and in a short time, to love you like a son."

The fear began to slowly drain from Edwin's body, like a balloon allowed to fizzle in a long, controlled screech of release. He blushed hotly, as though everyone could hear.

"You are," Adele went on, "quite possibly, the best thing to ever happen to my Roz-Roz, and although the two of you together have been not exactly the most accommodating to a mother such as myself: not inviting me to your wedding for example, deciding on a name for the baby without so much as a consultation . . ." Adele felt for the hair at the nape of her neck, smoothing it into submission. She continued: "Nonetheless, you're a good man. I know you make Roz happy. What more could a mother ask?" She turned right to Edwin then. "Well, there *is* more that a mother could ask." Her face seized with resolve. "I know, Edwin," she blurted, "I know. I saw the tree. I know it all." She waved a hand as if to quiet him until he'd heard her through. "I have thought about this day and night and I have come to a decision. I understand that this is as it is: you are not a Jew. I should have guessed it from the beginning, but a mother will delude herself. A mother will make herself not see what she doesn't want to see. But here is my decision: I will live with this knowledge. I know you will tell Roz that I know. That she couldn't tell me herself, well, it says what it says, no? I assume that is how you young people are with one another these days: honest, painfully honest. We of my generation, we are not like that. We are guarded. There are some things I shared not even with my husband, rest his soul. My daughter and I have not always been able to be open with one another. That is the way it is with a mother and a daughter . . ."

Edwin nodded his understanding and Adele continued. He would relate the gist of the conversation to Roz back at home later that evening, but there was something he would leave out of the retelling, something in Adele's tone, a stressed word, a portentous syllable, a stare of impending meaning. He wasn't sure why exactly he would leave it out. Maybe because Roz would make a fuss, and he didn't know if there was actually something to fuss about. It was only an inkling, and maybe it was just easier not to mention it, to let the story be a funny story, one they could tell again and again, laughing together at Adele's ardent eccentricity. It would be easier not to tell and save the story from becoming a mysterious source of anxiety. Edwin liked it simple. With Roz, everything became complicated anyway. He liked the idea of presenting her with a clean story, precise in its point, sharp of humor, nothing subtle or shadowy lurking symbolically below the surface.

The gravity in Adele's gaze suggested that she wanted to impart some confession, some offering unto her son-in-law. She said, "What I will insist on, a vow not to be broken, not after my death, you understand. Not ever. You will not tell them. Not even when I am gone, even if that time comes quickly and you are tempted. Even then, no."

Edwin nodded fervently. It was all he could do. He swallowed hard.

"God will forgive. He'll forgive you, and, God willing, he'll forgive me." She paused. "Mona," she said, letting her first daughter's name descend on Edwin like a shroud. She spoke slowly, emphatically, every word bearing a stress of its own: "Mona must never never know. You will go through with Joshy's bar mitzvah, we will prepare you, we will cover every corner." She had a glint of excitement in her eye, Edwin thought, a thrill from this secret mission. "No one—and especially never Mona and Joshy—no one will ever know the truth." She straightened up, composed herself again. "I must have your word on this, Edwin. God help me, I must have your solemn word."

"Yes," said Edwin, "of course. You have my word."

Adele pierced her stare into his for another moment as if to sear the oath into the pupils of his eyes. And then suddenly she came out of it, shook her head, breathed, and emerged like a hypnotic surfacing from a trance. She smiled at him, a veritably beatific smile, and then spun her head in search of something. "Waiter," she called. "Sir!" She grabbed her empty coffee cup by the handle and stuck it high in the air above her head. "Waiter, some coffee, please. Can we get some coffee here, over here, some coffee." She waved the cup back and forth in her hand, the fingers swelled with arthritis, jeweled in dark rings and gems that looked to have come from a treasure chest, and Edwin watched, imagining some ancient family stockpile unearthed from deep in the ground, beneath the frozen soil of the old country where it had been buried for many many years, and he imagined all that cold, impenetrable land, and somewhere so far, so deep within, a core, a core like the center of the earth. It was a core like a geode, and if you cracked it open, inside, under all the black encrustation and age, you never knew exactly what you might find.

4

THOU WAST THAT DID PRESERVE ME

"WHO EVER HEARD OF A SKIING NEBRASKAN?" ROZ said. "How, I ask you, did I happen to fall in love with the only downhill skier from a state with not one degree of vertical incline from Omaha to Ogallala?"

"It's an open border crossing into Colorado, you know," Edwin said.

"Goddamn democracy," Roz scowled. "Where are the fascists when you need them?"

"Plenty of skiing in Wyoming too," Edwin pointed out.

"Your parents couldn't have vacationed someplace sensible, like Kansas, and spared us this lunacy?"

Edwin's wedding present to Roz had been skis, boots, poles, a new down Gerry jacket, and a pair of stretch pants in a respectable shade of mustard that he'd hoped Roz would think fashionable but not gaudy, so that, on the slopes for the first time, she might feel composed but not conspicuous. For himself, Edwin would simply excavate the ski clothes that had been hibernating at the bottom of a duffel bag at the back of the closet, unworn in the years since his smashup on the Goat.

"What if we made it more than just a ski weekend?" Edwin suggested. "What if there were more to it than just skiing?"

"What in the name of god else are you going to make me do?"

"No, just, what if we went somewhere more interesting than Vermont or upstate?"

"Like Paris?" Roz perked up.

"I was thinking someplace with a little more vertical drop— like out West, maybe?"

Roz was softening fast. The devilishly scheming look of childish excitement on Edwin's face was beyond anything she could refuse. He so wanted to show her this crazy frozen ice-ledge world of his. And she was curious, she had to admit. A little. "I've never really seen the mountains out West . . . ," she conceded. The tickets were as good as booked.

JACKSON HOLE, WYOMING, INTO WHICH THEY FLEW aboard Frontier Airlines, was a one-moose town back in 1973. Teton Village, the little cluster of lodges at the very base of the mountain, was, compared with Jackson Hole, about an eighth-of-a-moose town. There were a few hotels, the operations office of the mountain, a few ski lifts that disappeared up the side of the Teton, which rose from the river valley like the fearsome and spectacular behemoth it was, and a little saloon called the Mangy Moose with elk heads on the walls, sawdust on the floor, and the best hamburgers Roz had eaten in all her thirty-two years.

"It's good to be here," Roz said, wiping up the last of the burger's juice with Edwin's french fries. "It is."

"Good," said Edwin. He smiled. He was glad to be on vacation, Roz could tell. It was easier for him than it was for her not to think of the baby. Who was fine. Of course. But still, she was not quite fifteen months, and they'd not been away from her for this long before. But it was good: good to have a break, some time to themselves . . .

"Let's just call quickly," Roz said. "Just see how things are."

Edwin laughed. He pushed back his chair and dug into his trouser pocket. He turned over a small pile of change into Roz's open hands. "Before it gets too late," he said. It was nearing midnight on the East Coast.

"OH, SHE'S FABULOUS," FRAN HISSED INTO THE phone. She was on the kitchen extension in Roz and Edwin's New York apartment trying not to wake both Miranda, who was asleep in the bedroom, and Adele, who had passed out on the living room couch halfway through Johnny Carson. "Miranda's an angel," Fran told Roz and Edwin, who were huddled in the Mangy Moose entranceway, their ears pressed together into the pay phone receiver. "Miranda's the easiest thing in the world. Your mother, on the other hand . . ."

"You don't even have to tell me," Roz groaned. "Fran, *you're* an angel. You're our greatest friend in the world. We'll make it up to you. I swear." For the week, Fran and Adele were living at Roz and Edwin's, sharing baby-sitting duty. While Fran worked during the day, Adele watched little Miranda, and when Fran got home in the evening, Adele could take a break, though when it came to her granddaughter, Adele wasn't interested in a reprieve. "The woman has written down every single thing Miranda has eaten since you left," Fran told Roz. "Every sound she's uttered. Every cute baby thing she's done. You're going to have documented for all eternity every diaper change the kid went through. She's mad. She's super-grandma. Is there any booze in this house? I need a drink."

"Top cabinet above the sink," Roz said. "I wouldn't trust the wine in the fridge. It's been there awhile."

"Too late. I've already polished it off." Fran was scuttling around the kitchen, opening and closing cabinets, shifting jars and cans, searching for the liquor.

"Above the sink," Roz said again, but Fran was one to whom

you could give directions a thousand times, knowing full well she would never get where she was going unless she figured it out for herself, trial and error, guided by maps, stars, a sixth sense, and her own bounty of wrong turns.

"Ahhhh," Fran sighed at last. Roz could hear a cap unscrewing, then the clinking of glasses and a gurgle of tumbling liquid.

"So everything's good?" Roz asked again. She had edged Edwin's ear away from the phone entirely, and he stood nearby now, kicking his boots against each other as if to shake imaginary snow from their treads. When Roz asked a question of Fran, Edwin looked up to try and read Fran's response through Roz's face. Then he returned to his boots.

"*Good?*" Fran repeated. "Is it considered matricide if it's not your own mother you're doing in?"

"Jesus, Fran, is she being that horrendous?"

"Oh, Roz-Roz, she's fine. She's a mother. She's a *grand*mother. She's off her noodle. I'm surviving." Fran paused. She lowered her voice. "Has she always been such a religious nut?"

"I think she's worse since Mona's Judaic enlightenment."

"Yeah," said Fran, "and what's up with this *Miriam* thing?"

"Miriam thing?" Roz repeated.

Fran took a large swallow of her drink, and her voice crackled into a rasp more pronounced than usual. "Yeah, she seems to have decided to rename your daughter."

"You're kidding."

"She calls the kid Miriam, what do you want from me?"

"Oh Jesus," Roz moaned.

"What?" Edwin hovered in closer.

Roz put a hand over the mouthpiece. "Nothing," she relayed to him, "Adele's just decided her granddaughter was named for Moses' sister, not Prospero's daughter."

Edwin's eyes widened, and he backed off again, stepping away from the conflict, away from the discord. He wandered off and studied the brochures mounted in a wall display.

"Well," Roz said after a time, laughing with resignation, "kiss little Miriam for us. And if you can slip it into conversation whenever possible that her grandma's crazy as a bat, it couldn't hurt to start her on that fact early . . . Thank you again, Fran, really . . ." She looked to Edwin, motioning him to the phone. He shook his head, waved it off; he didn't need to talk to Fran. "OK, yes, I'll tell him. Thanks . . . OK . . . Bye-bye." Roz returned the phone to its cradle. With a cunning flick of the head she motioned Edwin to her side. There she wrapped a puffy down arm around his waist and drew him close, winning him back. He warmed into her, his body loosened in her arms.

"What did Fran have to say?" he asked, resentfully obliging. He shut his eyes, awaiting the potential sting of the response.

"Oh, nothing," Roz teased.

"Come on . . ."

Roz smirked. "She said to tell you your scowl was unbecoming."

"Great," he scoffed. "I try to take a simple little vacation with my wife, and meanwhile Fran Kornblauser drinks us out of house and home—and then insults me!—while my mother-in-law decides to rename our child! She'll probably have the kid reading Hebrew by the time we get home. My daughter the rabbi!" Edwin buried his face in the shiny plush of Roz's coat. She stroked his hair kindly.

"There there, bubbelah," she said, laughing quietly.

GUNNAR, THE SCANDINAVIAN SKI INSTRUCTOR, MET Roz at the rope tow. He wore a red one-piece ski suit with a zipper up the front, and it seemed not unlikely that he would be completely naked underneath it. "Rhozz," he said, and it took her a moment to realize he was saying her name and not simply clearing the phlegm from his throat. Roz had parted with Edwin at the lift ticket window, and she was feeling a bit adrift. "OK, so we go up, we come down, we see where we go then, yes?" Gunnar regarded her eagerly, like a dog begging to be let outside.

"Yes?" Roz said, her voice pinched with uncertainty.

"We go!" And Gunnar edged himself over to usher Roz through the lift line ahead of him.

"We go," Roz echoed. *Down in a snow-flurry of death,* she thought.

FRAN SUCKED UNSEASONABLY AT A GIMLET DURING the nightly phone call from the mountains. "We had our first near close call today on the homestead," she told Roz.

Roz's gut hollowed out in momentary fear, the way it had on the tiny puddle-hopper of a plane they'd flown into the valley as the pilot eased toward the runway and Roz's stomach hung back in the clouds. Motherhood had already made her a ready mark for Fran's mocking; she didn't need to make it any easier. Roz attempted to feign distraction. "Oh yeah? Huh, so what happened?" She wasn't half the actress she wanted to be.

"Adele stuck the kid with a diaper pin this morning."

Roz let out a gasp which she then tried, rather awkwardly, to turn into a cough. "Everything OK?" she sputtered.

"Oh fine," Fran said. "Adele lost her head for a minute, but otherwise . . ." Fran could be an infuriatingly stingy tease when it came to desired information.

"Are you going to tell this story or am I going to have to coax it out of you word by word?" Roz snapped.

Fran laughed deeply. "Steady, Mama," she chided, and Roz wondered for a minute why they had ever trusted this woman with their baby.

"Fran, I *am* going to kill you when I get home from this godforsaken trip."

Fran caught the unsteadiness in Roz's voice and changed her tone. "I'm sorry," she said. "I'm sorry, I'm sorry. Your mother really is a piece of work, Roz. So, anyway, it's maybe seven-thirty this morning and I'm in the bedroom getting dressed for the office and I hear this cry of horror from Adele in the other room. So I'm in my bra and slip and I go running out there and Adele's standing over the changing table, this look of sheer terror on her face, holding up a yellow-duckie diaper pin like she's Lady Macbeth, screaming, 'Fran, I've stuck her! I've stuck her with the diaper pin!' Whereupon Miranda, like she knew her cue and was just waiting there silently in the wings for her entrance, lets out a howl to wake the dead—"

Roz cut in, "She's all right, though, Fran?"

"Miranda's peachy, darling. She squawked for ten minutes, then ate a zwieback. She's fine. But, so, my first thought is, OK, we disinfect whatever wound Adele has inflicted on the munchkin, so I say, 'I'll get the rubbing alcohol,' whereupon Adele lets out another cry and wails—and do you know, the woman appears to know the entire inventory of your medicine cabinet cold? Frightening. Anyway, she cries, 'They're out of rubbing alcohol!' So I go into the kitchen, come back with the gin, and we swab the kid down—she had to tell me where, you couldn't even see the pinprick—and then I pour Adele a tumblerful for herself and make her drink it before I leave the apartment. Nothing so dangerous, I swear, as a panicky grandmother."

At last Roz was laughing. "So where is she now?"

"Miranda's asleep, like any self-respecting baby would be at this hour. Adele took to her bed after the six-o'clock news. Nursing her nerves, I'd say."

"Jesus Christ," Roz sighed. "Only two more days," she promised. "We'll rescue you soon."

"How's life out there in Winter Wonderland?"

"Well, after three days of snowplow Gunnar decided it was time I try some 'stem christies,' but you get going fast that way, honestly, really fast, and if there's anything I've learned about myself on this trip, it's that fast and I, when it comes to a ski slope, do not get along." Roz peered out of the phone booth where she was seated in the hotel lobby to make sure Edwin wasn't yet returning from the bar, where he'd gone to fetch some drinks. He did not condone the paranoia that forced Roz to call home daily. He just looked at her with that bemused but disapproving stare, like he'd caught her doing something decadent and private, plucking chin hairs or drinking milk straight from the carton. He wasn't in sight, so she ducked back into the booth. "So here's the image I'll leave you with," she told Fran. "Me coming down the bunny slope trying with whatever control I could find to stop myself from picking up too much speed, with my Scandinavian slave driver shouting from the bottom of the hill, 'Rhozz, poot ze boots togezzer! Rhozz, poot ze boots togezzer!' And then, later, as we're saying adieu until tomorrow's torture session, he looks at me pleadingly with those gorgeous green eyes like I'm breaking his heart every second and he says, 'Rhozz, why you no poot ze boots togezzer?' " She paused for effect. "Such is my life," she said.

"All my sympathies, you poor poor dear," Fran cooed. "All day on the slopes with a Nordic playboy. You've got it rough, darling. Want to hear about my fun behind the typewriter today?"

"Oh, here comes the Wicked Husband," Roz said. "Gotta run."

"Yeah yeah," Fran said. "Ain't that always the way it goes."

"Love to Miranda."

"Of course, Mama."

"Talk to you tomorrow."

"Like clockwork, Roz-Roz."

ON HER LAST DAY OF SKIING, GUNNAR INSISTED THAT Roz leave the bunny hill for the first time and come with him once up the double-chair.

"We can still come down a green trail?" Roz pressed him.

"Rhozz, yes, we go easy, easy all the way."

"Funny, that's exactly what Jeffrey Berenbaum said to me. We were in the backseat of his father's Cadillac, one fateful night in 1958."

"Rhozz, my darling, we talk or we ski?" Gunnar looked at her in mock sternness.

"I'd much prefer talk," Roz said.

"Your husband, he pay me to talk?" Gunnar wagged his head slowly back and forth like a kindergarten teacher saying no. "Your husband pay me for skiing, yes? Come, Rhozz, we ski."

"What if I can't do it?" Roz asked. "What if we get up there and I can't ski down?"

"You can ski down. You poot ze boots togezzer and you can ski down." Gunnar, to his credit, was enormously patient.

"No, Gunnar, that's where you're supposed to tell me that you'll carry me down in your arms to safety and never make me participate in this godforsaken sport ever again."

Gunnar tossed back his beautiful blond hair, stretched that finely hewn jaw, and laughed. Then he took Roz by the arm and began pulling her, on her skis, toward the chairlift.

"This is entrapment," Roz cried. "This is unjust. Kidnapping! Forced downhill plummeting! I protest!" But, more or less against her will, Roz went up the mountain.

It was a stunning, exemplary Wyoming day: forty degrees, endless blue heavens, no wind, and a blazing sun that made Roz and Gunnar tilt their faces to the sky, lean back in the lift, and, against Roz's best intentions, enjoy the ride. It was such a nice day that Roz didn't even mind when the lift stopped for an inordinately long time and left them dangling a hundred feet in the air. It was almost like sunbathing, which Roz enjoyed infinitely more than skiing, and she was happy to put off what she was sure would be her downhill demise in favor of getting some color on her face.

"Gunnar," Roz said, her eyes still closed blissfully, the inner lids orange and warm. "Are you married?"

"I am," said Gunnar.

"Kids?"

"*Kinder?* No. But maybe we do. Maybe we do soon." Gunnar's English was such that he could respond when questioned and get people down a ski slope, but not much else.

"I have a daughter," Roz told him.

"Yes? Ah good, yes."

"Her name is Miranda."

"Ah good. Mir-an-da." He spoke slowly, as if savoring the sound. "A beau-ti-ful name, yes?"

"Thank you," Roz said. She was quiet for a moment. "I never thought I would, you know. I was never one of those women who just wanted to have babies, you know how some women just only want to have babies?" The air was clean as peppermint. The sun glowed deliciously.

"Ah," said Gunnar, "no?"

"But then I just wanted to. Or not so much wanted to, but thought: if I don't do this I'm going to regret it later on, and if I'm going to do it, I better do it now. So I did. We did."

"She is how many years? Mir-an-da?" Gunnar asked.

"Fifteen months," Roz said. "Just over a year."

"A little one, yes?"

Roz nodded; her eyes were still closed. They were sitting so close together in the steel-caged chair, Gunnar could probably feel her nodding even with his eyes closed as well. All around them the crags and drifts of the Tetons and their valleys sprawled into eternity. Roz could feel the warmth of Gunnar's body emanating through his parka, and it made her feel melty and tingly at the same time. There was nothing Roz could remember or imagine more glorious than this, this rush of well-being despite the ski run ahead of her, and the way her feet ached relentlessly inside the clamped torture of her ski boots, and the sudden burst of confusing, conflicted lust she felt for her married Scandinavian ski instructor, and the fact that in the last fifteen months her life had changed in ways that could never be undone, that no matter what

happened in the world—if she kept loving Edwin or stopped loving Edwin, if she started going to temple and lighting Sabbath candles and stopped swearing *Jesus* under her breath when something surprised her, if the Grand Tetons shook and crumbled and fell into the Snake River and washed away to the sea, if anything joyous, or horrible, or wrenching happened, anything that filled Roz with awe or wonder or terror or life—at the center of it there would be the one most essential thing: Miranda. And as the gears ground and the cables creaked and the chairlift roused itself to motion once again, hoisting them higher and higher into the sky, Roz thought: *I'm going back to my kiddo tomorrow.* She thought: *Tomorrow I get to see my baby.*

5

THE INCIPIENCE OF THEIR
DISCONTENT

ADELE ROSENZWEIG TOLD NO ONE, NOT EVEN HER daughters, about the cancer until it was too late for anything to be done. By the time she drew the family together to deliver her news, she would have less than a month left to live. She had waited, with excruciating and uncharacteristic patience and privacy, for two years, until she knew the cancer had spread far enough that no one would bother her with miracle cures or force her to eat bean curd and get radioactivation.

"Radiation! Radiation!" Roz cried. "Jesus Christ, do you even know what it is? Mom? It's just what they do. They cure it. It could still work . . ." They were in Adele's lawyer's office: Mona, Roz, Edwin, Adele, and Bernard Eisenstein, Esq., where they had been mysteriously summoned on a Monday evening in the fall of 1973. Roz was livid; she was beside herself. "How could you not tell us? How could you do that to us?" she screamed at her mother. She turned to Mona for assistance, or at least support, but her sister looked stoned, as if the whole thing were flying—*zzzhoom*—right past her pretty little head. Down the table, Edwin—her husband, her smart lawyer husband, practical and level-headed and rational—just seemed misplaced and distressed, here in this Jewish lawyer's offices, the smell of stale file cabinets and fried onions hanging in the air, exuding from the very creases of Bernard Eisenstein himself. Edwin looked like all he wanted in the world was for Roz to sit down and be quiet and discuss this calmly. But who the hell was he? Her husband, fine, but what the hell did he know about anything? This was her mother they were talking about! Her mother sitting there and making them hear that yes, she was dying, and no, she wasn't going to fight it, and so while she was still coherent and functional she wanted to get it all straight with Bernard about who would get what, so could they start with the big things, please—the apartment, the furniture—and get smaller? "I want them worn down a little before I have to listen to my daughters fight over the Tiffany," Adele told Bernard, for everyone's benefit. "The lamp, it's worth something now, no? . . . and the china, dinner service for sixteen. In all those years I broke only the one soup bowl, if you can believe—"

It was unbelievable. "I don't care about *things*!" Roz hollered. "I care about *you*! Is that so crazy? You tell me you're dying and that's it and there's nothing that anyone's going to do about it!?" She was quite nearly apoplectic. It was insane; it was like they were operating and arguing in dream-logic, which isn't logic at all if you're awake.

"Roz, darling," Adele said, and she looked tired as she spoke, and a little put out, the Queen of Hearts after a long game of croquet. "Roz, why must you make a federal case? This is what I didn't want. I wanted to come and talk calmly, with Bernard—come, Roz, put on a good face here for Bernard. He doesn't need to see you this way. Come, sit, my baby." Adele patted the chair that sat empty between herself and Bernard. She was wearing a boiled-looking lavender wool suit, heavy cameos festooned to her ears like dead ancestors still clinging on. Her mother did not look bad, Roz

thought. She looked like what she was: an aging Russian immi-
grant who'd known more than her share of unfairness, who in
forty years in the United States had managed to raise two daughters, bury a husband, find a good kosher butcher, and develop a
decidedly unnatural fondness for lavender. And now she was ready
to throw in the towel.

Roz leveled her most vicious glare at her mother's dark prag-
matic eyes. "You're insane," Roz spat. "You are not in your right
mind," she went on, gaining composure as she spoke, "nowhere
near it, Ma, and I'm not going to sit here and listen to it, OK?
Bernie"—she turned her attention to the lawyer, a friend of the
family for as long as Roz could remember—"Bernie, if you knew
about this and you kept it from us—if you condone this, this whatever she is doing, then you are a very very very sick man." She
paused, then turned on Edwin, as if he too were somehow part of
this macabre little plot. She said, "I'm going home," and she didn't
even wait for a response, just walked out of the office, down the
stairs, and into the street.

AT HOME, LORALEE HAD JUST PUT MIRANDA DOWN
for the night. Roz's key turning in the lock roused her right back
up again. "Mah-mee!? Mah-mee!?" she chirped from her crib.

Entering, Roz began to narrate Miranda's point of view.
"Miranda's saying, *All right! I knew that sleep thing wasn't for real,
we were just going through the motions, huh?*" Lately, Roz had found
herself assigning dialogue to Miranda the way other people did
with their pets, enabling the schnauzer and the Siamese to chat
amicably about the quality of food service. Roz looked at Miranda
and saw a little person who clearly had a lot to say but not quite the
vocabulary with which to do so. Roz tried to help her out.

Loralee laughed. "You're back quick," she said.

Roz took off her coat as she crossed the room, and threw it
down on a pile of boxes. They were at a point where there was no

reason to put anything away since they were just going to have to take it back out to pack before the moving truck came. Everything was everywhere. Except Edwin's suits for work, which hung in the bedroom closet as demurely as they always had.

"You OK?" Loralee asked. She turned off the TV, which she had been watching silently. She looked at Roz with concern.

Roz scooped Miranda from the crib and pulled her in, then sank down into the couch beside Loralee. She looked at Miranda, intently, inspecting. She put her hands on the sides of Miranda's head and held her like that, kissed the crown of her daughter's head, pointedly, meaningfully, a Godfather kiss. She did not turn to Loralee when she spoke, just kept staring at Miranda as if someone had threatened to take her away. "My mother's dying," she said, hearing the words as she spoke them, hearing the differences between what they sounded like and what they meant. She shook her head, as if the statement were more of a question. When Loralee said "Roz?" and touched her leg lightly, it was clear that Loralee had been talking and Roz hadn't heard anything but the voices in her own head.

"I'm sorry," she said to Loralee. "I'm sorry . . . What?"

"Oh, sweetie," Loralee said. It seemed like she wanted to reach in and hug Roz, but with Miranda on Roz's lap—thrilled to be the center of everyone's attention—there wasn't room for such a maneuver. Loralee just kept patting Roz's leg the way you'd pet a stray dog you didn't want to get too close to, not knowing where it had been. "What happened?" Loralee asked. "Do you want to talk about it? Do you want me to go?" She gestured toward the door, pushing herself up a bit from the couch as if to demonstrate to Roz how easy it would be for her to leave.

"No, no . . . ," Roz said. "No, no, stay . . . ," she repeated. She was having trouble making herself be present; she kept letting the focus of her eyes go soft, blurring little Miranda into a warm blob on her lap, losing sense of the dimensions of the room and of her own size within it. It seemed for a moment as if she were huge, a ballooning Alice, swelling until the living room wasn't big enough to hold her. And then the next moment she felt teensy, so small that the room and its contents loomed around her like skyscrapers in a strange and unfamiliar city. She felt seasick. Claustrophobic. "God, I can't breathe with all this shit in here," she said. "Why do we have so goddamn much crap? We're too young to have this much crap. I can't stand it here—can you breathe?" She turned to Loralee now for the first time, searching her face for something, like a tow rope, to grab on to. "How could we have made you spend the evening in this apartment?" she asked, suddenly horrified. "That was awful of me—this is unbearable."

Loralee's was just then the kindest face Roz could ever remember seeing; Loralee was a heating pad, an aspirin, a cinnamon bun of comfort. She said: "Let's get you out of here," whereupon she lifted Miranda onto her hip, hoisted Roz up with her other hand, and whisked them all down the hall to her own apartment before Roz could even think to argue or worry about being an imposition.

LORALEE'S APARTMENT WAS NEARLY AS MESSY AS ROZ and Edwin's, and Loralee wasn't moving anywhere. "I know," Loralee said as they entered, "I live like a warthog." She scooped a slump of wet towels off a kitchen chair and urged Roz into it, placing the baby back into Roz's arms. Loralee made for the liquor cabinet. "It really is brutal of you," she said, pulling down a bottle from the shelf and sniffing at it the way you might smell a carton of milk to see if it had turned. She seemed to decide against the bottle in her hand then and reached up to exchange it for another. "I mean, I used to go to your place when I needed to escape the encroaching messes. I don't know what I'm going to do without you here, Roz." The apartment into which Roz and Edwin and Miranda were moving was on the Upper West Side, a good ways away from Loralee.

"Oh, we'll be here all the time," Roz assured her, "or you'll be there. I'm not even worried . . ." Though as she said it she realized it wasn't true at all. She found herself then actively worrying about how they were going to stay close to Loralee, and why they were moving in the first place, until she realized it was a lot more pleasant to worry about something like that than it was to worry about your mother dying of a breast cancer gone to god-knows-what kinds of cancer which she refused to treat, and that sent her right back to worrying. "I shouldn't have left," Roz said. "I shouldn't have walked out like that . . ." She held Miranda to her with dogged insistence.

Loralee turned from the drink she was pouring. "It wasn't over?" she asked. "I thought you'd come home because—"

Roz cut her off: "No, I just walked out. I couldn't take it. She brought us there to say, *I've got cancer, I'm not fighting it, now if Mona takes the Pesach dishes, Roz-Roz, you can have the Blue Tree china.*"

"Is that a Jewish thing?" asked Loralee. "Like the Christian Scientists, the no-doctors thing?" She set the glass down in front of Roz and urged her, *Drink, drink.*

Roz took a long sip. "It's a stubbornness thing," she said, and she was aware of the real venom in her voice. "It's a distrustful, stubborn, martyrdom, guilt thing. It's like she's saying, *Don't spend the money on my cancer—that money is for you and Mona, that's the money your father left for his girls.* Which is all a sick, underhanded way of being the saintly, selfless one, sacrificing for her children even in her last breaths, at the expense of her own life . . . It's like she hears the obituaries in her head, the memorial services. She'll turn a goddamn lump in her breast into a fucking crucifixion!"

Roz was breaking down, a horrible sadness rising inside her to overtake the ire. She took another long drink, then looked at the glass as if it had just been handed to her. "What is this?" she said. "It's awful."

"Scotch," said Loralee. "Just drink it. Your other option is straight crème de menthe."

Roz nodded. She drank. From her lap, Miranda stared up at Roz as if she were trying to figure out what her mother was feeling but didn't yet know if all that puffing and red-faced commotion meant Roz was joyous or excited or indignant or pissed as hell. Miranda just gazed up, studious, interested in her mother's face.

"It's in her breast then?" Loralee said softly, and for a moment Roz had forgotten about Adele completely and could only think of Miranda—*What's in her breast, Loralee? She has no breast*—remembering Adele only when Loralee's hand moved toward her own breast as she spoke, as if to make sure it was still OK, still healthy, to protect it from the dangers it might face in the world.

Roz deflated. The tears welled to the surface; there was nothing else she could do. "It's everywhere," Roz said, and it all flooded out of her. "It's everywhere now."

SOMEONE WAS TRYING TO TAKE MIRANDA AWAY FROM her! "No!" She grabbed at the air, clutching for her daughter. "Miranda!"

"Sh sh sh sh sh, Roz, I'm just putting her in her crib," Edwin was saying. "It's OK, it's me . . ."

The room came jaggedly into focus. Roz was still wearing the dress she'd had on at Bernie's office. Something caught in the bed-spread and choked her. She pulled the medallion of her necklace out from underneath her. It had already imprinted itself on the side of her jaw. She felt dry-mouthed and wrinkly. From above, Edwin leaned down and pulled the blanket up a little further onto the bed. Miranda seemed to dangle precariously and limp-limbed in his other arm. Roz wanted to find the words to ask for her but she could not. It was just a need, grabby and selfish—she wanted to yank Miranda from him and bury her face in folds of powdery-smooth skin. The most comforting smell in the world: baby. Roz grabbed for her daughter.

"Let her stay," Roz whispered. "She's asleep." She sat up, arms held out to receive the child, but Edwin didn't hand her over, and he didn't look like he was planning to. Roz could feel a sort of panic rising in her. She imagined for a moment that she knew what it would be like for a mother to see her child imprisoned—a desperate, rabid incomprehension: *You may not take her! She belongs to me!*

"She'll be better off in the crib—look at her, she's out, she'll stay out."

"No," was all Roz could bring herself to say.

Edwin looked impatient, tired, like it had been a long day at the office he so disliked and all he wanted to do was crawl into bed with the wife that he loved even though she was difficult and made him stay at the treacherous and unending meeting with her mother and sister while she went home and boozed it up with the bombshell down the hall. Roz wanted to ask him how it had gone, but that made her think of Adele, which just made her want Miranda next to her all the more, and so she was unable to ask anything, other than for her daughter.

"Give her to me, Edwin. Please." Her voice was firm and uncompromising, but soft.

He was defeated, as usual. He passed Miranda to Roz guiltily, and with shrugging reluctance, like a child being forced to surrender an offending toy to his teacher knowing full well he won't reclaim it until the end of the day. He said, "You know how I feel about this, Roz," and there wasn't any of the Edwin-giving-in chuckle in his words, no sense that he didn't really mind.

"Yeah," Roz said, settling Miranda in her arms, "but the way you feel about it is exactly the way your parents thought about it, which has no bearing whatsoever on our reality right here."

"My parents didn't do such a terrible job, Roz."

Roz scowled. "How come whenever you get upset with me you say my name seven times in every sentence?"

Edwin's eyebrows went up with impatience. "That's a little bit of an exaggeration, don't you think?" He swallowed hard.

" . . . don't you think, *Roz* . . . ," she corrected.

He kept standing solidly beside the bed, a sergeant making nightly rounds. He did not move, but she could feel the tension in his body go slack by the way it seemed to make the room grow dimmer, his outline blurry. "Why are you doing this?" he said.

"My mother is going to die," she spat. It wasn't enough, so she said it again: "My mother is going to die."

And although he would normally have been so much more considerate—so much kinder, more supportive, gentle—that night he was not. He was tired. He felt worn. "Everyone's mother is going to die, Roz."

"*Roz! Roz! Roz Roz Roz Roz Roz Roz!* I know my own goddamn name, Edwin Edwin Edwin Edwin." Her anger was funneled through a stage whisper. Before she was done speaking she turned down toward Miranda, just to check that she was still sleeping OK.

"Goddammit, what is wrong with you?" Edwin bellowed, and it was then that Miranda started to cry. Roz pulled her close and cooed into her hair, and that set *her* crying once again too. At the sight of Roz's tears, Edwin broke down. He sank to the bed. "Oh—," he said, and then stopped abruptly, as if he wanted with every ounce of his instinct to say *Roz* but was forcing himself not to. "Oh, darling," he said instead, and it sounded ridiculous, both coming from him and being said about her.

"She could have told us . . . ," Roz sobbed. "She could have warned us. Even if she wouldn't help herself, she could have let us have a little time . . ."

"And you would have never left her alone until she agreed to fight it with the superhuman force that you and you alone, Roz, seem to possess on this planet."

Roz looked up, startled. Her eyes fixed him; her tears stopped completely, as if they had been induced by a spell that had now been recanted. "You're on her side?" she said.

"She has *cancer*, Roz, of course I'm on her side. Aren't you?"

The fury was rising inside her again. "That is *not* what I mean and you know it. Don't be snide like that." She cupped Miranda's head in her palm and drew it toward her as if to protect Miranda from the strange beastly man seated beside them on the bed.

"I'm not being snide," he said. "I don't know what you want from me . . . I go, I sit there while you run away. All I did now was come home. What do you want?" He was losing his control, his tone edging into the whine that made Roz cringe.

"Let me get something straight," Roz said, and she tucked her head down to give Miranda one more hushing kiss of a whisper. "Do you believe that it's just a fine thing for my mother to—"

He cut her off: "There's nothing fine about anything here at all."

"Let me finish," she ordered. "Is it a . . ."—she sought an appropriate adjective—"is it an *understandable* thing, do you think, for a person to not let her own daughter know when she is gravely ill?" Roz was speaking very deliberately, choosing every word. "Do you think it is wrong of someone to want her own mother to seek health care treatment for an illness which will certainly kill her if she does not seek said treatment?" She was wild-eyed now, everything straining in the restraint she was trying so desperately to maintain.

"Roz," he began, then stopped as if he wanted to erase himself, to start again. "I think," he said, "that your mother is a grown and sane and rational woman—"

Roz could not help the roll of her eyes.

"—a rational woman who, at her age, thought it best not to undergo a radical, invasive, or otherwise crippling 'miracle cure,' and, being the person that she is, didn't want her family fussing over her and making her feel like a sick person, wanted to continue living as she had always lived and go gracefully and in her own time." Edwin finished, his eyes on Roz pleadingly, but there was something satisfied in his lips, like pride in a speech well made.

Roz stared at him blankly, then her head snapped to. "You've got to be kidding me," she said.

Edwin seemed genuinely confused.

"That's a fucking load of absolute shit, *Edwin*," she sneered. "Is everything really that white-bread pristine in your little repressed corn-fed family? You're going to try to spare your family the pain of your own fucking death? What a load of shit!" She stopped short.

Edwin's gaze had shifted to Miranda, who was swaddled in Roz's arms, gaping with astonishment at the side of her mother's chin. She looked like she might at any moment begin to wail, or else to tell them both to shut the hell up so she could get some sleep, goddammit.

"Could we please put Miranda to bed now so you can yell at me to your heart's content and not sacrifice *her* night's sleep for it?" Edwin said.

"That's it! That's exactly fucking it! You want to tuck the children away, spare the kids, right? Don't let her be here when her parents fight, or get upset. God forbid she hear her mother cursing, swearing. God for-fucking-bid! That's not *family, Edwin*." Her voice dripped with saccharine sincerity. "That's bullshit. Maybe that's what kind of bullshit your family did, and my mother did, but I'm not doing that with Miranda—I'm not doing that *to* Miranda—and god help me, neither will you. She's a person, Edwin, she's a member of this family, and she won't be treated like anything but. I swear to god, you will treat her like a human being, not some little waiflette who's going to live in a fucking tower and see no evil, hear no evil. She is not Rapunzel. She's a person!"

Edwin, who had been cautiously holding his tongue throughout the tirade, took his first opportunity to speak then. "She's a *baby,* Roz," he said. "She's a baby and she needs to be put in her crib so she can goddamn go to sleep!"

And then as if on cue Miranda let out a wail far more terrible than anything issuing from her parents' mouths, and there was something about the pitch of it, or the intensity, or the duration, that stopped them cold, and they were silent, just listening to Miranda wail. It was as if the routine were somehow automated or choreographed, as though they had survived some sort of live onstage falter and now they were moving on, finding their place in the music, picking up the steps where they had fallen off. Roz began to stand, and as it was impossible to do so with a screaming infant in her arms, Edwin took Miranda, held her as Roz got to her feet, and then handed her back to Roz, who carried her into the next room and tucked her into her crib, turned the Humpty-Dumpty mobile on over her head, tucked the blanket in around her, and let Miranda finally get some sleep.

Back in their bedroom, Edwin was sitting on the edge of the bed removing his shoes. Roz unzipped her jumper and left it on the floor where it fell. In her underwear she slipped beneath the sheets on her side of the double bed. She shut her eyes against the light. Edwin stood in his socks, turned off the lamp, and walked to the door. "I'll just say good night to Miranda."

6

A Proper Farewell

EDWIN BECAME A LAWYER, ROZ KNEW, BECAUSE HE wanted to help people. But—and the full extent of this story wasn't anything Edwin had ever fully admitted, even to himself—he'd taken out loan after loan to finance his education knowing that once he passed the bar he'd be able to land a high-paying job to which he'd sell out just long enough to pay back the loans and then go on to do the good work, "civil rights," he'd always said, something "for the common good." But the loans were long repaid and Edwin still toiled at a ritzy Manhattan corporate law firm—mergers and takeovers and other things about which he couldn't have given a rat's ass back when he started. Edwin was someone who only ran at full power; if he did something, he did it well. He was smart, exceptionally quick, dedicated, conscientious, and Stattler, Burns and Monk was not going to lose Edwin Anderson without a fight. For years he vowed to quit, and every year the counteroffer they made to entice him to stay did just that. It was more money than he could sanely refuse, and, truth be told, though Roz hated the agony Edwin put himself through, she didn't mind the money itself, per se. It was with this money that they were renting a house *baby,* Roz," he said. "She's a baby and she needs to be put in her crib so she can goddamn go to sleep!"

And then as if on cue Miranda let out a wail far more terrible than anything issuing from her parents' mouths, and there was something about the pitch of it, or the intensity, or the duration, that stopped them cold, and they were silent, just listening to Miranda wail. It was as if the routine were somehow automated or choreographed, as though they had survived some sort of live onstage falter and now they were moving on, finding their place in the music, picking up the steps where they had fallen off. Roz began to stand, and as it was impossible to do so with a screaming infant in her arms, Edwin took Miranda, held her as Roz got to her feet, and then handed her back to Roz, who carried her into the next room and tucked her into her crib, turned the Humpty-Dumpty mobile on over her head, tucked the blanket in around her, and let Miranda finally get some sleep.

Back in their bedroom, Edwin was sitting on the edge of the bed removing his shoes. Roz unzipped her jumper and left it on the floor where it fell. In her underwear she slipped beneath the sheets on her side of the double bed. She shut her eyes against the light. Edwin stood in his socks, turned off the lamp, and walked to the door. "I'll just say good night to Miranda."

6

A Proper Farewell

Edwin became a lawyer, Roz knew, because he wanted to help people. But—and the full extent of this story wasn't anything Edwin had ever fully admitted, even to himself—he'd taken out loan after loan to finance his education knowing that once he passed the bar he'd be able to land a high-paying job to which he'd sell out just long enough to pay back the loans and then go on to do the good work, "civil rights," he'd always said, something "for the common good." But the loans were long repaid and Edwin still toiled at a ritzy Manhattan corporate law firm—mergers and takeovers and other things about which he couldn't have given a rat's ass back when he started. Edwin was someone who only ran at full power; if he did something, he did it well. He was smart, exceptionally quick, dedicated, conscientious, and Stattler, Burns and Monk was not going to lose Edwin Anderson without a fight. For years he vowed to quit, and every year the counteroffer they made to entice him to stay did just that. It was more money than he could sanely refuse, and, truth be told, though Roz hated the agony Edwin put himself through, she didn't mind the money itself, per se. It was with this money that they were renting a house in Montauk for the summer. And it was the money that would pay Roz's tuition when she, at age thirty-seven, began law school in the fall.

Each Friday night Roz and Miranda collected Edwin expectantly at the train station as though he might bear something more than a briefcase, a weary smile, and tales of the working-dad workweek. He walked toward them, arms open; Miranda propelled herself at him, hurtling—"Daddy!"—and Edwin swooped her up, swinging his daughter high over his head. Roz could not help but notice, as they whirled, how black with soot and dirt and newsprint Edwin's shirtsleeves became in the course of a single day in the city.

When they brought him back to the station on Sunday evening—or at the first crack of dawn on Monday morning, already re-dressed in Friday's suit, if he was particularly dreading his return to the office and had postponed his departure as long as possible—Miranda rode in the backseat of the car singing songs to accompany the occasion, her own soundtrack of good-bye. "*See ya, see ya, hope you had a good good time. Hope we get to say good mornin' to ya, hope we get to see you again . . ."* "*So long, it's been good to know ya, this dusty old dust is a-gettin' my home and I've got to be drifting along . . ."*

In the rearview mirror Roz watched Miranda as she crooned, marveling at her deep concentration, the intensity of Miranda's meditation on her words, which made her look not like a sleepy six-year-old but more like an actor, a serious stage actor, getting into character before the rise of the great red curtain. There was something dramatic also in the way Miranda bid her father farewell at the train tracks, something studied and a little bit too self-conscious in the way Miranda hugged him, clutching the lapels of Edwin's suit like a lover who might need to be forcibly torn from the arms of her beloved.

By late July Roz began to await Edwin's departures with a mixture of sadness, relief, and fascination. It was sad to see him leave, but also a relief to have him gone, to know the house was just theirs again—hers and Miranda's—for another five days: no one to comment on the wet bathing suits dripping from doorknobs or the sandy grit that collected in the bathtub, no one who wanted to have dinner cooked at home instead of happily trotting off to the crab shack every night, or gleefully relishing lunch at the drugstore counter where there were eight different kinds of milkshakes to choose from and the soup came in tiny single-serving cans. But mostly Roz was held in thrall by the expectation of Miranda's Sunday night displays: Which mournful ballads would their daughter choose for her serenade? What sort of farewell would she decide to enact? Once, early in the summer, Roz had made mention of Miranda's dramatics to Edwin, but he'd shown no response, seemed oblivious that there was anything out of the ordinary in Miranda's behavior. This only intrigued Roz more.

In August Fran took a week of vacation and came to Montauk for a visit. She didn't ride out with Edwin on Friday night, instead caught a train early Sunday morning, and when Roz and Miranda drove to pick her up at the station Fran was loaded down with bags from Zabar's. Roz felt a wave of pity for the other passengers, who'd had to sit for two hours next to a smoked whitefish and a pound of coleslaw on ice.

Miranda pounced on Fran's sacks as though she hadn't been fed since June: "Onion bagels? Did you bring onion, Fran? Did you remember onion?"

"*Did I remember onion?*" Fran repeated, aghast. "Is the sky blue? Does Miranda have a nose?"

Miranda nodded so emphatically Roz was afraid she might strain something in her neck. She reached out and rested a hand on the top of Miranda's head, steadying her. Miranda shook her off instinctively, like a cat who doesn't want to be petted. She pulled away and ran ahead of them, first backwards, then galloping in the direction of the car, an old hatchback they'd acquired use of along with the house. Roz wanted to call out to Miranda to watch herself.

She imagined another car in the parking lot suddenly backing out of its space, no warning. On impact, Miranda would fly, launched into the summer air like something nearly weightless, arcing over the black asphalt, slapping the hood of an overheated sedan on her way down, rolling off, skittering along the ground like a stone skipped across the surface of water, coming to rest with a thud— her small body suddenly weighted, as if tragedy had the power to bestow mass—*thwack* against the wheel of a parked cargo van . . . "Miranda," Roz cried out, the volume and fear in her voice at a pitch that shocked herself. "Miranda, watch where you're going please!"

Miranda's skip wound down into an obedient plod. She looked back at her mother with weariness and exasperation. Roz had sworn not to be an annoying mother, worrying Miranda's life away. But what the hell was a person supposed to do? If she had cats and lived on a busy road, would she not erect a fence to keep the cats on the lawn and avert possible catastrophe? Why did she feel the constant need to justify her protectiveness? As if keeping her child safe from harm was something she should feel guilty about! Edwin already thought she was ridiculous when it came to Miranda, and Miranda was old enough to see her mother as something of a wet blanket. And there was no way she was going to make it through a week of Fran without being crowned Queen Worrywart. She wasn't a worrier! Her mother had been a worrier, and Roz was most decidedly not going to follow in Adele's footsteps. It was deeply frustrating the way everyone insisted that Roz was so much her mother's daughter. She felt forced to walk a constant line between obsessive love and utter nonchalance, but she found it to be such a horribly thin line that she was forever falling off, to one side or the other. It made her feel a little like she had two personalities. She would be the fabulous mom-who's-more-like-a-friend-than-a-mom mom, the one who absolutely planned to let her daughter have sleepovers on school nights and go to bed late if there was a good movie on TV. The kind of mom who'd let her kid drink wine with dinner and wouldn't care less if her daughter wanted to dye her hair green and wear bustiers to school. But under all that fun and allowance, Roz was Adele, and she knew it. Whenever she left Miranda—for any period of time at all—upon return she inevitably imagined all the ways in which Miranda could have died while she was gone. It was a terrible thing to do to oneself, she knew, and certainly a terrible thing to do to Miranda, but the tendency—Adele's tendency, goddammit!—was a part of her as surely as Adele's nose was the one tacked onto Roz's face. I am the bane of my own existence, Roz thought. Could one be one's own bane? she wondered. It didn't matter; she was clearly going to become the biggest bane in Miranda's life. And soon.

Miranda adored Fran. Though Roz was embarrassed to admit it, she secretly believed in part that Miranda was drawn to Fran because she was big and smooshy and crude and laughed a lot, loudly. Once Roz had confessed this thought to Edwin, ashamed by what she perceived in herself to be a deep-seated fear of the fat and the jolly. Edwin had laughed and made a joke about those being the reasons that other people *couldn't* take Fran in very large doses. Roz had laughed with Edwin at the time, but didn't actually think it was funny at all. She thought a lot about that exchange. It weighed on her. Finally she figured out what it was that bothered her so much: Edwin was supposed to be the kind of person who'd stick up for someone like Fran, not put her down. Edwin was the morally conscious one who said and did the right and good things. It upset her more than she'd have expected, this idea of Edwin falling from grace. It upset her so much she confronted him about it.

"Fran?" Edwin had said, his eyes squinty and uncomprehending.

"Yes, Fran," Roz said. "I just felt like . . . I mean, you're her friend . . . I mean, if your friends and your enemies are saying the same things about you, wouldn't you start to wonder if your friends really were your friends . . . ?"

"I'm sure I was kidding, Roz," Edwin said, his voice at once defensive and mocking. He didn't even really distinctly remember the conversation, though it had taken place less than a week before. Roz felt as if she were being deftly condescended to, made to question her own perception of an event, to wonder why she'd just spent a week torturing herself over a conversation that hadn't even been significant enough to register in her husband's consciousness.

"Why would you kid that way about a friend?" Roz demanded, her sense of order not yet restored. If anything, she felt further estranged, further away from understanding.

"Roz, I love Fran, you know that," he told her, and though his voice was sweet and soft, it almost didn't matter at that point. Roz wasn't hearing the words anymore. Everything out of his mouth was sounding like *Roz, could you please stop worrying about every goddamn microscopic little thing . . .*

BACK AT THE HOUSE, ON THE DECK, THEY ATE BAGELS with lox and chive cream cheese and drank pink lemonade from concentrate that Miranda stirred into the pitcher all by herself. She showed off for Fran, leaping up from the table to turn a cartwheel or run to her room to fetch a picture or a book or a toy to display to Fran for inspection. Fran's stamp of approval seemed all Miranda desired for self-validation, and as Fran wasn't the most forthcoming when it came to praise, the fact that Miranda was able to extract as much of it as she did struck Roz as quite remarkable. Edwin was quiet throughout the meal, and when he excused himself afterward to go inside and look over some papers, Fran rolled her eyes at Roz. She had large eyes that were naturally droopy and she used them expressively, the way a dog might use his ears to demonstrate pleasure, want, woe, or guile.

"Hey, Miran," Roz said, "whaddaya say you go and mix up some more of your super lemonade and Daddy can have a glass while he's working . . . ?"

"Will you time me?" Miranda asked. You could get Miranda to do all sorts of things—fetch things you'd left upstairs, run down to the shore to test the water temperature, run out and grab your towel off the clothesline—if you agreed to time her while she did it.

Roz lifted her wrist and let the second hand make its way to 12. "On your mark," she said, "get set, and . . . go!" Miranda was off! Roz and Fran watched until she'd cleared the screen door, then lowered the backs of their deck chairs, passed the Hawaiian Tropic oil between them, and soaked up some sun. Roz untied the strings of her suit top and removed her watch, laying it down on the deck beside her chair. The air felt salty and smooth. Every so often a gull swooped by, squawking its way to the sea. It was nice just being there with Fran. It was relaxing. Easy.

"Shit!" Roz sat up suddenly, clutching her top to her breast with one hand and feeling around for her watch with the other. "What time did I start her at . . . ?"

As if on cue, Miranda burst back out onto the deck, a striped beach towel around her neck like a prizefighter, and the lemonade pitcher clasped to her like a baby. She reeled toward them, then stopped short, sending a splash of pink lemonade slopping onto her mother's toes.

"Whoa," said Fran. She stuck out an arm to steady Miranda.

"Careful, Miran, careful," Roz warned her. She studied her wristwatch. "Two minutes forty-five seconds," she declared, her voice full of unwarranted authority. She took the pitcher from her daughter's hands.

Miranda slumped to the ground. "Phew!" she sighed. She seemed pleased by her time.

Fran shot Roz a look of puzzled bemusement, and over Miranda's head, Roz shot one back to say, *Search me! But it makes the kid happy . . .*

With a burst of hidden energy Miranda leapt to her feet once again. "Can I swim now?" she yelped. "Can I now, please?"

"*May* I," Roz corrected her. She paused. "Come on, Mir, give me a little time in the sun, OK? A little Mom-time. When you've digested your bagels some, then I'll go with you down to the beach, OK?"

"You know," Fran began, "I heard somewhere they proved that was all bunk, all that don't-swim-for-half-an-hour-after-you-eat thing . . ." She grinned devilishly.

Roz shot her a look. "You'll be sleeping outside tonight, my dear."

Miranda was jumping up and down as if she had to pee.

Fran swung her feet to the ground and began to roll up the cuffs of her pants. They were billowy and black, as was most of Fran's wardrobe. "I'll go down with you, kid," she said. Smiling, she rose to her feet.

Roz shaded her eyes and propped herself up on an elbow. She was ready to give in, to take Miranda down herself, but something stopped her—the absolute content on both Miranda's face and Fran's. So all she said was, "Thank you, sweet." To Miranda she said, "Don't give Fran a hard time. You come up out of the water when she tells you . . ." But she knew Miranda would heed Fran's beck and call. Miranda was nodding furiously, bobbing like she was ready to shoot to the beach in a single bound, and Roz lowered her head back to the chair and waved as the two of them moved off toward the sand.

WHEN SHE COULDN'T REMEMBER THE WORDS TO A song, Miranda compensated with whatever appropriately syllabic fillers came to her. On the way to the train that night to drop Edwin off, the song was "Red River Valley," to which Roz thought she could remember square-dancing in college. They planned to stop for ice cream on the way to the station, so all four of them were squished into the car. Ice cream was the excuse for both Fran and Miranda to be there. Really, Roz just needed for Fran to witness Miranda's behavior so Fran could tell her if she was crazy or not. Edwin was quiet, licking at his Butter Brickle with mathematical precision. Fran and Roz chittered back and forth, swapping tastes from each other's cones. Miranda, who polished off her Rocky Road before they made it back into the car, resumed her singing. *"From this valley they say you are going. We will miss you and buys us your smile. And I say you have dated the sunshine. That was hiking a rathbone a Lyle."* Roz kept trying to shush Fran's conversation so she'd pay attention to Miranda's song, but Fran appeared to hear the whole thing as relative nonsense and Roz wondered if she would lend any insight at all to the strange phenomenon of Miranda's Sunday soap-opera dramatics.

"Comma say babasa if you love me. You not hate me you be me and you. Be right back here the Red River Valley. And alone you a lover so true."

In the driver's seat, Edwin leaned so he could talk to Miranda in the rearview mirror. "Missing a few lyrics there, kiddo?" he said.

Miranda looked taken aback before everything really registered and her face showed the hurt she felt. "I know it *pretty* well . . . ," she said.

"That's how the song really goes?" Edwin pushed, and Roz thought she could hit him, that's how angry it made her to see Edwin spoil Miranda's fun, question her, make her feel unlearned, silly, shown up.

Confident, her face fixed with determination, Miranda said, "Yes, Dad, that's how it goes," and Roz wanted to whoop and cheer when Miranda picked right back up where she left off, unwilling to let her father's doubt dissuade her from her project. *I love you,* Roz wanted to tell her, to hug her tight as she could and talk right to her face so she knew every word was dead-on true: *You're the greatest kid there ever was, my babe . . . You're the best I've ever ever known.*

It was hard to get Miranda to bed before the sun went down, and that night it was nearly ten before Roz and

Fran were able to collapse onto the living room couch and discuss the events of the day. The couch was an L-shape, and they lay with their heads together, feet apart. Fran lit a cigarette and blew smoke rings into the air above their heads. They had a magnum of red wine on the coffee table and they lifted their heads every few moments to sip from their glasses, refilling more often than necessary. Roz put an old Joni Mitchell record on the turntable and the summer night filled with *pling*ing strings and the imperative scream of fingers up and down the fretted neck of the guitar. *I had a king in a salt-rusted carriage who carried me off to his country for marriage too soon. Beware of the power of moons. There's no one to blame, no one to name as a traitor here . . .*

They sipped silently at their wine and stared up at the ceiling as if expecting a meteor shower. It was Roz who spoke first. "So is that bizarre, or what?" she said. "The way Miranda clung to him . . . It's like they're not particularly close in any way and then, Sunday night—boom!—she can't live without him. What do you think *that's* about?"

"Honestly?" With a few glasses of wine in her, Fran was about as tactful as a drunken sailor.

"No, *dis*honestly. Of course honestly." Conversations with Edwin were so guarded, his emotions so masked in a lifetime of politeness they'd lost the ability to affect him anymore. Fran, on the other hand, usually said whatever she felt, when she felt it, and the constant purging seemed to keep her thoughts true, the line between words and feelings taut and direct. Now Fran spoke like a teacher at parent conferences with bad news to break. "I just wonder," she said, "if she isn't trying to somehow set an example for you . . ."

"An example?"

"Well, you'll have to pardon me for saying so, Roz-Roz, but it doesn't seem to break you up much when Edwin departs again at the end of the weekend . . ."

Roz felt a sinking sensation. "You think Miranda's aware of

that?" she asked, but of course Miranda could sense it. How could she not?

"Maybe she's trying to let you know what a proper good-bye looks like?" Fran offered.

"OK," Roz said, her tone growing defensive, "I get it."

They were quiet awhile. Finally Roz said, "I'm sorry," but Fran didn't answer. Roz looked at her. Fran seemed to have fallen fast asleep. Roz refilled her own wine glass. Fran's sighs grew heavier, then deepened into snores. Outside the crickets buzzed. Roz could feel her heart thrumming with wine, like it was trying to make time with Joni's guitar.

7

THE MESS UNDER THE BED

Located in the heart of New York State's Adirondack Mountains, Camp Sunset Lake consists of "brother/sister" camps nestled on the pine-forested shores of a small private lake. Children ages 8 to 13 come from across the United States to spend eight challenging, fun-filled weeks each summer in a place where they can leave behind the conveniences (and the inconveniences) of the modern world and become part of a very special community. In the course of a summer, children are exposed to many new challenges and learn to develop new skills and talents. Sunset Lake is a community that believes in the power of community, and the deep respect and appreciation instilled in children through membership in such a community. A typical summer at camp includes much singing, gardening, hiking, canoeing, swimming, craftwork, field sports, waterfront activities, backpacking, sailing, and making great friends. It's also likely that campers might act in a play, ride a horse, feed a llama, cook dinner over an open fire, tie-dye a T-shirt, play tetherball, be in a jacks tournament, build a lean-to, fly a kite, catch a fish, and climb a mountain.

Dear Mom + Daddy, on Sunday to get into the dining hall for dinner we have to write a letter to our home so our moms and dads know we didn't fall off a mountain or something, that's what my counsler says so this is my Sunday letter even tho I wrote before anyway and you know I didn't fall off a mountain, not yet at leist. Camp is great!!!!! Next summer I hope I get to have the same cownseler Carrie becase she is great!!!! My pretty much best friend is Darrin (no she's not a boy if that's what you were thinking!) she's a girl named Darrin. She's in my cabin (did I tell you that allready?) We are swim buddys most days and she's a good swimmer as me almost. But its fun anyway!!!!!! My favorite activity is TRIPCRAFT where you learn how to do things to go on trips like tie knots and make fires and scrub pots with soap that comes out of the root of a plant called soap plant. My favorite song is leavin' on a jetplane and I know most of the words because we sing it when we walk back to our cabin when the other girls are still at the campfire because they're older. We sing all the time here! Every second we're singing. We sing when we wait for things and walk places. We sing when we pee! (ha ha, joke) but really we do! Next summer can I get the stasionery where they have the boxes you check off like Today was SUNNY RAINY   SNOWY (ok not really!)   HOT   COLD DRISZLLEY   WEIRD   The food is GROSS   EATABLE GOOD   WE HAVENT HAD ANY FOOD YET   IS THAT WHAT THAT STUFF WAS ON THE TABLE   and you check off what it was and there are other questions too. I wuld still write you a real letter to but those are fun for Sunday letters.   I LOVE YOU A MILLIAN ZILLIN GABRILLIAN   HUGS   AND   KISSES!   LOVE   AND MUSKITO BITES I HAVE 23 ON <u>ONE LEG</u> I COUNTED!

Your daughter,
Miranda Gert Anderson
Hatchling Bunk
Camp Sunset Lake

Hatchling Nest
Inspection Sheet
Thursday, July 10, 1980

Bathroom: ok—remember to stock TP
Clothesline: get dry stuff in before rain! (and get wet stuff
off rafters, back of cabin girls)
Sweep: ok except back, under beds (is that Miranda's bed
with all the mess under it?)
Beds: sloppy but fine. EXCEPT MIRANDA! (come on,
Miranda, what's the problem?)
Overall: 7 (come on, you guys, you can do better than that!)

Dear Mirand,
Thank you for writing us such super letters. I love to come
home from law school and open the mailbox and find a letter from my Miran—and I read it right away because I'm so
excited and anxious to know how you are and how things
are going at camp. Then when Daddy gets home I read it to
him out loud while he is having dinner and that's fun
because I get to go through it all again. I wish I were up
there in those mountains, swimming in the lake (even
though it sounds awfully cold! And are there really fish that
swim right into you or are you just pulling your old
mother's leg?) and playing tennis instead of going to school
and coming home in this hot and sweaty city. Daddy has
too much work (so what else is new, right?) but I am going
to go up to Tanglewood Music Festival with Fran this
weekend to hear some classical music. It's not as far north
as you are but we may have to bring sweaters for the evening. In the city it's too hot for anything outside, and then
when you get inside the air conditioners are always FREEZ-
ING and everyone gets summer colds from all the chang-

ing temperatures. Not me, though, not so far anyway. Wish me luck in staying healthy! We're so glad you love camp! We miss you too. Can't wait to see you on V Day! I love you, baby girl,
love,
The Sappy Mother
p.s. Hey, chicken, Daddy here, all that Mommy said x2! Love, Dad

Darrin—can I barrow your purple shirt for the sosial, the one with the fringe? Write me a note back.—M.G.A.

Miranda—yes. What else are you going to wear? How much time till rest hours over?—DEQ p.s. what is your middle name?

DEQ—thanks. Jeans shorts and my jelly shoes. I don't have a watch. Gert.—MGA p.s. what are you wearing?

For real, whats your middle name? I dont know what I'm wearing. I did not think about it I guess. What do you think I should wear?—DEQ

For real, it's Gert. I got named after some one in my dads side of our family. You can wear my haltar top that you like if you wanted.—MGA p.s. is the bell EVER going to ring?!?

MGA—thanks. I don't know. I'll see later I guess. It might be too cold to wear it at night. But thanks anyhow. What are you doing for afternoon activity? If it ever is time for it, I mean . . . Ha Ha—DEQ

DEQ—play rehearsal. What are you doing? If they ever let us out of this cabin that is.

MGA—climbing Sunset mountain with Carrie and making water color pictures on top. If we are ever allowed to talk ever again!—DEQ

DEQ—I wish I was going with you! Carrie is the BEST!!! Her boyfriend at boys camp is Bob. I LOVE BOB! p.s. rip up this note in tiny peices after you read it! Or else!

MGA—whose Bob?—DEQ

DEQ—WHOS BOB?!?!? You do not now who Bob is?!?! He's the gooooorrrrrggooouuuussss one that she's always with! DISTROY THIS PAPER WHEN YOU READ IT!!!!!—MGA

MGA—I dont think I know who he is. Oh well. They better let us get up soon or Ill scream!!!!!—DEQ

DEQ—I LOVE BOB! Don't tell. I have to pee

Miran—not much going on here, just a quick note before I'm off to class to say I love you. It's so hot here all I could bear to make for dinner was tuna sandwiches—I know, you hate them . . . Daddy is working late on a big case and we haven't seen each other hardly at all. It's kind of like he's away at camp too, only he doesn't get to have any fun.
Love, The Mommy

Hatchling Nest
Inspection Sheet
Tuesday, July 15, 1980

Bathroom: good
Clothesline: whose mudfight shirt is that still hanging there, Miranda Anderson?
Sweep: fine
Beds: Miranda, if you don't change your sheets by tomorrow you're going to spend afternoon activity doing it, so don't say I didn't warn you.
Overall: fine (except . . .), so: 6

Baby Girl—you sounded so sad still when we hung up the phone and I'm so sad thinking that I can't make you feel better. It's hard to be a Mommy from far away. I just hope you understand that Daddy HAS to go to this conference or else his bosses will be very upset with him. There's just nothing we can do, sweetheart, OK? You have to try and understand that, Miranda, that people can't always do exactly what they want to do. I know that you are sad, my girl, but we'll still have fun, even if it is just your old boring mom on V Day. I'm not sooooooo bad, am I? I hope not. I love you, sweet baby, and Daddy does too. We both do very very much. Love, Mommy

---

Dear Miranda, Mommy said you were upset about Visiting Day. I'm really sorry that I can't come. I was looking forward to seeing you and going for a swim with you in the lake. It sounds like you're having a very good time so far. Keep it up.

I know there's no excuse for me to miss something as important as Visiting Day, but I hope you'll try your best to understand. Sometimes in a person's life he can wind up in a place or a situation that he never meant to be in, but he's got responsibilities and can't just drop them. I know this probably doesn't make much sense to you right now. Maybe it's something you will be able to understand better when you are a grown-up and find yourself having to make similar, difficult decisions. I am thinking of you a lot and hope you are having lots of fun.

Write soon.

      Love, Daddy

DEQ—Where are you going to go with your parents on Visiting Day?—MGA

MGA—My parents can't come. Its too far away from Denver. I guess I'll hang out here at camp.—DEQ

DEQ—Maybe you could come with me and my mom if you wanted to—MGA

MGA—That would be so cool! Do you think I could really?—DEQ

DEQ—Ill ask—MGA

MGA—Are your parents divorsed?—DEQ

DEQ—No. Why?—MGA

MGA—How come your dads not coming?—DEQ

DEQ—He has to work.—MGA

MGA—Oh.—DEQ

DEQ—Really its beter any how. My mom can only yell at herself in the car now.—MGA

MGA—HA HA—DEQ

Dear Mommy, Hi! This is my Sunday letter sorry it is short. Love, Miranda

Dear Miranda, You know if you keep writing short letters I'm going to write short letters too. So there! We love you and miss you and wish you'd write US longer letters. Love, Mommy and Daddy

Dear Mommy, I'm sorry its just that were really busy here at camp. There is swimming and horsebackriding + tenis + softball + arcery + drama + dance + arts and craft + sailing + canoing + tetherball + pingpong + singing + soshils + hickeing + alot of other things too. Love, Miranda ps can my freind Darrin come with us for Visiting Day her parents arent comming ether becuse Denver is to far away.

Miran—Of course Darrin can come with us on V Day. You didn't tell me she was from Denver! Wow! We'll have a Girls' Day Out! Lots of studying to do—I'll write more later. Also Miran, will you please write a letter to Daddy—he's feeling really sad that you're so upset about Visiting Day. Please, baby, write him one of your sweet quick notes and cheer him up, OK? I love you, The Mommy

Dear Daddy, We had a soshual with the boys camp the other day. It was fun. I got asked to dance by two boys but one dosen't count because he is only my freind not my boyfreind. The other one is not my boyfreind ether but I like him his name is Scott Goldman and he is 9. We danced to the song I want you to want me by the musical group Cheep Tick. It was really fun. Soshils are when you get together with the boys and play music on the stareo in the red barn and dance to songs you like.

My 2 favorite cownslers here are Carrie (my couwnsler) and her boyfreind Bob who is a counseler at the boys camp. They both go to college in the year and camp in the summer and they have been going out since the begining of the summer. Darrin (my freind) saw them kissing. She said they didn't see her tho. FHEEW! That was close huh?! Lucky Darrin!
Well gotta run. See ya!
Miranda

Miran—Hi baby! I think maybe you'll be coming home just in time to catch your brain and put it back in school before it turns into a big pile of Jell-O. It will be funny for you to look at your letters to us when you come home I think, and you can see the deterioration of your spelling over the course of the summer. Maybe they should get a spelling counselor! (Just kidding—but it really will be interesting for you to see, I think.) Today I have to go to the bank and the post office and then I'm going to have lunch with Mona. Joshy and his wife had another baby in Israel. (I lost count of how many that makes.) If Grandma Adele were here she would send money to plant a tree there so maybe I will do the same thing and make my mommy happy.

Give my love to the mosquitoes!
Love, Mommy and Daddy

Dear Mrs. Anderson (I mean Roz),
I am writing to say thank you very much for bringing me with you on Visiting Day. I had a really good time. My mom and dad said to say thank you from them too for being so nice to me. They said that if Miranda ever wants to come visit in Colorado they would love that. Well, rest hour is almost over and we have to go SWIMMING! You are a very cool mom!
Love,
    Darrin Elizabeth Quaile, your Visiting Day daughter

Mom—Its Sunday and we have to have a letter home.
MIRANDA

Dear Miran—It was so good to see you this weekend and to meet Darrin and Carrie and everyone. It also made me really sad to fight with you like that, especially in front of Darrin. That's the kind of thing that I think you shouldn't do in front of other people, especially your friends who you don't want to make uncomfortable. I hope that you're not still upset with me, Miran. I'm not angry anymore and I wanted to tell you that: that I'm not angry, and that even in the times when I am angry I still love you. I don't know how much of what went on this weekend actually had to do with the ice cream thing and how much was because Daddy wasn't there, and I have been wondering if you think that you might be mad at me a little bit about Daddy not coming. I wish Daddy could have been there too, Miran. I wonder if it's wrong for me to tell you how sad and angry *I* am at Daddy for not coming. Maybe it's wrong to tell you that, but I've always been honest with you, baby, and there's no rule book that they give out on how to be a good mom. I wish there was sometimes! I'm doing my best, and as far as I know I think Daddy is trying to do his best too. So please, baby, cut us both a little slack. Please? It's a hard time, I know, and I think there are probably a whole bunch of things that you and I and Daddy should talk about when you come home, but for now baby you should just enjoy camp, enjoy everything you're doing, and your wonderful friends and that beautiful place and all the great stuff you're getting to do. And remember that I love you and Daddy does too.

Love, Mommy

Infirmary Report

Sunday 8/3 (only 4 more days on the teddy bear lice quarantine!)

Molly Rabiner—still here with PI. Should be OK to go back to cabin by Tuesday. Poor kid.

Miranda Anderson—complained to Carrie of stomach pain before dinner. Set her up here with some ginger ale and a bucket. She seemed fine when I got back from the dining hall, but I'll keep her the night anyway just to be sure. (check w/ Carrie—is something else going on w/ this one?)

TO THE CABIN INSPECTOR: MIRANDA WAS IN THE INFIRMARY AND SO SHE MISSED CLEANUP SO WE

JUST PUT ALL HER STUFF ON HER BED. PLEASE DON'T COUNT HER IN THE OVERALL SCORE. THE REST OF THE CABIN IS REALLY NEAT. THANK YOU, THE HATCHLINGS

Hatchling Nest
Inspection Sheet
Monday, August 4, 1980

Bathroom: good
Clothesline: OK
Sweep: OK
Beds: fine (exception noted—does she have small animals living under there at this point?)
Overall: 9

Dear Miranda, Haven't heard from you in a while, hope that means you're busy and having too much fun to write. We'll see you soon anyway. Can't wait to have you back home. I made a new comforter cover for your bed from those butterfly sheets we got at Macy's last spring, remember? It looks great! I hope you like it. Your room is waiting for you, looking forward to having its primary occupant back. I think it doesn't know what to do now that it's so clean. It says: Where's that messy girl? Where's all that dirty laundry? We liked that girl! When's she coming back? My hope is that MAYBE she's coming back as not such a messy girl (is that just wishful thinking? Or has the cabin inspection thing worn off on you? A little?) We love you and can't wait to see you!
Love, Mommy and Daddy

Infirmary Report
Sunday 8/10
Emily Harris—sore throat, salt-water gargle, Chloraseptic, Cepacol
Audrey Slesenger—calamine for mosquito bites
Zoe Frank—splinter removal, left heel, alcohol swab, Neosporin, Band-Aid
Miranda Anderson—the mysterious Sunday evening I don't want to write a letter home stomachache. What's going on with her? check w/ Carrie—worth a call home to her folks? Let her stay here for the evening, back to cabin to sleep.

Wed. 5 p.m.
Carrie— Just had a phone call in the office from Miranda Anderson's mom in NY, they haven't heard from her in a couple weeks, just checking to see if things are OK. Have Miranda call her at home this eve. bet. 7 and 8. —Sue

Thurs. 8:30 a.m.
Carrie— Mrs. Anderson called again—she didn't hear from Miranda last night. Concerned. Have her call home please. —Sue

Sue— Sorry, I sent Miranda up to call last night, but it looks like she didn't do it. I'll talk with her and then if she still won't call I'll call myself. Let her mom know we're on it if she calls back. Sorry you're getting stuck in the middle. Thanks, Carrie

Memo to All Staff: Buses arrive 7:30 a.m. Sunday morning. Departure time: 8:30 a.m. All duffels need to be up at the field under the shelter BEFORE DINNER on Saturday. Sleeping bags and day packs can come up with the kids to breakfast Sun. morning. Trunks to be shipped should go on the office porch. UPS will pick up on Mon. morn. Pick up Final Cabin Cleanup Checklists at office. Packing—Friday afternoon. Big Cleanup—Saturday. Final Sing and Awards—Sat. nite. Pls. have camper awards in to office by Sat. morn. Thanks, Sue

Hatchling Nest (Carrie)—Camper Awards

Zoe Frank—the When are we going to be there? Award
Paula Solomon—the Did someone say grilled cheese!!!!!? Award
Erin Garrity—the Lake Ness Monster Award
Miranda Anderson—the Was there an earthquake or is that just your bed? Award
Astrid Hazleton—the Calamine Kid Award
Darrin Quaile—the Emily Post Award for Impeccable Manners
Lauren Pappageorge—the "Lordy Lordy Hip Size Forty!" Award

Camper Report

Counselor: Carrie Specter
Cabin: Hatchling Nest
Camper: Miranda Anderson

Activities: Miranda spent a lot of time at tripcraft and at the ropes course. Then once play rehearsals began she got pretty consumed by that. Has a real talent onstage. Seemed to enjoy it. Loved waterfront activities, esp. swimming (see Ranks and Certifications). Too bad Drama stuff ate up so much time, I think she might've gotten further in diving. Rec. for windsurfing when she gets a little bigger.

Ranks and Certifications: Red Cross: Swimmer; diving: front dive; tripcraft: Firestarter, Tracker, Chef, Knots; ropes: Level 1 Climber.

Camper relations: Miranda is well liked, outgoing, made friends easily. Definitely a leader, occasionally bossy. Very close friendship w/ Darrin Quaile, overshadowed Darrin a bit, but Darrin's got a quiet strength, stands her own with Miranda, I think. Somewhat boy-crazy, but that might just be the age or all the girls feeding off each other's anxiety. They do seem awfully young, though, for the level of opposite-sex interest many of them seemed to express. (Or maybe I'm just getting old . . .) Only real trouble w/ others was in regard to Miranda's messiness, cabinmates became resentful when M's mess brought down inspection ratings. Don't know what to suggest there really: she just could not keep her stuff together and tidy for more than an hour after cleanup when she'd be all over the place again. I love the kid, but she's a slob, period. That's kind of the general feeling about her from the rest of the cabin too.

Health: Generally hearty, not a "sick kid," not a complainer. Complained of "stomachache" 2 Sunday evenings in a row and spent time in the infirmary, but that wound up being about not wanting to write letters home (Sunday dinner mandatory letter), not about stomach troubles (see General).

General: Miranda had a great summer in many respects. She loved camp, excelled at a number of varied activities, and made close friendships. She did, however, have some trouble with regard to her family back home. Not sure of the entire story. Her mom seems to be really involved and very concerned. Lots of letters from her all summer at least. They seem close. Not sure about the dad. But I think the mom's on top of it. Finally got her to talk to her mom on the phone. Lots of crying, but I think things are OK.

Other comments: I think it's highly likely that Miranda will be back next summer. She and Darrin are already planning for when they're old enough to be Spitfires(!).

8

WHERE YOUR PARENTS ARE

AFTER SCHOOL IN FIFTH GRADE, MIRANDA RIDES THE crosstown bus home to the West Side. She has her own set of keys to the outside lock and the two deadbolts on their apartment door. The building doesn't have a doorman. Miranda lets herself in, drops her bag and coat in a pile, and telephones her mom at work to let her know she is home safe. If Miranda hasn't called by three-thirty, Roz will go very nearly into cardiac arrest with worry. Miranda is the quintessential "latchkey kid." She sits alone in a locked apartment for four hours every afternoon, is intimately familiar with the plot twists on *General Hospital* and *Edge of Night*, knows every *Brady Bunch* episode verbatim, and could probably make a fortune on the game show circuit if given the opportunity. She does her homework to a constant backdrop of network buzz and waits to hear her mother's keys jangling in hand as she strides that telltale clomp from elevator to apartment.

If Roz is late, then it's Miranda's turn to worry. If *M.A.S.H.* comes on and still the elevator has not opened at their floor and the public-service spots begin their nightly campaign, "It's seven o'clock—do you know where your children are?" Miranda wants to call up the TV station and say, *How about it's seven o'clock—do you know where your parents are?* But then there is the *churn, clunk, pling* of the elevator doors, and Roz appears, maybe laden with packages, or papers she's had to lug home to work on, or bearing Chinese food from that really busy place on Broadway that has the best spareribs. Sometimes Miranda's dad gets home early enough to eat with them, or to play Miranda a game of spit or double solitaire before bed. Sometimes he gets home too late for that. Or just doesn't have it in him.

One evening after a dinner at which her dad arrived when they were nearly done, Miranda leaves the table to watch TV in the living room. Over *Family Feud* she can hear her parents talking in the dining room. Her dad is tired. He sounds old. When he came in from the office he'd gone straight to the kitchen to get a sponge and started wiping nonexistent fingerprints from the apartment walls before he even took his coat off.

"He's a good man," Roz confides to Miranda later that night. "He's a good, good man. But he's not a great man. He's too amiable to be a great man. And his brain works too methodically. He can't think expansively, he doesn't just *feel* things, the way you and I do. He has to puzzle them all out, and something gets lost." They are in Miranda's room, Miranda under the covers, Roz sitting on the edge by her side, her long spindly fingers combing the hair back off her daughter's face, cooling her after a choking bout of tears. Miranda does not understand all these things her mother says about her father, but Roz's voice is comforting, her hands soothing in Miranda's hair. There'd been a fight somewhere in between dinner and bed, Edwin angry with Miranda for something—an orange juice container returned empty to the fridge, a phone bill full of ludicrously expensive calls to Darrin Quaile in Denver, some perceived disrespect to her mother with regard to dinner, or dishes, or laundry, or bedtime. "He loves you very much," Roz says. "You know, sweetie, how much he loves you. He's going through a very hard time now. He doesn't mean to take it out on you."

"Why?" Miranda asks. "Why is he going through a hard time?"

"He's thirty-eight years old, baby. He's spent a third of his life doing something he never wanted to do, and he's asking himself why. He's not happy. This isn't the life he meant to live." She speaks softly. This is not a conversation meant for Edwin to overhear.

"So why doesn't he stop? Why doesn't he do what he wants to do?"

Roz smiles tiredly. "I don't know, babe. I wish I did. I think the problem is that he doesn't know what he wants to do."

Miranda doesn't understand that really. "How can he not know?" she asks.

"It's hard to imagine that, huh?"

Miranda nods, her forehead furrowed.

Roz thinks a moment. "Maybe think about it like this." She pauses. "Maybe think about it like if someone asked you what one of your friends wanted to be when they grew up. Like you and Darrin—say someone asked you what Darrin most deeply in her heart of hearts wants to be when she grows up, and you could probably know about things that it seems like Darrin's interested in, things she's good at. You could probably think of a bunch of things that you could imagine Darrin doing."

Miranda continues to nod.

"But you wouldn't know for sure exactly what she would say if that person asked her and not you, right? Or maybe if you knew this summer at camp that was one thing, but now it's changed, only you haven't heard about it yet. You live too far away, you don't get to talk or see each other all that much or anything. Think about Daddy like that," Roz says. "For Daddy to talk to his real self inside, the place that knows what he wants, it's like that self is as far away as Denver, and he keeps not calling, and then after a while he's lost the phone number and he's forgotten how to talk to that self of his way off in Denver, and then one day he realizes that he doesn't even know if that self is even still alive anymore, and he has no idea in the world how to go about finding it again, finding out what he really thinks in his deepest heart. He's been away from it for too long."

Miranda, without really realizing it, has begun to cry.

"Oh, sweet babe, come on, it's not a thing for you to be teary about. It's Daddy's thing, and it's Daddy who's got to figure it out." Roz's comfort is of an officious nature now: plump the pillow, straighten the blanket, hup, hup, hup, no room for crying here.

It all makes Miranda feel horribly, horribly sad.

"Come on, sweet, I shouldn't be laying this on you." Roz is ready to be done with bedtime, suddenly brusque, like a woman who's shared too much with a first-time lover. "Come on, love, it's late, late, late. To sleep with you, OK?"

Miranda nods, "OK."

"I love you." Roz kisses her once more.

"I know," Miranda says to Roz's back as she leaves the room. Miranda lies still in the quiet, her door the way she likes it, half open, half closed, a perfect wedge of hallway light cutting its way across the carpet, like sadness angling in through a crack in the door. Miranda lies in her half-dark thinking what it might be like for her father, out there, surrounded by the glare of bright, white sadness. She wonders if it's sadness he feels. It's been a long time since she has been able to ask him such questions. What could it feel like to be so far away from your self? Is it something that will happen to her too someday? Will she lose touch, the way you lose touch with camp friends or people who move away? Will she one day need her self and not have her self there to consult? She wonders how you stop that from happening, and then she wonders if that's just what growing up is: the process of that space between you and your self getting bigger and bigger and bigger until one can't see the other anymore, and you don't remember what it was like to be a kid, or what it was like to want something so badly that you can't ever imagine not wanting, least of all imagine wanting something and not knowing what that something is. And she feels bad for her father, because she senses he must be lonely, out there in the world without his self to keep him company.

AN ASHTRAY CRASHES TO THE FLOOR.

Edwin has started smoking again. He has placed an ashtray on the living room coffee table in deference to his weakness, but he does not use it since Roz will not allow him to smoke in her house. When he must, Edwin stands under the small awning at the building's entrance sucking in his carcinogens. Mostly, Roz and Miranda know, he smokes at the office, comes home at night exuding a cloud of his own smoke through the fibers of his suit and the pores of his skin. Roz makes him wash, brush his teeth, gargle with Listerine before she'll come within five feet of him. They dance around each other, a disdainful do-si-do, as he comes in the door and she shoos him off to the bathroom. His nicotine addiction has adjusted to a schedule: twelve hours on, twelve hours off. The ashtray sits on the coffee table, an open mouth, an empty stomach. *Feed me,* it says, *feed me.*

Miranda is experimenting with fake fingernails. This is the thing to do if you are a fifth-grade girl at the City Day School. It is not enough to paint her own; she must have length, shape, expanse. Lee press-ons are the staple. But Miranda is willing to explore the options. These afternoons her homework waits until five or six o'clock, until after dinner some nights. The afternoons are pure: soaps and nails. She sits in the living room wing chair, wrapped in a blanket maybe, or sprawled, feet over the arm. She pulls the phone to her side, assembles her snacks around her. Fritos, or Ho Hos, or Hostess chocolate cupcakes. The wrappers she hides in her schoolbag and deposits in the trash by the bus stop across town. Roz would have a fit to know what her daughter consumes during those long empty afternoons. There is no reason for her to know. This is, perhaps, Miranda's first true act of rebellion.

The fingernails, according to Roz, are distasteful, yes, but not detrimental to Miranda's health, so as long as she's buying them with her own allowance money they are permissible. Miranda's allowance is spent on junk food and fingernails: cotton balls, polish remover, press-on kits, emery boards and cuticle files, bottles of polish in shades of the eighties: sparkle, shimmer, glimmer, frost. Miranda has come, in school, to be known as the girl of the ever-changing nails. And now that she is known for this, she cannot stop: every day the color must change.

The space around Miranda's wing chair grows with clutter every afternoon: balled-up tissues, glasses and mugs half full of juice and water, papers and stationery and address books and loose-leaf doodles she does while on the phone with Darrin. They tell each other's fortunes from tricks learned in the school yard: lists of possibilities—future cars, husbands, homes, colors of wedding dresses, choices of bouquets, numbers of children, ages of death—whittled by scientific counting processes of elimination down to one true and inevitable outcome. They perform the ritual nearly every day. By the middle of fifth grade Miranda has been determined to live in each of the fifty states and to marry every boy she's ever known. The game is still fun: an unexpected outcome, the chance of a different life with every new round. As she talks she does her nails. Painstakingly. On TV: Luke and Laura, Frisco and Felicia, Holly and Robert, Brock and Bobbie. The ashtray on the coffee table fills with the detritus of the nail ritual: Q-tips and cotton balls stained bloody purple and sickly mauve, nail clippings, paper backings, wrappers and sales receipts and pieces of chewing gum folded into torn scraps of loose-leaf.

Tonight Edwin is home early. There is no explanation for this anomaly, just the fact of it. "Hello," he calls, opening the front door. Miranda, of course, thought it would be her mother, who is accustomed to Miranda's state of dishevelment when she arrives home in the evening. Edwin is not. Miranda says good-bye, fast, to Darrin, and hangs up the phone, but she doesn't want to move. She's happy where she is, nails drying, *What's Happenin'* reruns coming on the television. Her *dad* is home. She doesn't know what to make of that.

"Hello?" he calls again, as though perhaps he thinks no one will be there.

"Hi?" Miranda calls, her response as much a question as his.

Edwin comes to stand in the archway that leads from dining room to living room. He seems prepared to be pleasant, yet he doesn't appear to know what to say. This is not unusual. He is, around Miranda, tongue-tied more often than not. He looks at her as if she is a strange apparition in his living room. He looks as if to say: *What have you done with the last ten years of my life?*

"What time is it?" Miranda asks, straightening herself in the chair and craning to look at her father. He is still in full uniform, as Roz calls it—suit and tie—but he looks disheveled somehow too, wrinkled, thin.

"Nearly six," he says, preoccupied already, taking in the scene of the living room.

"How come you're home?" Miranda asks.

"Oh, just"—Edwin looks flustered—"just decided to come home early for once." His lighthearted reasoning is belied by his face. It's as if he'd come in expecting to be the one under scrutiny for his out-of-the-usual appearance. Instead he's faced with a scene he didn't expect: his living room a mess of teenage flotsam. "How long have you been watching that idiot box?" he asks, heading straight for the TV as if to punch its lights out.

Miranda, usually relieved to replace television with human contact, is suddenly threatened, defensive. "I was watching that," she says.

"Miranda," Edwin begins, the tone that leads inevitably to a lecture. But there doesn't seem to be anything else. Just disappointment. "Miranda." His eyes light upon the ashtray, and he picks it up, a tissue drifting away toward the floor. "What is this?" he says, shrill and accusing, not a question at all. "Is this really what you do all afternoon . . . ?"

Miranda hasn't prepared herself for this. She has imagined what she would do if Roz were to come home unexpectedly and discover Miranda with a Twinkie in her mouth, jawbreakers on her breath. She has never even thought to fear the surprise appearance of her father. She is at a loss.

Edwin picks up a clump of what is in the ashtray, but as he does so, he loses part of it, a few loose cotton balls that go skidding down the front of his suit, leaving perfect faint magenta trails in their wake. The ashtray flies from Edwin's hand, not accidentally, Miranda notes, for there is force behind it. Edwin swipes at his suit front. "Dammit, Miranda. Where's the . . . ? What is it? Baking soda? Seltzer? Roz!?!" he hollers, unaware that she's not home. "Roz!" He flies out of the living room, ripping off his coat as he goes, aims himself for the kitchen, where Miranda can hear him turn on the water, then turn it off again, muttering intermittently under his breath. Miranda sits in her living room wing chair, unmoving, without a sound. She has no idea where to go or what to do, and in the horrible frozen panic of that, the only thing that can happen happens. Miranda sits in the chair and cries.

WHICH IS THE SCENE INTO WHICH ROZ ENTERS: Edwin in the kitchen with his suit coat spread across the counter, the telephone crooked under his chin. "Well, I don't know," he is saying. There is a Yellow Pages open on the kitchen table. "Maybe"—Edwin is considering the lapel—"I don't know. I'm just going to bring it in. OK? Ten minutes, I'll be there. Just hold on ten minutes." He sees Roz and pushes past her. "I've got to get to Shim's before they close," he says, and is out the door before Roz can respond. She steps behind him from the kitchen into the dining room, from which she can see through to the living room, to Miranda, in her usual Miranda-seat, minus the TV. It takes a moment before she sees that Miranda is curled in her wing chair silently weeping.

"Baby!" Roz cries, rushing into the scene. "Baby, what's happening?"

But Miranda, at this point, cannot reply. Her tears become a sob, loud and uncontrollable, bellowing the let-loose of all hell, and until she has calmed down, the only thing Roz can do is hold her, stroke her, soothe her, *Shhhh baby, everything's OK, you're OK, baby, shhhh.*

IT IS A CALM TALK ROZ AND EDWIN HAVE LATER IN the night, none of the drama that the early evening might have foreshadowed. Roz is quiet in a way she would never have expected of herself. A quiet that speaks of shock. And of the promise of incipient and monumental change. It is so late when Edwin comes into Miranda's bedroom that even through her tears she has managed to fall into a sleep from which he has difficulty waking her. She is confused, and momentarily relieved to see his face— *Daddy!*—then not relieved at all when she sees his tears, when she sees that her father is sitting above her in the middle of the night crying as she has never seen a grown person cry.

"I'm sorry," he is saying, sputtering, "I'm sorry . . ." In the light from the hall, Miranda can see that her mother is standing in the door, arms crossed, her body rigid. The world has taken a turn that Miranda does not understand; she is not shifting with it, she is torqued, stuck, there is nothing that is sure anymore. It feels like something is breaking, cracking open, something that they hadn't realized was so brittle, like a baby who flings a vase to the floor and learns, through the action, what it means to be fragile.

When Edwin leaves her, retreating cautiously from Miranda's room as though she were already asleep, Roz is gone from the doorway, slipped away to bed deliberately, in deference to their privacy, Edwin and Miranda's. Edwin steps tentatively across the floor, then crosses the threshold, drawing the door closed behind him. Then he turns off the hall light, and Miranda can hear him go into the other bedroom and shut the door. She likes for her door to be open halfway when she goes to sleep, and the light in the hall left on to keep her company in the night. Edwin should know this. Miranda wants to call out to him, to come back, to make it right, but she doesn't. Somehow, tonight, it seems like this would be wrong: they've already parted, their good nights spoken, this episode finally put to rest. And somehow it is not right either for Miranda to get up and adjust things for herself, set the door open to its proper width, turn on the light so it comes in just so and she doesn't have to be scared. It's almost like tonight she's supposed to be scared. It's supposed to be dark, and she's meant to be alone, her parents shuttered far away down the hall in a different world.

9

WRESTLING JAILBAIT

THE THEATER CLUB HOLDS ITS FIRST REHEARSAL after school one day in October in the music room where Miranda normally has choir with the rest of the seventh grade. It is now packed instead with people she has only seen before from a distance. She's heard whispers of them in the cafeteria, their names mentioned in notes passed during study hall. They are high schoolers. Theater clubbies. They are girls in black stockings with so many runs they look like spiderwebs, their eyes traced in heavy liquid-black eyeliner, mouths darkened blood-red, or grim-black. Thick tarnished silver ankhs and mandalas hang from green velvet cords at their ghoul-pale necks. The boys are done up in antique tuxedo jackets, Dead Kennedys T-shirts, and wing-tip shoes. Or oxblood combat boots, and suspenders holding up tar-splattered army pants. It's like they've already been costumed, Miranda thinks, for a show that's months away. But these are their real clothes; this is just who these people are.

Enter the director, James. A senior, James already looks like a man, wears little wire-rimmed glasses and carries a clipboard. Miranda has heard people say that he is gay.

"Oh, Johann Sebastian . . . ," James calls out, crossing the room toward the old upright piano from which emanates an unfortunate rendition of Chopsticks. "Might I interrupt this moment of musical genius to ask a favor?"

There is a great crash of notes, and the piano bench screeches backwards. Two large hands plant themselves on top of the piano, deadening the chord, and the pianist rises.

"A small favor," James qualifies.

The response he gets is a skeptical stare.

"The scripts are ready. At the Xerox place. Can you run and pick them up?" James flashes a how-can-you-resist-me smile.

"Ask nicely," the piano player tells him.

"Puh-leeze," James begs, sweet and sickly, with puppy-dog eyes. "Please will you be so good as to retrieve our scripts so that we may begin to emote thespianically?"

"What's in it for me?" asks Chopstick-man.

"Me," James says, giving his own face a little Vanna White frame.

It's then, as the Chopsticks guy turns from James to the crowded room, that Miranda realizes who he is. Spencer Kagan. Standing across the room from her is Spencer Kagan, and he's looking straight at Miranda, and pointing. She freezes, and Spencer says: "How 'bout I take Miranda instead?"

James's hand flies to his poor, wounded heart. "I'm crushed," he swears, though he seems to recover quickly enough. "She's yours," he tells Spencer, and Miranda feels like she's just been auctioned off. From atop the file cabinet where she's perched, Miranda draws her chin back into her neck, eyebrows raised. She looks from James to Spencer, then back to James, and slides obligingly down to follow Spencer Kagan into the world outside school. A world far beyond the seventh grade.

HALFWAY DOWN THE SIDEWALK SHE ASKS HIM, "HOW did you know my name?"

"We hear you're a child prodigy." He nods in her direction as they walk. "Everyone knows your name."

Everyone? That freaks Miranda out. Older kids know who she is? They talk about her?

Suddenly Spencer stops walking, and steps in front of Miranda. She nearly trips over him as he stoops, hands on his thighs like a linebacker preparing to rush. Miranda can only stand there staring at his back, frantically trying to figure out what he's doing. She is panicking, convinced he's making fun of her in some way she doesn't even understand. She almost cries with relief when he finally cocks his head back around to her and says, innocent as sin: "Piggyback?"

"How'd *you* know *my* name?" he challenges on the walk back from the Xerox place, their arms laden with scripts.

"You're Spencer," she tells him, then sees how stupid she sounds. "Everyone knows who you are."

"Everyone?" He is making fun of her. She knows it.

"You practically have fan clubs." She laughs. It's true.

"Like groupies?" He ponders the notion. "I always thought it would be wild to have groupies."

"Like Sting," she offers.

"Sure, just like Sting." He laughs. "So who belongs to these fan clubs anyway?"

"Can't say," she trills, coy and singsong, trotting ahead of him. "I'd be breaking the vow of secrecy."

The play this year is *Pippin*, a musical: kings and queens, sons and lovers, the existential angst of a young man who can't figure out who he wants to be when he grows up. He tries lots of things: war, hedonism, domesticity, self-immolation—none strike him as a true calling. Spencer Kagan plays Pippin, son of King Charlemagne, and the words he sings ring close to Miranda's heart. Miranda, the only cast member who's not a sophomore or older, has been cast to play Theo, the very young son of Pippin's love, Catherine. In taking this neophyte on as a clubbie, the older kids turn her into a mascot of sorts, the little sister they never had. Miranda is the doll, the little girl who makes the rest of them feel even older and more mature than they are. This is all right with Miranda. For a time. For a time it is a role like any other: Catherine, Queen Fastrada, Theo, Miranda. At twelve years old, her position affords Miranda glimpses into another world, terrifying to teeter there on the edge, not welcomed in, not shut out either.

Miranda's mom was all gung-ho for Miranda to try out for the play, and supportive to a fault when Miranda actually got a part, but now that rehearsals have begun in earnest—lasting well into the evening some days, so that it's Miranda who comes home to find Roz propped up on her bed, half watching something on the TV—Roz seems saddened by the whole thing. Of course, she would never say so, but the way she gazes at Miranda, the glossy look in her eye when she says good night, the way she seems to be alternately adoring and then ticked off at Miranda for no real reason Miranda can discern—it all makes Miranda think that Roz is trying to convey something to her that as a mother she wouldn't be caught dead actually telling her daughter. She's doing, surreptitiously even to herself perhaps, what she has sworn she will never do: be a mother like other people's mothers. "If you want to spend time with me, then spend time with me," she often says, "but don't do it because it's Mother's Day or because you think you're supposed to." There are no enforced "family times" in Miranda's family—not even back when they were actually a family and not just Roz and Miranda, the mother-daughter roommates. She hears other people say things like *I have to go have lunch with my mom or she'll be pissed,* and that seems very weird to Miranda, who knows that if she blew Roz off, backed out of something they had said they'd do together, her mother would be sad, certainly, and she might feel rejected, or neglected, or hurt, but Miranda couldn't imagine her getting *mad*. She couldn't imagine how other people's mothers did it; did they yell *You'd better meet me at the Corner Coffee Shop and chat with me like I'm your best friend and you'd better act like you wouldn't rather be out with your own friends doing what normal teenagers do?* So when it starts getting to be seven or eight at night and they're still only halfway through the scene they need to block and everyone starts saying *Fuck, I gotta get home or my mother'll kill me,* Miranda just goes out to the pay phone in the lobby and calls Roz to tell her she'll be late, and she'll take a cab, so not to worry, and while she has the impression that other people's mothers say things like *Alexa, that's ridiculous, it's past eight, they can't keep you there like this,* or *I've had just about enough of this theater business,* Miranda knows that she'll hear the disappointment in Roz's voice—the deflated prospect of dinner alone, the quiet of the empty apartment seeming to echo through the receiver like ocean waves—but her mom will never say anything more than "OK, sweet, see you later, thanks for calling." It seems far more rational to Miranda than the way other people do it. Roz knows that Miranda would of course rather hang out with her friends, of course rather be at play rehearsal with cute Spencer Kagan and his crowd than sitting at home with her old mother, and that doesn't make her any less saddened by Miranda's absence, it just takes the blame off Roz for being "mean" and "unreasonable" like everyone else's parents and puts all the guilt right back on Miranda for being the one to decide to be a thoughtful kid, or not, to make her mother happy, or not, to be a disappointment like her father, or not. And it's in this way that Miranda thinks maybe her mother is, in her own way, the craftiest one of all.

. . .

"Could someone go find those guys," James yells out into the dark auditorium. "Act One, Scene Two! Are we or are we not trying to put on a show here? Where the hell is everybody? Jesus!"

Miranda is in the mezzanine. She slides down the banister, almost tumbling when she hits the floor. She glances around quickly, but it's OK, no one is watching. A whole slew of girls are hanging out in the lighting booth, where there is a space heater loaned to the club by someone's parents. November, and the school still refuses to turn on the heat for weekend rehearsals. The booth has become their sanctuary. Yellow gym mats lugged up from the basement line the floor and turn the cramped room into a little nest. It's littered with clothing, scripts, loose pages of libretto, and old takeout cups from the Greek deli on the corner, teabags dried into crisp cocoons. The clubbies spend more time in the booth than they ever spend on stage. But Spencer and the other guys aren't up there this afternoon: they've sneaked into the gym to play basketball.

The stairwell is dark as Miranda makes her way down to the basement. She pulls the sleeves of her sweatshirt over her hands, gliding her paws along the railing for direction, following sounds toward the gym: the slam of the basketball against the polyurethane floor and the boys' grunts and shouts echoing through the halls. During school the stairs are always noisy and crowded with students trying to take as long as possible to get from one class to another. Miranda finds something very empowering about the sound of her own footfall on each step. It's like having a pass to be in the halls when everyone else is in geometry. A special privilege.

Downstairs, she cuts through the girls' locker room, listening to the boys talk as they shoot hoops, catching the words not drowned out by bounces.

" . . . jailbait . . ." *Crash. Rattle.* Rebound off the backboard.

"Lay off, man . . ." *Screech.* Sneakers against shellac.

"Scam." *Dribble dribble dribble.* "Scum." *Slam.*

Miranda steps from the locker room into the gym. The ball flies through the air. Spencer swerves around the guy blocking him, dives under the ball and sends it up toward the hoop.

"Hey, you guys!" Miranda calls out from the doorway. Six heads snap around. "James wants you onstage now!" Six heads snap back to the hoop. The ball hits the rim, circles twice, and falls off the side, bouncing away meekly, like it's ashamed. The game disperses. Spencer grabs his shirt from the bleachers and lumbers over to Miranda. He is sweating, and the black hairs on his belly shimmer as he winds his shirt into a rattail and takes a swipe at her, dancing in a circle like a fighter, gleaming.

"What were you talking about?" she asks, leaning against the doorframe, arms crossed over her chest.

"You, jailbait," he teases.

"Yeah," she says, not quite sure what that means. "What'd you say about me . . . ?"

"That you're cute." He says it mockingly, taking another swipe at her.

"Cute?" Hello Kitty stickers are cute. Pom-pom tennis socks are cute. "I'm doomed."

"Hardly." He looks at her like *Give me a break*. "You watch out for those theater boys. They have no scruples." He flicks the shirt again, missing by a hair.

"*They* have no scruples?" she jeers, lunging at him, making a grab for the rattail. He takes off across the gym. "*They?*" She chases him through the boys' locker room and blindly up three flights of dark stairs. Crashing through the swinging doors into the auditorium, she slows, panting, but Spencer's still going. Racing down an aisle, he leaps onto the stage and launches into the middle of his scene without missing a beat. He had too big a lead. She'd never have caught up to him.

BY MID-DECEMBER SPENCER HAS TAKEN TO COMING BY Miranda's apartment on weekend mornings so they can ride to school together. He doesn't like the idea of her alone on the New York subway when there are so few people around. This seems to please Miranda's mother inordinately: Miranda doesn't have to ride the train alone *and* Roz gets to flirt, in her motherly way, with Spencer. She likes it when there are people around the apartment. Spencer's presence there on weekend mornings seems to brighten Roz's day. In the year and a half since her dad moved out, Miranda sees that weekends hang the heaviest for her mother. During the week she's got work and the world to keep her busy, but weekends, that's when people go to street fairs and share gyros and shish kebab and buy antique armoires with their lovers. They go to the movies and out to dinner and for late-night drinks in corner bars. Roz no longer has someone to do that with, and Miranda thinks it makes her sad.

On the subway Miranda curls under Spencer's arm. Across the car, a poster advertises confidential psychological counseling services. She closes her eyes.

"Oh, sleepy one . . ." A yellow wool scarf waggles in her face. It's her father's, one he left when he moved out; Roz forced Spencer to take it when he showed up that morning in an unlined leather jacket with a broken zipper on the coldest day of the winter yet. She wound it around his neck for him, which was embarrassing to Miranda, but Spencer bore it dutifully. "Up too late partying last night?" he asks.

"Yeah, right," she says. "Up late. Not partying."

"How come?" He jostles her.

Because I'm twelve, she wants to say, sarcastic as she can. Instead: "How come what?"

"How come you were up late?"

She sits straight to face him. She can't talk to him unless she's looking at his face. His voice is deep and his body next to her is overpowering. It's only his face that gives him away: still a softness to the sculpted cheekbones, like clay molded but not yet fired. His eyes are dark and very wide. She thinks they make him look lost, or awed. This is the part of him to whom she can talk. "My friends are all mad at me. They say I don't have enough time for them anymore. I'm always at rehearsal."

"Yeah, tell me about it," Spencer says. "I have a girlfriend who's ready to trade me in." He props his legs against the pole in front of him, and the thick wooden heels of his motorcycle boots make a dead clang against the chrome.

"Sarah wouldn't break up with you." Miranda's not sure if this is a statement or a question. She hopes it sounds informed. Sarah is a senior like Spencer. She wears dark green cowboy boots and is going to college in California next year. Her third-period bio class meets in the same room as Miranda's fourth-period life science. Miranda smiles at her every day now on the way out. She is working up to *hello*.

"No, I know," Spencer concedes. "She won't dump me, she's just pissed." He pauses. "She doesn't really understand, though."

"No one understands," Miranda says. "They think what I like to do is weird—that doing this show is totally bizarre. Like they'd never heard of anyone wanting to do theater stuff before. *I* don't get *them*, though. They all sit around shaving their legs together and drinking out of their parents' liquor cabinets. Like that sounds really thrilling."

"Once you start shaving you can never stop," Spencer warns. His beard is heavy. Disconcertingly unsavory if he skips a day. He has. "And don't start drinking yet, OK?" he counsels. "You have so much time."

"Yes, Dad." Miranda rolls her eyes.

"No really, I mean, I don't mean to be like that . . ." He looks earnest, apologetic. "Seriously," he says, "if you do want to, if you want to try it, you just tell me and you and I will have a drink together, OK? And you won't have to worry about anything, or anything." He reaches over and strokes Miranda under the chin like a cat, lifting her face like a parent would, so he can look into her eyes and know that she's heard him. She nods at him quickly, then burrows again, pressing her face into the black leather of his chest, like she can hide there somehow and wait until this growing-up stuff is over. It's the not-knowing that's most terrible of all—the worst feeling she knows, and she will do anything to get past it. The drinking and the dressing-up, trying to be older, it all seems so silly to Miranda, so misdirected, so *not* the answer to all these questions. Still, she knows she would willingly do *all* those things, look that foolish and naive—shave, drink, even have sex maybe—if she knew it would end the cluelessness and the desperately desolate sensation of being twelve.

For her thirteenth birthday Spencer takes Miranda out to dinner. They go to an Italian place up near Columbia and eat pizza with mushrooms and green peppers and green olives. Spencer orders a beer and the waiter doesn't even flinch. When their drinks come—his Pabst and her 7UP—followed by bread sticks to dip in hot marinara, Miranda decides the waiter must think that Spencer is her father. It's a somewhat plausible scenario: she might be able to pass for ten, he for twenty-three, they've only met once before . . . They toast Miranda's birthday and chatter aimlessly. When the pizza comes and Spencer orders a scotch this time, the waiter's eyebrows do go up slightly, but he's so swamped, the restaurant so busy, he doesn't even care. Miranda could probably order herself a rum and Coke without too much ado! It feels strange to know that, because it makes her think maybe she's supposed to, but she doesn't want to, and she just wishes she knew what Spencer was thinking, wishes she knew what it was he wanted her to do. She thinks she'd do it—whatever it was—just to please him, just to have someone's direction to follow. Miranda is halfway through her second slice of pizza, Spencer only a few bites into his first, when the scotch arrives. The waiter tears off to deal with other tables, and without a word Spencer lifts the scotch glass in one hand, Miranda's 7UP glass in the other, and tips a slosh of liquor into her drink.

"Happy birthday, kiddo," he says.

Miranda's eyes narrow and she squints at him, half confused, half smiling, and he grins back broadly, takes a sip of his drink, eyes twinkling with mischievous joy. Baited, Miranda raises her own glass, straw to her lips, and drinks. It tastes terrible, and she is relieved to remember that she still has a full glass of untainted water on the table. And awful-tasting as it is, this drink feels important. This drink will enable something. She has to drink this drink because it has things to teach her, things she's not going to learn on her own, without scotch, and without Spencer.

Whether she's high on tomato sauce, or Spencer, or half an ounce of alcohol, it doesn't really matter. By his second scotch Spencer's eyes are glowing the way Miranda imagines someone's eyes would shine if he was in love with you. He does nothing but ask her questions all night, like he wants to know every thought she has ever had. He asks what she thinks about school, the play, Alexa, James, himself, and she rambles on, stuffed with pizza, giddy in the atmosphere, the lights dim and low, the restaurant noise pleasantly deafening. She feels so warm and cozy, as if she could just melt right across the table and into Spencer, swirl herself into him, like creamer into coffee.

LATER THAT NIGHT, AT HOME, HER STOMACH UPSET from too much pizza and too many nerves, Miranda lies in bed, face up to the ceiling, her eyes shut against all shadow and danger. She tries, but she cannot make herself think of Spencer. A whole evening alone with him, and somehow once he put her in the cab toward home, she has been unable to draw his face clearly into her mind. Instead, all Miranda can think of is the night her father left, the night that everything really changed, not just theoretically but in tangible, unalterable reality. Somewhere in her scraps and shards of memory Miranda has this: her father, sitting at the side of her bed, his face contorted with tears, and through the sobs, his and hers, he is saying something that is sticky and hard and sharply true. He is saying that he has to go away for a while. That there is too much, that everything is too much for him, and it isn't Miranda's fault, it's all his own fault, every ounce, that Miranda is everything, and he loves her, and Roz, he loves Roz, but maybe love isn't enough. Wanting to be a certain person and actually being that person are two different things, and the things you did when you were young that you swore weren't just idealistic and naive whims—and you hated people, like your parents, for telling you so—they couldn't have been anything *but* naive and idealistic because maybe that's what being young was about. He doesn't know what being old is about, except seeing how wrong you were when you were young. He has to go away, he says, to think, to try and understand what he's doing with his life. And when Miranda remembers this speech it is impossibly locked to another memory, or the dream of a memory that she knows never actually happened: her father standing on the deck of a ship as it pulls away from a dilapidated pier on the West Side Highway and sails up the Hudson River to be gone at sea a long long time. Edwin waves from the deck, bawling, racked with the pain of his departure. Miranda thinks of this as the night her father left on a long cruise aboard a ship whose decks and levels he roamed like a spurned *Love Boat* suitor. He spends weeks, ages, wandering those decks, his mind rapt in philosophical entreaties and existential puzzles. All that time at sea, Edwin passes in thought. Because in reality, that's what he did when he went away from them: he thought. And then he came home again to Roz and Miranda, who had led a strangely empty, oddly free, and eerily liberated life in his absence, praying for his return and wishing at the same time for their lives alone to be so peaceful always. They greeted him with half-open arms and guarded hearts. And then, days later, he left again, to go back home to Nebraska and try to *really* sort things out. It was the beginning of the end, when there was still possibility: Edwin would work out his troubles and then he would come home and they'd take him back into their fold. But then time had gone by, phone calls and letters. There was a job in Nebraska. There were boxes to be shipped to a new address in Lincoln. Miranda remembers her mother packing those boxes. In that space before sleep, Miranda remembers this all as if it were the only part of her parents' divorce for which she was sober.

CLUBBIES ARE REGULARS AT THE ACROPOLIS DINER. Everyone sinks into booths along the window while Miranda hangs up her coat on the rack by the cashier and tugs off her huge winter boots. No one else in the cast seems to own a real winter coat. Or gloves. Not even a scarf that's made out of something other than mesh. In fact, Miranda's the only one of them who looks even remotely like she just stepped in from a blizzard. Of course, they're all sick, but they relish their colds. They're like branded martyrs: flourishes of horrendous nose-blowing; a take-out cup of tea with lemon and honey always in hand; a diet of herbal cough drops, Chloraseptic spray, and Marlboro Reds.

In the corner booth Spencer stretches himself out sideways, one arm draped across the top of the seat, the other hand clasped around a cup of coffee. He leans his back against the window, his head resting on the cold glass, and watches Miranda eat a bagel and cream cheese. She is very much aware of his gaze. As acutely as she is aware of the fine line between enjoying his attention and expecting it. She savors his stare secretly, directing her own as absently as she can past him to the older kids in the next booth. It's Alexa, who plays Miranda's mother in the play; Alexa's best friend Troy; Troy's sort-of boyfriend Trevor; and James. They are studying the color drawings on the paper placemats of all the mixed drinks you can buy after 5 p.m.: crazy concoctions spouting Hawaiian-print umbrellas and bulbous swizzle-skewered olives.

"Kamikazes—you can get so rocked off those . . ." Troy reaches across the table for the ketchup, uncaps it, and slathers her home fries. A curtain of dyed-black hair flops over her face, and she blows at it ineffectually.

"Do you remember that night at that skeezy bar by the seaport . . . ?" Alexa's got a cigarette in one hand and is waving a forkful of french toast with the other, trying to remember something about that night. "That guy . . ."

"Oh my god, yes, with that guy, oh my god, what was his name . . . ?" Troy reaches for the salt and gets her elbow in Trevor's plate. She holds it up to him and he sucks the syrup off her pale goosey skin. "George!" she cries suddenly, as though Trevor's lips on her arm have triggered her memory. "George, oh my god, it was George. With pickup lines like I have never heard before."

"George!" says Alexa, pieces of the night beginning to come back to her. "But not as bad as that time we did Jell-O shots in the Village—I didn't know who I was!"

"Great, next time I call rehearsal for nine and it's noon and you haven't shown up, I'll know where to look; you'll be passed out on the floor of O'Malley's bathroom with half the population of SoHo banging down the door trying to take a piss." James blows a big poof of smoke at Alexa and crushes down his stub in the overflowing ashtray. Troy grabs it, a shallow aluminum saucer with little indented ridges to rest a cigarette. She leans out of the booth.

"Ernest! Ernest!" she calls.

Ernest, middle-aged, with a handlebar mustache, approaches their table. He grabs the back of the booth and swings in toward the group with Fred Astaire flair. "What can I getcha?" he asks.

Troy tucks her hair behind her ear and looks up at him. "If you could, when you get a chance, empty our ashtray, that would be great."

"For you darlin', anything," Ernest says.

"Anything?" Troy asks, sex-kitten cute and practically purring.

Ernest looks at Trevor, next to Troy, shoveling in breakfast. "Trevor, buddy, keep me in line here. What would I tell my beautiful, loving wife of thirty-two years?"

"After thirty-two years I'm sure Carmen's wise to any excuse you could dream up." Trevor raises his coffee cup to Ernest and drinks.

"That she is. And thank god. Keeps me in check." Ernest dumps the ashes into one of his apron pockets and wipes the tray clean with a rag. "Thirty-two years. I tell you." He pauses. "You kids keep smoking the way you do, you're not going to live to see *twenty-two*."

"As long as I see twenty-*one*," Trevor says.

"Like it'll be anything you don't already do now." James distracts Trevor and steals a sausage link off his plate.

"Hey!" Trevor cries, and swipes a slice of James's toast. Mouth full and still chewing, he says, "Yeah, but there are things I won't be able to do anymore."

"Like what?" Troy challenges.

"Like . . ." Trevor draws out the word for dramatic effect. "Like have sex with sixteen-year-olds." He chomps into another piece of toast.

Troy turns on him, shoots up an eyebrow, and then flicks back around to Ernest. "This! This is what I put up with. Ernest, take him, teach him some manners."

"I don't know if you'd like mine any better, sweetheart . . ." Ernest backs away and spins flamboyantly into the beverage center to pick up the coffeepot and make his rounds.

Miranda pulls her eyes away, back to Spencer. "How do they know his name?" she asks.

"Who, Ernest?" Spencer drains the last of his coffee in one swallow. "Everyone knows Ernest." He shoves his cup away and hoists himself up to pay their check.

CIGARETTE BREAK IN THE SCHOOL YARD. CHRISTMAS vacation rehearsals are stressful, so Spencer's smoking even though he knows he shouldn't be. Miranda is drinking hot chocolate from a blue-and-white takeout cup with a picture of the Parthenon on it. Between the columns it says "It's a Pleasure to Serve You." Everyone is huddled against the school's brick facade trying to get their matches to stay lit, and Spencer and Miranda are sitting on the ground in an alcove sheltered from the wind. They are having one of their talks: Spencer talks, Miranda asks questions.

"How's Sarah?" Cocoa steam rushes from Miranda's mouth and it almost looks like she's smoking too.

"OK. She stayed at my place last weekend."

"That's OK with your parents?"

"No, they go away weekends. I've got the apartment to myself."

Miranda doesn't even like being home alone after school before her mom gets home from work. She turns on the soaps just to feel like there are other people around. "What does Sarah tell *her* parents?" she asks.

"She lies," Spencer says. "Says she's staying at a friend's, gives them Nicole's number. If they call, Nicole tells them Sarah's in the shower and she'll call when she gets out, and then she calls Sarah at my house . . ." Miranda starts to zone out, trying to imagine her own voice telling some story like that to her mom. But it's not her own voice she hears, it's some other voice. A voice she's created in her head before, the one she's imagined using to ask Spencer what it's like to kiss Sarah. How he knows when it's OK for him to reach up the back of her shirt, unhook her bra, bring his hand slowly around to her breast, to trace her nipple with the tip of his finger, around and around like Miranda does to her own nipples at night in bed when she's spacing out and doesn't even realize what she's doing until a little shiver shoots down her. A bizarre new sensation that sometimes turns her stomach. Her nipples just began to swell around Thanksgiving time. They are raised, and hard as new pencil erasers. Tender too, often sore. This she was prepared for, but also they itch.

In the courtyard beside Spencer, Miranda draws up her knees and rubs them hard against her chest through her coat and sweaters, trying to relieve the stretch and pull of that too-taut skin. She must look agitated because Spencer puts his arm around her and pulls her in close.

"Hey, what's up, sweetie?" he says. "Why so morose? You're supposed to be our smiling child of cheer. Are you cold? You want to head inside?" He crushes out his cigarette, stands, pulls Miranda to her feet, and stoops down in front of her.

On his back, she wraps her legs around his waist, and he grabs hold of her calves, tight, so she can feel his thumbs pressing into the flesh beneath her jeans. She wraps her arms around his neck. His hair smells like smoke. His ears are pink and cold.

JAMES CALLS REHEARSAL FOR NEW YEAR'S DAY because with a week until the show they have a lot to do. But his cast, it turns out, is so hungover they can only lie on the mats trading vomit stories of the night before. Miranda sprawls there with them, sometimes pretending to read *Lord of the Flies,* which she is supposed to finish before school starts again, but mostly listening. Finally, around eleven, Spencer appears.

"Happy New Year, kiddo!" he says, sinking down on the mat next to her. His eyes are bloodshot and ringed with gray. He hasn't shaved.

"Happy New Year," she says, distant, resentful.

"This is one messed-up bunch here," Spencer moans. "You should've seen us last night . . ."

But to hear about last night is more than Miranda can bear and she just cuts him off and starts talking— "When my dad still lived with us we used to go to Boston for New Year's and visit his law school roommate and his wife, and they have two sons, Ian and Todd." Miranda looks away, still talking, anything that comes into her head, just to keep the noise going, to keep him from telling her things she doesn't want to know. "They're a little bit older than me. Our parents would always go out to dinner and get really tipsy and come home at like two in the morning wearing party hats and blowing kazoo things and noisemakers and being really silly." And though this memory hurts, aches like a death, like something gone forever that she'll never get back, still she keeps going. "And even though it's so late, they wouldn't even care that we're all still up. We'd stay home and order out for pizza and watch *The Benny Hill Show* on television. And the whole time, we'd wrestle. We'd totally destroy the room, and I always wound up getting tackled and Todd'd be sitting on top of me and Ian would pin my arms down to the ground and count to ten. Last night I just watched the ball drop on TV. I tried to find *Benny Hill* even, but I guess maybe it comes on later or it's just on in Boston or something . . ." She trails off, unable to think up anything else to say.

"Wrestling, huh?" Spencer says. "You missed out on wrestling this year?"

Miranda nods.

"I'll wrestle with you whenever you want, OK?" he tells her.

"You're too big. I'd get squished."

"I promise I wouldn't squash you." He crosses his heart, hopes to die, sticks a needle in his eye.

"Yeah, right," she says. "You'd put one hand down and I'd be a pancake."

He reaches over and places one huge palm on her forehead, pressing as if to drive her right through the floor.

LATER THAT AFTERNOON MIRANDA IS STILL LYING ON the yellow mats watching from the window of the warm lighting booth as Spencer and Alexa rehearse the scene in which they kiss. When it's over everyone dashes outside for a cigarette. Miranda is left alone in the booth for a minute until Spencer enters, flops down on the mat, and starts to tickle her.

"Spencer . . . stop . . . stop . . ." She is laughing so hard she can't breathe.

"You said you wanted to wrestle . . ." He is relentless. She squirms into the corner, beating her feet against the wall. He doesn't let up.

"Say mercy . . . ," Spencer cajoles.

"Mercy . . . mercy . . . mercy . . ." She can barely get words out. He stops, still holding her down in case she tries to come at him. She is laughing, panting, trying to steady herself, probably melodramatically, she thinks, but it's wonderful. She draws a breath and looks up at him, and suddenly she is brave. "What's it like?" she asks. "Kissing Alexa? What does it feel like?"

His eyes register surprise, then something like a question. Her body tenses and his hands on her go soft as he leans down, moves a piece of hair from across her cheek, and tucks it behind her ear. Then he kisses her on the mouth.

He pulls himself away, flops back on the mat with calculated nonchalance. "That's what it feels like," he says.

Her backbone goes numb. The yellow of the mat is electric. "I wasn't concentrating," she says, more fearless than she ever knew she could be. "Do it again."

"Don't tempt me," he says, flicking her arm with his finger the way they shoot crumbs at each other across the table at Acropolis. "Jailbait," he teases. Flick. Flick.

MIRANDA AND HER MOTHER ARE IN THE CAR HEADING downtown after the final curtain. Miranda has explained to Roz the traditions of the theater club. The custom is for each cast member to tear down a publicity poster and hang it backstage during the last performance for everyone to write messages on. The traditional cast party is held at a rented loft downtown. Roz knows that Spencer will be there looking out for Miranda. Roz trusts Spencer: not because she should but because she can—because he is polite and large, physically, and because she does not yet worry about Miranda being taken advantage of as a woman since she is so clearly not yet a woman. Soon, Roz knows. But not yet. Trusting Spencer is not as hard as worrying about Miranda all night would be, so she has chosen trust. There is a lot she doesn't know. She doesn't know about the money skimmed off the concessions profits from the show each year to buy rum, and gin, and tequila. Miranda's told Roz that Spencer will put her in a cab when she wants to go home. Roz is nervous, but she agrees. She stops the car in front of a building in the East Village that looks like a warehouse. Miranda opens the door latch and leans over to kiss Roz on the cheek. "Thank you, Ma."

"You know, it was a lot easier when all you wanted to do was get up onstage and act and all the changes were make-believe." She waits until Miranda waves from the vestibule window before pulling away. Miranda's been buzzed in.

The loft is a fourth-floor walk-up. There is no railing and the fluorescent lights make her feel like she's in an incubator. People line the stairwell, leaning against the walls, smoking on the landings—people she vaguely recognizes from set and stage crew, and people she doesn't recognize at all, people who don't even go to her school. It's OK, though. She feels OK. She's worn all black tonight, and even though she cold-creamed off her makeup back at school, everyone can still tell that she was in the show. That she's one of them, and she belongs here. Miranda walks up the stairs purposefully, like she's looking for her friends. Nearing the fourth-floor landing, she spots Troy and Alexa and that whole crowd. She stops and says hi, and Alexa gives her a hug. Troy says it's great that Miranda came and that *her* mother would never have let *her* come to the cast party in seventh grade. James tells her to watch out for herself. Miranda asks if they've seen Spencer, and Trevor directs her into the apartment. Across the loft—through music, laughter, banging, yelling—she can hear Spencer's voice. He's drunk. Drunk off his ass.

SHE SHOVES HER WAY BACK THROUGH THE CROWD THAT has closed in behind her and pushes her way down the stairs, trying not to get branded by the orange-glowing tips of cigarettes. Some people try to move out of her way, but their limbs are slow and soupy. They blink at her.

Back on the street the cold air pounds at her head. She can see snow on the ground and her own breath clouding in a sliver of street light. Her lips are shaking. She remembers his: chapped, strangely muscular, somehow thick, like it was difficult to shape them gracefully into a kiss.

She hails her own cab. The vinyl seat is cold, and though Miranda can feel heat blowing on her legs through a vent near the floor, the driver has his window open and the frigid wind is shooting in. He has the radio on and a station is coming in static with Indian sitar music. It swirls through the car with a different kind of warmth—heady, like incense—as they speed up Park Avenue, every streetlamp they pass encircling the yellow cab in a fleeting orb of white light. Miranda unrolls the poster she's had clutched in her hand since she left the theater. She holds it up to the window and scans it in each splash of light. "You're the sweetest!" they've written.

"Don't ever change." "The star of the future!" "Keep smiling!" At a red light on the corner of Fifty-seventh Street she finds his message.

Hey Kiddo—
> *If only you were a little older . . .*
> *We'll still get married someday . . .*
> *You are my best buddy . . .*

I love you,

Spencer

Ellipses after every line, as if she is supposed to know what comes next. Or meant to figure it out for herself.

10

SPITFIRE

PLAYING JACKS ON THE SMOOTH WOODEN FLOOR OF the Spitfire cabin, Miranda and Darrin wonder if Roz will ever date again.

"It's been a couple years, right?" Darrin asks. "Tensies, back," she calls.

"My dad left at the end of fifth grade," Miranda says. The girls will begin eighth grade in less than a month now, and as the summer draws to a close they have begun to talk more about their lives back home, the worlds that await them there. They have begun the preparation for return. It's never an easy transition back into school, but this year they fear will be infinitely harder. They are the oldest, the Spitfires, the reigning queens of Girls' Camp. It's their last summer here, at Camp Sunset Lake, together.

"I kind of wish she would," Miranda muses. Her mom has always been on the overprotective side.

Darrin scratches on eightsies backward, scoops the jacks and ball together, and passes them across to Miranda.

"Sixes, forward," Miranda says. She is losing miserably. She tosses the jacks onto the floor between her straddled legs, studying the dispersal for convenient groupings. "Maybe she'd get off *my* case some if she was fooling around with someone herself." Miranda fumbles the ball on her second throw and has to go searching for it under Astrid's bed. When she finally hands it over to Darrin, it is slightly wet and attached to a dust bunny that trails behind it like a deflated parachute. Miranda flops down on her own bed to watch. Darrin has as good as won the game. "Not like *I'll* be fooling around with anyone," Miranda goes on, speaking as much to herself as to Darrin.

"Oh, right," Darrin says. Darrin has been slightly bitter all summer about Miranda's messing around with Jeremy Kinzer, a Splitrock guy over at Boys' Camp. Darrin hasn't hooked up with anyone, but Miranda knows that's not what's at the heart of her anger. Darrin doesn't want Miranda to have hooked up with anyone either. Darrin likes guys, it's not that she doesn't, she's just not curious the way Miranda is. Darrin's mind is filled with tear-jerking good-bye songs and sweet pine-needle memories. She's not ravenous the way Miranda is; she's ready to grow up in stride, and with a lot more grace, Miranda thinks. Miranda is too insatiable; all she can think of is the filling. Miranda knows that Darrin is actually afraid for her somehow, worried about what lengths Miranda might go to, driven by her impatience. The Spits—specifically those with boyfriends in the Splitrock Boys cabin—have been talking about a late-night rendezvous in the woods between the two camps, and Darrin has taken to leaving the cabin during such discussions. They hear her out at the bathhouse, Muck Pond, hand-washing a favorite shirt or a good Victoria's Secret bra. She sings "Leaving on a Jet Plane" aloud to herself, a sweet, lilting soprano, and the girls roll their eyes, "Darrin again," grinning at their friend's unreadiness—her unwillingness—to move on to this next phase of life with them. Miranda knows that in her own time Darrin will come around.

· · ·

THAT EVENING, THE SPITFIRES ARE A BEVY OF PEN-lights and flashlights meandering through the camp. It's a tradition, this August serenade, a farewell from the Spits who in another week will be leaving camp for good. They pause for a chorus beside each cabin, and though the sadder songs—"the homesick songs"—have been banned from the littlest in the Hatchling Nest, by the time the Spitfires have reached the senior cabins they are free to do "Fire and Rain," "Cats in the Cradle," even "Sloop John B." The oldest girls are famous for inducing their own sob sessions toward the end of the summer, and this year is no exception. Every Sunday night at Campfire Darrin begs to sing "Jamaica Farewell." *I'm sad to say I'm on my way, won't be back for many a day. My heart is down, my head is turnin' around, I had to leave a little girl in Kingston town* . . . Now her eyelashes are gummy with tears, and this is a source of pride: here at camp—so unlike home and school—here, crying is very cool. To come to breakfast Monday morning after Campfire with red, puffy eyes is enviable. Darrin has been waiting six years, ever since she was a Hatchling, to be a sniffling, bleary-eyed Spitfire walking slowly across the dining hall, a mug of steaming tea clutched between her hands.

By nine forty-five most of the Spitfire Girls are on their beds pretending to read or whispering across the darkened cabin. Tonight is the night. Miranda is ready to go, fully dressed beneath her covers. Darrin glances over at her suspiciously and Miranda confirms her fears with one telling nod. The plan is in motion now, and though she doesn't approve, there is nothing Darrin can do but play along. Anything else would make her a prude, or a priss, a Goody Two-shoes. It's too late for intervention. Miranda is dead set on going. For weeks she's had a knapsack packed: a blanket for the ground, bug spray, a pillow, a tub of baby wipes in case there's blood, and, of course, the famous condoms, which have been passed around the cabin so many times, hand to sweaty hand, that the cardboard box is soft and crumpled. Miranda wants to get this out of the way before school starts. She just wants to have the first time behind her.

The Spits' counselor, Posie, stops in to say good night around ten, then disappears for the rest of the evening. This happens every night. The girls don't like Posie much; she never seems all that interested in them. It's her first summer at Sunset Lake, and there's little doubt it will be her last. Camp doesn't suit her well, and that seems obvious to everyone. Of course that hasn't stopped her from snagging the cutest guy counselor at Boys' Camp as her summer fling. Miranda, like the rest of the Spits, has a mad crush on Walker, and most of their interaction with Posie revolves around him. All ten girls have declared themselves willing to bear Walker's children, and they are unceasingly flabbergasted by Posie's nonchalance toward him. She shrugs him off—"He's just a guy, you guys. A cute guy, but only a guy, you know?" she tells her cabin—and this only serves to fuel their disdain for her. What *is* good about Posie is that she's never around. They don't know exactly where she goes every night, or what she does, though they suspect it's with Walker whatever it is, but they do know that the window of opportunity for nighttime excursions lies between about ten-thirty and twelve-fifteen.

"Who all is going?" Darrin whispers to Miranda.

"Just me. Everyone else chickened out." She's a little peeved, but also proud: she's the only one with enough guts to really go through with it.

"You're doing it alone?" Darrin asks, her nervousness betraying her.

"It's probably safer anyway," Miranda says.

"You really want to do it alone?" Darrin asks again.

"I won't be *alone*. *Jeremy* will be there."

"How'd you get—"

Miranda cuts her off: "I sent him a note at lunch in camp mail. He'll be there." She is excited, and pleased with herself.

"Oh," says Darrin, who puts her head back down on her pillow as if to indicate that she wants no part in this. She can just go to sleep and pretend that none of it is happening at all.

As Miranda slips out the trapdoor at the back of the cabin that is the "fire escape" in case of an emergency, she blows Darrin a kiss. Darrin pulls the door shut, and Miranda makes her way down the trail toward the lake. She is nimble and surefooted, and tonight also feral, bounding through the woods toward the shimmer of water below. The adrenaline rush has infected her and she tears down the path, taking the ruts and roots in stride. Her feet know this trail as if it were part of her own anatomy. Six summers are coming to an end—she *does* know how Darrin feels—and the welling of loss that fills her is unbearable, so painful it's glorious, and that pain blooms and pulses inside her as she runs. Her feet move faster, lungs fill with balsam air, teeth grit back the tears she can't cry right now. She can't give in to the sensation, which makes it all the more poignant, puts her closer to the verge of explosion, the night around her dense with quiet, yet everything buzzing, her heart pounding in her chest like something fiercely and defiantly alive.

Emerging from tree-shadow onto the moonlit lakeshore trail, Miranda can see the boat dock and canoe racks, rows of orange life preservers slouched forlornly over their wooden pegs. There is no wind tonight, and out on the lake, tethered to their moorings, the sailboats look like obedient dogs, leashes tied to parking meters as they wait to be reclaimed by their owners. Miranda pauses by the boat dock, hands on her knees, head hung down to catch her breath. And then there's a gasp, but it comes from outside her body, not inside, and she lifts her head quickly, like a swimmer coming up for air. Her pupils are wide in the night, and when they meet Posie's eyes they lock into each other, and for a moment there is no breath anywhere at all.

.   .   .

WALKER HAS BACKED POSIE UP AGAINST THE LIFE preservers. In the night silence Miranda can hear the orange nylon squeak and rustle. Walker's hand is down inside Posie's overalls, his elbow drawn awkwardly back, legs bent slightly at the knees, like someone trying to clear the clogged chimney up at Main House, and Miranda knows that his hand is inside her, craned at that odd, unnatural angle, and the realization is so stunning it's as if, just then, a hand has wedged itself up inside Miranda too, like a plug, or a stopper, like a swift kick to the underside of her diaphragm, and then Miranda is sucking in a huge gulp of air, palpable as water; she can feel it rushing into her to slam itself against the pressure forced in from below. She feels pummeled, flattened in, meat tenderized and hammered into a docile slab. She cannot take her eyes from Posie and the hand stuck inside her like a burrowing animal. Posie sees Miranda, there is no question of that. But then it's like she simply decides, in her own head, that Miranda isn't there at all. Posie closes her eyes, lets herself melt down into Walker's hand, then flinches back and grabs a wooden life-jacket peg in each hand, bracing herself against the wall, and it's as if she has succeeded in making Miranda disappear.

It's not will or conscious thought that sets Miranda in motion again; it's adrenaline, pure and simple, and suddenly she is racing down the trail toward Birches, toward the boy who will—*Please, please, please, Jeremy, be there*—be there where the dark pine tree trunks give way to white shimmering birch, be there waiting at the lean-to, sitting out of sight, his back resting up against the peeled-log wall, the dirt floor cold beneath him. She runs toward that hope, her steps silent, cushioned by pine needles, and she feels, right then, for just that moment, that what she's doing is OK, that the things she feels are real, and that maybe, somehow, between this moment now and the time the big charter buses pull away from Sunset Lake and onto the black endless interstate toward home, maybe she will have something more than she has now. Maybe she will have managed to grab another little tiny piece of understanding amid all the things that make no sense to her at all. Maybe she'll have that—sex, she'll have sex—with which to start eighth grade, and maybe as she holds that knowledge it will fill her and protect her, a magic coat of armor to take her through this booby trap, trip wire, hidden pit, kamikaze world.

11

THE PERILS OF ORTHODONTIA

DR. STEVEN STONE IS THE ORTHODONTIST WHO CASTS Miranda's bite in plaster and entwines her mouth in a labyrinth of girders and cables that snag the insides of her cheeks and leave the skin there feeling like the shredded-pork schwarma at the gyro stand by the Fifty-ninth Street subway, which Miranda passes on her way to and from Dr. Stone's office. The only good thing about Dr. Stone's office is its proximity to Bloomingdale's, which means that after a hideous torture appointment with the good doctor and his clamps and pliers that wind her wires so tight she sometimes thinks her mouth might simply snap, the teeth caving inward like a building crumbling in an earthquake—after an orthodontist appointment like that, Miranda can walk over to Bloomingdale's and wander the aisles waiting for her Advil to kick in, making her way among the racks, feeling fabric brush against her skin, letting the warm milky lights lull her into a sense of sanctity. She likes to keep Thursday afternoons free, to give herself that recovery time, so that when she finally leaves the department store and makes her way uptown toward home, she is ready to face her mom, her homework, able to contemplate eating dinner, mushy as that dinner might need to be.

One Thursday late in the fall Miranda's mom makes plans to meet her at Dr. Stone's office after her appointment to go shopping together for something Miranda can wear to an upcoming Hanukkah party at her Aunt Mona's. The prospect of shopping with her mom is, to say the least, rather dreadful. Roz's fashion evolution seems, to Miranda, to have been cut short in about 1978. Miranda is, like any self-respecting eighth grader, mortified to be seen with her mother in public. But Roz insists. She's on a tight schedule, working as a paralegal, studying for the New York bar, and if Miranda is going to have something relatively presentable to wear, today is the day.

Roz is predictably early and Miranda is in the chair when she arrives, her mouth pried open in an embarrassingly vulnerable position that leaves her drooling on the bib Dr. Stone's assistant has tied around her neck for just such a purpose. It is this assistant who leads Roz in from the waiting room and directs her toward the chair in which Miranda sits tilted back, surveying Dr. Stone's stucco ceiling. She hears the assistant say, "There she is, Mrs. Anderson, in her finest hour," and Miranda vows to harbor a grudge against that woman until the day her braces come off and she can sneer at her with all the pure, nonmetallic venom she deserves.

"Hey, kid," Roz says, bending over to deposit a kiss on Miranda's upturned forehead.

"Eunngh," Miranda manages.

"I couldn't agree more," Roz says, and she whips off her scarf as if she were Grace Kelly standing atop the cliffs of Monaco, not Miranda's mother standing astride a dentist's chair next to a display case full of pink plaster casts of the overbites and underbites of a thousand other metal-mouthed teenagers like her daughter.

From behind her, Miranda can feel Dr. Stone swoop in like a vulture, his lab coat flying up behind him like a bridal train, instruments of pain clutched in his needly little hands. "Your daughter does have a way with words," he says, and Miranda truly wishes she were in a position to stick out her leg and send him sprawling into the instrument tray, pickers and prodders scattering in all directions, perhaps sending something particularly sharp and damaging straight for the face of the smart-ass assistant, who'd probably been born with her Vanna White smile and had never experienced the joy of closing her mouth around enough metal to set off the detectors at Kennedy Airport.

"How're the old teeth?" Dr. Stone asks Miranda, leaning over her, his stupid beard hovering menacingly inches from her forehead.

Miranda refuses to degrade herself with another spittle-choked attempt at a reply, to set them up for another chuckle at her expense.

"You don't say?" says Dr. Stone.

Roz leans in, her face shadowing over Miranda, a hand smoothing her daughter's hair. "Not so bad, right, babe?" she says.

Miranda moves her head with the indication of a nod. She rolls her eyes. Roz smiles down on her, and suddenly Miranda thinks she will burst into tears, right there in Dr. Stone's chair, under the glaring fluorescent lights. She wants to fall into her mother's outstretched arms, to rip off that moronic bib and run with Roz from Dr. Stone's office out into the streets of New York—*their* city!— where they'd buy crusty hot pretzels and taffy and apples and packs and packs of Bubble Yum and Hubba Bubba and cherry-flavor Tootsie Roll pops, and eat it all without a care in the world for brackets and rubber bands, and they'd sit on high stools in the Bloomingdale's lobby, fawned over by the makeup ladies from Lancôme and Clinique, and while they chose lip gloss shades and waited to sign the charge card slip they'd joke about Dr. Stone and his stupid scraggly beard and the dorky pictures of his kids on the wall and the cheesy holiday cards he sent out to all his clients, a big fat grinning Santa Claus with a smile full of tin that said *Hope you're BRACED for the holidays!*, and Miranda would never have to go back to his office forever and ever as long as she lived.

"Just a few turns of the screw and we'll have you on your way," Dr. Stone says, his voice edged with a maniacal quiver.

Roz wraps her scarf back around her neck. "I'm going to use the rest room, Miran. Meet you in the waiting room?" She pauses. Miranda nods. "I think I saw a *Ranger Rick* in there I haven't read yet."

Dr. Stone laughs again, like he's set on finding everything Miranda's mom says far funnier than it actually is. "Bye-bye, Roz," he says.

"B'bye," she calls back, and Miranda can feel the push of wind as the swinging door rocks on its hinges behind her.

BLOOMINGDALE'S IS RELATIVELY QUIET THAT AFTER-noon. Riding the escalator up to Juniors, Miranda regards herself and her mom in a mirror running alongside the moving staircase. She has Roz's lankiness, Roz's angles of nose and jaw. But she's lighter in coloring, thanks to her dad, her hair straight and flecked with gold. The freckles are Edwin's as well. Halfway up, Roz turns and faces the mirrored wall with Miranda, wraps an arm around Miranda's shoulder, and pulls her in, beaming back at their reflection as if it were a photo in an album that she could hold on to. As if that moment will be indelible somehow now that they have stopped and regarded themselves, and that notion makes Roz swell with visible pride. What she hasn't inherited, Miranda sees, is Roz's nostalgia. For all her practical maneuvering and tactical good sense, Roz is, somewhere deep down, a sentimental romantic who spends a great deal of time and energy attempting to conceal that very fact.

As they step off the escalator Roz takes a big breath, as if to savor the Obsession a group of dangerously gorgeous women are spraying into the air as liberally as if it were Lysol. Roz is preparing herself for the ordeal of shopping with her daughter, which, Miranda finds herself realizing, is probably no picnic for Roz either. She opens her mouth to say *Thank you, thank you for taking this time to take me shopping*, but Roz speaks first and leaves Miranda's words to clot in her throat like a wad of cotton from Dr. Stone's instrument tray.

"Mirand," Roz says. "Mirand," she says again, "there's something we need to talk about."

Miranda squints curiously at her mother. A momentary fear that this is going to be a sex talk of one sort or another rises in Miranda's gut, and she has the urge to turn and run the wrong way back down the up escalator. What Roz actually says could not have been further from Miranda's mind.

"So, I—your old bag of a mother—"

Miranda rolls her eyes, and Roz laughs at herself before she resumes.

"So," and then she just spits it out: "So I have a *date* tonight."

Miranda misses a beat. When she catches up, a smile is rushing across her face, a flush of goodwill toward her mom, who Miranda knows she is supposed to feel happy for at that moment. And even if the emotion inside her isn't quite happiness, she can't identify exactly what it is, and happiness seems readily appropriate. "No way," she says.

"I know," Roz says. "Hard to believe."

"*Mo-om*," Miranda chides. Roz knows she's still attractive. She complains about her sagging butt and her drooping chin, but with Roz it really is all somewhat humorous as well. When she stands at the mirror sucking in and stretching back the skin of her cheeks, it is with the knowledge that she will never, ever, put herself under the knife for vanity. Whatever insecurities her mom may have, she does know that she's an attractive woman. And she knows that Miranda knows she knows.

"OK, so here's the rub," Roz goes on, and as she says it, her face screws up small and twisty, like Miranda's response might be one she'll need to shield herself from.

Miranda's eyebrows are raised to say, *Out with it already.*

Roz takes another dramatic breath. "My date is with your orthodontist, Miran." She turns to Miranda, that squeamish look contorting her face, as though Miranda were a horror Roz can't quite bear to see.

Miranda's own face turns stony. "What?" she says.

"I have a date tonight with your orthodontist, Dr. Stone. Steven." Roz is beginning to speak more confidently now, standing a little straighter, more brave in her confession.

Miranda says the first thing that comes to her mind: "He has *kids*, Mom."

Roz smiles, a little sheepishly. "So do I, babe," she says.

Miranda takes that in, begrudgingly. "So he's divorced?" she demands.

"Yes. Of course. Yes, Miran, this isn't some illicit thing. It's all on the up-and-up here. Totally legal." Roz raises her arms as if Miranda might want to search her for concealed weapons.

Miranda just stands there staring, stunned. Her mind replays the day's appointment; she can't find the spaces in which any of this could have happened. She was there the whole time. There hadn't been talk of any date. "When . . . ? I mean, when did . . . ?" she tries, but she can't find the right question. "How did you . . . ?"

Roz, as always, knows exactly what Miranda's question is. "This isn't the first one," she admits. "I met him when I went with you for that first appointment when they made the cast of your mouth . . ."

Miranda shoots Roz a look of utter frustration, a look meant to say, *Get to the point already.*

"We ran into each other on the subway not long after that. I think I told you even."

"You told me you ran into him on the subway," Miranda hisses. "You didn't tell me that you were going out on *dates* together."

"We've gone out to lunch. Twice. And met once for coffee late one afternoon." Roz says this as though she is finally coming clean, every last sin accounted for. "We get along really well. I think we really like each other. It's been a while for both of us. It's awkward, a little, but it feels good too, Miran. It's nice to be a woman again, not just—"

Miranda cuts her off. "You know what, Ma? I can't hear this, OK? I just really honestly can't hear this." She looks around frantically for the down escalator. "I gotta go," she says. "I'll see you later, OK? I've just—I've got to go."

Roz looks like she wants to grab Miranda, to grab her and pull her close, and she's fighting every impulse and muscle in her body to keep herself from doing so. "Where are you going?" Roz says dumbly. "Where are you going to go?"

And Miranda knows this is just her mom, her regular mom, just wanting to know where her daughter is going to be, but for the first time in her life Miranda feels the instinct to lie, to deceive, to say *Nowhere*. To say *None of your fucking business*. But what comes out is, "Home, Mom. I'm going home, OK?" And she turns and flees, runs down the escalator and tears through the lobby, down underground to the subway station below. Waiting for the train, Miranda wishes she'd gone outside, wishes she could breathe some real air, but here is the N, too late for that, and she boards the car, squashing herself in against a thousand other random New Yorkers. And as she rides toward home alone on that filthy N train, rush-hour raincoats and mingled sweaty colognes clogging every inch around her, Miranda fumes, blindly, no idea what she's so angry about, exactly, except that she feels betrayed. Her mouth is throbbing with a pain that feels just and appropriate to the situation, and she has only a churning sense that her life is about to change in ways she cannot control and alter everything, forever, like a twist of the screw, the wire pulling tighter and tighter.

12

THE SS STEVEN STONE

WHEN ROZ CONSENTED TO PAY A VISIT TO ZINNIA, Mona's psychic, it was not because she felt bad about her own life but because she felt guilty about Miranda, who had been exercising no restraint in making it explicitly clear, on a more or less hourly basis, how exactly Roz was ruining her life. Roz Anderson and Steven Stone had decided to buy—jointly, in love, and against the pleading advice of more than a few friends, their lawyers, and the real estate agent who sold them the place—a three-story brownstone in Park Slope. *The market is right,* they said. *We're in this together,* they told their kids. *What a waste to keep sinking money into a landlord's pocket when we can be getting ahead on a mortgage at the same monthly rate.* For reasons related to Steven's custody agreement, he and his two kids had to live in Brooklyn within a twenty-block radius of their mother, Steven's ex-wife, a snippish, skinny woman named Felice. Neither Steven nor Roz was game for another marriage, per se. *We,* they boasted, leaning in for a kiss, *we have something better than marriage: unadulterated love and joint property holdings.*

The evidence was plentiful: moving to Brooklyn at the crucial juncture of ninth grade was obviously going to cost Miranda her future. Specifically, even if she survived all those trips on the subway to and from the city to see her friends (whom Roz couldn't expect she was going to just drop and abandon), even if she wasn't mugged, raped and murdered, or pushed into the tracks (the chance of which only went up with the frequency of subway travel), there was little point in remaining alive since leaving the City Day School basically meant giving up her chance of getting into a decent college. City Day kids go into better schools, Miranda said, and that was just a fact, plain and simple. It would appear to college admissions officers that this Miranda Anderson person hadn't been able to hack it at City Day when the real work of high school came along. So, whatever, Miranda told Roz, she'd just go to beauty school, or she'd bum around and see what happened . . . there were drugs to turn to, and she could become a dealer if it came to that. And there was always prostitution, after all. No need for Roz to worry about Miranda. *I'll find a way to survive,* she said, *somehow.* And then she'd skulk off to do her teenage brooding with an air of absolutely self-satisfied martyrdom. Steven, and Mona, and Fran, and anyone else Roz talked to about it said that Miranda was a resilient child—a young adult now really, fifteen almost—and would certainly come through all the stronger and more prepared for the shifting winds of change in life and blah blah blah whatever else they said . . . Nonetheless, Roz felt horribly guilty.

"You cannot live your life for your child," Mona said. "Nor," she proffered as an aside, "nor can you live your life *through* your child." Mona was fond of declarative statements. "You're in love," she told Roz, "you're in love with a man who lives in Brooklyn, and someday Miranda will understand the choice you are making to be with him. It's about finding a balance, Roz-Roz. Between who you are for her and who you are for you."

Which was all well and good for Mona to say, but Roz longed to confess to her older sister that she was uninterested in raising a child like Mona's Joshy, who now apparently went by Yehoshua and lived in a one-bedroom apartment in Jerusalem with an Israeli wife and, last Roz had counted, five children ranging in age from one to five. Mona kvelled with pride. It all made Roz very nervous. Mona's advice was something to be taken in extreme moderation.

"I'm betraying my daughter for a man," Roz said, cringing.

"And if you didn't"—Mona nodded in approval—"you'd be betraying yourself for your daughter, which would make about as much sense as being alone for the rest of your life." Mona was no-nonsense about some things, and when she cut to the chase, the discussion was over. Roz would very much have liked to point out that this advice was coming from a woman who (a) *had* chosen, for reasons she never made clear to anyone, to spend her life alone, and (b) had raised a son who never, as far as she knew, did anything that Mona found less than splendid.

Roz had been alone, and very much wanted to be not-alone. She had a daughter whom she loved so much it made her bones ache, but dammit, that daughter made her angry, and confused, and unsure of herself. Sometimes she thought she was as crippled by her love for Miranda as women in bad country songs were for their men. It was a desperately devoted kind of love, and she looked down on women who felt it for their cowboys. But to feel it for your daughter was a whole different story.

"Come with me, talk to Zinnia," Mona coaxed.

Roz rolled her eyes. "I already have a therapist, thank you very much. I don't need another fruitcake getting paid to listen to little dramas. Don't these people have anything better to do with their time?" Roz threw up her hands. "That's all I need: a psychic!"

Mona was undeterred. "Just because you've had a bad experience with some rigid, anal-retentive Freudian who probably just wants to get you into bed anyway—"

Roz cut in, "I wish!"

"—I'm not even entertaining that—"

"And who says it's been a bad experience?"

"I do," Mona said, resolute and unyielding. "Look," she said, "you can always go back to Dr. Everything-Wrong-with-You-Is-Probably-Your-Sister's-Fault, right? Just give Zinnia a try, see what you think. I'll pay. Think of it as a gift, an indulgence, something just for yourself, something pampering . . ."

"I wouldn't be arguing if you were offering me a spa treatment."

"Come on, Roz . . . She's wonderful, soothing, just come meet her . . . For me, Roz-Roz, come on . . ."

"There's a minor difference between a Swedish massage and seaweed wrap and a session with your crystal-ball swami . . ."

"Oh, but Roz," Mona said, wrapping her sister into her arms as if to hug, or maybe smother, her, "oh but that's just precisely where you are so very wrong."

ZINNIA'S OFFICE, SUCH AS IT WAS, COULD WELL HAVE been mistaken for an Indian restaurant. A few stone steps led down from East Fourth Street to a locked black wrought-iron gate. The door behind the gate was ajar, the doorway draped in curtains of linty blue velvet that hung to the floor like scuff-worn trouser cuffs. Mona pressed the buzzer, but it was impossible to tell if it had rung or not over the music which emanated loudly from an old boom box that someone had lashed with a chain and padlock to the outside stair banister. Mona looked as though she was trying to hum along with the tune—a choked cacophony of what sounded to Roz like kazoos and untuned violas—but couldn't quite pull it off. Mona was someone who could usually make anything look right. The kind of woman who'd dash out to the store one day in pajama pants and silk pumps because they were the first things she grabbed, and the next day everyone on the runways and in *Fashions of the Times* would be sauntering along in pajama bottoms and silk pumps. It was enough to make you do the things she did, no matter how bizarre they seemed.

Mona reached a hand through the wrought iron and poked it between the velvet curtains until she was engulfed up to the shoulder. It looked to Roz as if she were being sucked in, flitting her body, waving the arm. Roz wondered if it was like this when Mona came alone to consult with Zinnia; she could make anything look like a routine she'd been enacting her whole life.

Mona turned and smiled at her little sister. "It's so good you're here, Roz-Roz. You're going to be happy you came."

"So I hear," Roz said. She didn't smile. She lifted her eyebrows.

And then the blue curtains parted. Roz couldn't tell if it was the sight of Zinnia (who looked far more normal than she had expected) or the sight of Mona caught for a moment awkwardly, straining through the gate like a prisoner reaching for the cell key hanging just an inch beyond her grasp—but whatever the cause, Roz felt suddenly inspired, as if this whole thing maybe wasn't such a terrible idea after all. She reached out and took Mona's other arm to lead her away from the gate and caught Zinnia's eye at the same moment. The psychic was maybe forty, and looked more like a corporate secretary than someone who spent her days hunched over a crystal ball. Roz had expected Zinnia to be a wizened old woman who ate sunflower seeds as she worked, the chewed-up residue catching in her teeth and spittling off her tongue as she spoke. Her accent would be indiscriminately eastern European, and her draped shawls would exude the smells of the old country: hearth, earth, and onion. But this woman before her could have been a trader at Morgan Stanley. Roz decided she should try in the future to be less critical of Mona, who really was no ninny when it came right down to it. Zinnia pulled open the gate and ushered the women inside.

Zinnia and Mona exchanged a subtle, acknowledging hello, and then Mona stepped back as if to make room to introduce Roz. Roz smiled broadly, and the woman heaved the door open a foot farther and slipped through, closing the gate behind her with a click and a thud before she made her way up the steps and out of view.

"I'm so happy for you, sweetheart," Mona was saying to her. "I'm so happy you've allowed yourself to be here. I'm proud."

Roz felt a sudden loss of oxygen. "Don't patronize me, Mona. OK? I'm here, let's drop it. Done." Roz nervously touched the edges of her hairline, patting imaginary stray strands into place. She had a strong desire to kick her sister in the shin.

"There's our Roz!" Mona said, and slapped her tentatively on the shoulder, as if Roz were an old football buddy with a contagious skin disease.

Roz scowled. She glanced around perfunctorily. "The incense is an original touch," she said.

"And I thought Edwin was going to help you with that cynicism . . . ," Mona said.

"Edwin?" Roz said. "Edwin and I divorced three years ago. I assumed you knew."

"Before that," Mona said, her exasperation showing. "You know what I meant."

"He did," Roz told her. "He helped me tremendously. I got it all back in the divorce settlement, though. The kid, alimony, and all my cynicism returned to me, good as new."

Mona shook her head pityingly. "Roz," she said. "Oh, Roz."

AND ZINNIA WAS, OF COURSE, A PRUNEY OLD WOMAN with food-lint caked in the crevices of her dentures. She performed with a detached intensity, as if to attend to you best she needed to focus on something else entirely. She was somewhat dismissive and seemed put out to be doing another goddamned reading, but fifty bucks was fifty bucks . . . Did anyone mind if she smoked? she asked, the match already lit and poised. A few puffs later she let the cigarette languish in the corner of her mouth and took Roz's hand in both of hers. Her fingernails were ragged and Roz was afraid she'd get snagged, but she held her tongue.

"So who's got the boat?" Zinnia demanded, as though someone had promised her a schooner as payment and hadn't delivered.

"Excuse me?" said Roz.

Zinnia sighed.

Roz looked to Mona, who smiled knowingly from the corner where she sat.

Zinnia seemed perturbed. She sighed again, ever more deeply. "There is a man, no?" she asked.

Roz laughed, an exhausted snort: *this-is-ridiculous-what-am-I-doing-here.* "Where?" she said, and turned dramatically to check behind her. "I don't see anyone."

At this, Zinnia smirked unmistakably, and seemed to decide right there in that moment that Roz was OK. She was being let into the club. "So there's a man in your life," Zinnia said. "He causes you trouble—no, not him causing the trouble, but trouble from the journey you take with this man. OK?"

Roz raised her eyebrows: *OK, I'm still with you.*

"OK. This man, what? He owns a boat?"

Roz shook her head.

"No boat? Eh, OK, boat boat boat . . ." She drew on her cigarette, eyes rolling upward as if to search there for some meaning she'd lost, or only misplaced.

"Why a boat?" Roz asked.

"Because I see a boat," Zinnia told her. "Why else a boat? You ask me what I see, I say I see a boat, you say why a boat?" Zinnia shook her head, smirking all the while. Then she flashed Roz a wink. It was a sly one—Roz wasn't even sure if Mona could have caught it—but definitely a wink. She went on. "The water's bad, the weather is bad, but the boat, the boat is good. Strong. Sure. It's a good boat. It doesn't have a name, the boat. You know how they write on the side, or maybe in back, the name of the boat? Yes, well, this one there is nothing. The 'SS'—and then there's no more words there. The 'SS,' that's all." She paused, then began again,

"You're on a journey, it's a long journey . . ." Zinnia sounded as though she were intoning an incantation, words and phrases repeated many too many times. "Bumpy journey, rocky journey, long time at sea . . . OK? But, here's what I say: it's a good boat, this SS, OK? A good boat. It took you a long time to find this boat, I think, and I tell you don't give it up. The SS, she's your boat."

"The SS?" Roz said. "It's just called the SS?" She couldn't decide herself whether she was incredulous or simply disbelieving. She fought back the fourteen-year-old-at-a-Ouija-board, *you-want-to-dance-with*-me? awe rising in her. Awe like that turned you into a believer, and that was Mona, not Roz.

Zinnia fixed Roz in a stare that seemed to say, *Well, do you plan on speaking or not?* It was disarming.

"Did Mona tell you this?" Roz turned to her sister, then back to the psychic. "Do you already know . . . ?"

From the look on Zinnia's face it seemed that she couldn't even quite place who Mona was, let alone remember the things she'd said.

"The man I live with," Roz began, "the man I just moved to Brooklyn to live with . . ." She was testing Zinnia, she thought, trying to catch a hint of betrayal that this was all a story she'd heard before. But Zinnia looked the same as she had: impassive, and a little bored. "His name," Roz said, "just the whole thing with the SS and all—his name is Steven. Steven Stone."

"Well, of course it is," said Zinnia, about as impressed as a wall.

"And he's a good boat!" Mona chimed in from the corner.

"This is insane," Roz declared.

"That's fifty," said Zinnia. "You can pay cash?"

"I CAN'T BELIEVE YOU LET HER TALK YOU INTO THAT," Miranda said. She was spooning frozen yogurt into her mouth at an alarming rate.

"You're going to give yourself a headache," Roz said.

"*I'm* going to give myself a headache! Of course, it's my fault, everything's my fault, right?"

"I just meant the ice cream—slow down."

Miranda rolled her eyes. "It's not ice cream," she said. She held the lid out toward her mother, used her spoon as a pointer to underline the words as she spoke them: "Fro-zen yo-gurt."

Roz stood and fished another spoon out of the silverware drawer. She gestured toward the carton, and Miranda handed it over. Roz perused the ingredients superficially, then scooped herself a bite.

"So, what's your fortune?" Miranda asked. She leaned back in her chair, propped her feet up on the kitchen table.

"Oh, I don't know," Roz said. "It's probably a load of shit, right?"

"Probably," Miranda agreed. She waved her spoon at Roz: *Gimme back my fro-yo.* Roz ladled herself another bite and handed it over. She leaned back against the counter, the sweetness melting down her throat, and watched her daughter root around the pint unearthing hidden chocolate chips.

Roz crinkled up her brow, made her eyes like a puppy's. "Are you gonna hate me forever, Miran?"

Miranda rolled her eyes again. Then she seemed almost to be grinning somewhere there inside her shell, a smirk tucked under all that defiant anger. "Maybe not *forever . . . ,*" she conceded.

Roz could hear the pleading in her own voice, and it bothered her, but she couldn't seem to change it. "Because I think this is good, Miran, I really think this is good. I feel a way I haven't felt for a long time, you know, a way I didn't know I was going to be able to—"

Miranda cut her off. She stood. "Please, not another love lecture," she said, "I can't bear it." She sounded like a Victorian heroine, and her melodrama made Roz giggle in spite of herself. "Is that what the swami told you?" Miranda said, pushing, her teasing way. "That Dr. Steven is the true love of your life?" She put her hand to her heart. "Oh, it's so beautiful. I think I might faint."

Roz fixed her with a scowl, but kept smiling right through it. "How'd I raise such an obnoxious child?" she demanded. "Did no one ever teach you any manners?"

Miranda held up her hands—*I accept no blame for that one, Mother dear,* they seemed to say. *That one's all on you, Mama, all you.*

"Well, did no one ever teach *me* any manners!?!" Roz cried.

"Oh," Miranda said, "great, blame it on Grandma Adele. The poor woman's dead. Not even here to defend herself."

Roz softened. "She was a good mother." She shook her head, thinking. "No, Adele was a good mother."

Miranda looked embarrassed, like she wanted Roz to snap back to the game. "So what *did* Aunt Mona's psychic have to say for herself?" she asked. "Was it a total scam?"

"I don't know," Roz said. "Probably. Right? I mean: a *psychic*?"

Miranda nodded, but seemed interested to hear Roz continue.

"She said some odd things, though, like things that meant something to me that she didn't even know meant something to me. She just said what she saw, no idea what it meant . . ."

"What do you mean?" Miranda asked. She sank back down into her chair, ready to listen, one leg bent beneath her, the other foot on the seat, chin on her knee. "What did she say?"

"Well," Roz thought, "a lot of stuff. But basically, she said that this was right. She said I was riding in a boat over stormy seas, but that it was a good boat and would get me through . . ."

"And . . . ?" Miranda was growing impatient again.

Roz felt silly. She wanted to say this so it would ring for Miranda with the same note of inevitable truth that it sounded for her. She wanted this to come out right. "The boat," she began, but her voice was melodramatic and she didn't like it. She tried to modulate and started again. "You know how boats are named like the SS Something-or-other. Like the SS . . . oh, I don't know, the SS Something . . ."

Miranda was nodding. "Yeah, yeah, yeah, I know."

"Well, my boat didn't have a name. This great boat that I was finally sailing in, that I'd been waiting for . . ." Roz felt herself getting swept up in the romance of it, weaving these fragments into the larger story they implied. "My boat was just called the SS . . ." She felt herself opening up, wanting to give this to Miranda, this offering of peace, this irrefutable piece of the puzzle of their lives. "The *Steven Stone* . . ."

Miranda was silent for a moment, her eyes wide, fixed on Roz. Then she put her foot back down on the floor and pushed herself up from the chair. She pushed the chair into the table—something she never did—and held the back of it, as if for balance. Finally she spoke. "Oh. My. God," she said, so slowly each word became its own sentence. "Oh my god," she repeated. "Mom?" She looked at Roz intently, pointedly, craning her neck out as though to catch something she might not otherwise hear.

"What?" Roz asked, earnest and eager. "What?"

"You're even loopier than I thought you were!"

"Loopy?!" Roz balked, then found her footing, grabbed her balance, remembered her smile, the joke, the persona she had to keep up now around Miranda, the only persona Miranda seemed willing to see as her mom. Roz laughed, stuck out a hand, and pretended to whop Miranda, the way a mom in a sitcom might, one of those moms who was on such great terms with her daughter that they could kid like that, tease each other, take it all in playful fun. She whopped at her again. "Rotten child, I can't talk to you!"

Miranda nodded, slowly backing away toward the stairs, as if Roz were a rioting psych-ward patient, Miranda a lone nurse desperately trying to escape with her life. "It's all OK, Ma," she said slowly. "You're just fine. Everything's going to be just fine . . ." She reached the foot of the stairs, turned, and fled, bounding up, two at a time, and *shhhhhp* she was gone, like a tissue sucked up with the vacuum.

Roz put away the frozen yogurt, set the spoons in the sink. Business, business, taking care of business. No moping, no waxing rhapsodic for Miranda's childhood. Not allowed. No use anyway. What could you do? Lock the kid in a tower? Right. Roz could just see it: Miranda would grow her hair long, hack it off, braid it into a rope, climb down, and catch the first train into the city. A modern fairy tale.

And then she thought: *No.* She thought, *Goddammit, I'm the fairy tale:* fair Roz and her captain sailing the open seas aboard the SS *Steven Stone.* And, of course, there was a part of her that wanted to turn back, to climb over the rail, plunge down to the water below, and swim, swim, swim back to Miranda as if both their very lives depended on it . . . She had to stop herself. That was so clearly not what Miranda needed: her wet, bedraggled mother trudging up the shore, arms outstretched and dripping—*Baby, I've come back to you . . .* No. Besides, it was a good boat she was on, a great boat, a battleship tanker, a mammoth vessel of immutable steel. She was on the right boat. And there wasn't any turning back. She was already way too far out to sea.

13

ANY STRANGE BEAST
THERE MAKES A MAN

IN ALL HONESTY, LIVING IN BROOKLYN DOESN'T bother Miranda so much. It's kind of a pain, sure, and a bummer to be separated from her friends. At first she was genuinely bitter. Really honestly pissed as shit. But then something came along to temper that anger. Something unexpected, instantly sweetening the entire enterprise immeasurably. So even though her mother's completely off her rocker, and Brooklyn is simply not Manhattan, and Dr. Stone is a first-class boob, things just really aren't as bad as they seem. Though her new school seems low on cool and long on not-so-bright, within the first few months Miranda's already skipped ahead in math and landed an excellent role—her namesake, as a matter of fact—in the theater club's production of *The Tempest*. Plus, to make things around the house decidedly more bearable: Dr. Stone's son, Ben, happens to be very, very cute.

THE PARK SLOPE BROWNSTONE INTO WHICH MIRANDA and Roz and Steven and Ben and Jenny have moved is, as they say, "a fixer-upper." It's a three-bedroom house, with a basement they've handed over to Ben, the oldest, which Miranda and Jenny resent and understand at the same time, much the way the other Brady kids learned to cope when Mike and Carol let Greg have the whole attic to himself. Jenny and Miranda share the second floor—separate bedrooms with a connecting bath—and Steven and Roz have the entire top floor to themselves. None of the kids venture up there by choice; they're all a little frightened by what they assume goes on above them. By the time they actually move in, the first-floor kitchen has been remodeled, and the living and dining rooms are freshly painted, though the plaster underneath still threatens to crumble in a strong wind. Jenny's and Miranda's bedrooms have been painted too, and their bathroom, while hideous—candy-pink tile, black glossy trim, the sink and tub an awful aqua-blue—is at least functional, which is more than Ben can say of his, which consists of a toilet stuck haphazardly in an unheated closet. He has to come up to the girls' floor to shower: the price he must pay for basement-bachelor-pad luxury. It's all awkward and embarrassing at first—how much clothing must be worn, how much privacy can be demanded—but they adapt. It's sort of like being at camp, Miranda tells Darrin over the phone: you're all there, no one's leaving, so you just kind of get over it and deal.

AT THE EMMONS SCHOOL, A SHORT LOCAL BUS RIDE from the house, Ben is in the eleventh grade, Miranda the ninth, and Jenny eighth. Jenny is nice enough, if somewhat bland and uninspiring—kind of like her father, Miranda thinks. She's a girl who owns Fair Isle sweaters and argyle socks and drinks from juice boxes even when she's at home. And whether Ben is a product of his mother, Felice, whom Miranda has never met, or simply a freak of nature, a slap in the face of his own DNA, he is certainly unlike the rest of his family, at least as far as Miranda is concerned. Ben is a guitarist, but not in the every-teenage-boy-fancies-himself-to-be-Jimi-Hendrix sort of way; Ben just plays the guitar, all the time, alone in his basement. He's a mournful boy, always hiding behind his overgrown hair, sullen and cautious, watching. He's very private, it seems. But if Miranda sits in the far corner of the living room, in the chair next to the heating vent, she can hear very well down into his basement den, and she can listen to him singing old Townes Van Zandt songs, John Prine, scores and scores of Dylan. Sometimes the songs he picks out on the strings are fragments; stilted and tentative enough that Miranda imagines he is composing as he goes, and she imagines how it would be to have him write a song for her, about her, torn and tortured over a love that he knows he cannot have. In Miranda's mind Ben is like Joni Mitchell, pouring his simple sorrow through the soundhole on his knee. Lately it seems he is forever playing that Neil Young song, "Only Love Can Break Your Heart," and when she hears it, she feels it is something unspoken between them, a code, a bond. Ben, Miranda decides, is the reason behind all of this—the move to Brooklyn, everything. Whether or not Steven Stone is her mother's boat to end all life-mate boats, it seems fatedly and cosmically and unquestionably clear: this has all happened because Miranda and Ben are meant for one another.

He doesn't socialize much—not in the house at least—so it's hard to get to spend any time around Ben at all. He rarely eats dinner with the rest of them, and seems to operate on a schedule that, no matter how much Miranda alters her own—either slowing down or speeding to the breakfast table each morning, then dawdling like mad, walking different routes to the bus stop—she cannot manage to overlap. It's not that he's *un*friendly, or dismissive, or curt, he just always seems to be so far away, and all Miranda can think is that she wants to go to that place too—wherever Ben is. Miranda's world, which had felt a little unruly there for a while, is suddenly very very small and very very neat. She does not have to think about her mom, or her dad, or her creepy orthodontist, or the friends she's left behind, the new friends she has yet to make . . . Life, for Miranda, has become effectively compressed; there is Ben, and nothing else really concerns her at the moment.

BY DECEMBER, AFTER SPENDING THANKSGIVING WITH her dad and his family in Nebraska, Miranda is nearly out of her mind with love for this boy who might as well be her stepbrother. Coming home from school one Friday afternoon to find no one in the house and Ben's sultry guitar chords wafting up from the basement, Miranda sits for a long while by the heat vent trying to devise a way to approach him. She rifles through her book bag: gym shorts, sports bra, a rapidly disintegrating spiral notebook, a smushed box of cough drops, a copy of the new *Elle* magazine she'd bought at the newsstand that morning, her *Tempest* script from which she must have her lines completely memorized by Monday . . . Miranda snatches it out of the bag and hops up from the chair, smoothing the script against her stomach as she walks. She takes the basement steps at a trot, light on her feet, practically grinning with glee—how glorious to have a purpose! She pauses only for a half second of self-doubt, then raps intently on Ben's door.

Inside, the guitar stops abruptly. "Yeah?" Ben calls. "Come in . . ."

It strikes Miranda as bizarre how you could sit for months plotting how to get inside, and then one day you knock, he says come in, and you wonder if it would have truly been that easy all along. Slowly—as if she might be catching him in the midst of something compromising, as if she hasn't knocked at all—Miranda pushes open the door.

Ben is sitting on the end of the futon, guitar on his lap. He sets it down on the floor beside him. He's still wearing the same clothes he wore that day—ask Miranda any day and she can tell you which T-shirt to look for to spot Ben in the halls at school—but he's taken off his shoes and socks, and at first Miranda is afraid to look at his feet. Afraid she will find them suddenly repulsive, though she's seen them a trillion times before. Afraid too that she will find them so ardently arousing she will be unable to maintain the small bit of decorum she can still muster in his presence.

"Oh," says Ben. "Miranda. I thought you were Jen." He doesn't look disappointed, but she doesn't know what else he might be feeling.

"Why?" Miranda asks, though once she's said it she realizes it's an odd thing to say.

Ben crinkles up his face in a sort of amusement. "Because she knocks on my door all the time and you don't . . . ?" he offers. It's a question. Miranda smiles. "What can I do for you?" he asks. Polite! Oh, she does love him so!

She sticks the script out toward him, then pulls it back into her chest. She cocks her head, sheepish. "Are you busy?" she asks.

He gestures around him as if to indicate the lack of anything in his presence that might qualify as business.

"Could you . . . ," she begins—she should have figured out how to ask before she came downstairs!—"I've got to . . . Do you think you could maybe help me with my lines? I need to have them memorized by Monday and no one's home to read the other part, so I thought maybe if you weren't too busy and if you didn't mind too much . . ."

But Ben is already holding out his hand for the script. He looks like he wants to gesture her into a chair, but there aren't any in his room, just the mattress on the floor, so he straightens out the comforter, covering the sheet beneath as though he's trying hastily to restore the poor bed's modesty. Miranda leans one hand against the doorframe and pries off the cowboy boots she's wearing. She hopes to god her socks haven't gotten smelly. On the bed, she tucks her feet under her, just in case.

Ben flips open the script, scans some pages indiscriminately. "So who are you?"

"Miranda," she says.

"I know that much . . ."

"Oh, no," she says, realizing, "in the play. I play Miranda. I think that's the only reason I got the part. Because of my name. It's pretty dumb . . . ," she trails off.

The Tempest," Ben intones, "starring Miranda as Miranda," and she laughs, as though no one has thought to make this joke before, because honestly it has never sounded funny until now.

"OK," he says, "where from?" He flips pages again, as if it might be marked in red pen: *Begin here.*

"Um," she says, "um, how 'bout Act Three? I think I'm OK up till there." She feels daring asking this of him, as though he knows, as she does, that she's had her lines memorized for weeks. As if he knows exactly what happens in Act Three and why this is what she wants him to read. Really, he doesn't know a thing. He flips pages, finds his place, prepares. "*Enter Ferdinand, bearing a log.*" He laughs. "Should I find myself a makeshift log?" he asks.

She laughs back, shaking her head no.

He resumes, "You want me to read his whole speech thing here?"

She does, of course she does, but it's too much to ask, too unjustifiable. "Just the last couple lines to cue me," she says.

"*My sweet mistress / Weeps when she sees me work, and says such baseness / Had never like executor. I forget; / But these sweet thoughts do even refresh my labors, / Most busiest when I do it.* OK, you enter now, with Prospero, *behind, unseen.* Who's Prospero?"

"My dad," she tells him.

"Uh-oh," he says.

She laughs again. It is too much to say her lines with inflection in front of him, so she just plows through: "*Alas, now pray you, / Work not so hard!* . . ." And she's hardly aware of anything after that, the lines flowing out of her like a song she's known all her life, her attention only on his voice, his tone, the thoughtful way he turns the page, his attention to cues, and to line breaks, to stage directions, to her. When Prospero has a line, Ben reads it without pausing. A natural, she thinks, he was born to be her Ferdinand.

"*Poor worm,*" he says, hiding his mouth behind his hand, a gesture, to the stage note that says Prospero should speak his line aside, "*thou art infected! / This visitation shows it.*" He looks up to her, his index finger pointing to the text. "This is great," he says, "*poor worm,* that's excellent."

And Miranda thinks, *Yes, you don't even know the half of it, Ben, but yes.* "*You look wearily,*" she recites.

"*No, noble mistress, 'tis fresh morning with me / When you are by at night. I do beseech you, / Chiefly that I might set it in my prayers, / What is your name?*"

"*Miranda. O my father, / I have broke your hest to say so!*"

"*Admired Miranda!*" he begins, and doesn't balk at the speech ahead of him, just delivers it through so that she can listen to every line the way she listens to his songs through the vent, as if it were not Shakespeare or Neil Young or Woody Guthrie who penned those words, but Ben, Ben Stone, behind every line. "*. . . you, O you,*" he is saying. "*So perfect and so peerless, are created / Of every creature's best.*"

She does not know where to look as she speaks her lines. At him? At her hands? Off into some holy and distant horizon? Mid-speech, she manages to raise her eyes to his face, and mercifully he is reading along and she does not have to look him in the eye as she says, "*I would not wish / Any companion in the world but you; / Nor can imagine form a shape, / Besides yourself, to like of . . .*"

"*. . . Hear my soul speak! / The very instant that I saw you, / Did my heart fly to your service; there resides, / To make me slave to it; and for your sake / Am I this patient log-man.*" He chuckles at this, grins up at her: *log-man.*

"*Do you love me?*" Miranda asks quickly, before he lowers his eyes, and she holds him there in her stare for a moment, makes him break away first, back down to the page where he fumbles for his place, bumbles to get out the next line. He shifts awkwardly on the mattress as he reads, " . . . I, / Beyond all limit of what else i' th' world, / Do love, prize, honor you."

"I am a fool / To weep at what I am glad of."

And Ben, in his Prospero's aside: "Fair encounter / Of two most rare affections! / Heaven's vain grace / On that which breeds between 'em!"

Miranda begins her next speech, all too aware that the end of the scene is coming, a sense of panic overtaking her: *What do we do? What do we say after this?* And soon, so soon, it is done, *Exeunt,* and before she can delve into the embarrassment she knows is encroaching, it's Ben who speaks, the script in his hand, shaking it as though impressed by its weight. "They get right down to business in Shakespeare, don't they?" he says, smiling.

"Seriously," Miranda says, the breath rushing out of her too audibly; she is too visibly relieved. She shifts toward the edge of the futon, not because she wants to leave but because she doesn't know how to legitimize staying.

Ben looks a little confused. He holds the script out toward her. "You done? You want to do more?" he asks. She takes the script, standing awkwardly. "Are you OK?" he asks.

She tries to read his face to know if his concern is real or mocking, but she can't focus on anything but getting out of his room. "Yeah, no, no, that's great, I'm great. That was great. Thanks. Really . . ."

"Anytime . . . ?" he says, backing off, backing down the way you would around a crazy person, a loose cannon, *Don't get excited now . . .*

"Thanks," she says again, and flees, slamming the door behind her with far more force than necessary. She wants to shout *Sorry!* but can't—it's too inadequate, she's too intent on being gone.

Back upstairs—safe! The way she used to run from imaginary ghosts in darkened halls—she flops down into the heat-vent chair and hears Ben pick up his guitar again. A few chords strum through the tunnel toward her, and Miranda hears herself making a wager, a bet against herself, a double triple quadruple dare: if it's that song, the Neil Young one, then she'll go back downstairs and she'll kiss him. If it's "Only Love Can Break Your Heart," then she'll know exactly what she has to do. She waits through his intro as if her very life hangs in the balance, everything to be determined in Ben's musical selection.

When she hears his voice come through the vent it fills her with a rush, a thrill: that's it! The song! She strains to catch the words, but something sounds a little wrong, a bit off somehow. *"Now that you've found yourself losing your mind, are you here again? . . ."* But it's not until the chorus that she's completely sure: it's a different song. Still Neil Young, but a different song. What does that mean? Her bet hadn't accounted for contingencies like that. If he plays something by Crosby, Stills, Nash & Young, then she'll give him a hug three days from now . . . ? If he decides on anything written between 1969 and 1977, she'll tell him she thinks he's cute and leave it at that . . . ? The whole idea suddenly seems as ludicrous as it is. She sits in the chair and listens to his sad, sweet, beautiful, sometimes off-key voice, staring down at the script in her hands as if it were a dagger with which she might do herself in—until she hears Jenny's key in the lock and scrambles upstairs to her room before she has to face anyone, let alone Ben's little sister. That seems more than she should have to take in one day.

BEN GOES OUT THAT NIGHT; WHERE, MIRANDA doesn't know. Roz and Steven rent a movie—something with subtitles—and watch it upstairs in their bedroom. They invite Miranda and Jenny up to watch, clearly aware that the girls would rather stare at a blank wall for three hours than suffer the indignity of spending Friday night watching a foreign film with their parents. Jenny reads in her room. Miranda talks to Darrin on the phone until even *they* can't think of anything else to say to each other. She goes to her room and listens to "After the Gold Rush" until she cries, which doesn't make her feel any better at all.

She dozes off for a while, waking when she hears Jenny in the bathroom getting ready for bed. Jenny is the kind of person who always brushes her teeth, and lately when Miranda brushes her own teeth she has the sense that she's not doing so to prevent cavities, but to keep pace with Jenny. She hears the door to Roz and Steven's bedroom upstairs shut, and watches under the bathroom door to see Jenny's light flick off for the night. Miranda isn't tired at all anymore; in fact, she feels wired, her heart beating so quickly and insistently she is sure she can hear it echoing off the walls around her like in the Edgar Allan Poe story. She lies in bed watching tree shadows sway across her room.

When Ben comes home, she hears him stop in the kitchen, open the fridge, a cabinet, glasses clink, thud, the fridge closes, and there is the thump of steps down to the basement. And as Miranda pictures him opening the door to his room and flipping on the light, the first thing that hits her is: her cowboy boots! She left them there, that afternoon, by the side of his bed, and she thinks she has never been so grateful for something as that: a solid, substantial, legitimate reason to go down to his room.

She's still dressed; there's nothing to impede her sense of purpose, no time in which to doubt her intention or question her plan. She is silent on the stairs, sock-footed and stealthy. At the top of the basement flight she pauses, soft muted guitar chords slipping out through the cracks around the doorframe. It takes her only a few lines now to recognize the song. *"I was always thinking of games that I was playing, trying to make the best of my time. But only love can break your heart. Try to be sure right from the start . . ."* and it seems so clear that she is meant to hear this, meant to be at his door right now. She takes the last few steps toward the door and knocks softly. No response. She knocks a little louder. The music stops. "What?" he says. "Who is it? Hang on, OK, hang on a sec . . ." He sounds sort of panicked, a voice she hasn't heard in him yet.

Her hand is on the knob, turning. "It's Miranda," she says, cracking open the door as she speaks. The room is a haze of pot smoke, Ben standing helplessly holding a half-smoked joint as if he's trying to figure out where to hide it.

"Jesus Christ," he sighs, his chest collapsing as he sinks back down to the futon, the air flooding out of his lungs.

"Sorry," Miranda says. "I'm sorry. I didn't mean to scare you. I just wanted to get . . . I left my boots down here before, I just wanted to get them and I heard you come in . . ."

Ben is smiling incredulously now, shaking his head back and forth. He takes a drag on the joint and holds it out toward her. She accepts.

"What?" she says. "What's so funny?" She puts her lips to the joint, praying she won't sputter like she has when she's smoked in the past. She inhales shallowly, afraid to trigger a coughing fit. "What?" she says again, her voice escaping in a rush of smoke.

Ben looks at his watch, smiling broadly. "What do you have, a three a.m. rodeo date?"

"Oh!" She is startled, mostly by her own stupidity. Coming down to get her boots in the middle of the night! What was she thinking? "I just, I guess I just . . ." and then there's no use. Her protestations dissolve into laughter.

"Hey, pass that on back over here," Ben says, and as she transfers the joint from her fingers to his, their fingertips touch and Miranda feels a live-wire current rocket up the length of her arm. She nearly jumps back, awkward and thrown, and Ben says, "Hey there, steady. You OK?"

"Yeah," she says, "yeah, I'm OK, I'll just, anyway, I'll just get my boots. Thanks. Sorry. G'night. Sorry I scared you before." And once again, she flees his room as if she's swimming up to the surface from a long dive, unsure whether she's got enough oxygen to make it. Back on the first floor she sets her boots by the stairs and falls into the heat-vent chair, a mass of spent nerves. In the meantime, Ben has picked up his guitar and resumed the song. *"Yes, only love can break your heart. What if your world should fall apart . . . ?"* And Miranda, all Miranda can think is: This must be love. Because my heart is breaking. Do you love me? *Do you love me? O heaven, O earth, bear witness to this sound!*

14

HORROR

YEARLY GYNECOLOGICAL EXAMS MADE ROZ EXTREMELY
anxious. Stressed her out almost as much as the fear of a tax audit.
They were similar, really, she thought: you did everything the way
you were supposed to, followed all the rules, and still had the sense
that at any moment someone could pop in and discover that
somewhere back in line six you'd turned a seven into a one by mistake and, yes, they'd have to take the breast. She did cursory self-
exams once a month in the shower the way it said to in *Our Bodies,
Ourselves,* but she never really felt like she knew what she was looking for, so either nothing felt like a lump or everything felt like a
lump, depending on her state of mind. The idea of losing a breast
scared her more than she liked to admit; dying was more than she
felt able to address. Imagining what would happen to Miranda
sent her into paroxysms of anxiety, and then she'd realize that
whatever happened to her—cancer, heart attack, hit-and-run by a
taxi cab on Seventh Avenue—Miranda would survive, as Roz had
survived her own father's death, her mother's death. And that, in a
way, was terrifying as well. When her brain concocted terrible sce-
narios of Miranda's death, Roz could not imagine herself going on

afterward. She wouldn't become one of those mothers who took on the cause of her daughter's death—fighting sex offender laws, crusading for a leukemia cure, taking up the cause of handgun control. She'd just lie down and die right alongside her, and it was hard to imagine Miranda doing anything different if the situation were reversed.

Dr. Obelmeyer's office was on the fifth floor of a building in midtown Manhattan that overlooked Rockefeller Center. An elaborate system of strategically placed mirrors enabled a woman to watch the ice-skaters' reflections projected on the ceiling above her as the doctor did her thing—*Now take a breath, you're going to feel my fingers now, OK, now there's going to be a little cramping sensation, and* scrape, scrape, scrape, *there we go, all done now.* It was distracting, but also always gave Roz the sensation that with all those mirrors around someone else was probably also able to look at her, legs spread in Dr. Obelmeyer's stirrups. Roz appreciated the sophistication and sterile modernity of Dr. Obelmeyer's office, and if it meant that a pap smear cost two hundred and fifty dollars, well, she was willing to pay for some things. Once, in college, Roz had gone to a gynecologist who put socks over the ends of the stirrups so they wouldn't be cold and metallic. Roz spent the entire exam wondering whose discolored tube sock and lone burgundy argyle they were, and though a sliding fee scale and wholesale contraceptives and let's-get-together-and-look-at-our-cervixes consciousness-raising groups all seemed reasonable in theory, Roz never returned. Dr. Obelmeyer was Mona's gynecologist, and there were some things about which Roz had to admit that her older sister was right.

Dr. Obelmeyer had long, thick strawberry-blond hair that she wore back in a bun, giving the distinct impression that if she were to take it down and remove her lab coat, she'd become a Bond Girl: leopard-print panties and a looming black stethoscope. Her omnipotent sexuality lent a sort of insider's understanding to her medical authority. The woman believed in sex; she was trustworthy. When she reached under Roz's raised arm and felt for the lymph nodes, Roz had the sensation for a moment that she was not at the gynecologist's at all; she was getting a Swedish massage.

"Hmm," the doctor said, her manner brisk and concerned. She felt under Roz's other arm, then returned to the first. On the ceiling, a girl in purple leg warmers turned a double axel. Onlookers applauded with mittened hands. Dr. Obelmeyer's mouth was a grim line and Roz's stomach hollowed out with fear.

"What?" she said. "*Hmm* what?"

Dr. Obelmeyer laughed softly. "Roz, calm down. Let me just get a good feel here, OK? Shhhh, relax now, OK?"

Roz's armpit was suddenly a minefield. She wanted to grab it, to probe herself for whatever Dr. Obelmeyer was feeling. She tried to modulate her voice and wound up sounding like a psychopath. "Are you finding something unusual, Doctor?"

The doctor laughed again, less convincingly this time. Roz was deciding to hate her. She would find a new gynecologist, no more of this million-dollar charm. This woman was a cream puff. A sexpot. A goddamn Playboy Bunny! What in hell was Roz thinking, letting this charlatan paw so uncommunicatively at her breast. You couldn't knead someone's mammary glands making inquisitive grunts and not let them know what was going on. This was ridiculous. Roz would report Dr. Obelmeyer to the AMA as soon as she got up out of the chair!

"I'm feeling a little density, a little mass, and it's probably the lymph node, just a little swollen . . . Possibly a cyst . . ." She probed at Roz's right breast. She could have been a nail polish model.

"My mother died of breast cancer!"

"Roz," Dr. Obelmeyer chided gently. "Come on now." She turned her attention to Roz's file, flipping back in the records. "Now you're . . . what? Forty . . ."

"Five," Roz cut in. "Almost forty-six. Should I have a mammogram? Would that be the smartest thing to do, have a mammogram? Or a biopsy . . . I'm absolutely high risk—"

"Hold your horses," Dr. Obelmeyer said, and Roz pictured a team of Appaloosas straining in her flimsy grip. The doctor felt around Roz's breast once more, as if to confirm her conviction before she spoke. "Here's what you're going to do: you're going to make another appointment to come see me"—she checked the file—"in five weeks. For those five weeks you're going to cut out caffeine . . ." She looked at Roz expectantly to see if that was going to be a problem. Roz was nodding vehemently, so the doctor went on. "No caffeine—coffee, colas, tea, chocolate—and no fatty foods, fried foods, cut your salt intake . . ." Roz kept nodding. "Let's see where we are five weeks from now. If I'm still concerned about what I feel, then we'll move on to the next step—"

"Biopsy," Roz interrupted.

Dr. Obelmeyer maintained her even tone. "If I'm still concerned, we'll do a needle aspiration and see if what we're dealing with is maybe a cyst. We'll see if we can draw off some fluid then and narrow down the possibilities—"

"Can't we do that now?" Roz said, and her voice cracked like a teenage boy's.

"No," said Dr. Obelmeyer, so sternly that Roz was afraid to ask why not. There was a pause while the doctor collected herself. When she spoke again it was as a prophet, channeling her words from some holy and irrefutable source. "Eighty to ninety percent of these lumps are noncancerous. So it's more than likely that you are perfectly fine. I want you to relax. You will, I have no doubt, discuss this with people. They will all tell you stories. Please try to remember that stories are tales in which something happens. If nothing happens, there is no story to tell. In a situation like yours, eighty to ninety percent of the time there are no stories to tell. Ten to twenty percent of all lumps discovered actually become stories worth telling. Only a tiny fraction of those ten to twenty percent are actually horror stories. Think about movies," Dr. Obelmeyer suggested. "The world is not made of *Halloween 3* alone."

Roz was trying to remember if she'd ever seen *Halloween;* for a moment she almost forgot to remember that she was surely about to die.

THE SUBWAY LURCHED BENEATH THE EAST RIVER AND Roz thought about Edwin. Thinking of Edwin made her sad, always did. But there was also a relief: relief that he was not the man she was on her way home to find. Steven would rub her back and tell her everything was going to be all right. He'd understand her need to break down. Edwin wouldn't have known how to hold her; he'd have demanded from Roz a steely strength in the face of this adversity. He wouldn't have even allowed her to call it adversity until all the reports were in. It was eighty to ninety percent sure that Roz was not sick, and Edwin wouldn't have let her forget that for a second. In Edwin's world you were healthy until proven otherwise. Steven understood subtlety. He would understand the psychological toll, the emotional turmoil. The worry. Steven would bring her macaroni and cheese in bed and sit up with her watching late-night sitcoms and stroking her hair until she fell asleep in his lap. By the time Roz got home she had nearly convinced herself that in the whole scheme of things the purpose of this episode would be to illuminate her right choices, to make it clear, once again and to all, that divorcing Edwin had been the right thing to do.

Steven came home early on Fridays and was in the kitchen making pizza and drinking Beaujolais when Roz walked in. Immediately she burst into tears.

"Roz?" Steven asked, almost laughing. "Roz?" But his smile was too great, his mood too easy, and she couldn't find any words.

"Where's Miranda?" was all she could manage.

Steven looked perplexed, his grin unflagging, as though he were mocking her for weeping at a sappy movie, falling for Hollywood hook, line, and sinker. "They're all upstairs, our room. We rented *Psycho*," Steven explained. "I stayed to get Jen through the shower scene, then was sent away to make dinner." He used the cleaver in his hand to display a cutting board of diced onions, mushrooms, peppers, and pineapple chunks. A ceramic bowl stood on top of the oven, a checkered towel draped over its bulging rise of dough. Steven's eyes twinkled. They were living exactly the life they wanted to live.

Roz gasped, a sob caught in her throat.

"Sweetie!" Steven said, still uncomprehending, still smiling his confused, innocent smile.

"I'm just . . ." She choked. "It's just . . . oh, it's just hormonal, I guess . . ." She mumbled the words, swatting at her eyes. She dropped her bag and coat on the kitchen floor and started upstairs.

"Would you like some wine?" Steven offered.

Roz turned back, crying, smiling. "You're good to me, Steven," she said. "We're good." She stood in the middle of the staircase looking down on him from above. "It's a good life. This." She was sobbing steadily now, didn't even know if he could understand what she was saying, and from the look on his face it seemed he probably couldn't.

"Roz," he said, "what on earth is going on?"

"What if I have cancer?" she said.

"Cancer?" Steven's face only grew more confused. "Why cancer? What are you talking about? What's going on?" His tone was rising every moment, the fear lighting inside him now as well.

Roz sank down to the step on which she'd been standing. The sanitary pad that she'd taken from Dr. Obelmeyer's in case of bleeding pressed awkwardly against one thigh. Her pants leg caught on her boot and twisted. She felt like a child in a snowsuit, immobilized by discomfort. She put her forehead on her knees and wept.

Steven set down his wineglass and darted up the stairs. He sat beside her. "Roz, tell me," he pleaded. "Please tell me what's going on . . ."

· · ·

IN THE END THEY DECIDED NOT TO WORRY MIRANDA, at least not right then. The kid had enough to deal with already, they said; she was fifteen, and that was plenty to think about on its own. They would wait. In five weeks they would know something. Would it help anything for Miranda to also spend those five weeks in agonizing anticipation? The answer was clearly no. When they knew something more definite, then they'd tell the kids. Until they did, the fear was something Roz and Steven would share alone.

And it was strange, that secrecy. Strange to see how deceit changed you. Roz had never lied to her daughter before, and though she managed to hold her tongue those five long weeks, she swore she never would again. A lie, Roz thought, was like a moat. And this wasn't even a lie: it was a truth untold. But Roz didn't keep secrets—not from Miranda—and the deception surrounded her like a deep and murky swamp. Whether Miranda noticed any change in her mother was impossible to say. Miranda was a teenager; her moods were unpredictable, her demeanor alternately sweet and cankerous, babyish and rabid. It was hard enough to talk to a fifteen-year-old girl, harder still to keep something from her. Steven tried to convince Roz that to put some psychic distance between herself and Miranda would do them nothing but good in the long run no matter what happened. Roz told him she thought he was more full of shit than she'd ever imagined, and tried desperately to believe he was absolutely right. To tell anyone besides Steven made the not-telling-Miranda seem even more diabolical, sneakier, less explainable, more wrong. Roz kept her secret. Four, five, six times a day she called Steven at work, had a nurse interrupt him, pull his fingers from some crooked adolescent mouth so he could get on the phone and talk her down. She holed up at her office, working late, avoiding Park Slope. She cried often, made up stories about troubles at home to appease gossipy coworkers. Lies begat nothing but more and more lies, it was true. You told just one and spent the rest of your life with your hands on your ass trying to keep it from flapping in the wind. It was the right thing to do, but if the cancer didn't kill her first, the lying would do her in in no time.

In five weeks she lost seven pounds. "You worried, didn't you?" Dr. Obelmeyer chided. Roz's jaw was clenched. She didn't think she could move it to answer. She didn't know what in god's name she would say if she tried. "Or it could just be the water," Dr. Obelmeyer mused, "no salt, no coffee, that'll do it sometimes . . ." Roz nodded stiffly and the doctor busied about, snapping her gloves with distracted nonchalance, preparing her routine. It was a callous business, medicine, Roz thought. Made you steely. Made you hard. *Please God, let Miranda be a doctor. Make her strong. Give her the will to save herself from pain. Build her a turtle's shell and keep her heart locked deep inside.*

"Do you feel any changes yourself?" Dr. Obelmeyer asked. "Any discomfort, anything out of the ordinary?"

Roz's poor breast had spent five weeks under the closest scrutiny of its career. The poor thing had been squeezed and prodded and palpated within an inch of its very life. It ached with attention. It felt swollen from use. Roz shook her head no, shrugged, looked away and back again. She was completely at a loss.

Dr. Obelmeyer lay Roz down flat on the table and settled her arms by her sides. It was raining outside, and on the ceiling the skating rink was empty, a janitor moving slowly around the viewing areas spearing bits of trash on a long-necked skewer. Roz held her breath until the doctor reminded her to inhale. Her fingers worked their way around Roz's breast, kneading, pressing, testing.

"Feels OK," said Dr. Obelmeyer. She smiled and turned to Roz's chart on the counter beside her. "That's often all it takes," she mused. "It could wind up being a chronic thing. Some women do tend to develop these fibroid cysts, very sensitive to food, to substances." She was making coffee sound like heroin. "Or it could be random. We'll keep an eye on it, OK? Maybe we'll see you again in what? Six months?"

Roz nodded. Six months sounded OK. She would still be alive in six months! Roz thought of the horror movie her life might have become, but didn't: just a lot of fear, unbearable torturous suspense, and then nothing. "I guess I don't even have a story to tell," she said to Dr. Obelmeyer.

The doctor looked at Roz for a moment like she was someone she knew but couldn't place. Then a light of recollection crossed her face. She had been correct, and seemed pleased by this. But the thing Roz couldn't get out of her head was the story she'd already not told—the *not-story* she'd already not told—to Miranda. It was another lump inside her: probably not malignant, but worrisome all the same.

15

THE NIGHT AFTER THE NIGHT AFTER THE NIGHT AFTER THAT

DARRIN QUAILE'S FATHER IS A PSYCHOLOGIST, LENDing Darrin's amateur psych evaluations an air of informed authority. Her analysis of Miranda's obsession with Ben Stone is summarily simplistic, and probably uncannily accurate. "You only like him because he's the absolute one person you absolutely cannot be with," Darrin tells Miranda.

"You think?" Miranda asks, her face scrunched up, not wanting to believe.

"Duh," says Darrin.

"You don't know him, Darr, you'd die if you saw him. He's perfect. You'd so get it if you saw him."

"I *get* it," Darrin says. "It's not that I don't get it. It just seems like, OK: you know you can't like *date him* or anything, he's practically your brother, remember?"

"They're not getting married," Miranda says defiantly. "He's not ever going to be my brother."

Darrin is silent on the other end of the phone.

"I mean, it makes sense, right? If my mom's so in love with his dad, then doesn't it make sense that I would be in love with him too?"

"No," Darrin says, "what makes sense is that you know that there's nothing you could possibly do that's as bad as wanting to date your mom's boyfriend's son who lives with you. I mean really—what would your mom say? For real, what would her reaction be?"

"Well, I don't think she'd be *thrilled* exactly, but . . ." Miranda tries again: "*She's* the one who moved in with *my* orthodontist."

"Which means that she should understand why you want to jump into bed with his son?"

"Well . . ." Miranda laughs. "She is always talking about how liberated she is . . ."

"Yeah," Darrin says, "why don't you just run that one past her?"

"Yeah, but part of me is like, *what the fuck,* I mean, she didn't ask me before she hopped into bed with Dr. Stone . . ."

Darrin cuts her off: "Which is my point exactly! You're just into him to get back at her . . . right?"

But Miranda's not giving in. "Nooooooo," she whines, "I'm into him because he's amazing. It doesn't have anything to do with her . . ."

"Uh-huh," Darrin says. "Right."

"I swear . . ."

"Uh-huh."

"I am not making this up. I swear. I think he's there with it too, I really do. I don't think I'm reading stuff into it that isn't there . . ."

"OK, first of all," Darrin begins, "can I remind you that you *are* the same person who thought Andrew McCarthy was flirting with you *from onscreen* in *St. Elmo's Fire . . .*"

"I wasn't being serious about that . . ."

"Secondly: I'm sure you're right. I'm sure he *is* flirting with you. He's a boy. And you're beautiful. He can't help it. It's still wrong, Mirand. You still can't actually do anything. OK? Miranda?"

"What, *Mom*?"

"Promise me you're not going to do anything."

"What counts as anything?"

"Miranda!"

"Well . . . ?"

"Repeat after me: I, Miranda Anderson, do solemnly swear not to sleep with my stepbrother."

"He is *not* my stepbrother! We wouldn't even have deformed children . . ."

"Miranda, that is so *not* funny. You can't do this, OK?" Darrin is sounding too genuinely worried. This is ceasing to be at all amusing.

"OK OK OK," Miranda concedes.

"OK, why do I not believe that you're going to keep your hands off this boy?"

Miranda giggles, "Because I'm not . . . ?"

"Miranda! I swear to god! I think there are laws against that kind of thing!"

Miranda laughs. "Ugh," she says, "I should go. I've got a shit-load of math homework . . ."

Darrin's voice is serious again. "You're not going to listen to anything I said, are you?"

"Nope!" Miranda chirps. "But I love you anyway!"

"I swear to god, Miranda, someday this isn't going to be funny anymore. It's already not funny anymore."

"Shhhhh," Miranda coos, "shhhh. I'm OK. Don't worry, OK? I'll be good. I will. I haven't fucked up too bad yet, have I?"

"Ugh," says Darrin.

"I know," Miranda adds, "you love me too. Talk to you soon!"

Another moan from Darrin, and then just the dial tone.

THE PLAY KEEPS MIRANDA RELENTLESSLY BUSY, AND that's a blessing really, to have something to do aside from pine.

She hardly sees Ben at all, and when she does pass him—in the kitchen, coming out of the shower, in the cafeteria at school—they have pleasant, sweetly innocent exchanges, and these are enough to perpetuate, and tease, and strengthen the seemingly insatiable need she feels for him. By the time the show goes up in March, Miranda's agony over not having Ben has settled itself into a constant low-grade ache, like a hunger that will not be fed on mere food. Miranda knows at this point that even getting Ben will never sate her desire for him—it's moved so far beyond the issue of fulfilling a want. Whether or not she will get him—somehow, in some way—becomes a moot point itself; she will have him, unquestionably. It's what she will do then that eludes her. Once she has Ben, and Ben himself is not enough to quench the thirst he has aroused in her, then what will she do?

Ben comes to see *The Tempest* twice: once on opening night with Roz and Steven and Jenny, and then again, with some friends, two boys in his class whom Miranda only knows by sight. They sit up in the balcony, where they're in shadow even when the houselights are on, but she is as aware of his presence throughout as if the spotlight were on him instead of her. It is clear that this means something. By coming twice, Ben has made something known, and now without risk of complete embarrassment Miranda can put something of herself out there too.

On the final night of the show is the traditional cast party, held this year at the home of the boy playing Caliban, a boy named Oba whose house out in Bensonhurst has been conveniently parentally vacated for the week due to a timely conference in Singapore at which his mother, an economic historian, has been called to speak. Oba is not simply a theater geek, he's a baseball player and pretty political too, and the cast party quickly becomes much more than a party for the cast. It seems to Miranda that all of the Emmons School is there, packed into Oba's row house as if it were a bomb shelter. It's blisteringly, bone-numbingly cold, and with not a hint, not even a suggestion, of imminent spring. No one's even smoking outside; it's too cold for that. They're all just crammed in, doing what they do, and there's something about the proximity that makes it seem like they're getting drunk off each other—the way people catch colds from flying in airplanes—as if the alcohol content were recirculating through the air like in-flight oxygen, pot smoke getting pumped in and out of the vents.

Ben is there, leaning casually against a kitchen counter as if he weren't hemmed in on all sides, his hand around a can of Old Style. He looks more like he's at a backyard barbecue, the sun setting late and slow behind him, infinite possibilities of a summer's night stretching out in all directions. Miranda, three screwdrivers to the wind and even less inhibited than usual, sashays directly over, hoisting herself up to sit on the counter beside him. The kitchen cabinets stick out into her back and she has to hunch over awkwardly, which makes it hard to sip her drink, so mostly she just stares into it, the bottomless screwdriver, as if she could read the orange pulp like tea leaves and know what to do next.

"You were good," he says.

"Thanks," she says. Though she has cold-creamed off her makeup, her eyes are still bleeding black liner and she wipes at them now, checking her finger afterward for smudges. Her lashes feel gummy and that gives her a strange confidence, the sense that she is legit, she's authentic, Miranda Anderson.

He swigs from his beer, and although she doesn't watch him she knows his Adam's apple is rising and falling as he swallows and that thought is enough to make her have to close her eyes and pinch them shut and speak to him blindly, too pained to see his face as she says what she says: "Do you think you're too much like my brother for it to be all right for me to kiss you?" and then she holds her breath, waiting.

He says nothing, not a sound, and within seconds that silence—amid all the frenzied, congested blare of the party around them—is so deafening she has to look, has to know what he's doing. Her head whips around toward him, eyes flying open wide with fear. And there beside her is the same beautiful Ben, his posture the same, eyes trained down on his beer as if he's trying to burn through the tin can with the power of that stare. He does not know that her eyes were ever closed, because he *is* responding, *has* heard her question. His head is shaking back and forth as though it is a motion he has begun but is powerless to stop. All he can do is shake his head *no*, the smile on his face growing wider as he shakes, his head saying *No no no no no, no, I'm not too much your brother* and *Yes, oh yes! Score! Oh yeah!*

And then they are outside, on the street, having said their good-byes, pleaded their tiredness, all without a word to one another, on autopilot, all because it's so clear what they have to do. So suddenly there they are, on the street, in the frigid bitter cold, their mittened hands raised to the traffic, begging, *Cab, cab, cab, cab.* They've come no closer to one another than they'd been at the kitchen counter, just pushed themselves off, like swimmers from the edge of the pool, and sprinted through their musts and firsts and things-to-be-taken-care-ofs. A taxi pulls over beside them. Ben opens the door, Miranda slides in across the stiff cold vinyl seat, Ben sliding in behind her. She speaks their address as if through a dream, and the cab starts moving away from the world of school and friends and people who know who they are to one another, or at least who they are supposed to be. And then they are alone, in the yellow capsule of a cab speeding its midnight path across Brooklyn, New York—now, finally, it seems, they take a breath, the first since Miranda opened her eyes and looked at him in the kitchen, they breathe in as though they are one person, their breath so perfectly attuned, and when they release it is into one another, falling, without question, crumpling together against the backseat of that cab as though this kiss is all they have ever been hurtling toward.

There is no leader in this game, only followers; no decisions made, only gravity. It's unclear who does anything: who tells the driver where to stop, who pays for the cab, who unlocks the door, everything just seems to happen as if by some will of its own, or as though they have been working like this, together, forever, a well-oiled machine. Miranda drops her coat in the living room the way she always does. She climbs the stairs toward her room, turns on the light, flops onto her bed, pulls off her boots, stands, flips the light back off again, and closes the door, then slowly, quietly makes her way back downstairs. Ben is waiting at the foot of the stairs, a glass of ice water in each hand. He holds one out to her and she takes it. She turns off the hallway light, and they make their way silently down the basement stairs.

There's such a clear and single purpose about them that everything goes without saying. Miranda thinks the first words she can remember coming from his mouth since he told her she was good in the play are the ones he says as he is opening the condom wrapper, holding it to the light that cracks in through the tiny high windows from the streetlights—to see which way it unrolls. He is on the bed, on his knees, she on her back beneath him, when he says, "You've done this before, haven't you?" not in an accusing way, but in a tone that sounds relieved, and when she nods yes, hears her own voice for the first time in what seems like hours and may well be, her own voice saying "Once," and then his saying "I haven't," and her own saying "That's OK," as if that actually meant something, and then that's it, that's all the talking that happens that night in Ben's basement room, and if Miranda's sense of things can be trusted at all, if her perception of these events has any basis in reality, she thinks it is the last thing they say to one another until the next night, when they find themselves right there, downstairs, in his bed, again. And the next night. And the next night. And the night after the night after the night after that.

WHEN BEN TAKES HER TO HIS MOTHER'S HOUSE IT'S simply for convenience. "She's hardly ever home," he tells Miranda. "Where is she?" Miranda asks. They are on their way over to

Felice's, and as they walk Miranda gnaws at a stale salt bagel she grabbed from the bread bin at home as they left.

"Out." He grins at her.

Ha ha ha, she pantomimes.

"She decorates," Ben says.

"Hmm," Miranda says. She imagines a woman who is Ben's mom getting paid to stand around places improving the scenery.

"She's always off showing swatches and going to auctions."

"That sounds fun," Miranda says.

Ben shrugs, unimpressed. It's his mother, after all: how many seventeen-year-old boys are impressed by their mothers? "She's a bitch," he tells her.

Miranda pauses. "A bitch like everyone thinks their mother's a bitch, or really an actual bitch?" she asks.

Ben's voice is solemn in a way she hasn't heard before. "My mother's a bitch," he repeats, and it's clear that's all he wants to say.

They walk in pace, but at some distance from each other on the sidewalk. It's interesting, this thing with Ben, in that they're "together" in some ways, but since no one can know, they relate to each other so strangely. Often Miranda doesn't even lift her head when Ben enters a room. It's as if they can turn their relationship on and off, and it seems likely that this may spoil Miranda for the future, in which she imagines that people are forced to stand behind their own decisions, admit their lovers, concede to leading just one life as one constant person. The future—*that* future—is a dauntingly limited prospect.

It's not until they are safe inside the entrance to Felice's brownstone, the front door closed and locked behind them, that Ben pulls Miranda close and kisses her. Their furtiveness carries with it an excitement all its own, a surprise to it that takes Miranda's breath away every time. It seems clear that this too will spoil her: she will be someone who wants men to take her breath away, and they will not, and this will disappoint her. But for right now she's not analyzing, she's just kissing, the breath so pleasingly knocked from her windpipe by the suddenness of Ben's touch, and they stand there in the hallway, staggering weak-kneed to prop themselves against the wall, kissing and kissing and kissing.

IN THE THREE WEEKS THAT THIS HAS BEEN GOING ON Miranda and Ben have had only one condom mishap. They were done and he was pulling out of her and forgot to hold the end, and when he was out the condom stayed in, like a sock stuck in the leg of a pair of pants. "Oh shit!" He'd realized right away what had happened, and went down like a diver to recapture what had been lost. He had no trouble rescuing it from inside her—"right in the doorway," they joked—and there was still stuff in it and it didn't look like any had gotten out, yet Miranda had been scared, and Ben had seemed a little uneasy himself, and they've been super super careful since. So that day at Felice's house, up in Ben's old bedroom, on his old twin bed, when they are finished Ben holds diligently to the condom's end as he extracts himself from her, and they are both taken aback, and then smacked with relief at the sight of his penis, still sheathed in the condom, but then covered in a clotty film of blood.

"Is that what I think it is?" Ben asks, his voice rising expectantly.

"Yes!" Miranda cries. She thinks for a moment: "And right on time too!"

Ben stands up from the bed and carefully slides the condom off, then rolls it inside a wad of toilet paper big enough to hide a small animal and sticks the whole thing into an empty plastic bag before he wedges it into the trash basket. "Congratulations on not being a mother," he says, his smile weak but sincere.

"Congratulations on not having to pay for half an abortion," Miranda corrects him.

He smiles again, conceding, then goes into the bathroom that connects his room to Jenny's, the bathroom they used to share in the days before their parents' divorce.

Miranda pulls her T-shirt back on and finds her underwear on the floor. "Do you think Jenny has any Tampax or anything in there?" she calls to him.

The water is running in the sink, but Ben's face appears at the door again. "I think, actually I'm pretty sure, that Jen has, um, *not yet attained her womanhood,* as they say," he tells her.

Miranda laughs.

"Try my mom's room," Ben says. "Down the hall on the left."

Miranda climbs from the bed and follows Ben's directions. "So you're pretty darn sure your mother *has* attained hers, though?" she says coyly.

"Almost positive," Ben calls.

Miranda is surprised by the messiness of Felice Stone's bedroom, much more like her own bedroom than like Roz and Steven's, or any other parents' rooms she knows. There are old coffee cups on the floor by the bed, which is unmade in a flourish of down and flannel. The surface of the bureau is so cluttered it almost seems as if all the lipsticks and tissue balls and cardboard panty hose packages are actually arranged in the most precise disarray, delicately architectured as a house of cards. The floor is a hazard zone of capsized high heels and wadded-up workout clothes, aerobics sneakers with their tongues hanging out like overheated dogs. Miranda maneuvers her way to the dresser, riffling through detritus, just getting the lay of the land. It's the sort of mess where you just know that everything you need is right there somewhere, it's just a matter of figuring out where. Miranda's fingers graze dusty dishes of coins and safety pins and earrings and vitamin tablets; she pokes through a basket of papers, can practically see the worn white tube stuck there at the bottom, because that's absolutely right where a tampon would be, just out of sight and just within reach, but it's not. She lets the stack of papers and flyers and old *TV Guides* fall back into place, and as she moves away knocks the dresser with her hip. A book falls, and bending to pick it up, she spots a pad of yellow Post-it notes there on the floor next to the bed, the handwriting on the top sheet unfamiliar, but the snatch of content too intriguing to resist a second glance.

S—

You're sleeping/I have to go. Alarm is set. Late to meet the Gregorys. When will I see you? Life is ridiculous/Did we have to get divorced for sex to get so good?

—*F*

SHE IS ALREADY CRYING BY THE TIME SHE MAKES IT back to Ben's room, the note held out in front of her like something she doesn't want to touch. The Tampax search is forgotten. She holds the note out to Ben accusingly, swatting at her eyes with her other hand. She cannot see him clearly through the blear and salt-sting of her tears, and she imagines his expression at first to be smug, and condescending. "Did you know?" she demands, and when his face still seems blank and unyielding she only says it louder, her voice breaking with a sob: "Did you know?"

As he comes closer she can see in his eyes that he doesn't know—has no idea what it is he doesn't know, is about to learn, will never be able to un-know—and she surrenders the paper apologetically now, reluctant to end his ignorance. And then she thinks maybe it won't be so bad for Ben. *His* parents aren't the ones getting screwed over. What does *he* care for Roz? She's nothing to him, as little to him as she is to Felice.

Miranda realizes she's shut her streaming eyes only when she opens them again, and there is Ben before her, looming in like he's going to fall and crush her beneath him. His eyes are huge, shot suddenly with thin veins of red. In his hand he is crumpling the note, crushing it as if he wished it were a much larger, more weighty object than it is. When he flings it away from him, Miranda fears for a moment he has snapped something in his arm, pitching this feathery object as if he could tunnel it through the wall. In the frustration of that throw, Ben backs away, his head searching left and right, his foot flying out to kick the first thing he sees, the nightstand, which is cheap, made of plywood, splintering on impact.

"Fucking bitch!" Ben yells. "She's such a goddamn fucking bitch!" and then he is sobbing too, choked sobs studded with high-pitched wheezing noises, the sound and the sight both too horrible for Miranda to witness. She almost forgets her own devastation standing there watching his: the emasculation it causes him, Ben, shrinking, cowering, bawling in front of her like an old man, an old foppish man, thin like a dandy with his girly long hair and skinny little legs poking out like stilts from the oversized fabric of his boxer shorts. "I hate her!" he cries. "I fucking hate her! When is she ever going to stop ruining every single fucking thing she comes near? God, I hate her . . ." and he crumples then, at the edge of the bed, his face sinking down, burrowing in his hands, and the only thing Miranda knows to do right then is to hold him, to stroke his hair and whisper away his tears and rock him until he quiets, rock him until he's at peace. And it makes sense only then, for the first time, to them both, that they *are* brother and sister, born together there, in that moment, from that pain, on the floor at the foot of his childhood bed. Even the insatiability of her desire for him makes sense now in a way it otherwise never would have. They'd tried to sate it the wrong way, tried to turn it into the only desire they'd ever understood. Now it seems clear that they are something else to each other entirely, that they are bound in ways that sex could never join them.

Ben keeps saying, "God, I hate her," keeps repeating his hatred, like a terrible refrain, and each time it takes Miranda by surprise, perhaps because he hadn't seemed like someone with that much hatred inside. But also because Miranda is not thinking about Felice, she's thinking about Roz, and the feelings coursing through her are so complicated that when Ben says "hate," she thinks at times, *God, yes, I hate her.* Hate her for loving him, hate her for loving someone who doesn't love her back. Miranda hates that it hurts this bad to imagine her mother's humiliation. Hates her for being who she is and not protecting herself more, and for the silence Miranda will have to keep in the name of protection. It seems certain that she cannot tell Roz, that this is not someplace Miranda belongs, not something Roz can or will hear from Miranda, who has fought Roz's relationship with Steven from the moment it was made known to her. There's no recourse here but silence, waiting for her mom to figure it out on her own, and Miranda hates her for that, for not being swifter, savvier in the ways of love. It is wrong, Miranda thinks, to know more than your mother. To be put in this position, not allowed to just be an ignorant kid, uninformed of the goings-on of her mother's love affairs. Miranda doesn't want this knowledge, and neither does Ben, but they have it anyway, together, and it's just theirs now, to have and to hold. And that's all they can do there, that April afternoon on the floor by the bed where they've just made love the last time they ever will: hold their knowledge and each other, until Miranda realizes she's bleeding through her underwear and onto the floor and she has to extricate herself from him, has to get up and collect herself, and do something about cleaning up the mess.

16

LOV

A SUNNY SATURDAY. FALL 1987. JENNY WAS WITH HER grandparents for the weekend; Ben had gone to a football game, masquerading as a model American teenager. Miranda had gone into Manhattan with a friend to a crafts fair behind the Museum of Natural History. Probably, Roz thought, they would hang out in Sheep's Meadow surrounded by pot-smoking, white, imitation-Rasta men, dreadlocks hanging in deliberate disarray from beneath crocheted Jamaican-flag hats. At this point, all she could do was cross her fingers and hope that Miranda would make good decisions, hope she'd done enough to ensure that. Roz and Steven agreed on the way to raise children: you plied them in utero with brewer's yeast and folic acid and enough calcium to grow a giant; you talked to them like human beings from the moment they started breathing air; you taught them everything you knew to teach and gave them all the love you had to give; and then you sent them out into the world hoping you'd given them enough, hoping they were prepared. Roz and Steven complimented each other frequently on the successes of their parenting. They'd done well, pat-on-the-back, if they did say so themselves.

That autumn day Steven had gone to Long Island on a bulb-finding mission: a certain tulip he simply had to have for the garden next spring, and the planting season was getting away from him already. Bulbs needed to be in the ground before the first frost, and there were predictions of a cold front coming in the next week. So Roz had the house entirely to herself. Delightful. The sun was gloriously warm through the windowpanes, and she threw one open for a time to bring the smells of autumn inside: even in New York she thought she could smell burning leaves, fermenting apples, roasting chicory, molasses. Things felt very right. She was loving work as she hadn't in years, finally doing what she should have been doing all along. Jesus, she wasn't only doing what *she* wanted to do, she was doing what her *ex-husband* had always wanted to do. She worked for tenants' rights. She made enough money—not a lot, but enough. Edwin had never become the "good guy" he'd wanted to be, but now Roz had. Edwin practiced law in Lincoln, Nebraska, where he was apparently happy, engaged, in fact, to a woman named Kathy. A natural blond. Apparently he tried to do what pro bono work he could. But Edwin's life was another story entirely now.

In the upstairs bathroom Roz hefted the wicker laundry basket from the floor and wandered through the bedroom picking up stray socks and crumpled boxer shorts and tossing them in the hamper. She fancied herself a trash collector, wishing she had a long-handled pick, like the Parks Department men who ambled through New York's green spaces in their sturdy green uniforms spearing evil bits of garbage and removing them from the public eye. Later, Roz would remember those feelings of such grand goodwill with morbid irony. She would relive that morning again and again like a bad TV show in syndication. Some tired old plot line you can't believe they're getting away with again: the Terrible Discovery. All seemed well, skippity-do-da, hum-dee-dum—*but then:* Roz grabbed a pair of Steven's jeans from where they were draped over the back of a chair. As she slung them into her basket, some change flew out of the pocket and onto the floor. Roz set down the hamper, retrieved the change from the carpet, pocketing it. Two pennies, a quarter. She picked up the jeans and dug her hands into each of the pockets—she hated the noise of coins clanging around in the clothes dryer. Of course it was the last pocket she checked—of course. A tiny little yellow Post-it note, maybe one inch by two, folded onto itself, sticky side in. Roz saw *e you*. It wasn't Steven's handwriting. She flipped it over. *I lov.*

SUFFICE IT TO SAY THAT THE LAUNDRY DID NOT GET done. The thing was this: Roz would have liked to be a person who went and did the laundry anyway. Who washed the bastard's dirty goddamn underwear and folded it in tidy piles at the end of the ironing board. And then maybe poured him a drink when he came home, made it just the way he liked it, then poured one for herself before she dumped the rest of the bottle over his lying-sack-of-shit underwear and tossed a kitchen match into the pile.

Maybe there was a time when she would have been that person. When she would have at least tried to be that person. She thought back on the morning, on that pulsing sense of rebirth, the strength she'd felt inside her like a glowing ball of sun, and it all seemed like such a lie. Such a dreamy, wishful, complacent, stupid lie. That morning she'd fancied herself a phoenix, and by noon it was so clear—so stupidly, idiotically, blatantly clear—that she was nothing more than a calf, a colt, a spindly-legged, pink-eyed, furless pathetic fawn hobbling around on raw, new hooves, like Bambi in the forest bleating, mewing, crying out for mama.

Who?!?! she should have screamed. *Just fucking tell me who!* But the person who could have said those words was worlds away, so far away she'd become another person entirely. Roz could only imagine herself there, as if in a movie. Full costume, makeup, lights, sound, roll 'em. Like a childhood memory retained only through the telling but lost to any visceral recall. Horrified at herself, Roz wandered dumbly through the house: they'd repainted the living room, stripped the doors down to light grainy wood. All that horrible wallpaper gone. Ripped out two bathrooms, more seashell-pink linoleum than anyone should ever have to contend with. Roz ran her hand along the stairway banister, its smooth smooth wood cool to the touch, realizing as her fingers slid the length of the rail that, at least to start, there wouldn't be any screaming. She realized she was going to be someone for whom she could harbor no respect. Someone who yelled nothing—who *said* nothing—and waited. She'd be passive-aggressive. She'd try and make him prove his love for her on his own. Worse: she'd be a woman who made excuses. Somewhere inside her brain they were already formulating. The jokes to which *I love you* might be the uproarious punch line. The joke *I love you* might have been unto itself. Steven's joke. With someone else. It was a note from Jenny. From Steven's mother. It was someone else's note entirely; Steven had the scoop on someone else's trysting heart. And because inside Roz knew that none of that was true, she realized that she would be the lowliest of all these forms. She knew what she would do the moment Steven walked in the door carrying his sacks of tulip bulbs—his *Angelique*, his *Apricot Beauty*, his *White Dream*, his *Angel's Kiss*. She would cry.

So it went:

Steven came home. Five in the afternoon. Roz had poured herself a third glass of Chardonnay—so wholly inappropriate, Chardonnay, the wine of garden parties and galas held upon great lawns. It was all they had, though, and it was necessary. Steven entered whistling—so ghoulish—of all things, "Put Another Log on the Fire," and Roz could track him as he made his way through the house. She was upstairs in their bedroom, on the bed, wine in hand, knees pulled into her chest in a pose she knew the self-help books would call "protective" and "withholding." Steven set his packages down by the back door that led to the garden, his whistle fading in and out of earshot as he made his way to the bathroom, *Put another log on the fire, cook me up some bacon and some beans, and go out to the car and change the tire, wash my socks and sew my old blue jeans, come on, baby* . . . The faucet went on and it was as if Roz could see him, one flight below, because she knew exactly how he washed his hands, like the doctor he was, scrubbing in when he first arrived home. More fastidious in ways than Edwin, Steven washed his hands before he and Roz made love, something she'd always found sweet and caring, as if he understood the delicate bacterial balance of a woman's body and cleansed himself out of respect for that natural perfection. Now when she thought of it, it all seemed cold and clinical, as if it had been she and not Miranda who was Steven's patient. As if it had been Roz, not her daughter, bound in, these last years, by the metal wires and silver-steel cages of Dr. Steven Stone.

He left the bathroom, went to the kitchen. The fridge door swung open. *Fill my pipe and then go fetch my slippers, and boil me up another pot of tea, then put another log on the fire, babe, and come and tell me why you're leavin' me.* There was a clinking of beer bottles, the door shutting with its suction catch, hands riffling a drawer, flick, clink, a bottlecap flipped onto the counter. *So sit here at my feet 'cause I like you when you're sweet, and you know it ain't feminine to fight.* And the *clop, clop, clop* of his feet as he mounted the stairs toward the bedroom.

The look that crossed his face as he entered was not *I've-been-caught* concern, but actual concern. That is, if Roz's judgment could be trusted anymore, if her interpretations of Steven had ever been anywhere near accurate. To what extent could one delude oneself? Roz wanted to know. They'd bought a house, made a life together. Would *all that* have to be reevaluated now? Had something been wrong all along? The sight of Steven, his body language easy as he swung into the room thinking he'd flop down, have his beer, catch up on the day with Roz—the sight of Steven's face changing as he realized something was wrong, that was what did her in: the caring in his face.

"Roz," he said, surprised, the afternoon's scenario shifting in his mind and on his face. "Roz, what's wrong?" He came right to her, sat beside her at the edge of the bed. The beer bottle got set down on the night table, Steven's arms came around her. "Are you OK?" he was asking, a hint of fear rising in his voice. "Has something happened?" He was thinking of the kids, of cancer, Roz's family, their friends. The fear was palpable.

"Who?" Roz wept, her voice almost inaudible. "Who is it, Steven? Who is she? Oh god, why? God, just who? Who?"

Steven's breath caught in his own throat. The world-weight in his eyes grew suddenly heavy. He knew. The shit he didn't want to deal with, the problems he thought he might be able to ignore— they were all there, now, and whether he was ready or not he had to answer to them. He had to answer to this woman whom, in many ways, he did love.

"Felice," he said, and his voice was soft and grave. "Felice."

"Felice?" Roz asked, because this didn't make sense. She didn't understand. Felice was Steven's ex-wife, the mother of his children, the woman to whom he paid exorbitant alimony checks each and every month. "What do you mean Felice? I don't understand. Felice?"

And by then Steven was crying too, as if broken, everything inside ready to spill. He cradled Roz in their bed, and she let him, and they rocked together, not soothingly, but back and forth, back and forth, as if they could rock away the pain. "Yes," Steven said. "Felice." He took a breath. "It's been Felice. Oh god, Roz, it's so much more complicated than it seems . . . Moving in . . . our kids . . . And I didn't expect . . . neither of us did. And when the cancer scare . . . when you were so . . . when everything was so awful, I just needed someone to talk to. And then I had no idea how to tell you, how to break this. But it seems so clear. So clear that we . . . that she . . . that Felice and I can't just undo all those years. That we're still the ones who know each other best. But how could I tell you? There's been so much going on . . . I just didn't know how . . . We were just getting settled . . ."

But Roz couldn't hear any more. It was too much information, too many readjustments and reevaluations to make. She would have had to live the last year all over again in her head, replaying every scene under these new lights, considering every move in view of these new facts. And she didn't want to do it. It was too much work. She didn't have that kind of energy. She felt supernaturally tired. It would have been like renovating the house, again. That much work: ripping off the new wallpaper, taking an electric sander to the stairs, cracking the tile out with a sledgehammer in big rubbled chunks. It seemed clear: the job could not be done.

"Please," she said to Steven, her voice taking on its first semblance of control, "please make it go away. Tell me it's over and we'll never bring it up again. Not until we're old, not until we can deal with it. It didn't happen, OK? Just tell me it never happened."

The look on Steven's face was impossible to read. His eyes were uncomprehending, as though he didn't understand what she was asking, only he did; it wasn't Steven who was confused, it was Roz. Because what she hadn't heard in his speech, in his confession and his plea, what she hadn't heard was exactly what he was trying to say. Which was, and would always be, then and forever: *I love her more.*

17

CHRISTMAS IN LINCOLN

WHEN MIRANDA TELLS BEN SHE'S SPENDING CHRIST-mas in Lincoln his fingers move up the fret of his guitar and begin an old John Prine melody. *"It was Christmas in Lincoln and the food was real good . . ."*

Miranda stops his strumming hand. "It won't be," she says.

"Won't be what?"

"Good. The food. My grandmother brings Jell-O salad. Every-thing else is made with cream of mushroom soup."

Ben flashes a terrible smile. They are sitting in the Emmons School basement, leaning against orange metal lockers, waiting for the fifth-period bell. "I know!" he says, as though he's got a great idea. "You can come share the holiday with us! I know how much you enjoy Steven and Felice . . ."

Miranda's tongue lolls out of her mouth as if in death. Then she snaps back. "Is that really a song?" she asks. " 'Christmas in Lincoln'? I still need a gift for them. Could I find that at Tower?"

Ben laughs. "You probably could, but I don't know how much they'd appreciate it."

"Why?" Miranda says.

"It's really 'Christmas in Prison,' " he tells her.

Miranda doesn't miss a beat. "That might be an improvement," she says.

ACTUALLY, LINCOLN IS PRETTY NICE. IT HAS SUR-prised Miranda each of the few times she has visited. She doesn't really mind going to see her dad. It's hard to hold the past against him, like blaming an unmedicated schizophrenic for his erratic behavior. Now it's as though he's finally found the right drug cock-tail, or discovered the secret formula for well-being. The Midwest becomes Edwin Anderson. The morose man from the Upper West Side is gone; in his place: a calmly handsome lawyer with a general practice on the outskirts of Lincoln, a tasteful ranch house nearby with a treeless lawn, and a soon-to-be wife named Kathy who works ridiculous hours as an emergency room nurse and seems to know how to take care of Miranda's father.

Edwin picks Miranda up from the airport in a red Dodge Shadow. He has heat blasting out the vents, and the radio tuned to what Ben would call Pepto-Bismol jazz.

Miranda gives the car a once-over. "Midlife crisis on a budget?" she smirks.

Edwin raises his eyebrows in response. "It's Kathy's," he says by way of explanation.

"Fan-cy." Miranda smiles.

They make their way through the requisite conversation topics: school, friends, theater, summer plans . . . "How's your mom?" Edwin asks, as though he'd like it to sound casual, an incidental question. As if he'd just remembered, *Oh, right, you're Roz's daughter, aren't you?* Still, underneath his tone is sincere.

"Shitty," Miranda says.

Edwin's face contorts in empathetic pain. "Oh no," he says. "Why?"

"She and Steven split up," Miranda tells him.

"I didn't know." He seems at a loss to say anything more.

Miranda wants to say, *Well of course you don't, how would you?* Instead she tells him, "It was only like two months ago or something."

Edwin is silent for a time. "You didn't like Steven much, did you?" he finally asks.

Miranda shrugs. "He was my orthodontist." This seems explanation enough.

Edwin laughs in spite of himself, and Miranda can't help but wonder what sorts of emotions lie behind that laugh. If she had to guess, she'd say the look on his face has something to do with awe, like what he really wants to say is that only Roz would fall in love with her daughter's orthodontist, as though he still regards her with some amazement. *What a wild lady!* he seems to be thinking. *Can you believe I was married to such a wild wild lady?*

What he does eventually say comes out as though he's emerging from deep reflection on the subject. They are at a stop light, and as it turns green and Edwin lets up on the brake he says, "Roz will find someone new in no time."

It seems that this is meant to be reassuring to Miranda, but all she can think is, *What the fuck does that mean?* He makes it sound as though Roz goes through men with abandon. As if she's some dating fiend, always with a new man waiting in the wings. But Edwin doesn't have anything to be bitter about. There wasn't anyone preparing to take his place the minute he stepped out the front door.

"She doesn't do the dating thing very well," Miranda says, but then immediately feels bad. She doesn't want to make her mom sound pathetic either. Doesn't want her dad to think he's got the upper hand somehow. This sort of rivalry has never actually been a problem between Edwin and Roz themselves, it's only Miranda who feels a sense of constant competition. She does not want to be the one sitting between them, weighing them for one another, yet that's exactly where she almost always manages to position herself. Inadvertently, and to her own chagrin.

"No?" says Edwin. "I'd imagine Roz does fine for herself. She's so outgoing, so gregarious. Such a people-person."

Roz? Miranda wants to say, and it's like she can remember the Roz whom Edwin is talking about—the woman who sauntered into Dr. Stone's office and turned everyone's world upside down—but she's been so sad in the wake of Steven that it's hard to summon the image of that vibrant woman whom Edwin recalls. It seems good, though, that he thinks of her like that, and Miranda decides she should do all she can to uphold the image. "Yeah, you're right," she says. "I'm sure she'll be great." She doesn't sound believable, but her father seems not to notice at all.

"She always was," Edwin says, and his voice has that dreamy lilt to it, like he's talking about some aging screen idol who's captured his attention all these many years. Miranda wonders this: *Is it possible that my dad is still in love with my mom?* It has never even crossed her mind the other way; it's clear that the person Roz loves—or, now, *loved*—is—*was*—Steven. She's just assumed that the person Edwin loves is Kathy.

The car makes its way up an entrance ramp and onto the highway, one lane blooming into four, and as Edwin checks over his shoulder—look, merge, look, merge—Miranda feels that her thinking has widened too, like the road. There are so many lanes, and once you leave one, that doesn't mean it disappears, it just goes on without you. And you without it. This seems suddenly, stupidly clear to Miranda. When you left the scenic drive for the interstate it wasn't necessarily because you liked the big road better. Sometimes to get where you were going you needed to get on the highway. People did what they had to do. Some people got carsick if they drove the windy mountain roads. Some people liked speed too much to compromise it for tranquillity. Others wanted to go places only accessible by bumpy gravel-churning trails. You might not enjoy traffic lights and congestion, but if you liked the city enough you might be willing to bear those things. You took the roads you thought you had to take. Sometimes you got lost. You took wrong turns. You stopped by the side of the road to pick raspberries. You hit a deer and totaled the car. You stopped for gas, changed the oil, bought air freshener. You kept driving. And all the while, you could still only ever be in one place at one time, which didn't necessarily mean it was the place you most wanted to be, it just meant that was where you were.

KATHY IS A SUPERDOER, THE SORT OF WOMAN WHO should teach first grade or organize labor unions. Or be an ER nurse. She is decidedly one of those women who come home from a fourteen-hour shift and then sit at the kitchen counter crafting Martha Stewart balsam garlands until 4 a.m. The house is a decorator's fantasy, not at all gaudy with Christmas: the lights are all white and none are blinkers, and the boughs and bows and mistletoe sprays seem not merely to be ornamental but to have sprouted from deep within the walls and mantelpieces like midwinter foliage.

Festivities begin early here; a few days before Christmas is the first official gathering, and relatives of all derivations have come in from Omaha, Beatrice, Grand Island, and Des Moines for tree-trimming at Kathy and Edwin's. There are probably thirty people milling about the house, chatting, drinking eggnog, offering Edwin advice up on his ladder, arms in the branches—*No, no, a little to the left, closer to that snowflake thing, perfect!* Every so often Edwin calls out to Miranda for an opinion, and from her armchair in the corner of the room she calls back over the crowd, "More tinsel," or "There's a bald patch by your knee . . . other knee." Although Edwin will be Kathy's first husband, she does have a twenty-year-old daughter named Shaunna, who herself has a fourteen-month-old baby girl and an on-and-off live-in boyfriend whom Miranda has never met. Miranda is holding court in the corner of the living room with soon-to-be stepsister Shaunna and soon-to-be stepniece Brittney. These relationships feel very abstract to Miranda, like mathematical theories gone unproven. She can think of very little to say to Shaunna, who is bouncing Brittney on her lap and quizzing Miranda about New York fashion.

"What's really in style now?" Shaunna asks. "What are people wearing there? What's cool?"

"I don't even really know, honestly," Miranda says. "I guess I'm pretty out of it about that stuff." Shaunna wants what's-in-the-department-stores fashion, and Miranda feels like she doesn't have the energy, or maybe the heart, to tell Shaunna that what's "cool" isn't what's cool at all.

"No way," Shaunna is saying, shaking her head. Her eyes dart up and down the length of Miranda's body, taking her in, as though committing her outfit to memory. There is something in this gesture that pumps Miranda's ego but also makes her uncomfortable—the sheer regard on Shaunna's face, her unabashed desire to directly imitate Miranda's style. It is exactly what Miranda does—sees someone at school, like Jenn Tate or Elise Martowski, and studies exactly how it is that Elise wears her jeans, how wide the ankles, how slouchy the waist—though Miranda must wait weeks before she can actually attempt the outfit herself. This mimicry feels intensely shameful to Miranda, as though to be caught at it would be to reveal herself as a fraud. She is embarrassed at Shaunna's lack of shame, and then even more embarrassed by her own deceit. Great, she thinks, so we're both copycats, but at least Shaunna's honest about it. This thought makes Miranda want to make it up to Shaunna somehow, to apologize for herself. She wants to ask Shaunna something that will force Miranda into the passenger seat, enable Shaunna to be the expert. Then it dawns on her: Brittney. The words are out of her mouth before she thinks another thought: "So what's motherhood like?"

Shaunna's smile is too bright, her nodding seems compulsive. "Awesome," she says, too quickly, and without anything to back up the declaration she just sits there nodding and making Miranda feel worse than she did before.

"Really?" Miranda says, trying not to sound surprised, just inquisitive.

"Sure," says Shaunna, "it's really cool . . ." She fades off.

Miranda feels like Barbara Walters. She has no idea where to go with this but forward. "Is it what you thought it would be like?" she asks.

"I guess," Shaunna answers. She doesn't seem annoyed at Miranda's questions at all, just slightly unsure of her own responses, as though she hasn't yet thought about how she likes motherhood, as though no one has ever asked her such questions before. "I guess I didn't really know what it was going to be like, but it turned out OK." She pauses. "I guess it's like a lot of things where you don't really know if you like it or not until you try it."

This logic strikes Miranda as irrefutably true and absolutely bizarre at the same time, and she nods for lack of response. *Well of course*, she wants to say, *but what're you going to do if it turns out you're just not really into it? What the hell do you do then?*

"I'm lucky, I guess," says Shaunna, bending her head to kiss Brittney's fat neck. "I guess I could've hated it, and that would've sucked . . ."

Miranda nods again. Shaunna's right, certainly, but her whole way of thinking is so different. To Miranda, a bad decision is like a catastrophe; the idea of being stuck is terrifying. Miranda suddenly wishes Roz were there. Roz would know what that difference was. Roz would be able to tell her what distinguishes the way Miranda thinks from the way Shaunna does. She tries to channel Roz, the way she imagines Kathy channeling Martha Stewart— *Now how would Martha approach the arrangement of this hors d'oeuvres platter?*

"Oops," says Shaunna. She lifts Brittney by the underarms, away from her own body. "Think someone needs a diaper change," she coos. "'Scuse us," she says to Miranda, and spirits Brittney away toward the stairs.

Sitting alone in the corner, at the mercy of any overzealous relative who might choose to come chat her up, is far worse than the awkward conversation with Shaunna, and Miranda knows she must escape before she is ensnared. Across the room, between the pile of presents on their plaid blanket and the sideboard display of greeting-card trees, Miranda spots the telephone perched on a small wooden table. The grandfather clock in the hall has just rung seven, which means eight in New York. Roz just might be home from work, maybe.

The line rings three, four times, and then the machine picks up. Miranda hears her own voice, like a squeaking child, lisp from the other end, "Hi, please leave a message for Roz or Miranda after the beep. Thanks. Bye." It takes her a second to talk, to figure out how to speak to herself. When she does, in contrast to the outgoing message, her voice sounds reassuringly mature. She steps back to try and sequester herself from the party a bit, but her foot hits something and she stumbles, catching herself against the sideboard. Steadying, she looks back to see what she's hit. "Shit," she says, then realizes she's speaking into the receiver. Realizes she's speaking to her mom, sort of. She laughs. "Hi, Ma." She giggles again. "I think I just trampled the baby Jesus . . ." More giggles. "Ugh, where are you when I need you?" She lowers her voice even further, turns her face to the wall. "Damn, I wish you were home. Well, I'll try you later, I guess. God, I wish you were here. Ugh. OK, anyway. Um, we'll talk soon, OK? Love you. Bye."

As she hangs up the phone, Edwin's voice is the first she hears, coming down from above, from the top step of the ladder where he seems to be stranded. He calls to her, "Miranda, help your old dad out here! Find us the star. Do you see it down there? We're ready for the star!" And it's nice, just then, to have a purpose, rooting around on her knees through poofs and puffs of molting tissue paper.

BY THE TIME SHAUNNA RETURNS WITH A NEWLY diapered Brittney, Rod, the child's father, has arrived. He is a big guy, in work boots and a wool hunting jacket. He looks like the kind of guy who isn't around much. When Shaunna sees him, standing there by the hallway coatrack with Miranda, her face lights up and Miranda feels a rush of sadness, her heart going out to Shaunna, who will, in her life, surely be nothing but hurt and disappointed by this big, thoughtless lumberjack of a man whom she appears to think the world of.

"Hey, honey," he says, taking Brittney from Shaunna with practiced ease. He holds the child in one arm, wraps the other around Shaunna's shoulder, and kisses her forehead with a tenderness Miranda doesn't expect at all.

"Hey," says Shaunna, nestling into him. Miranda just stands before them smiling despite herself. If she didn't know anything, she'd say they made a lovely tableau of a family. And then, for the second time that night, she thinks that maybe she really doesn't know anything about them at all.

"You-all want to take a drive?" Rod asks. He peers at Brittney, as if the question is just for her. "Go see the lights? All the pretty Christmas lights?"

Shaunna answers, "Oh, Brittney, you want to go see all the pretty lights, don't you? Mommy promised you we'd go look at all the pretty Santa Clauses and the reindeers, right?"

Rod turns to Miranda but directs his question to Brittney, perhaps because he can't seem to remember Miranda's name. "Does your little friend want to come with us to see the pretty lights, Britty?"

Shaunna turns to Miranda, her eyes eager, smile full. "Oh yes, come, please. This'll be great. I'll get Britty's coat." And she's off again, up the stairs.

Miranda shrugs. Rod shrugs back at her. "Why not?" she says.

"Why the hell not?" Rod agrees. He hefts Brittney a little higher on his hip and stuffs a hand into the pocket of his jeans to try and dig out the ring of keys bulging under denim.

THE LIGHTS ARE DECADENT—BLOCKS AND BLOCKS of elaborate luminary displays on front lawns, across roofs and porches. Afterward they go for hot chocolate at a coffee shop in town. They are not gone more than two hours, two and a half at the most, but when Rod slows the truck outside Kathy and Edwin's house to drop Miranda off again, she can see that the only light in the place left blazing is the tree. The cars are all gone from the drive and from the street out front, and it's clear that Kathy and Edwin have gone to sleep. Miranda shuts the truck door as quietly as she can and says good night with a wave through the window as Shaunna readjusts herself in the seat, sleeping Brittney cradled in her arms. The truck rumbles and lumbers off down the street as Miranda makes her way up the walk. The difference, she thinks, between her and Shaunna is that even if Miranda hated being a mother she'd still compulsively strap her kid into the car seat. She thinks maybe she just takes everything more seriously than Shaunna does; every choice she makes feels to Miranda like life and death. She thinks maybe she is even a little envious of Shaunna, who seems to take things easier, far more capable of rolling with the punches than Miranda thinks she could ever be. She wonders for a moment why it is that she thinks the decisions she makes are so damn important. Then she remembers Edwin, once too tortured by the weight of his own life to make any choices at all, and her own caution begins to make nothing but sense.

Inside, the air is heavy with sweet cinnamon, such a contrast from the crisp chill of outside. Miranda locks the front door behind her. The house has been returned to its immaculate, preparty state of crafted casualness, and Miranda can't help but wonder for a moment if the evening has really taken place at all. But the tree is trimmed, its shimmering silver star reflecting the lights of a thousand tiny bulbs. Miranda yawns exaggeratedly. It feels good to be so ready for sleep. She crosses the living room and bends down to unplug the tree lights, and it's only then that she notices the Nativity scene again, there on the floor tucked in by the mounds of gifts. Like the rest of the house, the crèche has been completely restored, all the shepherds righted and everyone replaced in their spots in the manger. When she looks closer, she sees that even baby Jesus, who'd lost an arm in the rumble earlier, has been neatly Super-Glued back together. He rests atop his little cushion of hay, convalescing.

18

Youth Dew

Roz might have been able to categorically ignore the holidays that year had it not been for Esther. Her ex-mother-in-law out in Omaha didn't ask for much, but made it undeniably clear that Christmas presents arrived at their destinations prior to December 25 or simply did not count. And if they didn't count, then you had effectively neglected, on Christmas, the woman who planned to pay for your daughter's college education, and that was simply someone you could not afford to scrooge. Miranda would not return to New York until after New Year's, so Roz could shop for her at the after-Christmas sales (which was not *the* reason but certainly *a* reason that Roz so willingly relinquished custody of Miranda during the holidays). But the package for Esther was sitting in the hall, ready to go to the post office; all Roz had left to pick up was the requisite bottle of Estée Lauder Youth Dew for which she'd left room between the annual pair of Chinese bedroom slippers Esther lived in and couldn't find in Nebraska and the new Metropolitan Museum's Book of Days for the coming year. The lox, Zabar's shipped directly.

Roz hated to brave Bloomingdale's, especially during the Christmas season, but this really was just a one-stop in-and-out;

she wouldn't even have to tackle an escalator, just go straight in the Third Avenue door, directly to the Estée Lauder counter, and then down into the Lexington Avenue subway to catch the train home to Park Slope. She was tired, and somewhat depressed at the prospect of spending another Christmas alone. Which was ridiculous, she knew; she was a Jew for god's sake. Still, the house was empty, and that was sad unto itself. She almost wished she was from one of those big Christian families in the suburbs, roofs festooned with glowing crèches, thousands of nieces and nephews running around the tree, the tinsel sticking by static to their fuzzy footie pajamas, the carpet an aftermath of plastic battery-operated toys and outfits ordered from pages of the Sears Christmas Wish Book. Oh, those jolly old families! Roz thought: *Well, if I'm not just the Good Cheer Grinch.* She pushed in from the windy street, through the revolving door, and entered the department store.

Bloomingdale's was literally frothing over, oozing with Christmasness: balsam, holly berry, cinnamon, pine, Bing Crosby, fruitcake samples. Elves wearing bells peddled Dixie cups of eggnog, and gigantic snowflakes dangled from the ceiling and loomed at Roz like acid flashbacks. It was enough to make her dizzy, but she plowed forward, through the crowds, toward Estée.

The salesgirl was in her thirties and looked it, her makeup layered on so thickly she may as well have been wearing a latex Halloween mask. It made her heavily shaded eyes appear recessed into her head to an unseemly depth. She looked exhausted and Roz was glad, in the midst of the holiday hubbub hell, to have such a simple request for this poor worn-out clerk. The girl wrapped up the transaction she was working on, then turned to Roz. She'd been at the job long enough that she could say *Can I help you?* without opening her mouth—it was all in the eyebrows, really—which meant she was probably not far from toting a semiautomatic rifle to work in her seafoam-green Estée Lauder tote bag and opening fire, wiping out Clinique, Lancôme, and Chanel in one huge retail bloodbath.

"A bottle of Youth Dew, please." Roz was making a valiant attempt to speak spiritedly. "The largest one, please. With the pump."

The girl didn't move. "I'm sorry," she said. "We're sold out of the Youth Dew. It's an extremely popular item around the holidays."

"But I get it here every year," Roz said, as if establishing herself as a regular Yuletide Youth Dew customer would send the girl scuttling off to the private stash kept for just such emergencies. The salesgirl wasn't moving. "I always get it here," Roz said again.

"I'm sure you do," the girl said. "We *are* getting on in the season. Perhaps you're doing your shopping a little later than usual this year." She was attempting patience, but didn't have much of it left. Who could blame her?

"I always come at this time," Roz said. "The week before Christmas. You always still have Youth Dew."

"Well, ma'am, this year we don't." The salesgirl waited.

Roz threw up her hands in frustration, racking her brain for some idea of what tactic to try next when she heard someone saying her name.

"Roz?" The voice came from behind her. "Roz? That you?"

She turned. It had been nearly three months since Roz had laid eyes on him, since he'd moved himself and his kids out of the house and back in with Felice.

"Hello, Steven," Roz managed. The salesgirl sighed wearily and turned her attention doggedly to the next woman in line, who was pushing past Roz and worming her way up to the counter. Roz relinquished her spot and stepped with Steven into the heavily trafficked aisle.

"Roz," Steven said again.

"Stop saying that," she said.

"I'm sorry, I'm . . ." Steven was flustered. "I . . . How are you?" he stammered.

"Fine," Roz said, her voice pitching in an attempt to sound cavalier. "Just doing a little Christmas shopping . . ."

"Yeah? Me too!" said Steven, as if this constituted a great coincidence.

"You don't say?" Roz said, her mouth beginning to curl into the sneer she knew Steven deserved.

Steven looked to the ceiling like he was praying something might drop into Bloomingdale's and beam him up. "So how are things?" he said, nervous. "How's Miranda?"

"Good," Roz announced. "Great," she amended. "Great. She's with Edwin for the holiday . . ." Roz was out of things to say.

"Yeah!" he said, with more enthusiasm than warranted. "That's what Ben said."

"Ben?" Roz said.

Steven paused, tentative. "My son . . ."

"Oh, shut up, Steven, I lived with the kid."

Steven just stood there, his shoulders hunched as if to say, *Well, what then?*

"How does Ben know?"

"From Miranda?" His answers were questions too, uncertain as to what she was asking in the first place.

"Ben talks to Miranda?" she blurted, loudly. Loudly enough that even amid the jingle-bell din, a few shoppers turned toward the noise. Roz lowered her voice. "Since when do Ben and Miranda talk to each other?"

Steven's face read like he thought she'd lost her mind. He spoke slowly, as though Roz were deaf, or foreign, or just a complete moron. "Ben and Miranda talk to each other all the time, Roz . . ." He looked like he was expecting her to freak out at any moment, attack him, or run screaming through the Christmas-shopping throngs. "Ben and Miranda are close. I mean, they lived together that year too, right? They go to school together. Our kids are close . . . really close." Steven was saying it all incredulously, like it was unfathomable that he was having to *tell* these things to Roz. She felt like the weekly amnesia victim on *One Life to Live.*

"Our children are close?" Roz squeaked. And suddenly she was so unbearably hot that she thought she might die. She started pulling at her winter layers, scarf and gloves and hat, letting them fall to the slush-puddled marble floor. "How close? What do you mean *close*?"

Steven watched anxiously. "What're you . . . ?" He glanced around; Roz let her coat fall onto the pile, reached to unclasp the collar of her blouse, get some air on her neck, try to breathe.

Roz swallowed furiously. She wanted to speak, but how could she? Steven Stone, asshole—sleeping-with-his-ex-wife-while-living-in-Roz's-house asshole—Steven Stone knew more about her own daughter's life than she did! Miranda and Ben were friends?! Were Miranda and Ben more than friends? She thought she might gag; she felt bile climbing up the back of her throat. When she finally spoke, her voice was a pinched rasp. "You might have let me know, Steven," she said slowly, deliberately, trying to make sense of the words as they issued from her mouth. Her tone was awkwardly formal, elevated and contrived. "You might have called and told me."

"Call you?!" Steven cried. They both knew full well that she'd have hung up at the sound of his voice. "To tell you something it would never have dawned on me you didn't know?" he challenged. "There would be no reason for me to tell you . . ." Steven stammered. "How can you have not known, Roz? They talk on the phone. They hang out. You have to know that. You can't not know that. Ben's over at the house all the time. Roz, there's no way you could not have known."

"*The* house?" Roz screeched. "*Which* house?"

"*Your* house," Steven said. "*That* house. The house where we all used to live."

"*My house?*" Other customers were no longer surreptitiously glancing in Roz and Steven's direction; they were outright gawking.

Steven looked ready to die of humiliation. "Roz, Roz," he said, coming closer as if he might be able to keep her from flying completely off the handle, to keep things contained there, between them. "Roz, honey, please—please calm down—let's . . . why don't we, let's go sit somewhere. And talk. Let's go get a cup of coffee?" Steven bent down and started gathering Roz's things from the floor.

"Don't touch that coat." Her voice was modulated. She stood rigidly, and though her tone was steady, there was something shrill and frightening below the surface that made Steven do as she said. "Go away, Steven. Get away from me right now. Stand up and walk away. Now."

He looked up and could see she was deadly serious. Probably sane as well. He dropped the scarf and hat back at her feet and stood up slowly. His face, Roz thought, seemed to have aged since she'd turned to him by the Estée Lauder counter. Without another word, Steven Stone let himself disappear into the Bloomingdale's sea of identical gray raincoats. Roz just stood there and watched him go, the crowds flowing alongside her, parting to pass her like a river coursing by a boulder, polishing the edges in its wake.

19

NEW WIVES AND OLD HUSBANDS

ROZ HAD ONLY ONE THOUGHT IN HER HEAD: *I AM too far away from my daughter.* It seemed suddenly imperative that she reach Miranda. So much had gone on without her noticing. It was not only plausible that Miranda had been involved somehow with Ben, it seemed probable, inevitable maybe. She sought out a pay phone like an animal hunting meat. The holiday bustle left her consciousness altogether; her purpose now was singular: call Miranda. In the basement she spotted a phone across the aisle and darted for it, intent on starting immediately to make up for lost time. There had never been lies or secrets or untold truths before Steven, and now Steven was purged, gone for good, and she felt relieved to imagine that she and Miranda would never have to lie to each other again.

Roz leaned against the wall beside the phone and shuffled through her date book for the number in Lincoln. She hated calling Edwin's house, hated the way it made her think. There was something devastating to Roz about encountering someone with whom she'd shared so much, faced with the stark reality that they shared nothing anymore. Except a daughter. And a past. But even that was negligible. She wondered if in fact they did share the memory of their life together, or if by then their separate versions and interpretations had so completely eclipsed the actual events that Roz and Edwin might as well have lived them separately. She wondered, too, how Steven would tell the story of his time with Roz. Was she a blip he'd rather forget about? Would he think of Roz as the person he'd most egregiously wronged in his life?

The phone rang in Edwin's house in Nebraska, more than a thousand miles away. Roz shrugged the receiver to her shoulder and looked at her watch. Quarter to nine. Quarter to eight in Lincoln. She couldn't remember what time she'd left work. Everything seemed off: compressed, and then stretched out. How long had she talked with Steven? How long had she been wandering through Bloomingdale's? The feeling of claustrophobia returned. She fanned at her face with the date book in her hand. On the other end, someone picked up the phone.

"Hello, Merry Christmas," said a woman's voice.

Roz said, "Kathy?"

"Judith?" said Kathy.

"What? No. Sorry. No, this is Roz. Roz . . ." and it seemed absurd to call herself Roz Anderson to this woman, who would soon be Kathy Anderson herself—but who was she then? "It's Miranda's mother," she said.

"Oh! *Roz*. I'm so sorry. You sounded like my sister for a minute there. But she's in Hawaii. Couldn't figure out why she'd be calling from her vacation!" She laughed. "How are *you*, Roz?" But before Roz could say anything, Kathy was off again. "I'm so sorry, Miranda's not here. She left with Shaunna and Rod and Britty to go see the light displays . . . oh goodness, when did they take off? Half an hour ago maybe? Is it something important? Should I put Eddie on the line for you?"

Roz cut her off, abruptly, but not intentionally. "No," she said, and she knew her voice sounded urgent.

Kathy laughed again. "You know, I can't take that either. Talking to Shaunna's daddy. Doesn't seem to matter how long goes by, it's still hard. Why *is* that, do you think? I mean, it doesn't even seem to matter if you've had a perfectly amicable parting. Duane and I were like you and Eddie, no bad blood really, just changes. And still, the thought of having to carry on some normal conversation with him just makes me jump in my skin, you know?" She paused, and Roz felt it was her turn to say something but she couldn't seem to find a way to make her mouth move in the right formations. It was actually comforting to listen to Kathy talk. It was the way she might have liked to call up her own sister and just prattle on about things. But Mona wasn't that kind of sister. And talking to her was never comforting in the least.

Kathy seemed—as Roz usually was herself—unable to metabolize silence, and she jumped right back in. "Oh, here I'm yammering along, all on your dime! Roz, can I have Miranda call you when she gets in? Do you want to try her back a little later? I think Eddie's already asleep on the couch . . . We might both be asleep soon, but I could sure leave a note, even if I've hit the sack by the time she gets in . . ."

All Roz could think to say was exactly what she then said. "What happened to Duane?" she asked Kathy.

"Duane!" Kathy said, her voice full of exasperation and fondness. "Duane's mostly in Omaha, when he's somewhere at all. Which isn't all that often. Duane's not what you'd call a real stable guy."

"Like Edwin," Roz suggested, and they both laughed then at the absurdity of that statement.

"Oh, right," Kathy giggled. "If only Eddie was a little more predictable . . ."

Roz felt her muscles loosening, an ease spreading in her bones. She had an urge to sink right down along the wall and sit on the floor, her bags around her, in the basement of Bloomingdale's and talk on the phone to this woman she didn't even know out in Lincoln, Nebraska, who was about to be the new wife of her old husband. She let herself slide down the wall, until she was sitting, knees curled to her chest. "How *is* Edwin?" she said. She thought her voice sounded sort of dreamy and far away, imagined the scene swirling to a blur, twinkling xylophone music announcing a flashback sequence. "Does he still fall asleep with his glasses on?" she asked.

Kathy broke in, "Glasses on, lamp blazing, on top of the covers, middle of a show on the TV . . ."

Roz laughed. "I used to think I was lucky if I got his shoes off him! I always thought I'd get kicked in the night with a wing tip . . ."

"I *have* been kicked in the night with a wing tip!" Kathy cried.

"He can be dangerous . . ." Roz added, and they both laughed again at the thought of that: Edwin Anderson, dangerous.

It was Kathy who spoke again. "I'll just leave Miranda a note right here on the counter for when she gets in . . ." Roz could hear her scrambling around for paper, something to write with. "Should I have her call tonight, Roz, will you be up awhile?"

"No," Roz said. "No, you know, I'm thinking maybe don't even bother. I'm just being a silly mom, missing my girl, who'd probably rather I didn't bug her anyway . . . I can just see her rolling her eyes at me now . . . You don't even have to let her know I called at all. So long as she's doing well, having a good time . . ."

"Oh, Roz, she's a super kid," Kathy said.

"Yeah," Roz said, "she's all right . . ." and they both laughed again. "Ach," Roz scowled, "I'll probably last until tomorrow, then give in and call her anyway. What's pride to a mother anyhow?"

"It's a lost cause, Roz, is what it is," Kathy declared, and Roz wondered if the habit of saying a person's name in every sentence you spoke to them was something she had picked up from Edwin, or if Kathy and Edwin were really two found peas, come together in their pod at last.

20

THINK ABOUT IF YOU WANT

IN JUNE, AFTER HER SPLIT WITH STEVEN, ROZ DECIDED it was absurd to be living in a three-story house alone with Miranda, and set herself to the task of taking in some boarders. She moved from the third floor down into Jenny and Miranda's old "suite" on the second. Miranda got Ben's basement. The plan was to rent the top floor and share the street-level kitchen, living room, and entrance. That summer they took in a couple, triathletes who left unexpectedly after three months to train in Colorado. Roz was annoyed. She didn't have the time or energy to devote to tenant-hunting. Then, one afternoon in early September of her junior year, Miranda called Roz at work to say that the new English teacher at school had just moved from Oregon and she and her boyfriend were living on a friend's couch while they looked for a place, and could Miranda bring her over to the house to check it out and maybe meet Roz too if she could get home from the office at a reasonable time?

"Sweetie," Roz said, "maybe think about if you really want your English teacher in your kitchen on Saturday morning?"

"Oh, I see," Miranda snapped. "My orthodontist's OK, but you draw the line at my English teacher?"

"Miranda."

"She's not *my* teacher, anyway. She teaches eighth and ninth. Besides, she's like twenty-three. She's really cool."

"By all means, then. You should've said so in the first place."

WING MCARDLE, ROZ HAD TO ADMIT, DID SEEM rather cool. She was smart and articulate, and looked at least thirty, though Miranda had been right about her actual age. The childhood she alluded to—Oregon seacoast, horseback riding, an airy outdoor upbringing of sunburns and Solarcaine—explained her premature crow's-feet and the lines around her mouth that kept laughing even after she had stopped. She wore a linen jumper with big flour-sack pockets and clunky black shoes with bulbous steel toes that looked dangerous enough to ward off potential assailants on the streets of New York. She streamed through the brownstone gasping as though heartbroken at every alcove, exposed brick wall, and original wood molding. She appeared to love the house even more than Roz did. The things she complimented were all the things in which Roz took special pride, and Roz liked her, right off the bat.

"We'll come back tonight, if that's OK," Wing said. She was taking the place, just had to collect her boyfriend, Alexander, way out in Williamsburg from the home of a person called Stoker, with whom they'd been staying. Stoker, according to Wing, had a studio apartment, a pet python to whom he fed live rats once a month, and nothing in his kitchen cabinets but a jar of solidified Cremora. "I can't even begin to tell you what a relief this is," Wing said.

"Do you guys need any help moving?" Miranda asked, and Roz had to turn around to make sure the person leaning in the kitchen doorframe and *offering* to do something for someone else was in fact her own daughter.

"That's sweet," said Wing, who was casting about in her shoulder bag for change. "We've got so little stuff, though. I think we'll be fine."

"Oh, to be young and nomadic!" Roz cried, and Miranda shot her a look like Roz had just broken into song.

Wing laughed. "And all this time I thought we were just poverty-stricken!"

"What does Alexander do?" Roz asked.

"Good question." Wing paused. "Alex," she said, as though he were a student whose record she was trying to call to mind. "Well, at school he was in film studies . . . Let's just say that Alex is still on the job market . . ."

Roz leapt in: "I didn't mean . . . I'm not asking because of the rent, I was just curious."

"Oh no, no, no, I didn't take it that way at all," Wing assured her. "Alex, he's just, put it this way: I set up this teaching job for myself from school last year. But in Alex's field . . . He came out to New York right after graduation—I still had credits to finish up in the summer session—Alex came out in June to find a job and a place for us to live." She smiled and gave a little nod by way of punctuation. "Let's just say he's been about as effective on the job market as he was with housing." Wing looked to Miranda. "You solved one of our problems—maybe you've got a hot lead on a job for Alex too?"

"I'm on the case," Miranda said, resolving to check the classifieds.

ALEXANDER HORLICK WAS A BROODING YOUNG MAN with dark, narrow eyes and exquisite cheekbones. He spoke little, preferred to stand in the corners of rooms, and touched Wing at every available opportunity. That first night, while Wing stuck a few things in the fridge—milk, margarine, a loaf of cheap sliced bread—Alex went to look at the upstairs. Miranda leaned in the entranceway as usual, as if to fully cross the threshold was more trouble than she was willing to take. She looked at her mom like she knew exactly what Roz thought of Alex: she thought he was a loser. But Roz, who was about as defiant as her daughter, was loath to fulfill Miranda's expectations. Wing shut the refrigerator door, and as she passed by, Roz slid an arm through hers, a maternal gesture, drawing Wing in. "He's *gorgeous!*" Roz whispered, her mouth exaggerated. Miranda strode from the kitchen and began to drag herself up the staircase with such laborious effort she might have weighed four hundred pounds, and Roz and Wing were left in the kitchen, arms linked, smiling awkwardly after Miranda under the glare of the ticking fluorescent light.

Alex had enough left in a dwindling trust fund to keep up with his share of rent and groceries and still maintain a near-perpetual high, and it wasn't that Roz minded her house smelling suddenly as savory as it had twenty years before, what bugged her was that Alex never offered to share. When, once in a while, Roz worked at home for the day, she had to focus on the appraisal of court briefs, enduring the saintly green waft of smoke that permeated the house. Periodically, Alex himself emerged from the third-floor den for sustenance. He fed the way Steven's son, Ben, had: he was that same kind of bottomless, adolescent skinny that made it incomprehensible to imagine where all that food went once it got inside. On his way to the fridge, Alex passed Roz's desk, sock-footed, and gave a quick spasm of a military nod in her direction. This made her nervous and edgy. He was like Steven Stone: good-looking, aloof, judgmental. They were men who operated like one-man "in crowds," men who had the power—to whom she *gave* the power, for Christ's sake; she was embarrassingly complicit, she knew—to decide who was "it" and who was not. Not that their lives looked particularly enthralling—couch-potato stoner, philandering orthodontist—but it was through their sheer remove that they could make you feel like you were being left out of things you weren't sure you'd have wanted to be part of in the first place.

. . .

ONE SUNDAY MORNING THAT FALL, ROZ AND WING sat at the kitchen table with coffee and the *Times,* waiting for Miranda to return from the bagel place. Alex, who hadn't once seated himself for a meal with them, padded into the kitchen as usual for his snack, gave them each his little nod, and then turned to go, spoon in one hand, raspberry Dannon yogurt in the other. At the door he paused and turned back around. The women looked up from their papers, and all three were still for a moment until Alex did an odd little flat-footed jump in the air, turned on his woolen heel, and accompanied himself up the stairs with a jubilantly whistled chorus of the Skippy jingle. From the landing he called back to them, his voice a deadpan mockery of glee: "Happy! Happy! Joy! Joy!" And then he ducked back into the recesses upstairs.

Roz turned to Wing, her face scrunched up in bewilderment.

"Ren and Stimpy," Wing explained, then realized that wasn't quite enough of an explanation for someone like Roz. "From a TV . . . his favorite cartoon . . . it's got rabbits, or mice, or some-thing . . ."

There was something in Wing's tone—disapproval, or frustra-tion—that emboldened Roz. The words were out of her mouth before she could edit herself. "What exactly do you see in him?" she asked.

Wing didn't seem surprised by the question. Roz guessed it probably wasn't an uncommon one. "He's different than he seems," Wing said.

"So was Ted Bundy," Roz said, reaching for her coffee.

But Wing had her defenses down. "He's horribly insecure. Really really really shy. He's self-conscious to a degree that's liter-ally debilitating . . ."

"Which is why he's not supporting both of you as a J. Crew model?" Roz said.

Wing looked a little confused, like she thought that not at all an obvious thing to think about Alex, and Roz could see her tucking it away in her mental store of curious things she might take the time to ponder one day. "His work . . . What he was doing in film—in theory—really it's excellent. Bergman's influence—the early work especially—on David Lynch . . . ?" Wing offered, but it sounded as though she'd said it so many times it didn't matter whether she believed it or not.

"Well," Roz said, for she felt she had to say something, "you know what they say about still waters . . ."

The front door clicked open, then shut with a bang, and Miranda stepped into the kitchen waving a sack of bagels. Wing smiled; all that had been said seemed forgotten and not even in need of forgiving. She dipped a knife into the tub of cream cheese and brandished it toward Miranda. "And you know what they say about the early bird . . ."

MIRANDA, FOR HER PART, REALLY LIKED ALEX HOR-lick. Roz usually didn't get home until seven in the evening, and Wing stayed at school until about the same time, advising the drama club, grading papers, and just staying on top of her teaching load. Thus, it was Alex, reigning sloth-king of the third floor, with whom Miranda spent free time after school that year.

"Does it bother you?" Roz asked Wing one evening when they were still at the kitchen table finishing a bottle of not-terrible red wine. Miranda was upstairs with Alex watching TV. "If you minded having Miranda up there all the time you'd say something, wouldn't you?"

"I think the question should be whether you mind Miranda being up there all the time under the questionable influence of my great American stoner-boy?"

Roz wiped a finger through the spaghetti sauce on her plate and sucked it clean. "I think I'm declaring myself officially through with having a say about who does or does not have an influence on my daughter. It's good training for when she goes to college. Ha! There's a job for Alex! Professional empty-nest preparation for parents. He could get people to pay him to come live in their houses and corrupt their children and let them grow gradually accustomed to being impotent in their kids' lives." The thought of her own impending impotence in Miranda's life filled her with a dueling sense of horrified relief.

"I think," Wing laughed, "that you may be the only parent in America who'd actually go for a scheme like that."

WHEN ALEX HIMSELF TROMPED DOWN TO THE KITCHEN that evening for a microwave veggie pocket, he was quite obviously stoned out of his tree. He programmed the microwave, stepped out of its nuke-ray path, and leaned back against the counter to wait for the buzzer. Roz could see Wing regarding him, and it was fascinating to try to read her face: in her eyes a mix of deep love and sadness, on her mouth a hint of defiance, the lips slightly pursed, teeth clenched, the breath held, showing restraint. Alex's face was flushed, his eyes two slanted lines with dots of dark iris glimmering out from between the folded lids like polished gem-stones. He also had a shining, domed pimple beneath his left eye, a heartening imperfection on his customarily flawless face.

Roz said, "Are you up there getting my teenage daughter stoned on marijuana?" How odd it was, Roz thought, that although she felt annoyed, she wasn't terribly worried.

Alex nodded his military nod. "Yes ma'am," he said.

The microwave's buzzer went off and Alex flung open the door and removed the steaming pastry, joggling it between his hands.

"Paper towel?" Wing offered, holding one out before him like a fireman's net. He tossed it on.

"My savior," he said, collecting his dinner and pausing to lean in and plant a kiss on Wing's forehead.

Roz had stood up; she moved across the room, opened a cabinet, and started fumbling through. Unearthing a bag of pizza-flavor Goldfish, she held them out toward Alex. He reached for them with one hand, and with the other placed his hot veggie pocket over his heart. Roz tugged open the fridge. "Take some OJ too," she said.

"I am deeply moved," Alex said, looking to Roz like she was breaking his heart. "A mother's concern for her child's munchies." He accepted the juice and backed out of the kitchen, bowing all the way.

Roz stacked Wing's plate on her own, and carried them to the sink.

Wing looked as if she'd been carrying on a conversation inside her head and just started to speak it aloud. She said, "Giving Alex a hard time now would be like kicking him when he's down."

Roz wondered, briefly, what Alex might be like when he was up. She turned on the water and squeezed some Joy into a sponge.

"I get accused of going yuppie, getting suddenly obsessed with money, being a fair-weather girlfriend . . . Sometimes," Wing said, laughing at herself a bit, "sometimes I think I wish that I'd get home from school one day and find him in bed with Miranda, or with you—"

"Oh please," Roz cut in.

"I know," Wing said, disappointed, resigned to Alex's fidelity.

"Need I point out that finding a *philandering* guy isn't usually the problem? I know quite an accomplished one, if you're in the market . . ."

Wing laughed, but her heart wasn't in it. "But you *wanted* Steven," she said. "You wanted him to be faithful. God, I'm sorry, I shouldn't bring up . . ."

Roz waved off the apology, sending out a little spatter of dishwater. She left the sink, forgetting the running water, and sat. "If you want Alex to leave, you'll tell him to leave."

Wing blushed graciously.

Roz leaned in, her face not a foot from Wing's, her breath warm with wine. "I didn't kick Steven out," Roz whispered. She put a soap-sticky hand on Wing's forearm. The water faucet ran in the background like white noise. "I was so far from kicking him out." The tears rose in her eyes as if to spite her. "I asked the fucking bastard to stay. That's how sad . . . that's how pathetic, you don't even know . . . I begged that fucking bastard asshole to stay . . ."

Wing's face registered disappointment, then shifted toward pity, and the truth suddenly didn't matter so much to Roz, the truth of who she was, who she had been. Even though the truth was turning the look on Wing's face to something like disdain, it wasn't disdain for Roz, necessarily, but for the Wing she didn't want to become. Then suddenly Wing's face lit with relief: a memory, a piece slipping into its place. "But you thought you had *breast cancer*! You were a wreck! *Of course* you asked him to stay."

A momentary panic. "Please, Wing, please don't mention it to Miranda. It would take so much explaining now." She paused. "Anyway, it's no excuse. I was on my feet again by that time." Suddenly Roz felt as if she were posing Wing with a dare. "You can do it," she said. "Walk upstairs, turn off his friggin' television, and say, *Alex, we need to talk.*" Roz could see it in her. Wing was almost there, almost ready; she needed one last nudge.

"Miranda's up there . . . ," Wing said.

Roz stood and strode to the stairs. She craned her head up into the darkness. "Miiiraaaandaaaaa," she called, her voice lilting, giddy. She sang out again: "Miiiiiraaaandaaaa!" Then she noticed the water faucet still running and practically skipped to the sink to shut it off.

They waited a minute in silence but Miranda didn't appear. Finally Roz started waving Wing up the stairs. "Just go," she said. "Just go. Send her down when you get there."

"OK," Wing said. And she went.

Roz leaned back against the sink. She wished there was just one more glass of wine, but the bottle was empty. Maybe she could coax Miranda into helping with the dishes. Yawning, she raised a hand to cover her mouth. Her fingers smelled of Joy, and she held them there beneath her nostrils until she was heady with lemon.

The feet on the stairs were too springy to be Miranda's. Roz opened her eyes to Wing in the stairway threshold, one hand on either wall, leaning into the kitchen light. The posture was young, a little sheepish. She spoke before Roz could. "They're stoned beyond coherent thought." She laughed, as if to admit the light and futile irony of her thwarted mission and to chuckle it off. "You want to come up for *Moonlighting*?" Wing asked, then hung in the stairway the way Miranda did, awaiting a response.

Roz shut her eyes again, and the world was milky cobalt and orange inside with flares and shadows of light. She rubbed one eye and tried to ease away her anger. "I'll just set some of these dishes to soak."

Wing turned to bound back up the stairs, then looked back to Roz like she wanted to say something, like thank you, maybe, only she didn't, just smiled again, a smile in which Roz thought she saw apology, and appreciation, and desire, and resignation, all at once. Wing turned again and climbed the stairs two at a time.

Roz resumed washing the dishes. Wing wouldn't leave Alex any sooner than Alex would leave Wing. No more willingly than Roz would have left Steven. Miranda would go off to college, and Roz and Wing and Alex would stay here, in the brownstone in Park Slope. And Alex would smoke pot and watch movies and think about the theoretical implications of the zoom shot, while Roz took the subway into Manhattan each morning and back each night and tried to change the world, one landlord at a time, in the hours in between, and Wing taught *Lord of the Flies* to kids like Miranda who would grow up and do the brilliant and horrible and mundane and extraordinary things they were destined for, always waiting for something to happen. For the world to tilt, to quiver, to buckle beneath their feet and deposit them, blinking and afraid, into lives other than their own.

21

ENTER CERTAIN NYMPHS

IT BEGINS AS A GAME.

MR. LORIMER IS TWENTY-THREE. HE ISN'T DREAMY, but he is intense, and there's something sad about him that Miranda is immediately drawn to, the way you follow your own reflection passing in the window of a store. Miranda isn't positive—not entirely, anyway—but she has the feeling that he's setting her up to meet the challenge. It's not standard curriculum for seniors to read *The Tempest;* he's petitioned for it. And there's something about the way he called her name on the first day of class, the way he didn't have to look around to see which hand might go up in response to "Miranda Anderson." He'd known who she was, clearly. There hadn't been a question attached to her name; instead he'd seemed almost pleased when he read it, as if she were a student he'd had in class before, as if he were saying *Hello again.* But she hadn't been in his class fall term, and that was his first semester at Emmons. What seems most likely to Miranda is that Mr. Lorimer is hot for Wing, whose desk sits across from his in the English Department office, and that he thinks his position as Miranda's teacher might well afford him some alternative access to the elusive Ms. McArdle. Miranda is his "in," and she's ready to have some fun with that, because when it's spring semester of your senior year and you've already gotten into college there's not a lot to keep you awake during a class that meets after lunch in a windowless room in the school basement. Anyway, Wing could use a better boyfriend than Alex, and though Miranda's not sure Mr. Corbin Lorimer is the one, he's decently cute, and that seems like as good a reason as any to give his mettle a little test and see what he's really capable of. So on that first day when he calls her name and looks her dead on with his blue-blue eyes behind those black-rimmed glasses, she has the gumption to stare him back and say without the slightest hint of modesty, *"Here, master."* Then she adds, *"What cheer?"*

He almost doesn't flinch. *"Good,"* he says, his smile smirking its way toward mischievous, *"speak to th' mariners; fall to't yarely, or we run ourselves aground. Bestir, bestir!"*

Miranda laughs. The rest of the class is looking at her and Mr. Lorimer like they've just stripped naked and danced a jig.

"We have a Shakespearean scholar in our midst!" Mr. Lorimer announces.

"No," Miranda says, "we just did it freshman year."

"Here at Emmons?" Mr. Lorimer asks.

Miranda nods.

"A thespian then. And who did you play?"

She waits a minute, not sure if he's serious. "There's only one woman in it," she says. "Miranda." She feels dumb, like her own joke has backfired on her.

"Of course," says Mr. Lorimer, grinning broadly, magnanimous, ready to take on the world. "There *is* only one woman here on our uncharted isle. Daughter of Prospero, lover of Ferdinand, Miranda's the only lady around."

Jud Blumberg pipes in then from the other side of the room,

ever the smart-ass comment on hand. "What about Ginger and Mary Ann? Now those were some ladies!" And there's laughter all around before Mr. Lorimer finds his place and resumes the roll call. But already something's been established, a precedent set. The semester might turn out to be more fun than she'd thought.

DURING THE SUMMER OF 1971 ON A WEEKEND ESCAPE to the Catskills, Roz and Edwin Anderson went to see a regional theater group do an open-air production of *The Tempest*. Roz's pregnancy was just beginning to show, and as they'd lain on the quilt they'd spread over prickly grass, Edwin's hand rested lightly across Roz's abdomen, as though he wanted to be the first one to know if anything started squirming around in there. They were, by then, already deeply absorbed in an ongoing round of the Name Game. "If it's a boy . . ." they'd pinned down early on: Jack, for Roz's father, who had died before she'd ever really got to know him. But as for girls, they were still at a loss. Both their mothers were still alive, and even if they weren't, no child of theirs was going to be forced through life as an Adele or an Esther. Edwin was unfortunately fond of some insipid girly names that Roz wouldn't even discuss—Amanda, Jessica, Melissa—and though they both liked Jenny, so did the vast majority of the pregnant American population and that almost seemed in its own bland way as cruel as choosing something freakish or pigeonholing like Blue, or Peaceblossom, or Iolanthe. Roz favored some hippie names— Ginger, Angela, Georgia, Jocelyn—and Edwin accused her of being obsessed with the "juh" sound, which hardly seemed like something one should rightly get accused of, but Roz backed down in an effort to keep whatever peace they still had. They had been arguing the subject over dinner, but a bottle of red wine had mellowed them since, and when the lights rose and the play began, their repose in the grass was tender, Edwin's hand rubbing softly over Roz's belly.

It was the middle of Scene Two before Prospero spoke her name aloud—*"Thou hadst, and more, Miranda . . ."* and Edwin's hand stopped its circling. A few lines passed. Roz's ears pricked up. *"Twelve year since, Miranda, twelve year since . . ."* Roz and Edwin turned to each other. Neither of their faces registered emotion. Not a word nor a nudge was exchanged. If anything, Roz's face betrayed a mistrust, a wariness, a skepticism that said, *It's too good to be true.* And then they turned back to the play. Something had been decided.

"OK," Mr. Lorimer begins, "so who've we got here? Let's try and get some of the characters straight before I send you all home to try and make sense of this on your own. We'll get some basics out of the way. Because Shakespeare's a lot easier if you know the story ahead of time. It's not about 'what happened,' it's about the language." He says the word "language" as if it is a foreign term, as if the idea of being interested in the "how," as he puts it, "and not just the what" might be a strange and novel concept to these students. It strikes Miranda as a little patronizing— they've been reading Shakespeare for years now: *Richard III, Romeo and Juliet, Macbeth,* and that's surely something Mr. Lorimer should be aware of. Instead he appears to think his *Tempest* is their first, by a long shot.

"OK, so we're on a remote tropical island. And the only people who live on this island are Prospero, his daughter, Miranda"—and he makes a sweeping gesture toward the side of the room where Miranda sits chewing on her pen cap—"and their slave, a 'savage,' a 'native,' Caliban." Mr. Lorimer speaks some words in quotes as if to mock them, but he never stops to explain why some words are ripe for such treatment.

Of course Mr. Lorimer has her read the part. Mrs. Blaunik had let Juliet Abrahms read Juliet the year before, and Richard Little-ton read a little of Richard III in tenth grade before he got mono and was out for the rest of the term. It seems only logical that if she wants Miranda she can have it. They blaze through Scene One the first period; Mr. Lorimer seems profoundly uninterested in the Boatswain and the Shipmaster. He sends them home to read Scene Two for the next day, and Miranda and Simon Ramirez are assigned the extra task of preparing to read some of the scene aloud as Miranda and Prospero.

"MR. LORIMER WANTS TO GET IN YOUR PANTS," Miranda tells Wing that night at home. Wing has decided that Alex may no longer smoke in the house, and has made him go outside to the yard for a cigarette. Wing is making tea, and Miranda sits at the kitchen table, *The Tempest* open before her.

Wing turns from the stove to face her. "Don't even joke about that, Miranda," she says sternly.

Miranda snorts and turns back to the book. Wing is, at times, a decided pain in the ass. Miranda's lip curls into an insipid little snarl as she mouths a mimic of Wing's response. *Don't even joke about something like that, Miranda.*

Wing must be in a shitty mood already, because usually she's a keep-the-peacer at all costs. Today she snarls back. "Act your age, Miranda," she says, and leaves the room.

"PMS much?" Miranda yells after her, and it's here that Wing breaks.

"Miranda, I am going to throttle you," she yells back, and their peace, Miranda knows, is patched.

THE NEXT DAY MR. LORIMER WEARS JEANS TO SCHOOL, and a checkered shirt with a sweater vest on top. Miranda comes in a little late from lunch and sits in the first chair she can find, which is next to a girl named Ciely Fuchs, whose miniskirt is the size of a lettuce leaf. Ciely crosses and recrosses her legs every thirty seconds. Mr. Lorimer is in the midst of a spiel about something, and when he turns to write a line up on the board, Ciely sighs audibly and leans toward Miranda. "Don't you just want to bite his cute little butt?" she says. "Don't you want to sink your teeth into that? Aaach," she shudders, eyelids fluttering in mock-orgasm.

Miranda's sense of propriety leaves her suddenly, and she laughs out loud, a sputtered guffaw that turns every head in the room. Mr. Lorimer stops what he's saying and, on the cusp of exasperation, turns in the direction of the laughter. But as Miranda and Ciely come into view his countenance shifts and his voice comes out teasing instead of reproachful. There's a pause first. Then: *"Dost thou attend me?"* he asks.

Another moment of silence. Ciely seems either thrilled or mortified, it's unclear which. Miranda doesn't know how to handle the situation—she's not usually the bad kid in class—but she does know the next line, and it seems the appropriate thing to say, so she does: *"Sir, most heedfully."*

"Good," says Mr. Lorimer, and he turns, pleased, back to the board.

For the rest of the period they make their way through Act One, Scene Two. Simon Ramirez gives an astoundingly soporific performance as the most lethargic of Prosperos, perking up only when he gets to refer to Miranda as "wench." Except for Ciely, who either is on speed or has the worst case of ADD Miranda's ever seen, the rest of the class is slouched in a collective food coma. Cafeteria Philly cheese steaks and fries, and all their brains go numb for a good hour and a half. They have to ditch Simon halfway through his Prospero since he's practically snoring out the lines; finding someone else who's willing to read the part is no easy task. There's a struggle every time a new character enters because no one will volunteer to read. Finally Mr. Lorimer stops asking and starts dictating, and that goes decently until Ferdinand's entrance toward the end of the act. Mr. Lorimer calls Jud Blumberg out of a reverie to read the part, but he's so lost and his speech is so slurry that Mr. L. lets him off the hook and calls on Eric Sonner, but *he* appears to have forgotten *how* to read, so in the end Mr. Lorimer just does the part himself. "Out of respect for old Bill S.," he tells them.

"*My prime request,*" booms Mr. L., "*Which I do last pronounce, is (O you wonder!) / If you be maid or no?* OK," he says, "and Miranda says yes, '*certainly a maid,*' so what does that tell us? What's he asking her? This guy who takes one look at her and falls in love, what's this most important question he has to ask of her?"

There's dull silence from the room. A few kids shift in their chairs. Mr. L. looks like he's ready to start pitching desks, only it would take too much energy so he's just going to outwait them. "Come on," he says, "get it from the context. Use your brains. What does Ferdinand need to know about this woman he's falling in love with? What does he have to ask her?"

Still nothing.

"Miranda?" he asks, desperate.

Miranda acts as bored as the rest of them. "If she's available," she says. She yawns woefully.

"Yes!" cries Mr. Lorimer. "He needs to know: Is she single? Is she a virgin? Can he even allow himself to want her?"

For the first time, a hand goes up. It's Ciely. Mr. Lorimer acknowledges her excitedly. "Yes, Ciely?" he pips.

"Yes," she says.

"Yes what?" he asks her.

"Yes, he can allow himself to want her." Ciely's eyes pulse a little larger, as if she's eaten something too big for her windpipe.

"OK. And what does Miranda tell him?" Mr. Lorimer scans the room. "Jud? What does Miranda tell Ferdinand?"

Jud looks perturbed. *Why do you insist on calling on me, Mr. L.,* his eyes seem to ask. He doesn't even speak, just raises his eyebrows in defeat.

"Come on, people, it's right there in the text. What does Miranda tell him? What do you know about her? *Is* she available? Is she already promised to someone else? What's the role her father's playing in all this? People, are we all reading the same play here or what? And I'm not calling on Miranda Anderson, so don't even think you're getting out of this that easy." And he so pointedly does not look in Miranda's direction that it's almost as if he'd stood her on a pedestal before the entire class with a sign around her neck saying "Genius." Miranda feels her face go hot and her hands cold.

"Well," Jud begins grudgingly, "if Miranda's the only female on this island . . . ?" He speaks as if he thinks this moment of effort is the last one he'll have to put in for his semester's C plus. He's probably right.

"Yes, Mr. Blumberg, that's true. But what does that tell us? She could be boinking every Tom, Dick, and Harry in the place. No?"

A twitter of giggles from the class. The girls in back are waking up, sitting straighter in their chairs. Ciely is beaming like Miss America.

From the other side of the room a hand goes up. Aubrey Frazier is a smart girl, but she never talks in any class, seeming to find the discussions beneath her. She looks as frustrated as Mr. Lorimer did a minute before. "Page forty-nine. Line four-forty-five." Aubrey's voice is beleaguered with ennui. Meanwhile, Mr. Lorimer looks like he's so happy that people are talking, he's about to pee in his pants.

"Read the line for us, Aubrey, please, if you will," he cries.

Aubrey rolls her eyes. Without a gram of inflection she opens her black-lipsticked mouth and intones, *"This / Is the third man that e'er I saw; the first / That e'er I sighed for."*

Mr. L. picks up the call before she's even finished: "The third man she's ever seen!" He looks around expectantly. "Who are the first two?"

No takers.

"Come on, people! She's standing onstage with one of them!"

"Her father!" Ciely calls out.

"Yes!" says Mr. L. "And although this is Shakespeare, I think it's safe to assume that Miranda's not shtupping her dad."

A gaggle of giggles erupts once again.

"And who's the other man on the island?"

Jud is perking up as well and he speaks now as he raises his hand, letting it flop down to the desk when he's done. "The slave-guy. What's-his-name?"

"Caliban," Mr. L. provides. "And what do we know about him?"

Jud again: "That he tried to get with Miranda but she negged him."

"OK, so here we've got Miranda, the virgin, setting eyes on the love of her life for the very first time. It's romantic. It's cheesy. It's a John Hughes film. We're all supposed to be eating it up." Mr. L. has the fever and he's plowing on. "And what's Prospero's reaction? What's his deal with all this love stuff?"

Ciely: "He forbids it, right?"

"Does he?" asks Mr. L., his head cocked, mouth pursed expectantly.

"No," Miranda calls out, surprised at the sound of her own voice. "He says he does but really he wants them to get together."

"So why's he forbid it then, as Ciely tells us?" asks Mr. L.

Miranda speaks again, as if the conversation were just between the two of them there, no one else in the room. "Because," she says, "because the best way to get someone to want something is to tell them they can't want it." It's not a lot of words to say, but the effort leaves her breathless anyway.

There's a pause in the room, silence, then Mr. L.'s hand going up, his finger pointing straight at Miranda like a laser beam. Like the touch of the fairy godmother's wand. "Bingo," he says. "Give the little lady a prize."

And then there's the bell.

Mr. Lorimer's senior English class meets next on Friday afternoon, a week into the new term. As the kids file into the room, chugging the dregs from soda cans and unwrapping

Blow Pops to suck during class, Mr. Lorimer is uncharacteristically seated behind his desk at the front of the room. He does not even look up as they enter. On the blackboard behind him is written:

In-class writing assignment: LOVE. Think of movies you've seen or plays or books you've read where people fall in love at first sight. Maria and Tony in *West Side Story*, Nellie and Emile in *South Pacific*, Romeo and Juliet, Cinderella and Prince Charming, Sandy and Danny in *Grease* . . . Think about the scenes where the lovers first set eyes upon each other. Why is that moment so important? What does it mean? In the Middle Ages many people believed that you could see through a person's eyes and into her soul. What is the significance of the first glimpse of two lovers given this idea? Prospero says (page 49, lines 441–42), "At the first sight / They have changed eyes." Why is this a particularly striking line, given what you know of the emotional states of Miranda and Ferdinand?

When the period is over, they stack their loose-leaf pages on his desk, the corners folded over and torn in lieu of staples or paper clips. Mr. Lorimer barely acknowledges anyone, his chin resting in his hand as he corrects a stack of papers that might as well be the Magna Carta for the intensity of his ostensible concentration.

THE EMMONS THEATER CLUB'S PRODUCTION OF *FID-dler on the Roof* is scheduled to go up at the end of February, so already they are rehearsing every day after school plus weekends. Miranda is Hodel, the daughter who leaves home to be with Per-chik, the man she loves. That Saturday morning, when the strag-glers are still making their way in from the January cold, steaming takeout cups of coffee and tea in hand, Miranda and Joe McSweeney, both seniors and longtime devoted theater club members who come to rehearsal on time, are going through a scene. There is an emotional exchange, the culmination of which sends Hodel running from the stage and out through the audience to the rear exit. A dramatic flight, largely orchestrated to get Miranda to the correct side of the auditorium for her next entrance. It's rather fun too, tearing out through the audience like that, and Miranda is excited to do it for real next month, the spotlight tracking her through the darkened theater, the rags of her costume flying in her wake. For today, though, there are no trailing babushka scarves, no granny boots to clack down the stage stairs. Just Miranda in Levi's and sneakers, her ponytail bouncing up and down like a cheerleader's as she runs from the auditorium and out into the chilly hallway. She runs clear to the far wall, stopping herself against it with her hands and pausing to catch her breath. From inside the auditorium she can hear someone call, "Take half an hour, you guys!" It is only when she looks up that she sees Mr. Lorimer standing at the end of the hall with a look on his face like he's just sold his firstborn child into slavery.

"Miranda—," he says.

"Mr. L.?" It seems for a minute like this can't actually be him, a trick of the eyes, a head rush, but not him, certainly. "What're you do—?" but he cuts her off.

"Will you talk to me?" he asks. His tone is plaintive, almost scared.

Uncertain as to where anything is going, Miranda tries to maintain a sort of perky oblivion, but she sounds like a simpering pep rally when she speaks. "Sure!" she says brightly. "We're on break anyhow!" She feels like a complete moron, but she follows him when he turns and rounds the corner toward the English office.

No one else is working at school on Saturday except the theater club adviser, and he's a bio teacher, his office three floors up and across the school. Mr. Lorimer closes the office door behind them and takes his seat behind a desk. Miranda sits in the student chair on the other side, the way she would if this were a regular conference during regular school time. She perches on the edge, stares down at her hands as she laces and unlaces her fingers. Mr. Lorimer is silent, waiting, as if she's done something wrong and he knows and he's waiting for the confession. And she knows that's not it—knows that's not at all what this is about—but the gall of being wrong about his intentions, the terrible moment that would ensue if she were the first to broach the idea, that's what keeps her silent, keeps her thinking, *Maybe this really isn't what I think it is.*

"I knew it was you," Mr. Lorimer says finally, letting out his breath as though he's been holding it forever.

Miranda raises her eyes to his for the first time. She squints slightly, her brow furrowed.

"I knew when I got it it was you," he says again. He looks so desperate to Miranda, so alone.

"What was me?" she asks. "What did I do?"

Through his trauma, he smiles a little, a flash of his usual flirtatious smirk. "Do you want this to keep being a game, Miranda? I thought your note meant that you were tired of playing it as a game. We can keep up the game if you want. I *am* infected. I'll keep playing." He's so earnest Miranda doesn't even know how to begin asking what she needs to ask.

"You're *infected*?" she says, cautiously. "What do you mean you're *infected*?"

His look is shifting from apoplexy to puzzlement. As if it is his last resort, the last trick he has up his magician's sleeve, he pulls open his desk drawer and reaches down into its depths. His hand comes up bearing a small scrap of paper torn from a loose-leaf pad. He passes this across the table to Miranda, so careful not to touch her hand that he drops it from a good half foot above her hand and it misses her, instead wafting to the floor at her feet. She has to bend down to retrieve it.

Poor worm, reads the note, *thou art infected!*

"I didn't write this," Miranda says. She looks at the paper again, then passes it back to him across the table. This time their fingertips brush, and Mr. Lorimer snatches back his hand as if from a hot pot on the stove he'd reached for unthinkingly, and without a pot holder.

"You didn't write it?" he repeats, almost to himself.

"No," she says.

He looks up at her again, his eyes sharp, like someone snapping out of a trance. "Would you tell me if you had?" he says, quick and pointed, then stares down again, like he's bracing himself for a response he's not going to be able to bear.

Slowly, deliberately, Miranda waits for him to raise his head again. When he does, what she says is: "Yes," and they stare at each other then for a long time, trying to read what that yes might mean in one another's eyes.

It's Miranda who speaks first. She smiles a little, offering: *"You look wearily . . ."*

A wave of relief crosses his face and he speaks gratefully. *"No, noble mistress, 'tis fresh morning with me / When you are by . . ."*

Another minute of silence goes by. He is gearing toward something, plotting, blocking it through in his head. "I'm twenty-three years old," he admits, as if this explains something.

Miranda nods.

He tosses up his hands. "I can't just go around deflowering my students!" he cries, his voice an impassioned whisper.

Miranda cocks her head at him, inquisitive: "You've slept with students before?" she asks him.

"No, no, no, of course not, no, that's not what I mean, I mean I can't just go and be with a student. It's totally unethical, it's . . . I can't do it. I've been driving myself insane for months. *You've* been driving me insane for months . . ."

Months? she thinks, and knows then that he's already written her far deeper into this than she's had any idea.

"I think," he says, his guard dropped and surrendered, "I think I want you so much I don't even know what's right or wrong anymore. I think I'm losing my fucking mind over—"

Now Miranda cuts him off, catching her own breath first, as it seems to have escaped her. Her stomach goes light, as if her body has been relieved of all substance. "I'm eighteen. Legal," she says, and as she speaks she can feel the confidence flooding into her blood like oxygen, her laurels sliding in beneath her like they were made for resting upon. "And you'd have had to come along about five years ago if you wanted to be the one doing the deflowering."

Mr. Lorimer looks at her, definitely surprised.

"And you're not in time to be number two either, but I could still fit you in as number three if you'd like . . ."

He laughs for real then, and the sound is a relief to them both. Then Miranda starts to say something but he stops her before she can. "Watch it, I might be forced to propose marriage to you immediately. Just be warned . . ."

"Whoa," Miranda says, her smile broad and sure and sly. "First things first."

22

Just Like a Pretty-Boy

Alex was beautiful. Darrin had to give Miranda that much.

"He's a sweetie," Miranda said.

Darrin pondered that. Alex seemed too oblivious to be sweet. "I guess," Darrin said. She was lying in the trundle bed watching Miranda get ready for school. Alex wasn't a jerk, just sort of flaky and cute, with a superficial intensity and an annoying way of responding to everything with a smirky, vague "Right on" that sounded almost like a question the way his voice rose at the end of the phrase. He said "Right on" as if to indicate that "Right on" might be what he'd say if he were to answer you. Darrin had known a boy like that the previous summer at an arts program in Los Angeles. He was from Santa Monica. Once they'd gone for a hike together, and he'd moved with the slow awe of Dorothy seeing the world in color for the first time. Passing a grove of manzanita, he'd paused dramatically. "What if the trees moved and, like, talked, and they were all, *Hey there,* and we were all, *Hey, how's it goin'?* and they were all, *Fine, thanks,* you know, and we just kept walking." This seemed to strike him as something he'd need to really think about in depth sometime. Darrin spent the rest of the summer hanging out alone or with her roommate, Grace, a violinist who found sitting in a coffee shop and reading the *New York Times* together a perfectly companionable activity.

"Well," Miranda said, hefting her book bag up to her shoulder so that she slouched seductively under its weight, "I'll be home by three. There's food in the fridge, TV, books." She gestured to the bookcase that lined the wall of her bedroom. "And if you want to hang out with Alex, just knock up there. Good-bye, love," she said, tossing a kiss in the vicinity of Darrin's cheek. "Have fun!" She closed the bedroom door behind her.

It was February. Darrin and Miranda were seniors in high school. Back in Denver, Darrin's school had a week off for "midwinter recess." Miranda's school in Brooklyn, as she put it, "didn't get squat." Somehow, though, when Miranda said it she made that sound far cooler than having a week's vacation. But Miranda had a way of making most things she did—even if they were things that everybody did on a regular basis—sound fun, and always somewhat daring. Miranda had, in the years Darrin had known her, been able to make braces seem fashionable, a broken arm look sexy, and her parents' divorce sound like a Woody Allen screenplay. Miranda could make dental floss enticing.

The day before, Darrin had gone to school with Miranda, gotten special dispensation to attend her friend's classes, and finally put faces with the names she'd been hearing Miranda talk about for years. But today Darrin was staying home with Alex. She pulled on a pair of Miranda's sweatpants and made her way up to the kitchen. On the counter was a note from Roz.

Mir & Dar—

    I'll bring home sushi tonite from the city? Call me @ the office. Is it maki we like? Are those the little rolls?

What do you say if you want them with the rice and the little sesame seeds on the outside the way they do that? Call me.
XOXOXOX,
Mom (aka Roz)

Darrin adored Miranda's mom. She was wacky and neurotic and doting and Darrin found it discouraging that Roz didn't have a battalion of suitors beating down the door. One night the previous summer when Darrin had gone with Roz and Miranda to the Cape for a week, Roz had gotten kind of drunk on homemade daiquiris while they all played Scrabble and listened to tapes of Roz's old scratchy records—Laura Nyro, Melanie, Joni Mitchell, Janis. "There it is," Roz had chimed in during some Joni Mitchell tune. "There's the explanation of it all." She was lying back on the couch, staring off the screened porch to the water and smoking, deeply, a Marlboro Light, which she only did, she swore, when she got drunk in a cabin with two seventeen-year-olds. She hopped up and rewound the song, hushing the girls until her line came around. *"You don't like weak women, you get bored so quick, and you don't like strong women 'cause they're hip to your tricks,"* Roz sang to Darrin and Miranda.

"Well, *there's* something no one thought of before," Miranda said flatly. Miranda was perfectly lovely to Darrin's folks when she visited Colorado. To Roz, though, she could be a serious bitch. Or just a sullen pain in the ass. But sometimes they got along brilliantly, laughing, teasing, more friends than relatives, and at those times Darrin was envious. Her own parents were just her parents, no more and no less, as she was sure they'd always be. Miranda's situation—however much Miranda might complain about it— seemed far more sophisticated than Darrin's would ever be.

"It's not the idea, Miran," Roz had said, blowing smoke rings into the air above her head. She closed her eyes the way Darrin's father did when he listened to opera on the radio. "It's the way she says it. The simplicity. The clarity. It's just so . . . right."

"My mother," Miranda said to Darrin, "is drunk."

"Your mother," said Roz, "of whom we all now happen to be speaking in the third person, is quite certainly not sober in the slightest."

Miranda and Darrin laughed. Roz did too.

Later, upstairs in their room, tucked into their twin beds like Jan and Marcia, under the emboldening spell of darkness, Darrin said, "Your mom's amazing."

"She's a piece of work all right," said Miranda.

"She's fabulous," Darrin countered.

"She's certifiable," Miranda said, yawning.

"Why are you such a bitch to her?" Darrin said, and they were both a little taken aback to hear such a line come out of Darrin's mouth. Immediately Darrin regretted it, feared making Miranda upset or angry, feared causing a rift between them in a place where no rift should be.

But Miranda hadn't been upset or angry at all; in fact she'd seemed sort of pleased and—Darrin knew this was weird, but couldn't help feeling it—almost relieved. She said, "She's my mom . . ." like it was a question. As if she wanted to check that she'd given Darrin a suitable answer. It was an odd and strangely important shift in the dynamic between the girls, and it still had a somewhat mystifying effect on them both.

DARRIN TOASTED A BAGEL AND DRANK WHAT WAS LEFT of a pot of coffee someone had brewed earlier that morning. There was a disheveled *New York Times* on the table, and she flipped through, the pages sounding loud as thunder in the morning quiet. She skimmed headlines wondering how things might be different if she'd done her growing-up here, where the tight urban density seemed to press people thin and mature them fast. Render them prematurely chic. Darrin was still waiting to hear from colleges. What she really wanted was to go to art school; she was even more determined to do so in Manhattan. She'd applied to Cooper Union, NYU, Columbia, and Barnard. Now it was just a matter of the wait.

BY THE TIME ALEX WANDERED DOWN TO THE KITCHEN Darrin had filled in everything she could on the crossword puzzle, scanned the stock reports, and practically memorized the day's TV listings.

"Hey," said Alex.

"Hey," Darrin said. She folded the newspaper hastily, as if to conceal what she'd been doing. Alex's presence was daunting, mostly, Darrin thought, because he was so freaking beautiful. She tried to imagine herself being as unfazed by Alex as Roz was: above that sort of silliness, so far past girly. But Darrin's reaction to Alex was base, so instinctually reactive it wasn't something she had time to check before she was plunked inside the feeling itself. Wanting Alex was like those Schoolhouse Rock sketches that used to come on between Saturday morning cartoons on TV when Darrin was little. There was one about the nervous system. *There's a telegraph line, you got yours and I got mine. It's called the nervous system. And everybody understands those telegram commands and you know that everybody better listen.* Like swatting a fly or pulling your hand away from a hot stove, desiring Alex seemed to be something her body just did on its own. Darrin wasn't sure her brain was involved at all.

Alex poured himself a bowl of cereal and sat down at the kitchen table across from Darrin. His mouth full, he gestured to the ill-folded newspaper using his cereal spoon and the arch of one eyebrow. It was a coy gesture, and Darrin noticed for the first time how like Miranda this man was. Unassumingly sexual in even the most mundane movements. Darrin wondered if Alex knew this about himself. If Miranda did, for that matter. If they used it, consciously, in whatever ways they could, or if it was a power more like sight: you opened your eyes and you saw.

"So," said Alex, "just visiting from out of town?"

"Yeah," Darrin said, "just visiting." She wished she had something to do with herself there at the kitchen table. Like smoke, or knit. Learn a foreign language. "How long are *you* here for?" she asked. It didn't seem to be an illegitimate question.

Alex gestured again with his spoon, circles spiraling out into the infinity beyond an arm's length. He swallowed. "I'm going to Guatemala at some point," he said. "Mexico, Nicaragua, El Salvador. My girlfriend teaches, so maybe summer, but maybe I'll go by myself. We'll see . . ." It was just like a pretty-boy, Darrin thought, to make some deliberate mention of a girlfriend three seconds into any conversation. *I know you're thinking about me,* it said, *but don't. I'm taken.* And they were always taken by some girl who was clearly so much cooler. Some girl, like Wing, who you'd think could have any man she wanted. The women of the pretty-boys were always gorgeous, but in an interesting, imperfect way. They had crooked noses, or heavily blond-downed upper lips, childbearing hips, intriguing scars. They were smart and driven, confident, outspoken. And hopeful. You could practically see the hope rising in them like yeast feeding on any drop of sweetness tossed its way. Their breastbones pushed up against their skin like something trying to break through. They looked at their pretty-boys with an expectancy bordering on desperation, the way a parent watches a disabled child for any sign of progress, any indication of movement toward normalcy. Eventually—well, Darrin didn't know what happened eventually. Maybe they stopped hoping. But she wondered if that meant they gave up on the boy, or gave in to him. *That* she just didn't know.

When he finished his cereal, Alex pulled a pipe and a rolled-up Ziploc baggie from the pocket of the frayed, splotchy khakis he'd been wearing the night before when Darrin and Miranda had gone up to watch TV with him and Wing.

"Dube?" Alex said.

"Excuse me?" said Darrin.

"Smoke?" he asked again.

Darrin didn't smoke. She looked at her watch. "Little early," she said.

"No such time," Alex corrected her. "No such time," he repeated. "That's cool. I respect that," he assured Darrin in a way that was neither assuring nor respectful. He grabbed a box of Strike Anywheres from the shelf above the stove. While Alex smoked, Darrin reclaimed the crossword puzzle. She filled things in because they fit, not because they were right.

"So you're a friend of Miranda's?" Alex squinted across the table.

No, an old college buddy of Roz's, she wanted to say. Moron. She nodded instead.

"Cool," Alex said. *I, Alex, deem you cool.* It wouldn't be long, Darrin thought, before his personality so devalued his aesthetic appeal that she'd be able to look at him without any shortness of breath at all.

It was maybe twelve-thirty when the doorbell rang. Darrin and Alex had moved out to the living room, where Alex put an insipid Phish bootleg in the tape deck and sprawled himself across the couch, where he lay tapping his fingers against his sternum in a sort of reciprocal beat with the music. Darrin had pulled a book off the shelf—*What Color Is Your Parachute?*—but continued to stare up at the towering bookcases that lined the wall. She already knew what color her goddamn parachute was. Alex's presence was beginning to compel her to swear, rampantly. She wondered what that meant. Roz's bookshelves were crammed full, the contents arranged according to no overriding structure, thematic, alphabetical, or otherwise. Darrin wondered if any of them were Miranda's dad's, remnants of that once-upon-a-time marriage. You couldn't have pinned down a singular individual from looking at those bookcases. There were self-help books and texts on economic theory, LSAT prep courses and Shakespearean plays interspersed with *Snoopy Digest* and old copies of *Poetry Northeast* and *SKI* magazine. Darrin hadn't drunk enough coffee that morning, and her body could tell. Phish rankled through the weedy air and she could feel her eyes wanting to close. Titles loomed out from the bookshelf and then receded, and she found herself fitting the words she read to the tune she was hearing, titles morphing into parodies of themselves: *Fear of Flying Where the Sidewalk Ends, Rabbit Run To the Lighthouse, A Very Young Dancer For Whom the Bell Tolls.* Darrin giggled despite herself. Then the doorbell rang. She thought maybe she'd go make another pot of coffee.

Alex bounded up from the couch like an anxious teenager waiting on a date. He was, in fact, Darrin knew, only twenty-three.

"Sto-ker!" Alex shouted, flinging open the front door. There was a moment of backslapping and cheek-kissing camaraderie that you only ever saw between hippie boys, the same men who wore Indian print skirts around the house and didn't seem to share the pervasive phobia of being mistaken for homosexual that afflicted the majority of the straight male population.

Alex led his friend into the living room and introduced him. Alex did, to his credit, attempt a sort of politeness, cloying and fractured as it was. "Hey," he said, "this is my good friend Stoker. Stoke, this is—hey, I apologize, tell me your name again?"

"Darrin," said Darrin.

"Sweet," said Stoker. He turned his attention back to Alex. "Dude," he said. "So, dude, what's been happening?"

This man, who could not have been younger than thirty-five, made Darrin feel like a grandmother. Or maybe like someone's old maiden aunt. Her voice, when she spoke, had a patronizing cast she found she was aware of but oddly unable to control. "Can I get you some coffee, Stoker?" She said his name like she was June Cleaver talking to Wally's friend, Eddie Haskell. "I was just going to put up a pot."

"Yeah," said Stoker. "Sweet. Thanks."

Darrin turned to Alex.

"I can't have caffeine," he said. "Too intense." He grinned. He might have just stepped off the pages of *GQ*. He was truly stunning.

Darrin turned toward the kitchen, and something came out of her mouth, and as she found the filters and measured out the French Roast she wondered if she had actually spoken the words "Very well then" as she retreated. "Very well then," she repeated, flicking the coffeemaker on. The water began to gurgle inside. "Very well then," she said again. She couldn't tell how she felt about the sound of those words in her voice. She thought perhaps it was somewhat pleasing.

When Darrin came back out of the kitchen bearing two cups of coffee, a third person had joined Stoker and Alex in the living room. He was splayed across Roz's Turkish rug and appeared to be already completely stoned.

"Would your friend care for some coffee?" Darrin's disdain was growing more and more apparent.

"Yeah," said the friend. "Thanks." He reached up to take one of the cups Darrin was carrying. She passed the other to Stoker and went back to pour another one for herself. She slammed a cabinet, clanked the silverware drawer shut. Silly, she knew. They were not boys who sensed when someone else was feeling a little offended.

Darrin carried her coffee back into the living room and sank down into the armchair opposite the bookcase. Peripherally she could see the boys, lounging, drumming, sitting up occasionally to sip at their coffees. Darrin stared at the books. *Looking for Mr. Goodbar Out on a Limb*. She snickered to herself. *Our Bodies, Our-*

selves Our Gang. She wished she could share these with somebody. Wished Miranda and Roz were there to laugh with her, goad each other on to funnier, more outlandish conglomerate titles, outdoing themselves each time. *Learning to Love The Naked and the Dead, The Joy of Sex Of Mice and Men, The Joy of Cooking Sons and Lovers.* Like knock-knock jokes, or bad puns, or misheard song lyrics. If Roz and Miranda had been there, Darrin would be so content. It wasn't what you did, she thought, but who you were with that made all the difference.

Stoker stretched, glanced around. "Anyone got the time?" he asked the air.

"Near two," said the friend.

"I gotta head out soon, man," Stoker said.

Alex stood up as if he'd heard his cue, disappeared up the stairs, and returned a minute later carrying an assortment of plastic baggies in one hand and what looked to Darrin like a postal scale in the other. He set everything down on the coffee table and plunked himself down cross-legged, rubbing his hands together like someone about to enjoy a huge meal, or execute some devilish scheme. From the bookshelf, titles rose out at Darrin like she was wearing 3-D glasses. *I've Had It In the Shadow of Man, The Family of Women Learn to Say No.* She laughed out loud, realizing only as she heard it herself.

Alex looked up from his weighing and parceling. "What's funny, Funny Girl?" he said, and without waiting for a response turned back to Stoker. "How much can I do you for, bro?"

There was a pause while Stoker dug out the contents of his pockets and counted up the cash. Darrin looked quickly back to the bookcase, then spun on Alex. "What the hell do you think you're doing?" she demanded.

Alex smiled up at her blandly, as if awaiting patiently the punch line of the joke.

"You're dealing drugs out of someone else's house?!"

Alex's face relaxed into a smarmy and patronizing grin of

understanding. "Chill, sweetheart." His voice veritably oozed sincerity. "We're all friends here."

"You're not *my* friends," Darrin shrilled, "You're not *Roz's* friends, asshole."

"Chill *out*, sweetheart," Alex said again, more imperatively this time.

"Don't . . . ," Darrin started, "just don't even . . ." and she wanted to throw them all out right then, only that seemed absurd; it wasn't even her house. Alex was, in addition to whatever *else* he was, a rent-paying tenant. And suddenly there just wasn't any more she could say or do, struck by the ridiculousness of it all. She simply pushed her chair out of the way, set her mug—still full of coffee—down on the table, and went down to Miranda's room, where she crashed onto the bed, and in the blindness of her fuming rage she promptly fell asleep.

WHEN SHE WOKE, THE CLOCK BESIDE THE BED SAID ten past three. Miranda would be home shortly. The house above was quiet, and Darrin crept up the stairs and peered into the living room. Stoker and the other friend had gone, and Alex lay alone on the couch, his head tossed back in sleep. As Darrin watched the sprawl of Alex's beautiful form, every few seconds his body gave a twitch, the spastic jerk of an arm, a leg. Like a hyperactive child, Darrin thought, lurching down to a nap, and she couldn't help imagining herself lying there beside him, naked, their bodies tacky with sex and sweat. She imagined what it would be like to be the woman he loved, watching him there as he twitched in sleep, shots of static energy shooting sparks through his limbs like devils forking their way into the world.

23

INCLEMENT WEATHER FOR TRAVEL

ALEX FINALLY LEFT AT THE END OF MAY TO TRAVEL IN Central America, and Wing was by turns ecstatic and apoplectic. Though Roz hated to see her so distraught, something about being turned to for advice in matters of the heart made her feel maternally valuable. Whatever romantic sagas her own daughter might be embroiled in, Roz was clearly not the person to whom Miranda confided such things. And Miranda knew how it hurt Roz to be at a distance from the goings-on of her daughter's life. Miranda played this leveraging advantage as her trump, performing alternately as a huffy, eye-rolling teenager and as a pouty only child who was about to move away from home in a few months and whose mother seemed far more concerned with the welfare of a total stranger than she was with her own daughter, *sniff sniff, pout pout. Two can play at your game, Miranda,* Roz wanted to say. *Touché.*

As a high school graduation gift, Roz had wanted to rent a cabin in the Adirondacks, take Miranda and Darrin away for a weekend to their old camp stomping grounds. Miranda and Roz seemed to get along much better when Darrin was around, and whether it was that Darrin brokered a peace between them, or kept them in line with one another, or just raised their spirits, it worked.

The awaited Adirondack weekend was only a few days away when Darrin's mother called from Colorado. Darrin's grandmother had passed away, and with the funeral Darrin wouldn't be able to come East after all. The cabin slept three, and Roz knew they'd need to fill that third bed if she and Miranda were both going to live through the weekend. In a panic to find someone to run interference on such short notice, Roz invited Wing, who had been at loose ends with way too much time on her hands since school had let out for the summer.

"Great," Miranda said, "some graduation present. A weekend cooped up with you two."

Roz sent up a prayer for the weekend not to turn into a complete nightmare.

It had been years since Roz last drove this route upstate to the Adirondack Mountains. The Visiting Day route is how she thought of it. As they moved north, everyone's mood improved, even Miranda's; she seemed so excited by familiar landmarks pointing the way to camp that she forgot to be pissy. Just past Glens Falls, the profusion of Lake George signs came into bloom and I-87 became the Adirondack Northway ("America's Most Scenic Highway 1968"). The towns got smaller, the hills bigger, the hills now mountains, the blacktop on which they drove so clearly an intrusion upon this green-growing land. Miranda, in the backseat, swore the name of every town sounded familiar— Schroon Lake! North Hudson! Elizabethtown! She shrieked with glee at each passing road sign, then tried to temper her enthusiasm when she saw how vicariously happy it made Roz.

"God, you know what's so weird," Miranda said, "just that all this *stuff* exists." She gestured out the car windows. "At camp it's like the whole world is camp. You don't imagine anything outside of it. Like people who actually live in the Adirondacks. To us the Adirondacks *was* camp. Plus a Tastee-Freez where we went for ice cream once a summer, and some rock-climbing gear store where the counselors shopped on their days off. And then, like a trillion miles away across Lake Champlain, in Burlington, there was Ben and Jerry's. But that was it practically."

Roz remembered that Ben and Jerry's all too well, the scene of an unfortunate temper tantrum one Visiting Day long ago. God, how she'd worried then that Miranda was on her way to becoming a very high-strung little girl . . .

"God, and the mountains!" Miranda was saying now. "We totally thought of the mountains like they were people . . ."

Roz was happy listening to Miranda prattle on. It was this quality in Miranda's voice that she missed. The voice that wanted to tell Roz *everything*, to narrate the whole world as it unfolded around her.

"Some mountains were big and friendly," Miranda said. "They fed you gorp and wild blueberries and had names like Jo and Esther and Giant's Wife. And then there were the intimidating, cowboy mountains saying, like: *Climb us if you can.* Like Macomb and Dix . . . Saddleback, Hough. Or the really terrifying, totally irresistible ones like Gothics and Whiteface and Wolfjaw. And Wright—"

"Wright," Roz said, "that rings a bell . . ."

Wing, who had been quiet in the passenger seat, chimed in now. "There was a plane crash on Wright if I'm not mistaken," she said.

In the rearview mirror Roz could see Miranda's expression sour: this was her story, not Wing's. Wright was *her* mountain. Roz directed her question to Miranda as if Wing had never spoken at all. "What happened on Wright, Miran?"

Miranda seemed to derive some odd pleasure from seeing Roz spurn Wing. This fascinated Roz: how Miranda could be so elusive and opaque about some things, and then such an open book about others, so easily charmed, so unbelievably gullible.

" . . . When we climbed Wright, Rattlesnake year at camp, no, maybe it was Sugarloaf . . . ? No, no, it was Rattlesnake, 'cause we had Brenda . . . anyway, so when we did Wright, Astrid found a whole clump of wires from like the cockpit or something that were all scorched or something. It was really creepy. You can see the whole engine, it's totally embedded in the rock on top right where it crashed into the mountain . . ."

Miranda went on with her tale of Wright Peak—an Air Force bomber meandering miles off course during a winter storm—and her voice had the runaway frenzy of a child. Roz wondered if Miranda's friends ever got to hear this voice. Or did they just get the cool one, the voice of a Miranda reticent with disdain? And guys—when Miranda talked to boys, what voice came out of her lips then? In front of her teachers Roz had seen Miranda display a mixture of earnest regard and ditsy subservience. But the teachers already knew she was smart. They saw the papers, the grade reports, the files. But the boys—Roz was certain they found Miranda cute, but what did they make of her when they got beyond cute?

When they stopped for a bathroom break, Miranda ran ahead toward the convenience store. Roz and Wing ambled over, chatting. Roz said, "Now that she's graduated from Emmons, do we get to break our nondisclosure pact and gossip about my daughter?" They pushed through the doors, Wing smiling fiendishly. Miranda was already on her way out, crossing the store in long strides. Passing the candy rack, she grabbed a sack of Skittles and pitched them to Roz, who reacted in a split-second shift and caught it. "Snacks on you, Mamacita?" Miranda called back, but it wasn't a question. She was already gone, a whoosh of golden hair and the *ding ding ding* of door chimes.

.   .   .

IT WAS EVENING WHEN THEY ARRIVED AT THE LONG Lake cabin, the air already cooling to that nighttime chill Roz remembered well from Visiting Days at Sunset Lake. You could be running around all day in the sun, swimming in the lake in the heat of the season, and then at night the temperature could dip so low you'd need hats and wool socks, long underwear even. As they walked down the pine lane toward the cabin, setting-sun rays streaking across the lake, Miranda was overcome— "The smell of camp!" she cried ecstatically. Roz grinned. Miranda was in her element. This was how Roz had envisioned the trip: a weekend for Miranda in the place where she had always been most herself.

The house was a North Country standard: a rustic cabin outfitted like an old Adirondack camp: heavy pine furniture, the requisite deer heads, heavy woolen blankets, kitchen shelves stocked with mismatched stoneware, a steep herd-trail of a path leading down to the lake, an aluminum canoe hitched to a withering dock. The house smelled of pine, and of mothballs and must, and before anything else, Roz made her way around the place opening the shuttered windows to let the lake air blow in through the screens. Struggling to uncleat the sailor's knots that kept the shutters battened and then to hoist the ropes that would raise them, Roz couldn't help but think of Edwin. She could almost see him there in the role that Wing took on now, following Roz around with a broom, cleaning cobwebs from the corners of the screens.

As the house aired out and Roz unpacked the groceries they lugged in from the car—the "camp food" Miranda insisted on for this trip: marshmallows, Bisquick, hot cocoa mix, and individual packets of flavored oatmeal—Miranda and Wing dug out their swimsuits for one quick jump in the lake before dark. Miranda's suit—a new cotton bikini flowered pink and white with dots of yellow and green leaves—was not something Roz recognized, and when Wing complimented Miranda on it she spat out something about its being a gift from a friend and then went hurtling into the chilly lake. A friend, Roz thought. A friend who gave her skimpy bikinis? She had a question: *Who is he, Miran?* She felt mischievous: there was a little teasing to be done.

Roz cornered Wing while Miranda was in the shower. She felt vaguely criminal in a rather delightful way, completely unable to stop herself. "Does she have a boyfriend?" Roz asked. Her own voice was flirty, she knew.

"Not so far as I know," Wing said. She thought a moment. "There was that thing with Ben Stone, right, but you told me about that. Before my time at Emmons . . ."

Roz shook her head. "You know, and I still can't figure out if they were just friends or what?"

"Or if they just bonded over everything with you and Steven . . ."

"Exactly," Roz said. "But I'm starting to think there's someone now. Tell me that isn't the kind of suit a boy would buy just to see her put it on?"

Wing laughed. "You're enjoying this, aren't you?"

Roz opened the fridge, held a beer out to Wing, who accepted. She reached back in for another. A flick, flick of caps and they clinked lite beers.

"I'll torture it out of her," Roz said. "Ve haf vays uf maykink zem talk, you know . . ."

By the time they ate dinner Roz had cracked out the Joni Mitchell. The lite beer had gone quite nicely to her head, and with towels draped over banisters, magazines scattered on tables, and bratwursts sizzling under the broiler, the cabin began to feel cozily inhabited.

Roz sang her way to the table with a plate of cucumber salad, swinging her hips through the kitchen doorway. "*I used to count lovers like railroad cars, I counted them on my side. Lately I don't count on nothing, I just let things slide...*" She sidled up to the table, presenting the platter before Miranda like service for the queen.

"Someone's drunk," Miranda said.

"Am not," Roz said, sliding into her seat, a slice of cucumber already in her mouth.

Wing came to the table with a bag of hot dog rolls, and she tossed one to Miranda, who had to lean out of her chair to catch it.

"And she's running for the end zone..." Roz did her sports announcer voice. "Is that where they run?" she asked.

Miranda shrugged. Wing laughed. They ate. *Good,* Roz thought. *We're OK, we're good.*

Her mouth full of food, Roz had a thought, started to speak, thought better of it, and finished chewing. Miranda and Wing waited. Finally, after a swig of beer, Roz said, "Edwin loved bratwurst." She started to laugh.

Miranda rolled her eyes.

Roz felt a sudden, irrepressible desire to drink her daughter under the table and make her stay there awhile. "May I get you a beer, darling?" she asked, diabolically sweetly.

Miranda stuck out a hand and felt her mother's forehead for fever.

"Oops, that's illegal, isn't it?" Roz remembered herself.

Miranda and Wing nodded.

"I'd plead self-defense," Roz claimed.

"Well, it's OK with me," Miranda said. She grabbed Roz's bottle and started to drink.

Roz followed her first instinct and swiped the bottle away from Miranda. Perhaps she did so with a little more force than she intended—she would turn this over in her brain a long while before she fell asleep that night: how much guilt she needed to feel, how much was Miranda and her dramatics. Roz snatched the bottle back from Miranda's hand, and as she did, the bottle knocked against one of Miranda's front teeth. Roz heard the sound, pulled her hand back immediately, utterly sobered by her concern. "Oh!" she cried. "Oh, Miran, I'm sorry! You OK, kid?"

But Miranda had already taken up a cry of her own. "Fuck!" she said, loud, and mean-sounding. Like she *wanted* to sound mean. "Ow! What the fuck, Mom? Ouch." She held onto her front tooth with her thumb and forefinger, testing its hold in her mouth. Roz felt a wave of panic, like sickness, rushing over her.

"Miran, let me see. Babe, let me see, please . . ."

Miranda's countenance was nastily angry. She let go of the tooth, and it seemed that she was fine. No blood, no tears. It looked like she was fine. "You could try to be a little carefuller," Miranda said, her voice curt with indignation.

And there was something about her tone—so haughty and disdainful and mocking—and that must have been what compelled both Roz and Wing to do what they did next, because it *was* mean of them. Because they *were* dropping to Miranda's level. "More careful," they corrected her in unison. And when they heard themselves—the grammarians!—they both dissolved into laughter.

Of course, it only made Miranda madder. "Fine," she said, now audibly riled, "crack my tooth and then correct my fucking grammar."

Roz felt suddenly stern. "Miranda, watch it," she said.

"Fuck you," Miranda told her.

Wing just sat tight-lipped across the table, smiling inwardly, waiting for the turmoil to pass.

"Don't," Roz said. "Please just don't, Miranda. Can't we just have a nice time here, please . . ." She could hear her own voice bleeding into a whine, and Roz knew that all Miranda could be thinking was: *Lame.*

Miranda pushed herself away from the table and stood. "Whatever," she said, stalking off upstairs to her room. "En-joy," she called, smarmy and vicious, from the top of the stairs. Then she turned on her heel and slammed the door.

Roz and Wing sat in stunned silence at the table, their

bratwursts looking up at them like forlorn worms. After a minute, feeling whipped and nearly winded, Roz spoke. "*What* just happened?" she asked.

"I have no idea," Wing said, shaking her head in disbelief.

They both laughed then, seeing themselves, stranded there in the wake of Miranda, Hurricane Miranda, having wreaked her havoc, raging silently upstairs now, downgraded to a tropical storm. It was true that when it came to Miranda, Roz often felt like a traveler: stuck at the airport, watching the weather, estimated time of departure unknown.

24

THE ARDOR OF THE LIVER

THE SUMMER BEFORE SHE GOES TO COLLEGE MIRANDA gets a job scooping ice cream on the Upper West Side of Manhattan at a Häagen-Dazs that happens, conveniently, to be quite near the home of her friend Judson Blumberg. The Blumbergs are a laissez-faire sort of clan: during the summer Judson's mother rarely leaves the family's Hamptons beach house, venturing into the city only when word reaches her of a fabulous closeout sale at Kenneth Cole or a markdown on Prada bags. Judson's father is a high-powered something or other who likely keeps a few trophy girlfriends handily stashed in case he should find himself in need of one, the way a diabetic might tuck hard candies into purses, drawers, and coat pockets in anticipation of an emergency. It seems equally likely that Judson's mother gets herself regularly laid by her tennis instructor or her golf pro or some other such person with very white teeth and terry-cloth wristbands. Judson is the youngest of four—two older brothers and a sister—and his folks have tired of doing the parental thing. This relative freedom has engendered in Judson an independence that is not so much reckless as it is grandiose. Judson is a big talker, but when his house comes to renown as a dependable spot for debauchery, Judson himself is neither the debaucher nor the debauchee. He is the master of ceremonies, the keeper of the brothel, the maître d'. He is the professional and attentive concierge: there's always orange juice in the morning, Sara Lee pastries in the freezer, and clean towels in the bathroom, and Judson, at all costs, protects his guests from discovery and disclosure. He is a good friend and a bad enemy, and it seems clear that Judson Blumberg will one day make a valuable confidant and ally to politicians, mafiosi, and other wealthy incognitos.

It is convenient, Miranda tells her mother—for convenience is always something Roz can appreciate—that Judson lives so close by the ice cream shop, because Miranda can thus work the late shift, for which she will be better paid, and then go crash at Judson's. Roz has known Judson since his prepubescence, finds him a decent boy somewhat frightened of girls, and won't mind particularly if her daughter *is* having sex with him (though Miranda surely is not). The plan is agreed upon by all. Especially Judson's mother, who takes the opportunity to chat up her manicurist and her tennis partners and the ladies with whom she lunches at overpriced cafés about the "little chickadee" that her Judson is having as his last high school fling.

Of course, none of that is true. A block from Judson, in a prewar apartment building whose dank, marbled lobby has the aura of an eastern European bathhouse, lives part-time bicycle racer and neighborhood Humbert Humbert: Corbin Lorimer, English teacher.

AT MIDNIGHT WHEN MIRANDA'S SHIFT ENDS SHE SLIPS into the employee bathroom and strips off her Flavor T-shirt (usually STRAWBERRY, printed boldly across the back as if it were her name and she a baseball player and not a minimum-wage worker up to her elbows in Swiss Chocolate Almond) and changes into something specifically suggestive yet casual, offhandedly alluring, and provocatively nymphlike but not too childish. Then, when she's closed down the store and padlocked its steel window fencing until morning, Miranda walks down Columbus Avenue past the bistros whose clientele spill out from the sidewalk tables into the street, and the all-night Korean vegetable markets where young men sit on upturned milk crates shelling peas or bunching fresh-cut tulips.

Judson's door is not often answered by Judson himself, but by Dean or Chris or Kirk or another of the pack of boys who seem to have taken up residence at Judson's side. Most of them just graduated, guys who've stuck around to do summer school, guys who drink too much and manage consistently to fail some course or another during the regular school year. At Judson's, cans of Bud crack open with the frequency of gunfire in a bad neighborhood, and the boys are engaged in an ever-ongoing game of poker that Miranda suspects they play not because they enjoy it but because they imagine it a mature thing to do.

Never planned or choreographed, the seduction ritual varies. Each time it happens they have to pretend they don't know it will happen: perhaps Miranda will rise from the poker table at one-thirty or two, do a few dishes in the kitchen sink, and make motions toward the door. Maybe then Mr. Lorimer will check his watch, fold his hand, mumble something about an early appointment the next day. Or maybe they'll be more bold, and potentially less suspicious: Mr. Lorimer going out to put Miranda in a cab home, for it isn't ever a good idea for a young woman to be on the street alone so late. No cab will be hailed. Mr. Lorimer slides his key ring round Miranda's finger and she jingles the bunch of keys as she walks away, back to his apartment to wait until Mr. L. can make an innocuous exit from the soiree at Judson's and come expectantly ringing his own doorbell.

"Hey," he says, his eyes eager, body drawn back in calculated restraint.

"Hey yourself."

"What've you been doing?" He digs a hand into his pocket, turns the contents out into a bowl by the door: nickels, dimes, his poker earnings of the evening.

"Nothing."

"Nothing?" he says. They talk like this.

"I leafed through last October's *Esquire,* ate seven green grapes and a dill pickle spear from your fridge, and tried to open the bottle of wine on the counter but I couldn't figure out how to work the corkscrew thingy." She leans against the entrance to the kitchen.

"Seven grapes? You *ate seven* grapes?"

She nods dully.

He comes in close, threads a hand through the hair at the base of her neck, pulls his body in toward hers. "Who said you could eat seven grapes?" he whispers.

"Fuck you," she says.

"Yes, please."

"Pig," she teases.

"Hmm," he grunts, turning away, feigning disinterest.

She stretches out an arm and catches the back of his shirt, tugging.

"So you *like* pigs now, do you?" He spins around to her.

She scowls.

"Maybe you just don't quite know *what* you like . . ."

Miranda cocks her head, eyes rolled in disgust. "Do most women let you get away with lines like that?"

Mr. Lorimer laughs earnestly. "You're hardly most women, Miranda."

She feels inexplicably hurt for a fragment of a moment. Then she goes self-righteous. "At least you realize that then," she says.

"God, Miranda." He shakes his head at her, disbelieving their situation. He wants, it seems, to make her understand the way it looks through his eyes. "You just don't even know . . . You have no idea what this is . . ." There is a plaintive current to his voice, like he is nearing a place of unsure footing.

"Apparently, no. No, apparently I don't."

"Why can't you see it? How can you not see it?" and it is as if he so wants to be the child himself, to look to Miranda for some sort of explanation. It makes him so silly and foppish and she wants to tell him not to be that way, not to lose his edge, not to crumble and supplicate like all the men she can think of except for the through-and-through assholes who you could never really be with anyway because they don't want girls like Miranda; they want slinky fuck-bunnies, girls with kaleidoscope cunts. They don't want what Mr. Lorimer wants. And he knows what he wants: he wants them whip-smart and old for their age. He wants his girls savvy and sassy, with muscular calves and bony shoulders. He wants Miranda.

And she wants him. Sometimes.

He pulls down her underwear there in the kitchen and it feels like a scene from 9½ Weeks, which she likes because it makes what they are doing recognizable; she's seen someone onscreen do something like it before. Sometimes Mr. L. seems too sure in his moves, like he's read a book on lovemaking and memorized the techniques. Other times it seems like he acts that sure because he thinks Miranda is exactly everything he wants. And it feels strangely amazing to be someone's perfect-ness, to be the place where everything comes together right, all the pieces of his desire meeting in Miranda, like a broken china plate held together so all its points of fissure meet and erase the scar. When he pulls her underwear down and lets it hang off her ankle, hoists her other leg up and holds it from under the knee, grinding himself against her—while he does that: she is everything he wants her to be. If she doesn't think too much, or talk, or try to make sense of all the pointed-dart thoughts streaking around her mind. She always manages to break the spell anyway, somehow. It's not intentional, it just happens: she'll have to pee before they do it, or she'll say, "We can do this in the kitchen if you want, but if you don't put on a condom I will kill you and so will my mother," or later, afterward, she'll squirm away in the night, back to Judson's to sleep in a guest room, fully clothed, as if she might at any moment be roused in the darkness and called to action.

BACK IN BROOKLYN, THINGS ARE GRIM. WING IS spending her summer in intensive and informal psychoanalysis with Roz, who comes home from work each evening and counsels the troubled and perennially indecisive Wing until they are both too tired to understand their own psychobabble. Most everything Wing says begins: "I feel like I'm beginning to have an understanding of—" or "I know that having been with him so long discredits my judgment in your eyes, but—" Roz cuts in on the middle of Wing's every thought: "Wing, honey, just listen to what you're saying." They are so well suited to one another that it relieves Miranda, lets her off the daughter hook. Roz finally has someone who willingly takes her advice and actually seems to benefit from it. Miranda doesn't know exactly how Roz would respond to the thing with Mr. Lorimer, but she doesn't think Roz's input, whatever it might be, would lend much clarity to the situation. It isn't that her mom would be Mom-like or stodgy about it; Roz seems to pride herself on nontraditional parental reactions. But Miranda has simply no idea where Roz might come down on this one. She can't talk about it with any of her friends from school for obvious reasons, and anyway, she's starting to think that she doesn't actually really *like* any of her friends from school very much. Darrin is in London until August, being her usual productive, creative, motivated self. Miranda never talks to her father about anything except school and travel plans and weather. Which leaves Judson, who probably already knows pretty much even if he doesn't know *officially* about her and Mr. Lorimer. But Judson has the romantic

IQ of a fire hydrant. Which leaves—although it's awfully problematic and will be complicated for them both—Wing.

Miranda, certain that word of her and Mr. Lorimer must already be spreading through Emmons gossip chains, waits for Wing to confront her (in that concerned way that she must surely be picking up from Roz) and ask just what in hell is going on. But Wing—out of politeness or what, Miranda doesn't know—never says a thing. So one morning at the end of June when Roz has left for work Miranda finally decides to bite the bullet and bring it up herself. They are in the kitchen—Wing reading the paper, Miranda puttering around annoying her—and Miranda drops hints just to see if she can prompt Wing into addressing the thing first.

"So," Miranda begins, hanging half inside the refrigerator looking for something to snack on, "do you hang out with any Emmons people now that school's over?"

"Mmmm, a couple," Wing says, not lifting her eyes from the *Times*, "sometimes, yeah."

Miranda pulls a Coke from the back of the fridge and cracks it open. It fizzes and she catches the spray with her upper lip. "Like who?" she asks. She wipes her mouth on her sleeve.

"Uhh, Karen—Mrs. Hausman," Wing corrects herself. "Trini Holland, Manny Edelbaum, sometimes Fauzia."

"Hmh," Miranda says decisively, as if she's just been handed a very interesting and pertinent piece of classified information.

Wing sips her coffee, eyes glued to the Metro section.

"And what are they all doing for the summer?"

Wing lifts her head. "Well, aren't you just Encyclopedia Brown of Park Slope," she laughs.

Miranda does too. "So I've got some time on my hands . . ."

"Whelp, uh, Karen's busy being very pregnant; Fauzia's translating at Berlitz. Manny does some kind of catalogue mail-order business thing with his cousin so he's in and out of town in the summers, traveling around on business. Trini's teaching summer school at Emmons . . ."

"How about like Ms. Casper and those people from English?"

"I think Rosette's away—maybe the Cape, something like that. Who else is there? Sandy—Mr. Barber—works at a summer camp upstate. Gretchen Laub has a fellowship in Ireland until August."

Miranda sips her Coke. "How about Mr. Lorimer?" she says.

"Corbin? I think he's around the city."

"You should date him," Miranda suggests.

"Mmm, fun," Wing snorts. "I could go watch him bike racing in those tight little shorts . . ."

"You don't think he's hot?" Miranda asks.

"In a sort of a way, I guess . . . Why, Miranda dear? Do *you* think he's hot? Yet another member of the Corbin Lorimer fan club?" Wing taunts.

"Hardly," says Miranda.

"Oh, of course, *hardly,*" Wing teases. "No," Wing says, shaking her head, "no, you're right, though, he's totally the teacher I would've had a crush on as a student. I can completely see that."

"I don't have a *crush* on him," Miranda says.

"Right," says Wing, "of course you don't."

"But *you* should go for it," Miranda says. "I mean, Alex is gone. Why not? You should start dating other people." Miranda thinks: *I sound like my mom.*

"I'll take it under advisement."

"I heard he once got a student pregnant . . . ," Miranda says.

"Has there ever been a remotely attractive male teacher who *wasn't* rumored to have knocked up a student?"

"You never know, though," Miranda says. "It does happen . . ."

"I'm sure it does," Wing says. She flips a newspaper page and looks like she wants to reabsorb herself in world happenings.

There's silence then, Miranda fiddling with her soda-can tab. She breaks it off, then runs it down the side of the can, leaving indented tracks in its wake. "Or maybe," she says, "maybe it's that you've *already had* Mr. Lorimer. Maybe you're just way past all that by now . . ."

"Yeah, that's it, Miran. Corbin and I. While you were messing around with Alex, Corbin Lorimer and I were getting it on in the teachers' lounge."

"I never fooled around with Alex," Miranda says.

"I think this conversation is crossing some lines we probably shouldn't be crossing," Wing says.

"I didn't, though," Miranda insists. "I honestly never fooled around with Alex. I wouldn't have done that. He was your boyfriend. I didn't, ever."

"I know," Wing tells her. "I was kidding. I know. We really shouldn't joke like this, though. It's unprofessional of me, it really is."

Miranda hates it when Wing gets all proper and stodgy. It's like she suddenly forces herself to recall that she's a grown-up and Miranda's just a kid. "I guess," Miranda says. The silence feels awkward now. "You know," she says, "Mr. Lorimer plays cards with the guys who hang out at Judson's house. I mean, he's over there a lot, you know? Just hanging out, shooting the shit, playing poker . . ."

"You're kidding." Wing looks truly shocked.

Miranda shakes her head.

"Ugh," Wing grimaces. "That is so distasteful."

Miranda nods as if to agree, but what spins in her head is not accord.

"God, that's pathetic," Wing says, the implications of the story hitting her one by one. "Does the guy not have friends his own age?"

The front door lock clacks open in the hall and Wing and Miranda both lift their heads to the sound like animals, ears perking at the approach of danger. There is a thudding of things to the floor, then the door slamming shut more forcefully than necessary. "Dammit," they hear, and the voice is Roz's.

"Mom?" Miranda says. She is already pushing out her chair, as though sitting at the table with Wing is an act in which she shouldn't be caught.

Roz enters the kitchen in a state of barely controlled rage. She speaks as if she's been planning her opening line all the way home. "I think a bomb threat at the subway station is a perfectly good excuse to work at home for the day, don't you?"

"You're kidding." Wing says. "At our stop?"

"Oh yes," Roz says, her head waggling in disbelief, eyebrows raised to say: *Of this I wash my hands completely.* She glances around the kitchen, surveying the scene, getting the lay of the land, then plunks down at the table in defeat. Her face seems to ask for distraction: *Someone just start talking please and distract me from my fury!*

Wing answers the call. "So what do *you* think, Roz, about a fresh-out-of-college high school teacher playing poker with students during the summer?"

Roz looks genuinely relieved at the prospect of having something else to think about. "I didn't know you were a gambler, Wing," she begins.

Wing laughs. "Different fresh-out-of-college high school teacher."

"They're mostly graduated," Miranda says. "The guys. The students he plays with." She hovers next to her chair.

"Great," Wing says, dripping with sarcasm.

"It's all guys?" Roz asks. She is treating this like a riddle, a brain-teaser, and she's determined to collect all the relevant facts.

"Pretty much." Miranda slides back into her chair, now a reluctant participant in this coffee klatch.

"Is he a homosexual pedophile?"

Miranda and Wing answer at the same time.

"No," says Miranda.

"Not that we know of," says Wing.

Roz considers. "So he's just hanging out with a bunch of them . . . ? That seems pretty innocent to me," she decides.

"Thank you, Mom," Miranda says, pleased.

Roz turns to Wing. "You think it's not?"

Wing scowls. "It's just lame."

"It's no lamer than you hanging out with me," Miranda says, suddenly confident. Suddenly pissed off by Wing's judgment. Her proclamations. Her superior notion of herself.

"Totally different," Wing says, brushing away the comment like toast crumbs from the counter. "Not the same thing." And they are siblings for a moment, fighting for the place of rightness in Mom's eyes.

Miranda shrugs. "Whatever," she says. She gets up again, pushes in her chair, and makes for the door. Mr. Lorimer has always seemed a little crazy to her, on the edge of something, not quite balanced in himself, but she hasn't before thought of him as lame. Hearing it now from Wing makes the assessment fit perfectly, like learning someone's astrological sign and seeing, *Oh, of course you're a Scorpio, how could I ever have thought anything else?* Miranda thinks of Darrin, the way Darrin looked at her so quizzically throughout the Mr. Lorimer story, how Miranda hadn't been able to tell what exactly Darrin's reaction was, and now it seems clear that Darrin had thought what Wing thought: pathetic.

"You don't think you could love me, but I think you're wrong." They are sitting on the fire escape of Mr. Lorimer's building one night in early July and Miranda can feel the sweat trickling down her stomach inside her dress. It's after eleven and she hasn't eaten dinner. He'd stopped in to the store at six that evening when Miranda was getting off work and they'd gone back to his house straight from there, too freaked that someone might see them together to stop for something to eat.

"I think that's a Paul Simon song." She is dying for a sliced turkey sandwich but can't bring herself to insist they get some food.

"Goddamn you—why does it always have to be some sort of dis?"

It embarrasses her when he speaks with slang, like when her mother uses some hip little phrase and sounds like an overgrown camp director. She doesn't answer him.

"Do you want to leave, Miranda? Do you just want to go? Fine. Go. I can't do this. You're a fucking baby, what the fuck did I expect?" He stands, and ducks through the window back into his living room. For a moment Miranda is afraid he means to close the window and leave her hanging there on the side of his building in an Indian sundress and no underwear, but he just turns and strides into the darkness on the far side of the room. She climbs through after him.

"If you're going to start pulling the 'baby' stuff again, then I am leaving," she tells him. She is trying to sound logical, not mean, but instead it comes out whiny and distorted. She can feel him looking at her like she's just stuck out her lower lip in silent defiance.

"I don't want you to leave," he says. "I don't want you to stay either, not really. Yes I do. Jesus Christ, I don't know what I want." He runs his hand through his hair, laughing bitterly at himself, at his utter defeat. "This is insane."

She comes to him then, on the sofa, curls her feet in under her and feels the grosgrain of the slipcover pressing in lines into her shins. She is softer now. She knows her voice will come out warm and slow. "It's not so insane," she says. "This is good. Sort of. It's good in its ways. You wanted this. *I* wanted this. And that's OK, right? Isn't that OK?"

Mr. Lorimer lets his head fall back against the wall, and he stares up as if the ceiling were a sky. "I may have to kill you," he says.

Miranda chuckles, sadly. "I know," she says, "just try and make it not so painful, OK? Gunshot to the head or something. Just be done with it, you know?"

"Don't patronize me, Miranda, all right?" His face is long, his voice steely again. "That's a little more than I think I should have to take right now."

"Look, I'm not patronizing, you're being schizophrenic. What am I supposed to do exactly?"

"Oh, just go, Miranda. Just fucking go. You're going to go eventually anyway, why don't you just go now."

She picks up her bag by the door, slips into her sandals. "Well, now that's very logical," she says, and steps into the hall letting the door close firmly behind her. The last word means a lot, to both of them. It's sort of cheating to walk out and claim a last-word victory, but at this point she doesn't care. Pride is pride, and she's got more of it than he does right now. Except that she still isn't wearing any underwear.

Miranda rides the elevator down to the lobby, which is cool as a tomb even in the stultifying heat of the city. She almost wants to stay there, lay her cheek against the stony floor, and fall asleep in gray shadows. If she weren't so hungry she might do just that, but as it is, her stomach is grinding at itself and she pushes through the heavy front door and out into the steamy street thinking desperately of a turkey club with fries and coleslaw and a chocolate egg cream.

THE THREE BROTHERS RESTAURANT IS RELATIVELY busy still serving late dinners, not yet on to postbar greasy breakfasts to soak up the booze before people make their way home for the night. Miranda pushes through the door into the blasting-cold air-conditioned air. A chime on the door announces her arrival and the onset of the cold. The sweat on her body seems to freeze instantly and she feels like she has a fine layer of icicle coating her, as though she's been dipped like a Dairy Queen cone.

Along the left-hand wall of the diner runs the lunch counter and beyond it the grill and the kitchen. The right wall is lined with booths two rows deep separated from the counter by a low ground-glass partition. As she enters Miranda glances down the counter stools. There's plenty of room for her, but she shifts abruptly and scurries off to a booth in the back corner. At the counter, undoubtedly satisfying their pot-induced munchies, sit Kirk Dunfree, Chris Robleski, and Dean Berger, the Judson Blumberg cronies.

Miranda slumps down in her booth, waves away the menu offered her by an aging waiter who's clearly worked the Three Brothers late shift since the beginning of time, and orders as if her very life depends on as fat a turkey club as they can build. She curls her legs up underneath her, then remembers to try and not flash the entire restaurant and checks to see that her dress is tucked in around the edges. Her arms are bare, and they goose-pimple in the AC. She tugs her ice-cream-stained T-shirt from her bag and pulls it over her head. CHOCOLATE. It's not high fashion, but it is another layer. She considers putting on her sunglasses too in the hope that she can disguise herself from recognition by the boys at the counter but decides her tiny blue-lensed John Lennons won't do much by way of camouflage. At the next table over, a group of girls eat and jabber among themselves. They have braces, and heads that seem oddly large for their bodies. They talk about a movie they've just seen, about the stars, the boys they like, the clothing they wish they owned. It's such a clichéd teenage conversation it's hard to believe it's not television. How depressing, Miranda thinks, how ridiculously predictable everyone really is. Anything you do is somehow exactly what you're supposed to be doing right then in your life. It makes her wonder why anyone bothers to do anything when it's already clear what you're going to do every step of the way anyhow. Maybe that guy, John Calvin, who thought everything was predestined—maybe he was right. She wishes she had something to read. The place mat on her table is the same kind they have at every diner in New York: drink specials she's sure no one has ordered since about 1950. Blue Hawaiis and gin fizzes and champagne cocktails frouffed up like tulle-ridden ballerinas. She remembers how distantly awed she had once been, back before they moved to Brooklyn, back at City Day, at the Acropolis diner where she'd hung out for hours nestled against Spencer's body, listening to the older kids talk, watching them down their coffee, watching the smoke from their cigarettes puff across the table into each other's faces. She's older now than they'd been then! That seems impossible, but it is irrevocably true. She supposes that's just the way things go: you never get to the place you once looked up to because once you're there you're no longer looking up and you realize that maybe it only really existed if you caught it on an angle from below. But then she supposes also that she has become her own version of that elusive, daunting maturity. To the marionette girls in the next booth . . . God, back when she was their age she would have been utterly bewildered by someone like herself: eighteen years old and fucking her English teacher.

Mercifully, her egg cream arrives. Miranda pounces on it like a scavenger, sucking in through the straw, all the energy in her body concentrated on the intake of sweet and cold. Her eyes are cast down, watching the foamy head sink lower and lower in the glass, but as she hears the entrance bell chime her eyes flick up instinctively and she is faced with the sight of Mr. Lorimer standing in the doorway, scanning the restaurant. He's come after her. And there she is, without her underwear, in a Häagen-Dazs T-shirt, sipping soda through a straw like some *Happy Days* teenybopper.

He sees her and starts toward the table. Miranda half expects one of the guys at the counter to spot him and call out in overzealous salutation, but they are engrossed in the last bites of their meals and Mr. Lorimer passes right by them in his beeline for Miranda. He holds her stare as he crosses the room, and there is something dramatic about him, crazed and unreal. That's what

Miranda loves about this—the total insanity of it: this grown man plowing into a diner late at night, his young lover sitting disheveled in her booth. In the fantasy, people turn to stare. In reality, Miranda isn't sure if they do or not, she's so caught up in the sweep of it all: his determination, his frenzy. Her own aura of ravaged, waiflike lostness.

"Miranda . . . ," he begins.

"What?" she demands. "What?"

He sinks into the booth. He is sweating, his face drawn and pained. Something has been sucked out of him, like the heat has gotten inside and leeched on. He looks at Miranda like he is asking to be saved, and she can't think for the life of her what the right thing is to do in a situation like this. "You just left . . . ," he says.

"You told me to," she says.

He takes a breath as if to speak but then deflates before any words come out. He looks like he might let out a sob, and Miranda turns toward the counter, toward Kirk and Chris and Dean. Chris has lit up a cigarette, and Kirk rests with his head on his arms, done in by his meal. Dean's stool is empty, and it strikes Miranda to wonder whether he's gone home to his own house or to Judson's. In that moment she wonders too what Dean's parents are like: if they know where Dean is those nights he doesn't come home, if they rest comfortably in their son's lies the way Roz accepts and relies on Miranda's for her peace of mind. Or maybe it's different for boys. If Judson were a girl, she thinks, would he get left alone in the city for weeks on end?

When Miranda looks back to Mr. Lorimer the expression on his face has gone from despair to apoplexy. He seems to be looking straight through her, but as she tries to search his eyes for some clue to his thoughts, she realizes he isn't looking *at* her, but *over* her. She straightens, as if to turn, but her movement makes him start and he bristles a look forbidding enough to say, *Under penalty of death will you turn your head.* She crinkles her forehead: *What?*

Two things happen then at the exact same time. Mr. Lorimer's face morphs before her eyes, like a Claymation figurine: his features lift, like the cartilage beneath them has rejuvenated spontaneously and he's suddenly animated again, restored—albeit in a sort of sick, Halloweeny way—to the man she knew before she really knew him.

The other thing that happens is Dean Berger's voice from behind her saying, "Hey, Mr. L. What up?"

Miranda doesn't mean to turn around per se; she will describe it later as a reflex: you hear a noise behind you and you turn to it. So she turns to it and watches as Dean's reaction shapes itself on his face. First there is: *Hey, Miranda,* then: *I didn't realize that was you sitting there,* and then the more complicated—but ultimately so simple—calculation of *him, plus her, equals . . . and all those nights playing cards at Judson Blumberg's, and the looks you wrote off to Miranda Anderson being a big flirt, and the rumors that you've heard about Mr. Lorimer but who haven't you heard those rumors about so you didn't really pay any attention, and how suddenly it all makes a lot of sense here in the Three Brothers Restaurant that Miranda Anderson wasn't just flirting, she was fucking Mr. Lorimer . . .* and while all of that riffles across Dean Berger's face, he is at the same time composing himself, collecting his cool-guy persona as though he were drawing a coat around himself on a blustery winter day. Because nothing would be so awkward as to show his surprise, and nothing less suave than to let on that this coupling could faze him in the slightest. So all Dean actually says as he passes by their table on his way back from the men's room that night is, "Blackjack tomorrow, 'round eight," and with a flick of his chin in their direction he saunters by, out the door with its *ding ding* and onto the street where Chris and Kirk already stand waiting in the heat. And then they are gone and it is just Miranda and Mr. Lorimer again, but in that one short moment everything has changed, and Mr. Lorimer stands now, that same phony ease masking his face like putty, and turns and walks out of the restaurant, and *ding ding*, as if to announce its arrival, Miranda's turkey club sandwich lands with a clatter on the table before her, some fries sliding off the heaping plate.

"Anything else for you tonight now?" says the old waiter, and Miranda shakes her head no, her mouth already too full to speak.

WHATEVER HAPPENS NEXT, IT CLEARLY HAPPENS FAST. The very next evening, finished with a long shift and not due back at the store for another two days, Miranda slumps into the Brooklyn house, exhausted and badly in need of a shower. She starts down the stairs to her basement room and hears a shout from upstairs, "Miranda, is that you?" Mercifully, her mother is out for dinner with Fran in the city.

"Hey, Wing, yeah," Miranda calls, continuing down.

"Miran—can we talk when you have a chance?"

She stops. "Yeah, OK, I'm just, I just need to take a shower, OK?"

"You hungry?"

"Sort of, yeah. Yeah, I'd eat."

"'K . . ."

Miranda drifts down to the basement.

WING'S IDEA OF DINNER IS TO CUT UP EVERY GREEN thing in the house, add any canned bean, vegetable, or fish she can find, toss the whole thing up with lots of olive oil and red wine vinegar, and sprinkle on something crunchy, like sunflower seeds, or chow mein noodles, or Bran Chex cereal. Which is fine; it's far too hot to cook anything real and certainly too hot to ingest it. She makes iced tea from a mix, which tastes like powder but is cold and sweet and good despite itself. Wing serves herself a hefty mound of salad, then passes the tongs to Miranda.

"Hey, so, Miran . . . ," Wing begins offhandedly, as if to segue into what she wants to address, but she is segueing from nothing, which sort of defeats the point of a segue.

"I'm pretty sure I know what you're about to say," Miranda tells her.

"Oh good," Wing says, palpably relieved, "then you say it and spare me from having to."

"Uh-uh," Miranda says. "I already tried to talk to you about this once and you just totally didn't get it at all."

"What? When? You wanted to set *me* up with him. We never talked about this . . . I didn't know anything until—"

"I tried, though," Miranda says. She shoves her mouth full of lettuce and carrot chips enough to keep her chewing for a while.

"Miranda," Wing begins again, trying to be composed, as if reminding herself what *adult* is supposed to mean. "Miranda, Trini Holland called me today . . . she's teaching summer school—"

"I know." Miranda cuts her off. "I know I know I know."

Wing looks indignant, a bad impression of a mother's exasperation.

"I mean I know she's teaching summer school. You told me."

Wing takes a breath. "I'm not trying to be confrontational about this, I'm just . . . I'm concerned, it's not . . . I mean, are you OK, Miran? What's going on? Trini's got Dean Berger and those guys in class now and they're in there today going off about dirt they've apparently got on someone and it's not exactly difficult to get it out of them, and she called me not to be nosy or to get into someone else's business but because from what those guys were saying, whatever's going on sounds like it's not going on well and she was genuinely worried that you might be in over your head." Wing is trying hard not to sound like a guidance counselor but not doing a very good job. Guidance counselors are always trying not to sound like guidance counselors, which is precisely what characterizes their speech so distinctly.

"I don't think I'm the one who's over my head," Miranda says.

"What? I don't—"

"I don't think I'm the one everybody should be so worried about."

Wing looks truly puzzled. "What are you talking about, Miranda? Would you please stop being cryptic. You wanted to talk about this. I'm sorry I didn't realize that before. So let's talk about it. *What* is going on?"

"Did you already tell my mom?"

"No." Wing pauses, attempting to modulate her voice. "No," she says again. "I came to you first. Please tell me what's going on."

"It's OK if you tell her," Miranda says, and suddenly this becomes true. God—it hits her like something hard in the gut—God, she really wants to talk to her mom.

"Let's deal with that later, OK?" Wing pleads. "Could you please just let me know if you're OK and what's happening, please?"

"I think," Miranda begins. She is afraid of sounding like a cocky little shit. She tries again. "I think that in the scheme of things I'm not the one who's getting the most hurt. I think Mr. Lorimer's really a lot worse off than I am and I don't know if you know him well enough to ask him or if you know someone who does because I don't mean to be a bitch, I really don't, but that's been the way our dynamic's gone and it's just gotten so complicated now." It is getting easier to talk as she goes on, as the story of the situation takes over and eclipses the situation itself. It makes a better story than it does a relationship, and Miranda will wonder later if that is something she was aware of all along, or if maybe that's just the way most things are: you do the things you do because you like telling yourself about doing them. It keeps you interested in the story of your own life, wondering what might happen next.

Wing still looks monumentally confused, like she isn't willing to take anything for granted and will ultimately settle for nothing less than the whole story, end to end. But before Miranda begins there is a disclaimer to establish, like a warning or an epigraph, instructions: How to hear the story I am about to tell.

"The thing is," Miranda says, "I'm out of here, you know? We'll go to the Cape, and then I'll be getting ready for school, and then I'll be gone, into an entirely different life. I mean, it's like witness relocation or something. You know? I get to start over. And he doesn't. And that doesn't seem fair." She really wants Wing to believe her on this, and she hopes she sounds the way she feels. "It's just that he's a good guy really, I mean he's a good person, and, I don't know, I just . . . just, be nice to him if you can. He's really really not a bad person, OK?"

25

THE GOOD PEOPLE OF NEW YORK

ON THANKSGIVING MORNING MIRANDA TAKES THE train in from Providence and Darrin meets her at Grand Central so they can ride the subway together out to Brooklyn. The train car is as close to deserted as Miranda has ever seen it.

"All right," Miranda sighs, flopping across two seats and propping up her legs. Her wool socks, she sees, are two different shades of gray. "OK," she says, "prepare me," and she pinches her eyes shut. Darrin has met Sandy Schecter; Miranda has not. "He's an artist . . . ," Miranda prompts.

"And an art historian," Darrin adds.

"A prof?"

"I think," Darrin says. "Columbia maybe?"

"So he's single?"

"I guess his wife died."

"How?" Miranda asks.

"Breast cancer."

"Hmm," Miranda says softly, and they are quiet around that for a minute. "So what's he like?" Miranda tugs at the waist of her jeans; they are her roommate's and have a tendency to slip down to an indecent degree. She's been living in this pair of Levi's for the last month, and has specifically worn them home today because they make her feel like the person she wants to be. She worries that being back at home will turn her into a teenager again, the minute she steps through the front door of the Park Slope brownstone.

"He's totally sweet," Darrin tells her. "He's attractive, sensitive almost to the point of New Age–ness, but not annoying, just really PC and nonoffensive and in touch with his feelings. Good stuff. He's successful—teacher, artist. He thinks your mom is about the greatest thing since the cat's meow . . ."

"Ugh, I bet she's so all over him . . ."

"So all over him?" Darrin says. "Where are you from? Venice Beach?"

Miranda is still surprised when Darrin mocks her. It's a new dynamic between them, and it is strange. Darrin hasn't changed, per se, or suddenly grown up or anything, it's more like she's finally giving voice to the things she should have always been able to say to Miranda but never did. Darrin has always been the more mature one, more together; Miranda never had Darrin's self-possession, her assurance, and yet Darrin had always deferred to her. Now, it's as if things are finally being set straight, each of them falling into the roles they were actually meant for. It feels like the Levi's feel: right.

"It's not my fault I got a surf bum for a roommate," Miranda says. "Speech patterns are so infectious."

Darrin's expression is a spoof of concern: "You should really go get the shot at Student Health," she says. "Protects against the most contagious of dialects. You won't be completely immune, but aside from serious Jersey and South Boston it'll keep you pretty safe."

"When did you become sarcastic?" Miranda demands. "*I'm* the cynic. *I'm* the one who does that."

"You're out of practice," Darrin says. "Providence, Rhode Island? I mean, really. They wouldn't know what to do with sarcasm up there. You'd be firing into a void. Four years and you'll be soft as mush."

Miranda shakes her head vigorously. "Once a New Yorker, always a New Yorker."

Darrin laughs.

"So where's the but?" Miranda asks.

"The what?"

"The *but*. What's wrong with this guy? Heroin addict? Convicted felon?"

Darrin laughs again. "He's an absolutely lovely man."

"But . . . ?"

Darrin considers. A little guiltily she admits it: "He's no Noam Chomsky."

Miranda doesn't miss a beat. "Well, who the hell wants to date Noam Chomsky?"

"My point exactly!" Darrin cries.

ROZ HAS PAINTED THE BROWNSTONE'S ENTRANCEWAY since Miranda left—a crepey sort of beige, "a *breathing* color," Darrin calls it. Sometimes Miranda worries that Darrin, like Roz, is beginning to push the New Age line a bit far. It seems a little like a conspiracy. They both look wonderful too: vivid and artsy and very chic. The outfit that had seemed, that morning, to capture a sort of offhandedly sexy bohemianism is now making Miranda feel like the Holly Hobbie backwoods cousin come to the big city for Turkey Day.

Roz's hair is short and straight, a crop that's almost dykey, and she has on big flowy pants and a tunic-type sweater that drapes her body in hues of wine and mulberry. Literally, Miranda thinks, her mother glows. She's heard people talk of sex's afterglow but has never fully understood; she always feels a little skanky after sex, stinky and stringy-haired. She thinks of her poet-boy back at school—Dov, a junior who lives quietly, alone, at the end of Miranda's hall—and pictures the two of them sitting at Ruby's Diner, holding hands across the table, waiting for their eggs and coffee. He made her wait to sleep with him; he made them take things slow, which at first seemed contrived and forced to Miranda, but then, when they finally had sex, just the week before, it *was* a different thing than it had been with Mr. Lorimer and the others. Sitting at Ruby's the morning after that first sex with Dov, Miranda knows she did not glow. She probably looked terrible—unwashed and grimy—but so did he, and she found him all the lovelier for it, so who knew? Maybe that *was* the glow: the beauty you saw in someone who was not beautiful. But Roz is beautiful. And she is distinctly aglow.

Roz hugs Darrin at the door like a bear. Seeing Darrin with her mom that way, hugging, like friends, it seems that they really share something, something separate from her, and that makes Miranda feel a little immature, and irrelevant. When Roz lets Darrin go she swoops in on Miranda, then pulls back, holding her at arm's length, a parody of the American mother welcoming home her scholar. "How's my hippie chick?!" Roz cries.

"Oh good grief!" says Miranda, but it is all, for once, in good spirits. "Well, if you don't positively ooze well-being," she adds.

"Well, if you don't positively ooze patchouli!" Roz counters.

And then there's a voice from outside the still-open front door. "What's everybody oozing about?" Through that door, from the autumn streets of Brooklyn, enters Sandy Schecter.

He is not what Miranda expected, she can say that much. He glides in, confident but not supercilious, and kisses her mother from behind, on the back of her neck, a deceptively innocent gesture pointing toward something much more intimate. Miranda feels riveted, her attention glued to them, to that space between their bodies, the way you might be transfixed by a car wreck or a porn movie: you know you shouldn't but you can't get enough. Sandy is far more attractive than she'd imagined. He has the Waspy good looks of a descendant from an old New England clan, a little rugged, as though he should have been—or *has* been, what the hell does she know?—a fisherman in Maine or on Cape Cod. But he's a

Jew from Denver, she knows that much. A Jew from Denver? He is awkward in a way that could certainly come from being an outsider, as if he's sure he's offended someone. Miranda tells herself to stop being so judgmental. She should be more patient. Besides, he likes her mother.

"So, Sandy," Miranda begins, deliberately casual, like a father interrogating his young daughter's date. She reaches across the table for the mashed potatoes, half standing in her chair, a proprietary gesture, claiming the expanse of table as her realm. She ladles herself an extremely large portion. She's acting weirdly macho, but almost can't help it. There's something about Sandy that, despite his good looks and apparent friendliness, makes her feel like the only real man at the table. *Stop,* she reminds herself. *I'm being nice, refraining from judgment, being open-minded, pretending I'm Darrin, nice.* She musters nice, like a pep rally, a nice rally: *Go, Miranda! Nice! Nice! Nice!* "So," she says again, her mouth now full of potato, which she knows is rude—god, she can't stop herself!— "so how long have you lived in New York?" she manages to get out, and then leans back, pleased with herself, waiting for his answer, arms proverbially crossed at her chest. *God, I'm awful!* she thinks.

"Hmm," says Sandy, brow furrowed, "I believe it's thirty-seven years this fall." He takes a bite from his plate and loses a few peas in the process. They go rolling onto the floor behind his chair. He seems not to notice.

Across the table Miranda can see Darrin snicker, but she can't tell if it's at Sandy and the peas or at Miranda. Thirty-seven years! He's twice the New Yorker she is!

Miranda falters for another question to ask. Her manly bravado seems all wrong now and she feels herself slipping into girly mode. He's clearly not a talker, this Sandy, and not one who carries his share of the ball. Girly seems more appropriate: the dumber Miranda acts, the more confident he'll be by comparison.

"Darrin told me you do art, and I was wondering what kind of art you do?" *Shit,* she didn't sound dumb, she sounded patronizing. Roz was going to kill her. Was it so hard to be civil and decent for one afternoon, Roz would demand. I guess so, Miranda would snap back, part of her wanting just to say, *Mom, I'm sorry,* but not a part attached to her mouth or accessible to words. She is stuck with bitchy. It appears to be all she's got.

"It's hard to talk about art, don't you think?" Sandy says, so earnest Miranda thinks he must be kidding. She has to bite her lip to keep from laughing. "It's so personal, everything that comes out is a part of me inside, and to talk about it . . . I'm not good with words. I think in images. Words always seem wrong somehow . . ." He drifts into a drumstick as though it is the only logical conclusion to his thought.

Miranda knows her eyes must be wide. She can't bear to look at her mother. She expects a swift kick under the table—from anyone actually: Roz, Darrin, Wing, Sandy himself . . .

"I," Darrin announces mercifully, "am going in for seconds," and she gets up and starts for the kitchen.

"I am so all about seconds," Miranda says, pushing back her chair and racing to slide through the kitchen door ahead of Darrin.

"*So all about seconds?*" Darrin repeats, but then says nothing more. In the kitchen they fill their plates with too much food they don't actually want to eat, and the silence is bad, like a smell you can't pretend not to notice.

"I'm being a bitch, aren't I?" Miranda says, her voice hushed.

"Uh-huh," Darin says, nodding, not looking at Miranda.

"I can't help it," Miranda whispers. "He's so odd."

Darrin lifts her eyes to Miranda's now, her mouth a sad, frustrated, teeth-gritting half-smile. "Hmm," she says, apologetic, but as if she's throwing up her hands. *I'm awfully sorry you feel like that,* the look seems to convey, *you selfish little brat.* Darrin shrugs then, like she doesn't have any idea where they can go from here.

She chews her lip a second, then gestures to the door: *Shall we?* Miranda follows her through.

In the dining room, Roz is standing, making motions toward clearing the table.

"Don't you even try that, Mother dearest," Miranda says. "Darrin and I haven't even begun to eat." There is always food to the rescue.

"Oh god no," Darrin agrees, overly vehement, glad for a diversion. "Back in Denver that would've just been hors d'oeuvres so far. We've got courses to go here."

Roz sinks back down in mock exhaustion.

"Denver," Sandy says.

"Oh my god," Miranda realizes, "you're both from Denver."

"Brilliant deduction," Darrin says, not altogether nicely.

"You don't *like* Denver, do you?" The question has popped out of Miranda's mouth involuntarily, and though she's clearly speaking to Sandy, it's Darrin who answers, ridiculously—she knows *Darrin's* take on Denver. "It's not so bad. It's like any other city. Except warm, near water. Mountains . . ."

"It was home," Sandy says, as though his affection for Denver is something beyond his control, an inherited gene, a family trait.

In leaps Roz, savior of the century: "Do you have that attachment to it, Darrin? Or are you pure Manhattanite now?"

Darrin laughs loudly, more Roz's laugh than her own. It is a laugh to keep Miranda out of the conversation, and it is working. "I'm still on the hormone therapy," Darrin jokes, "but after the operation, you won't be able to tell the difference."

"So you're not loathing New York, even growing up in a decent part of the country?" Wing asks. Though she is tolerating life in Brooklyn, she almost never goes into Manhattan and seems to be biding her time until she can figure out where her life is going to take her next. Miranda really hopes it isn't to Alex in Central America. Wing is too cool for that. Definitely too cool for Alex at least, who has yet to resurface from Latin American parts unknown. Wing jokes that he is probably in some Third World prison awaiting trial on drug charges, but Miranda got a postcard from Antigua around Halloween. She was surprised to hear from him at all, and had read it to Darrin over the phone. Darrin still doesn't believe that Miranda never slept with Alex. Miranda wishes *someone* would believe that she'd never slept with him. She probably deserves it, though. Maybe she belongs with someone like Alex.

"New York is not as bad as everyone says." Darrin defends this town. New York seems truly to have come to be hers to defend. "I mean, look at you two." She gestures to Roz and Sandy. "That's like *the* perfect New York story."

Wing says: "You met in the library, right?" which is clearly for Miranda's benefit since there is no way Wing has heard this story any less than eighteen times.

"In the main branch of the Public Library," Roz clarifies. "In the reading room."

"So you were. . ."—Miranda hazards a guess—"fighting over a book?"

Sandy smiles at Roz from across the table. They are nauseatingly happy. Or maybe they're just happy, and it's Miranda who's nauseating. It's all she can do to keep from standing up and walking out of the room. She wishes she'd stayed at school for Thanksgiving. Or gone home with Dov. He'd invited her. What is she doing here in the midst of this . . . ? She doesn't even know what *this* is.

Sandy says: "We saw each other across a crowded room—"

Miranda can't take it anymore. "Um," she interrupts, "does anyone know what time it is?"

They all stop short in their merriment, like children caught in forbidden play. Roz looks a little perturbed, but checks her watch anyway. "Four-fifteen," she tells Miranda soberly, as though what she really wanted to say was, *Grow up, Miranda, OK? It's time.* Miranda thinks maybe she agrees. She wishes she knew how.

"Eek," Miranda says, standing, pushing in her chair. "'Scuse me, I've got to make a phone call." And she turns and walks upstairs, more relieved than guilty, but a little guilty anyway. The table is silent. Miranda pulls the phone into the bathroom, closes the door, and sits against it. She dials Dov's dorm room number out of habit, then hangs up, stands again, and digs in her pocket for the scrap on which she's written his number at home. She stands before the sink as she dials, the phone crooked between her neck and shoulder. She stares at herself listening to the ring. She narrows her eyes, glares. A man answers the phone, and there is much noise and revelry in the background.

"H'lo?" he says.

"Is Dov there?"

Before the question is fully out of her mouth the man is shouting away from the phone and into the fray, "Doe! Hey, get him, Lisa, get your cousin," and there is much mumbling and the knocking of receiver against something hard. "Doe-Doe: you." Miranda can almost see this man gesturing to the phone. She cannot decide if he is doing so absently or with an it's-your-little-girlfriend smirk. It unnerves her not to know which. She focuses instead on herself in the mirror. She wants to look the way she thinks she looks to Dov at school, the way she looks when she feels like herself, but that sensation is elusive right now, growing fuzzier with every minute she spends in her mother's house.

"Hello?" He doesn't know it's her, could be just another phone call.

"Hi. It's me."

"Miranda!" At least it's not a question. At least he knows who "me" is.

"Hi," she says again. She hates her face in the mirror at that moment. She looks like her mother, that wishful gaze, and it makes her feel sad and silly.

"Happy Thanksgiving," he says brightly.

"I guess," she says.

"Sweetie"—his voice is all concern—"what's going on?"

"Nothing, just my family . . . How're you?"

"Great," he tells her, "great. I'm great." And there's too long a pause then, Miranda staring herself down in the bathroom mirror. It's clear that this isn't going to help at all. She is the same indefinite person she was before he picked up the phone. The same person she was before she met him, and he doesn't know who that is any more than she does, which means that sometimes he knows some things and sometimes he has no idea at all. "How's the boyfriend?" he asks.

It takes her a second to realize he means Sandy. "He's OK, I guess," she says. "I'm sorry, I shouldn't have called, you're busy, you're having fun . . . I should go back to them all anyway. I just wanted to say Happy Thanksgiving and all . . ."

"Are you OK, Miranda?" he asks again, gentle, and considerate, but so ineffectual right now. None of this has anything to do with him. Maybe Dov and Miranda will stay together awhile, and maybe they won't, but even if they do, even if he comes to mean something real to her, he still won't have anything to do with this: this family, this brownstone in Park Slope, this girl staring back at her from the mirror.

"Yeah," she says, and tries to make her face look like she means it, "yeah, I'm OK. It's just I should go. I'll see you on Sunday, I guess . . ."

"We can talk before then if you want . . . ," he offers.

"OK," she tells him. "See you Sunday."

Back downstairs the conversation has picked up again, and when Miranda reenters it doesn't falter, as if all present are determined not to let her mood spoil their day. Roz is in the middle of some story that everyone is hanging on, bleary-eyed with laughing. She's really quite a force, Miranda thinks. Like Crazy Glue. Or a supermagnet. Flypaper. She draws things to her, and they stick. But they stick because they want to, not because they can't leave. If Sandy adores Roz half as much as Darrin and Wing do, Miranda thinks, then maybe her mother is a damn lucky woman. Roz has always been searching for a match, someone to meet her as she is. As an equal. But maybe in the end it's going to come down to the fact that no one is a match for Roz. Miranda wonders if the same will be true for her, or if she'll be luckier than her mother in that regard. There is something about Roz that sets her apart, a kind of understated greatness, an inner strength so stalwart it can't be broken. It keeps people at a distance, Miranda thinks. Everyone loves her, but from a few steps away. And if there are men out there who have the same kind of strength that Roz has, Miranda can't say she's ever met one. Her mom has spent years waiting for her prince to come along and doesn't realize that not even a prince will do. Roz is in another league entirely.

When the story is over, and the laughter has subsided to a dull sniffle and gasp, it's Darrin who breaks the spell.

"I want pie," she declares.

"Oh!" Wing hops up from her seat. "That's my job." She had been designated dessert-maker when she insisted on sweet potato instead of pumpkin pie. Sweet potatoes, she claims, are the perfect food. As long as she promised fresh whipped cream for the top, Roz had been quite willing to concede. Wing disappears into the kitchen and Darrin starts to clear the table. Then Roz gets up to use the bathroom, and Sandy stands up to help with the dishes but Darrin shoos him back to his chair.

"Sit, sit," she says. "I got it. Rest. Relax. Take a load off."

Sandy sits back down obediently. Miranda, beside him, is picking walnut pieces out of the stuffing bowl. He turns, catching Miranda's eye. "You know," he says, "I'm pretty crazy about your mom."

Miranda laughs nervously. She looks around to see if anyone can help her out, but there is only the wine bottle. She pours. "That's what I hear," she says. *Here we go,* she thinks, *and boy, is this going to be some chat* . . . But Sandy just sits there, satisfied, apparently having said what he wanted to say.

"Well, you *are* the boat," Miranda tells him.

"The what?"

"The boat," Miranda says. "My mom didn't tell you about Zinnia . . . ? The SS . . . Zinnia, Mona's psychic . . . ?" But Sandy Schecter still shakes his head no. "Well, you'll have to get her to tell you about the boat." Sandy wants more, but is also visibly thrilled to have this little quest before him. He seems almost grateful. He knows something now that Roz doesn't know he knows, and this makes Miranda his ally in a way. It's no skin off her back, and peace is better than not-peace. Maybe that's what you learn in college, she thinks: how to make peace when you don't actually have to but you might as well.

"Hey, Miran," Wing calls from the kitchen, "are there spoons on the table?"

"Yes ma'am," Miranda hollers back. Darrin comes back into the dining room and surveys the table for more to clear. The toilet flushes in the other room, and Roz comes swaying out, a blurred but lovely vision in mulberry. She ambles over and plunks herself down beside Sandy just as Wing pushes through from the kitchen, her back against the swing door, a pie in each hand. And then suddenly, out of a patch of sated, candlelit silence, Sandy grabs his wineglass with a rather unsteady hand and lifts it dramatically to the sky. He rises on rubbery legs, his chest puffed like a rooster, voice booming, deep and low, and so different from every other voice in the room that night. He says: "To the good people of New York," and he holds his pose, as if waiting for the room to rise and join him in a standing ovation.

Miranda's eyes bulge with the effort it takes not to bust out laughing. The look that Darrin shoots her across the table is no longer mean—Darrin is trying not to laugh herself—and the moment they share is the way it's supposed to be with them: near hysterics, Darrin invoking the temperance, *Don't you dare laugh, Miranda Anderson, or you'll make me laugh too,* and the relief Miranda feels at that, at knowing that in some ways Darrin will always be on her side, that relief is everything she needs. There they all are, trying not to double over, even Wing, busying herself with the pies, the way any good teacher would, feigning oblivion until the awkward moment has passed. Miranda herself is frozen, happy right there, right then, in that bursting moment where it's like they're all just poised on an intake of breath, waiting to see what will happen.

It is Roz who does something: plants her feet, levers a hand against the table, and pushes herself up to standing. Taking a wineglass from the table, she raises it alongside Sandy's. "Yes," she says. "To the good people of New York."

Miranda does finally laugh then, but it comes out as a flood of relief, a gush of good tidings, not a jab at her mother, but a sign of all that is well and fine and OK with them. All that is not perfect and never will be, but is all right—more comfortable than it could be, not as difficult as it has already been, and maybe not as easy or as trying as it will be again—because they're still there, still there with each other. Miranda laughs when Roz speaks, the way Darrin might laugh, or Wing, and there is nothing dismissive or malicious in her tone, just release. She curls her feet underneath her and rises to her knees on the chair. "Cheers," Miranda cries. "To the good people of New York." Whereupon Wing, loath to be uncooperative, raises her pie-cutter in an apple-crumb-crusted salute: "To the good people."

And then Roz reaches back with her other hand and grabs Darrin's arm, pulling her from her place in the background, her arm circling 'round Darrin's shoulders in a grip that said, *You are here, Darrin, you are here, and we're not letting you go.* And then somehow there is a glass in Darrin's hand too, her fist raised to the center of the table where four pieces of crystal stemware and one silver-plated pie-cutter clink together in a glorious twinkling. "To the good people," Roz says. "To the good people of New York."

Acknowledgments

Huge thank-yous to Jenny Minton (who is more than I ever knew an editor could be), Adam Pringle, Amy Robbins (whose eye and ear as a copyeditor put me to shame), Eric Simonoff (the greatest agent in the world), Erin Ergenbright, Evan Shopper, Allison Amend, Jane Rosenzweig (with special thanks for her name, which I swiped off a workshop phone list before we'd ever met, unaware of what a dear friend she would become), Michelle and Pat Forman (tale-tellers extraordinaire), Myra and Tony Nissen (for their stories and their love and for that great week in Costa Rica, where they let me sit by the pool and scribble on yellow legal pads without raising an eyebrow as their courtship and early married life were rendered in fiction), the Vermont Studio Center, James Michener and the Copernicus Society of America, and the Iowa Writers' Workshop. And to Chris, for the Rose Main Reading Room and everything after.

A NOTE ABOUT THE AUTHOR

Thisbe Nissen is a graduate of Oberlin College and the Iowa Writers' Workshop, and is a former James Michener Fellow. *Out of the Girls' Room and into the Night,* her first published book, won the 1999 John Simmons Short Fiction Award, chosen by Marilynne Robinson. Her stories have appeared in *Story* and *Seventeen* magazine. A native New Yorker, Thisbe now lives in Iowa.

A NOTE ON THE TYPE

This book was set in Minion, a typeface produced by the Adobe Corporation specifically for the Macintosh personal computer, and released in 1990. Designed by Robert Slimbach, Minion combines the classic characteristics of old-style faces with the full complement of weights required for modern typesetting.

Composed by Dix, Syracuse, New York
Printed and bound by Quebecor Printing, Fairfield, Pennsylvania
Designed by Virginia Tan